WHERE
WE LIVE
A Benefit for the Survivors
in Las Vegas

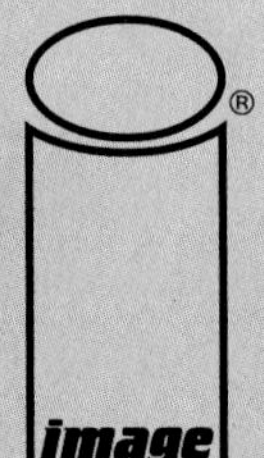

WHERE WE LIVE, A BENEFIT FOR THE SURVIVORS IN LAS VEGAS TP. First printing. May 2018. Published by Image Comics, Inc. Office of publication: 2701 NW Vaughn St., Suite 780, Portland, OR 97210. Printed in the USA. For information regarding the CPSIA on this printed material call: 203-595-3636 and provide reference #RICH-789148. For international rights, contact: foreignlicensing@imagecomics.com. ISBN: 978-1-5343-0822-0.

A LONG WAY FROM HOME

an introduction by J. H. Williams III

My wife, Wendy, aptly named this book, WHERE WE LIVE. It has the surface meaning of just what it says, but it goes so much deeper than that. It speaks to where we all live, not just in our houses and apartments, towns and cities, our states and our country, but also where we live in our minds and hearts, in our very souls. It also speaks to how we choose to live, and how that matters. Ultimately, it's about what we will accept into our lives.

The Las Vegas, Nevada, on October 1st 2017, a mass shooting killed 58 people, and injured well over 500 others at a concert attended by thousands of music fans. Many of those who witnessed this horrific incident are still dealing with the massive psychological effects left in its wake. So, we're talking about thousands of people who will have lasting after-effects for a very long time to come.

There are a number of reasons to read this book. First and foremost is to help those in need; 100% of the proceeds of this volume will go to victims of this terrible crime. The amount of funds raised by other various organizations has been very impactful, but it's not enough for the long-term needs of survivors. And while raising money is an important goal, another key reason is to get some informative understanding and human perspectives of the problems and issues around the proliferation of guns and gun violence in America.

What happened here in Las Vegas that awful night does not stay here in Las Vegas. There has been so many deaths and wounds from gun violence across our country to make us all sick. We have to ask ourselves as a society 'how many Sandy Hooks or Sutherland Springs or Las Vegas or Parkland incidents have to occur before we say enough is enough?' There had been over 300 mass shootings in 2017. So many that the news cycles couldn't keep up. 2018 is shaping up to be at least as bad. How sick is that? I don't have an answer that fully explains that question. I just know we have to ask ourselves as a nation, as a civilized society, at what cost is any of this adherence to loose gun laws worth? Is it worth the hundreds of deaths, the thousands of injured and traumatized? Is it worth all of this death and destruction?

No. It never is.

But yet, we somehow have found ourselves living in this nightmare of our own making. I often hear it referred to as the "new normal". I'm sorry, there is nothing "normal" about this. It's an abnormality that is symptomatic of deeper issues we have to face. Stricter gun laws alone won't fix our deeper societal problems, but we have to start there when it comes to stopping gun violence. You often hear that it's not the guns that kill people. In some ways I understand that statement, guns don't pull their own triggers. But we have to be honest with ourselves. The types of guns we allow into our society certainly make it easy to mow down people in large numbers. Even some military personnel are publicly saying assault rifles are weapons of war, nothing else; they are super-efficient killing machines designed specifically to kill as many people as possible in the shortest amount of time. They are designed for one purpose: to rip flesh apart. Period. People are killing people... with guns.

I'm not saying we have to ban all guns; this isn't about taking away people's Constitutional rights. But there needs to be reasonable controls put in place.

The laws as they currently exist are not good enough. We've made changes to our law before when they didn't fit the times we were living in. There is no real reason not to do it again. Facts show every other country on Earth that has dealt with getting certain types of weapons off the streets do not have this mass gun violence problem. And by having done this, they're saving lives every day.

Even though WHERE WE LIVE is designed to help the victims of the Las Vegas shooting, it's also designed to take a deeper look at the problems we face as a society. It's for where we live, but it's for the nation as well. Incidents like what happened here in Las Vegas, and in too many other communities, are affecting everyone much more profoundly than we yet realize. The entire country is hurting. Through stories and art, we want to ask the questions and address the problems we face as a country, as a people. To get the conversation moving in a direction of dealing with how out of control things have become. We can't just let this slip into the ether anymore. By creating an engaging and thoughtful book that talks about the various nuanced problems that got us here, we hope to contribute to that conversation.

What you're about to read features a wide variety of perspectives on the issues from some of comics' top creators, as well as many local Las Vegas talents sharing their points of view on what happened here. The stories are personal, biographical, fictional, and allegorical. Many feature true-life accounts from people who experienced that awful night and how it has affected them. These stories are all delivered in a wide range of content and styles: from comics, to essays, to poetry. All of it from the heart of every single person involved in this book. It's a way to raise funds to help others the best way we know how, by creating art that conveys messages. Messages that might be hard to hear, but need to be heard all the same.

Wendy and I are thankful to all who joined us in this endeavor. We thank Editor Will Dennis and assistant Michael Perlman for their diligent efforts. And we're very thankful to the courageous witnesses who wanted to tell their story in this unique format: Sarah Angelo, Savannah Sanchez, Autumn K, Leala Tyree, Rachel Crosby, The Patterson Family, Stephanie Ballou, James Ochsenbein, Chad Perkins, Aubri, Bonnie Hilts, Daniel Hernandez, Lee Shoeppner, Jason Harris.

Our hopes are that this book helps our community and our larger national community in a variety of ways. If WHERE WE LIVE can change one mind or start one new conversation about this, it will all be worth it.

J H WILLIAMS III
Las Vegas

TABLE OF CONTENTS

"WHOA, YOU'RE FROM VEGAS? WHAT'S THAT LIKE?"
BY WARREN WUCINICH
PRETTY MUCH EVERYONE ASKS THAT.
ALL LAS VEGAS NATIVES GET THAT QUESTION.
A LOT.
AND WHILE NOT ALWAYS GENUINE, I'VE ALWAYS GOT AN ANSWER...

2002
IT'S JUST LIKE THE MOVIES. I SWEAR.
I DON'T KNOW. I'VE NEVER BEEN FROM ANYWHERE ELSE.
DUDE, IT'S CRAZY. ALL I DO IS GAMBLE AND GO TO *CIRQUE DU SOLEIL*.
IT'S HOT.
VERY HOT.
IT'S LIKE ANYWHERE ELSE BUT WITH MORE BOOZE AND SLOT MACHINES.
I CAN'T REALLY BLAME TOURISTS FOR ASKING. VEGAS IS A WEIRD PLACE.
LAS VEGAS CARICATURES
IT'S UNIQUE.
BUT AT THE SAME TIME IT'S AN ALIEN VERSION OF OTHER PLACES.
EXAGGERATED.
WELCOME TO Fabulous LAS VEGAS NEVADA
A PARODY.
I GUESS PEOPLE EXPECT **ME** TO BE DIFFERENT, TOO...
DO YOU LIVE IN A HOTEL?
DO YOU SEE LOTS OF CELEBRITIES?
ARE YOU REALLY GOOD AT GAMBLING?
ARE THERE SCHOOLS HERE?
SO DO YOU GO TO STRIP CLUBS ALL THE TIME? SHOOT MAN, I WOULD IF I LIVED HERE.
...AND SURE, IT'S FUN TO PLAY IT UP.
WELL, IF YOU'RE TIGHT WITH THE MOB THEN LIVING HERE IS PRETTY COOL.
BUT IF I'M BEING HONEST, LIVING HERE ISN'T THAT DIFFERENT FROM LIVING IN OTHER CITIES.
24 HRS
BAR
SURE, STORES AND RESTAURANTS ARE OPEN LATER...
...AND YOU CAN GET A DRINK ANYTIME.
THAT KIND OF STUFF.
BUT THE REALITY IS, LIKE ANYWHERE ELSE, YOU GET UP, GET STUCK IN TRAFFIC, AND GET TO WORK.
AND LIKE ANYWHERE ELSE, VEGAS CAN BE PRETTY DULL.

BUT THAT'S NOT REALLY WHAT MOST VISITORS WANT TO HEAR.

PEOPLE VACATIONING IN A PLACE THEY *THINK* IS EXCITING DON'T WANT TO BE TOLD IT *ISN'T*.

AND THEY ***DON'T*** WANT TO BE LECTURED TO.

OH, AND IT'S "NEV-***AD***-A" NOT "NEV-***AH***-DA."

VEGAS SELLS ITSELF AS SOMEPLACE CRAZY AND AMAZING.

IT SELLS ITSELF SO WELL...

...THAT NO MATTER WHERE ELSE YOU GO...

WHOA...

*...*YOU'RE FROM VEGAS?

...PEOPLE WONDER.

WHAT'S *THAT* LIKE?

BUT IT'S NOT SO BAD. I MEAN, IT'S ALWAYS SOMETHING YOU CAN TALK ABOUT WHEN MEETING NEW PEOPLE.

WHOA, YOU'RE FROM VEGAS? WHAT'S THAT LIKE?

IT'S A GREAT ICEBREAKER.

IT CAN GET TO THE POINT THAT YOU DON'T EXPECT ANY OTHER QUESTIONS.

WHOA, YOU'RE FROM VEGAS? ARE YOU *ALRIGHT?*

JAN 2, 2018

SO...

...WHAT'S IT LIKE TO BE FROM VEGAS?

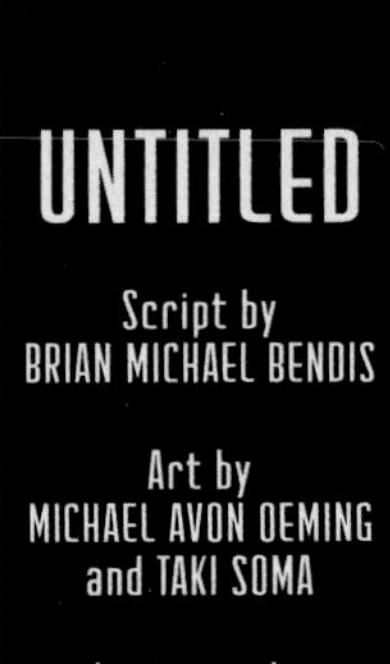

UNTITLED

Script by
BRIAN MICHAEL BENDIS

Art by
MICHAEL AVON OEMING
and TAKI SOMA

Lettering by
BERNARDO BRICE

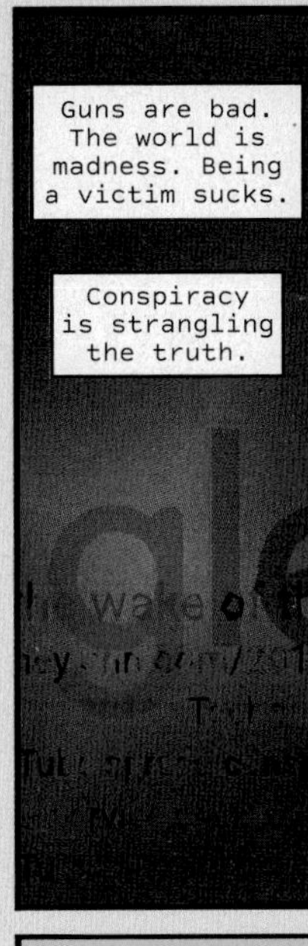

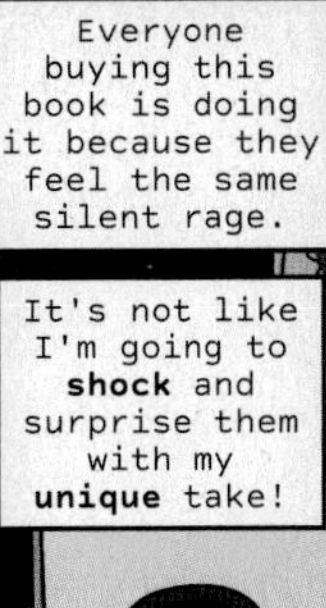

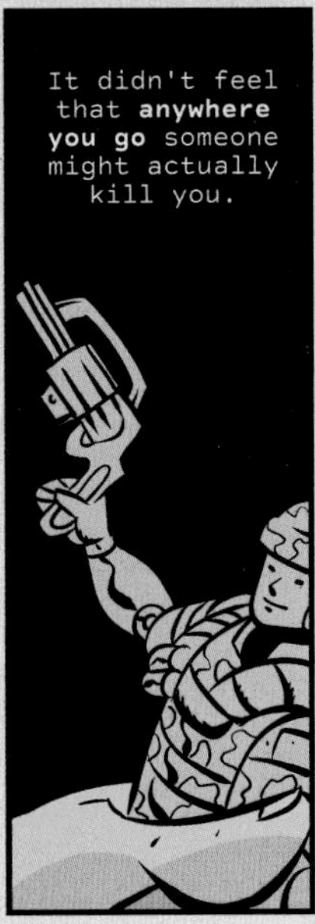

I was going to write a piece about how the news keeps conspiracy alive because they can't actually wrap their heads around the truth...

But everybody knows that too.

I was gonna write a piece about following a bullet to its horrible conclusion.
Backsp
Delete

Everybody knows where the bullets come from and we know where they go!
Backsp
Delete

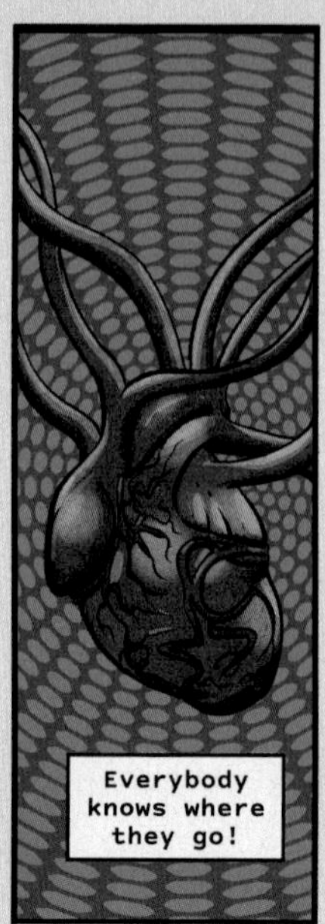
Everybody knows where they go!

And we know why... Money.

Guns are money.

Money is more important than humans.
We think that's not true but every day that **I've** been alive...

The only thing that connects the bubbling madness of Vietnam all the way to this shit is... **Money.**

I was going to write over and over again: When will it stop? When will it stop? When will it stop?

But it won't! It will never stop. Don't believe me? Sandy Hook.
The end.
49

Oh! Need another? Congress was attacked by a gunman while playing baseball--
--And they **still** won't do a damn thing.

Someone shot **them** and they won't change their minds!
Little kids, teenagers, **them...**
Nothing budges them.

I was going to write a piece about how the Parkland kids inspired us to do better...

But I'm **mad at myself** that I'm one of those middle-aged people all excited that the Parkland kids are getting up and doing something.

Something that we should have done a year and a half ago...

And by "a year and half ago" I mean about **40 years ago!**

We're so lost to this new madness that we turn to children!
We put all of this on their shoulders and hold our breath, and hope for the best?
That's the plan?
Even I was going to do it.
Shameful.
When will it stop?
Because I really want to know.
I really do.
Goddamn it!
END

ALL THE POSSIBILITIES OF PAPER
written by W. Haden Blackman
art by J.H. Williams III
lettered by Todd Klein
My daughter holds up a piece of blue construction paper
She is nine
And I imagine all the things a nine-year-old
Could make out of that blue sheet
She could create a night sky,
Stars and a moon and even planets
Drawn in white and yellow crayon
Or an ocean filled with sharks and whales and clown fish
She could fold it into a paper airplane,
Or an origami horse
She could roll it into a pirate's spyglass
Or cut it into ravens to decorate her walls
While spinning in circles in the kitchen
She tells us that the paper is the perfect size
Not for the cover of one of her hand-written story books
Or for a flag to hang in the hideout she built with her big sister
Or for a makeshift tent for the fairies who live in our backyard
She tells us the paper is the perfect size
To be taped over a small window
This is her job, she tells us
Because she is one of the taller kids in class
She will practice her job all school year
Whenever the alarm sounds
My nine-year-old daughter
Who knows the differences between ravens and crows
Who writes stories and talks to the fairies
And always defends her big sister
Will stand on her tiptoes against her classroom door
The door I know couldn't possibly stop a bullet
And tape this piece of paper
Over her classroom window
So the shooter can't see inside

"WHEN I WAS A KID IN THE 1950s, I OWNED A DAISY RED RYDER BECAUSE I WAS TOO YOUNG TO HAVE A REAL GUN.
TRAINING B-B RIFLE

"I WOULD TAKE THIS RED RYDER INTO THE WOODS AFTER SCHOOL WHERE I SHOT AND KILLED **COCHISE** AND **GERONIMO** MANY TIMES, LET ME TELL YOU.

"WHAT I'M SAYING IS THIS: YOU CAN'T TALK ABOUT SELLING **THE AR STYLE RIFLE** IN AMERICA UNLESS YOU TALK ABOUT THE FANTASY OF THE AMERICAN GUN.

"IN THE EARLY 1980s THE GUN INDUSTRY STARTED SEEING SALES IN HUNTING WEAPONS DROP. THEY TRIED TO KEEP THE MARKET ALIVE BY PITCHING THE SEMI-AUTOMATIC RIFLE AS A 'MODERN SPORTING RIFLE'.

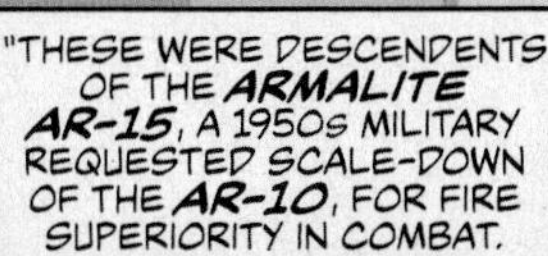

"THESE WERE DESCENDENTS OF THE **ARMALITE AR-15**, A 1950s MILITARY REQUESTED SCALE-DOWN OF THE **AR-10**, FOR FIRE SUPERIORITY IN COMBAT.

WE DON'T CALL 911

"HANDGUN SALES WERE ON THE RISE, BUT IF THE CUSTOMER BOUGHT ADD-ONS FOR A HANDGUN, AMMO AND A HOLSTER, IT MIGHT BE ABOUT $50.

"THE **AR** KNOCKOFFS HIT THE MARKET WITH A LOT MORE ACCESSORIES: CARRYING CASES FOR HUNDREDS OF DOLLARS; MILITARY-STYLE OPTICS FOR UP TO A GRAND, AND SO ON.

Attention Politicians
OVER 5,000,000 SOLD
THE WORLD'S LARGEST ARMY AIN'T IN CHINA.

"THE ACCESSORY TAB COULD EASILY EQUAL THE COST OF THE GUN. THE ECONOMIC INCENTIVE TO PUSH **AR RIFLES** INDUSTRY-WIDE IS OBVIOUS.

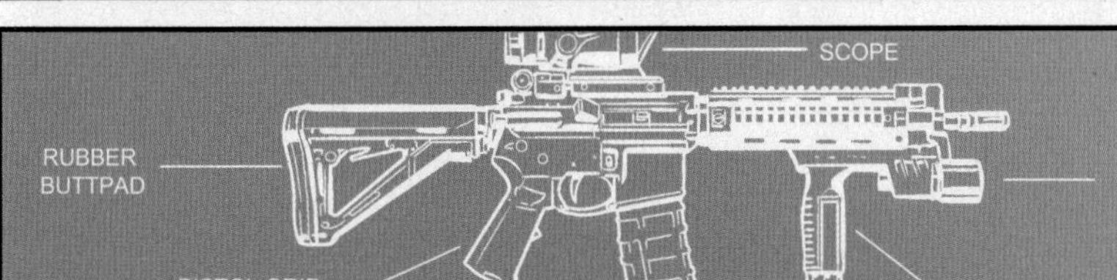

SCOPE
RUBBER BUTTPAD
PISTOL GRIP WITH INSERTS
VERTICAL GRIP
"BUT IT TURNED OUT IT WAS THE SPORT OF HUNTING ITSELF WHICH WAS IN DECLINE, AND NO GUN COULD SAVE IT.*
"TO KEEP SELLING THE PROFITABLE AR RIFLES, THE GUN INDUSTRY NEEDED A NEW MARKET TO OPEN."

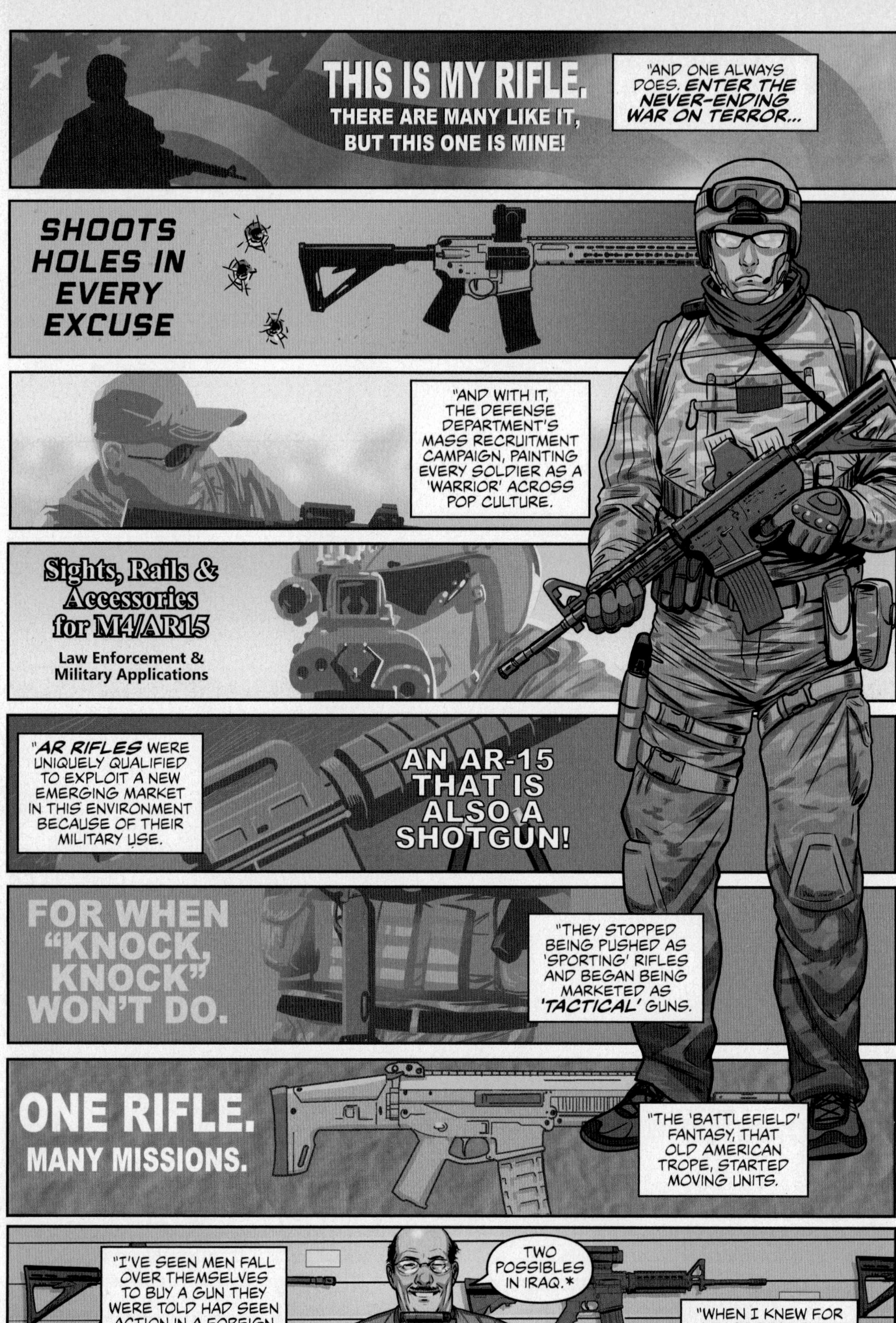

*AR style rifles confirmed kills: ***Sandy Hook*** - Twenty children between six and seven years old. ***Pulse Nightclub*** - 49 dead, 58 wounded. ***Las Vegas Music Festival*** - 58 dead, 546 wounded. ***Stoneman Douglas H.S.*** - Seventeen dead, fourteen wounded.

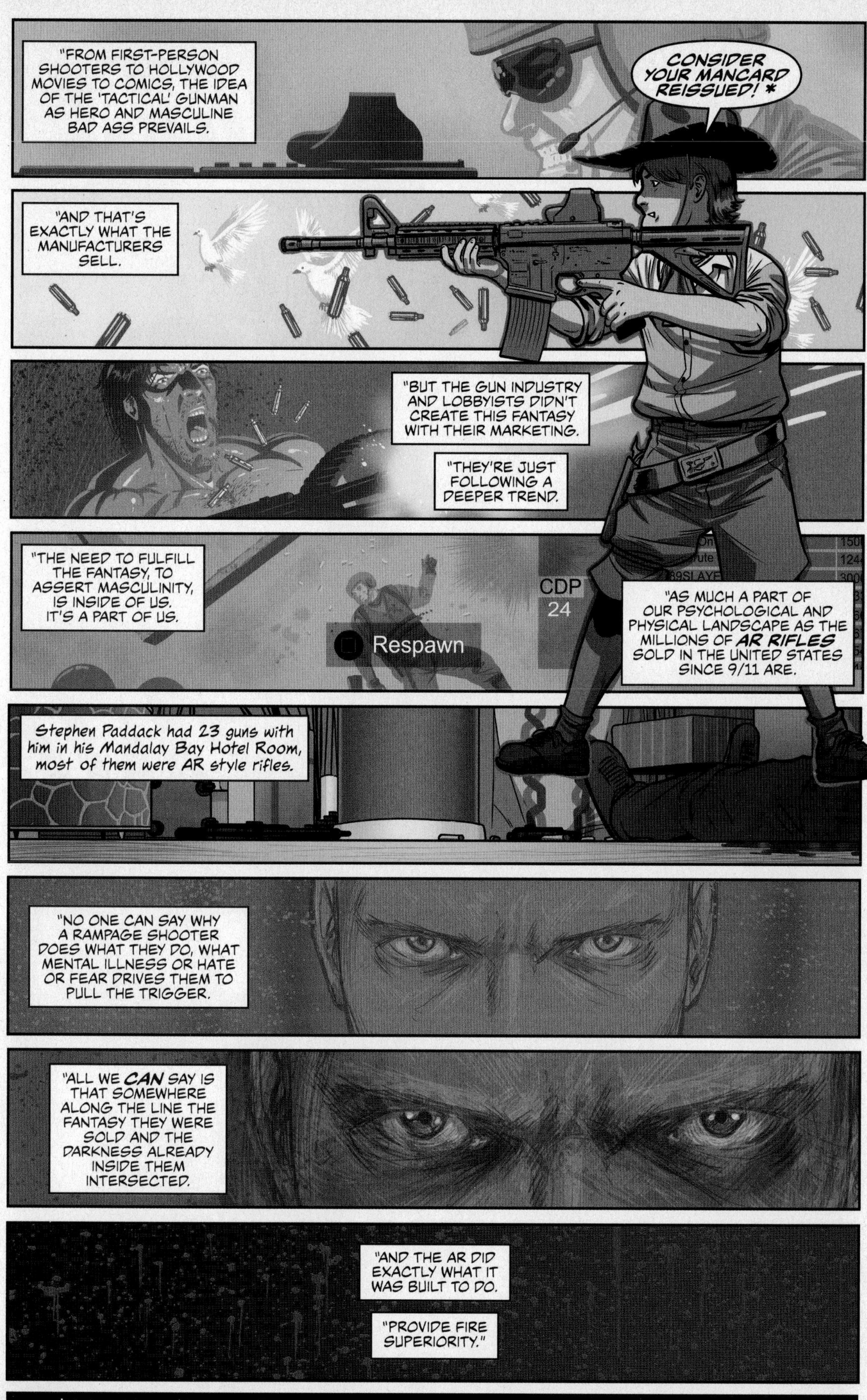

*Actual ad copy for **Bushmaster.** Makers of the AR-platform rifle used in the

Michael R. Weisser is the author of the "Guns in America" series and an ex-gun retailer. He has spoken on gun violence to the New Yorker, New York Times, Huffington Post, and others. His blog, mikethegunguy.com, is a must for understanding all sides of the gun issue

GOING OUT WITH A BANG

BANG

I HEAR YOUR SOUND AND IT'S DEAFENING...

I PRAY YOU NOT TO WHISPER IN MY EAR THAT YOU LOVE ME, FOR I WON'T BE ABLE TO HEAR IT.

I SEE YOUR BRIGHT FLASH AND IT'S BLINDING...
..., AND FOR ONE BRIEF MOMENT THIS IS ALL I SEE.
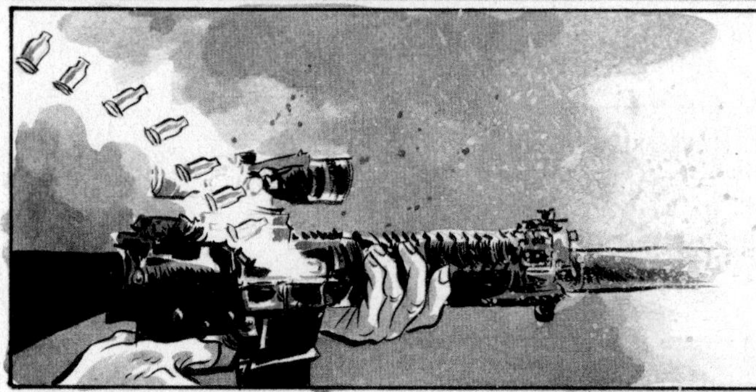
I PRAY YOU NOT TO COME MEET ME NOW, MY LOVE, FOR I WON'T BE ABLE TO SEE YOU.

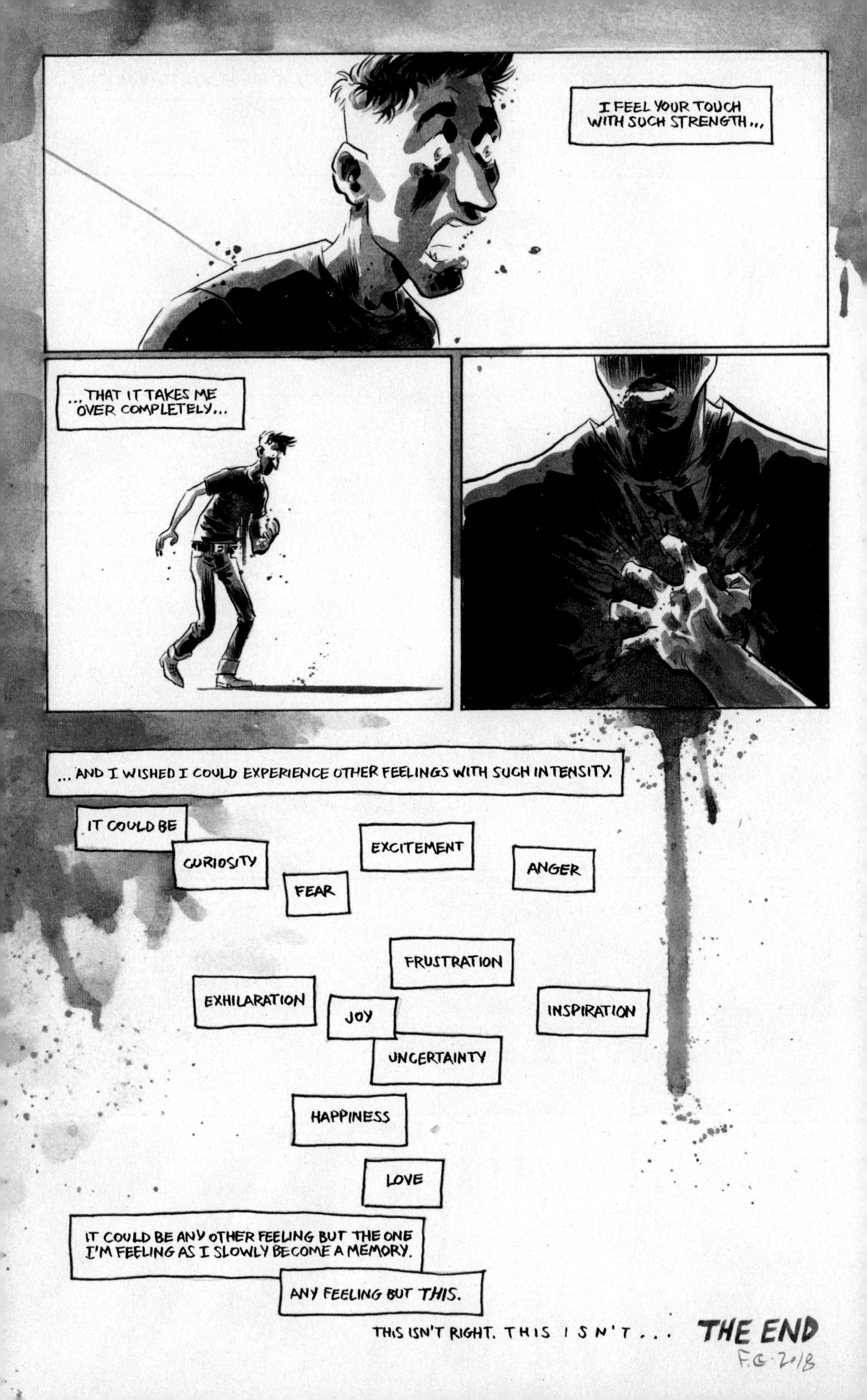

I FEEL YOUR TOUCH WITH SUCH STRENGTH...

...THAT IT TAKES ME OVER COMPLETELY...

...AND I WISHED I COULD EXPERIENCE OTHER FEELINGS WITH SUCH INTENSITY.

IT COULD BE

CURIOSITY

FEAR

EXCITEMENT

ANGER

FRUSTRATION

EXHILARATION

JOY

UNCERTAINTY

INSPIRATION

HAPPINESS

LOVE

IT COULD BE ANY OTHER FEELING BUT THE ONE I'M FEELING AS I SLOWLY BECOME A MEMORY.

ANY FEELING BUT *THIS*.

THIS ISN'T RIGHT. THIS ISN'T...

THE END

F.G. 2018

Lee

MY NAME IS *LEE.* THIS IS MY STORY.

AS YOU CAN IMAGINE, OCTOBER 1 *CHANGED* EVERYTHING.

HAUNTED

Story based on an interview with eyewitness **Lee Schoeppner**
Writer: **Alex Segura** • Art: **Marco Finnegan**
Colors: **Kelsey Shannon** • Letters: **Janice Chiang**

WELC
TO Fabulous
LAS VEGA
NEVADA
THAT NIGHT, A VENUE FULL OF CONCERTGOERS BECAME A *WAR ZONE.*

WHEN I THINK BACK, I *SEE* STATIC IMAGES.
I GUESS THAT'S MY MIND'S WAY OF *COPING*—AS IF THE ORDEAL WASN'T *REAL.*

I DON'T *SLEEP* ANYMORE.
HNGH!
I HAD *NIGHTMARES* FOR WEEKS. THE IMAGES WOULDN'T *FADE AWAY.*

MY *THROAT* SWELLS UP.
BREATHING BECOMES *DIFFICULT*. I COULDN'T GET IT *OUT* OF MY HEAD.

MY WIFE ZULY, OUR FRIEND LAURA AND I WERE ATTENDING THE ROUTE 91 FESTIVAL.
WE'D PARTIED THE FIRST TWO NIGHTS, BUT WERE TAKING IT EASY THAT EVENING.

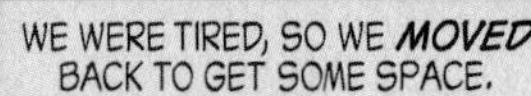
WE WERE TIRED, SO WE MOVED BACK TO GET SOME SPACE.

SOME BREATHING ROOM.
THEN JASON ALDEAN TOOK THE STAGE.

POP! POP! POP!
WHAT WAS THAT?

"FIREWORKS?" PEOPLE ASK.
POP! POP! POP!
NO. NOT FIREWORKS.

WE'RE UNDER FIRE.
WE NEED TO GO–NOW!
I RECOGNIZE THE SOUNDS IMMEDIATELY.
AUTOMATIC GUNFIRE.
I'VE FIRED HANDGUNS AND RIFLES–EVEN AUTOMATIC RIFLES.
THE SOUND IS UNIQUE.

WE'RE UNDER FIRE.
FLASHES IN THE PAVEMENT. THEY DON'T REGISTER RIGHT AWAY, BUT I KNOW NOW THEY WERE BULLETS RICOCHETING.
TCHK!
TCHK!
TCHK!

WE CUT LEFT. OUR HEARTS PUMPING LIKE CRAZY.

WE SEE THE SEVEN-FOOT CINDERBLOCK WALL AND I HESITATE FOR A SECOND.
BUT THE NOISES– THE SCREAMS, THE NON-STOP GUNFIRE...

THEY REMIND ME WE HAVE TO RUN. CLIMB. ANYTHING.

GUNFIRE ALL AROUND US.
MY BODY IS SCREAMING ONE WORD AT ME: RUN!
BUT PEOPLE NEED HELP GETTING OVER THIS WALL.

WE HELP. WE HAVE TO HELP.
HOLD ON!
T-T-THANK YOU, THANK YOU.

I HELP OUR FRIEND LAURA AND A FEW OTHERS OVER THE WALL.

I FEEL AN ACHE IN THE PIT OF MY STOMACH.

WHERE'S ZULY?

ZULY?! ZULY?!
NOTHING.

THEN I SEE HER, AND MY HEART STARTS TO BEAT AGAIN.

THE SOUND OF GUNFIRE CONTINUES, A POUNDING RHYTHM AROUND US.

BUT I FIND HER. WE FIND EACH OTHER, IN THIS ENDLESS DARKNESS—
A SPECK OF LIGHT.
LOVE.

There is no greater love than this.

My love,
I know you could have danced up that
entire stretch of desert road,
your palms aloft like fronds above
the fount where that oasis grows
straight out of the asphalt strip,
where I hoped you'd fall in love with
the way our voices sound together.
You touched your hands to my shoulders
and let me lead you through the crowd,
singing aloud, your face aglow
beneath the calico marquee lights that
glimmered off the concert stage,
you turned to me as if to say
How can this be?
That we can live so perfectly.

But sometimes the heat plays tricks on me.
All around me I began to see
shells where there was no shore,
slaughter where there was no war,
tearing through the air like claws,
I stepped into that twisted mirage
when the chandelier of stars had shattered
I grasped the only thing that mattered,
and realized what I saw was true,
knowing what I had to do,

I wrapped my arms around you
when it ripped my heart in two.

He didn't take my life,
I gave it freely,
and if you ever really
doubt that you were kissed
or that you are truly missed,
remember when I showed you.
There is no greater love than this.

— by Talia Hershewe,
Home means Nevada to me.

Illustration by Jock. Lettering by Bernardo Brice.

U N T R A N S L A T A B L E

Greg Lockard script Tim Fish art
Michael J. DiMotta colors Sal Cipriano lettering
IN MADRID, I TEACH ENGLISH AS A FOREIGN LANGUAGE AND I WORK WITH A WIDE VARIETY OF STUDENTS ACROSS THE CITY.
EVERY CLASS BEGINS WITH CASUAL CONVERSATION PRACTICE OR A GAME.
COMPARING POP CULTURES IS COMMON...
JAYZ
CHER
FOOTBALL VS FUTBOL
GAME OF THRONES
...BUT DISCUSSING CURRENT EVENTS, NO MATTER HOW DIFFICULT, IS WHERE MY STUDENTS ALWAYS IMPRESS ME.
TRUMP
BREXIT
CATALON
WHEN A SHOOTING HAPPENS IN THE U.S., I GET QUESTIONED. THIS HAS OCCURRED MULTIPLE TIMES IN THE SINGLE YEAR I HAVE BEEN TEACHING.
HOW DOES THIS HAPPEN?
DOES EVERYONE IN THE U.S. HAVE A GUN?

THE DISBELIEF ON THEIR FACES IS THE ALWAYS SAME.
NO! BUT IT'S VERY EASY TO BUY ONE.
TRUMP
BREXIT
CATALO

HOW CAN I FULLY EXPLAIN THIS TERRIBLE ELEMENT OF OUR NATION?
BOOM!
BOOM!

I USE A PERSONAL EXAMPLE OF MY MOTHER, AN ELEMENTARY SCHOOL TEACHER, LEADING ACTIVE SHOOTER DRILLS WITH HER YOUNG STUDENTS.
3,000 MILES AWAY, I WONDER WHY THOSE CHILDREN CAN'T LEARN IN PEACE.

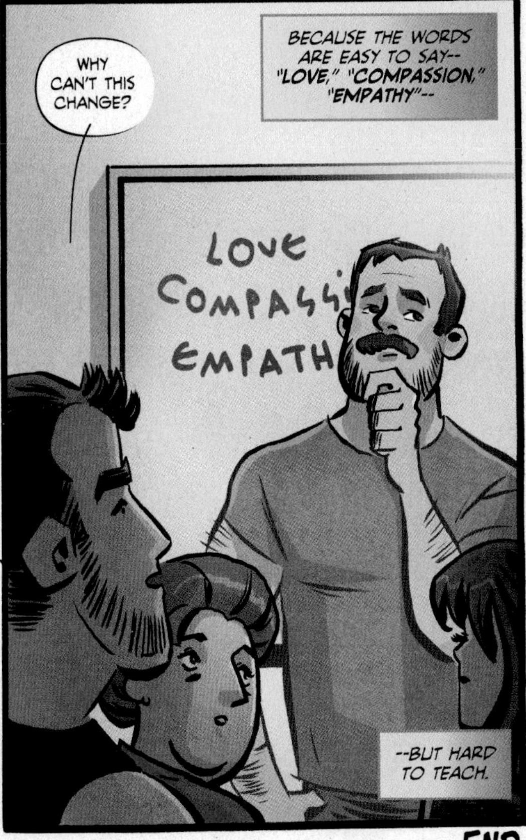
WHY CAN'T THIS CHANGE?
BECAUSE THE WORDS ARE EASY TO SAY-- "LOVE," "COMPASSION," "EMPATHY"--
LOVE
COMPASS
EMPATH
--BUT HARD TO TEACH.

END.

INVOLUTION

[GUSTAVO DUARTE]

CULTURE

Written by
RYAN BURTON

Art by
TONY PARKER

Colored by
DEE CUNNIFFE

Lettered by
BERNARDO BRICE

Wesson, Bene

DOB: 10/17/

Time: 22:15

MATER SEMPER

SO BEAUTIFUL.

!
WILD BIL
BURGERS
TAKE AIM, PARTNER!
MATER SEMPER CERTA EST.
MATER SEMPER CERTA EST.

A EST
NEW
YOU ARE YOUR MEDICINE
COME AND GET IT
HOSPITAL

AND
GET IT

BEAUTIFUL.

SO BEAUTIFUL.
End.

LOVE AND FEAR
SCRIPT BY AARON DURAN
PENCILS & INKS BY JOE MULVEY
COLORS BY JULES RIVERA
LETTERS BY BERNARDO BRICE
IT'S 1992. I'M A SOPHOMORE IN HIGH SCHOOL.

THAT'S ME OVER THERE. THE FAT ONE WITH THE SHOVEL.
I KNOW WHAT THIS LOOKS LIKE. SOME ODD RURAL INITIATION THING.
I GUESS WE ARE PERFORMING A RITUAL. A DEEPLY PATRIOTIC RITUAL THAT WILL ENSURE OUR WAY OF LIFE FOR GENERATIONS TO COME.
BILL CLINTON HAD JUST BEEN ELECTED AS PRESIDENT. AND SO, MY FRIENDS AND FAMILY ARE DOING THE ONLY SANE THING IN SUCH A FRIGHTENING WORLD.

WE'RE BURYING GUNS.
COOL.

THE U.N...
...LIBERAL COMMUNISTS...
...GOTTA BE SAFE...
AT THAT MOMENT, I DON'T FEEL FEAR OR PARANOIA. I FEEL GOOD. I FEEL SAFE. BUT MOST OF ALL, AS MY DAD HANDS ME A BEER, I FEEL **LOVED**.

IT WAS ONLY A FEW PRANK CALLS TO MY HOME. BUT IT WAS ENOUGH TO IGNITE THE FEAR IN ME. SO HERE I AM, DOING WHAT I'VE BEEN TAUGHT TO DO. DOING WHAT I'M EXPECTED TO DO.
I SHOULD BE WASTING MONEY ON A CAR STEREO, OR A NEW GAMING SYSTEM, OR A MYRIAD LIST OF WHATEVER 18-YEAR-OLD AMERICAN BOYS DO.
YOU'D BE AMAZED WHAT A FIVE-MINUTE FORM AND $50 EVERY TWO WEEKS FOR THREE MONTHS WILL GET YOU.
IT DIDN'T MATTER THAT THE PRANK CALLS HAD LONG SINCE PASSED, BARELY A BLIP ON MY FAMILY'S MEMORY.
I REMEMBERED. I FELT THE FEAR. THE GUN FIXED THAT.
SOLD
SOLD
--BECAUSE HE'S STILL A CHILD, THAT'S WHY!
YOU'RE RIGHT, AND IT'S TIME HE STEP UP AND BECOME A MAN--
NO! YOU DON'T PULL THIS MACHO SHIT ON ME. HE'S EIGHTEEN, WHY DOES HE NEED A GUN? AND DON'T TELL ME HUNTING. HE FREAKING HATES HUNTING!
I TOLD THEM I LIKED TO TARGET SHOOT. AND I DID.
STILL DO.
I DIDN'T WANT TO BE AFRAID.
BUT THAT ISN'T WHY I BOUGHT IT. I WAS AFRAID.

THE GUN DID FIND ITS USE IN MY LIFE.
IT'S AMAZING HOW QUICKLY YOU CAN MAKE A BUCK OFF A GUN WHEN TIMES ARE TIGHT, EVEN LEGALLY.
THOUGH NOT AS MUCH AS ONE WOULD BELIEVE, BUT A MONTH OF GROCERIES AND A PAID 90-DAYS-PAST-DUE ELECTRIC BILL IS NOTHING TO SCOFF AT.
THERE WAS NO SHADOW GOVERNMENT. NO REASON TO BE THAT KID IN 1992 ANYMORE.
THE ONE THAT BURIED GUNS IN THE DESERT TO PROTECT HIMSELF AND HIS FAMILY FROM THOSE THAT HATED HIM.

IT FELT GOOD TO LIVE WITHOUT **FEAR**.
AND WITH PENNSYLVANIA ALL BUT COUNTED, WE'RE CALLING IT FOR DONALD H...

...THE SO-CALLED ALT-RIGHT...
...NEO FASCISTS...
...WITH PEOPLE OF COLOR FACING...

SO HERE I AM. A LIFETIME REMOVED FROM THE SCARED CHILD BURYING GUNS IN THE DESERT. OR AM I?
PREPARING THE ONLY WAY I'VE BEEN TAUGHT.
WONDERING WHAT WILL WIN.
LOVE.
OR FEAR.

Larime & Sylv

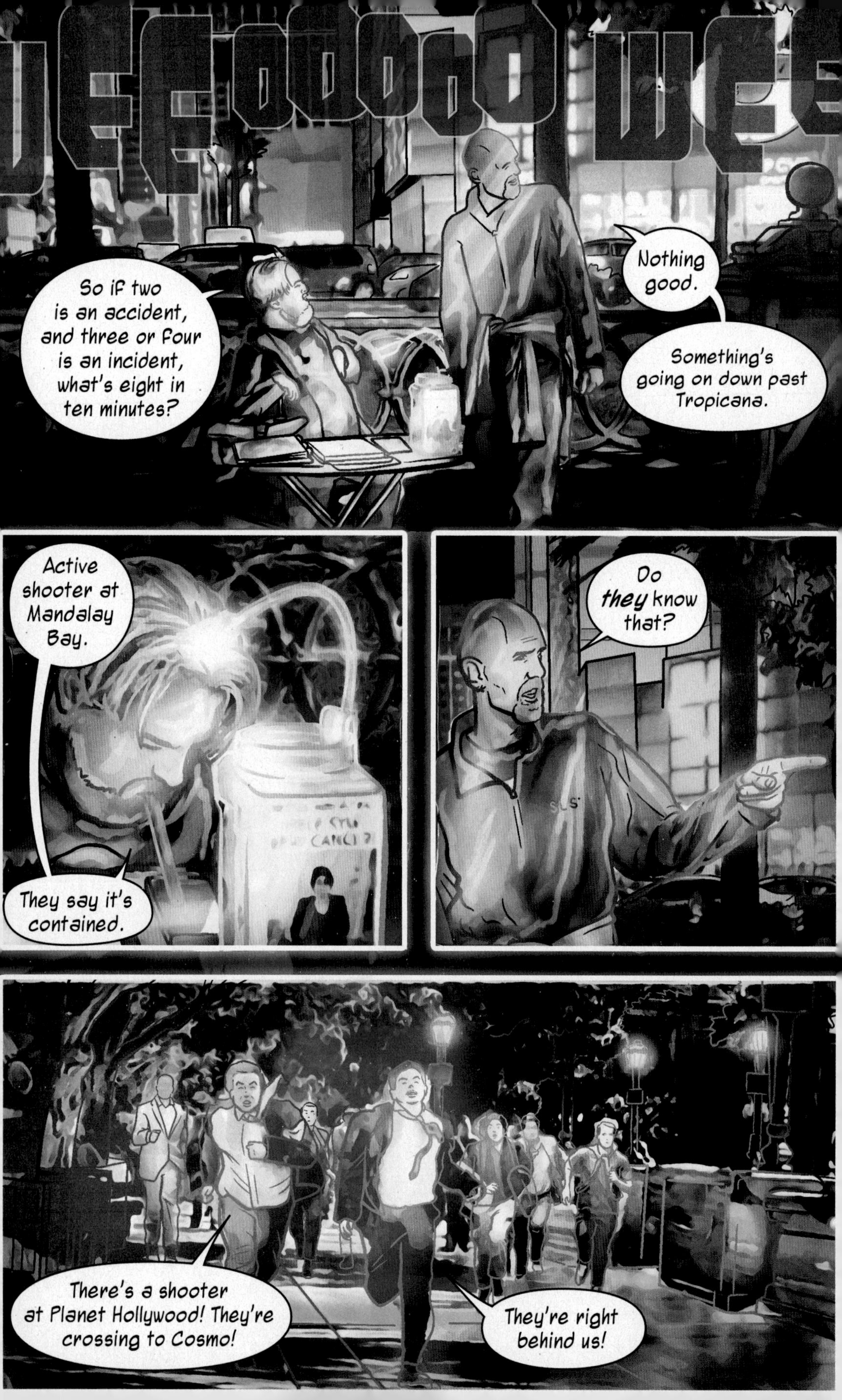

So if two is an accident, and three or four is an incident, what's eight in ten minutes?
Nothing good.
Something's going on down past Tropicana.

OOOOO WEE OOOOO

What's going on over there?

Are you guys ok?

Where are you right now?

Are you safe?

Are you working tonight?

There's a shooter on the strip!

We heard there's two out there!

Is Larime at home??

m e a n w h i l e

Another Day in Paradise

by Larime & Sylv Taylor

Good to go. Be safe.
Thanks, Drew. You too.

It's kind of creepy.

I've lived here five years, and I've never seen the Strip empty.

Like something out of a zombie apocalypse movie. I sit in the elevator a long moment, just watching.
Police randomly drive by in all directions, like they're chasing ghosts. There's a part of me I'm not proud of that wants to just sit in this dark elevator and watch what happens.
But it's not the most surreal part.

...Can I cross?
POLIC

randoxxx: Why aren't the cops there yet??

They're securing each area, it takes time.

helpfulguy321: Maybe they need help?

They don't know which reports are real or fake.

tryhard76: They need good guys with guns out there too.

They won't know you're a good guy.

patriot21: I carry, I should go down there.

All they'll see is a rando with a gun.

realmurican13: Yeah, they won't shoot if people are fighting back!

You're going to get killed.

realistfedora: If everyone was armed this wouldn't happen.

My husband might get caught in the crossfire!

scoobydoo552: We need to do something!

...

Any word on what's going on? I thought it was just Mandalay Bay.

There may be multiple shooters.
I think we got one at New York, New York.* Get home safe.
*I was told this by an officer from Metro that night. It was false.

The whole Strip's shut down. There's an active shooter.

I tried.

We heard on the scanner there might be a shooter in the Bellagio.
You work out front, right?
Yeah. I just left there. Wow.

Hey Zelda. Daddy's home safe, little butt.
Sylv? I'm home.

It turned out, in the end, that the second gunman was just a rumor, a game of telephone gone dangerously wrong. "I heard something!" turned into, "I heard him!" and "He's down the Strip!" to, "He's right behind us!" But the fear was very real. Real enough to cause panic, stampedes, and confusion on the part of everyone from tourists to security. Real enough to send Metro on wild goose chases throughout the Strip, as every hotel guest had their own story about a crazed terrorist, fueled by instant internet speculation that literally went viral.

In the days that followed, everyone had more questions than answers, and when the answers didn't come quick enough, people came up with their own. All we know is, officially, that one gunman smuggled suitcases of guns into his suite, and shot into a crowd of concert-goers, without interruption, for 10-15 minutes, and 58 people died. We don't know why. We might never know.

POWERFUL
STORY BY RAFAEL SCAVONE
ART BY RAFAEL ALBUQUERQUE
COLORS BY TRISH MULVIHILL
LETTERS BY BERNARDO BRICE
IT'S ENOUGH.
I'M SO TIRED OF IT ALL THAT I CAN'T GO ON ANYMORE.
IT TOOK ME SO MUCH TIME TO REALIZE THAT IT WAS ALL IN VAIN...
THAT THERE'S NO WAY BACK FOR ME...
THIS MACHINE KILLS FASCISTS
God Bless America
...FOR US.
FOR ALL OF US--
SINCE YOU'RE GONE, ALL THE THINGS I UTTERLY BELIEVED GRADUALLY CHANGED...
...AND NOWADAYS I CAN'T EVEN RELY ON MY OLD BROTHERS.
THOSE ONES WHO GAVE THEIR OWN BLOOD AND SUFFERED RIGHT AT MY SIDE.
THEY'RE ALL GONE...LIKE YOU... ON THAT DAY.

IT'S HARD TO BELIEVE THAT THE PLANS WE USED TO MAKE JUST VANISHED AWAY WITH YOU.
ALL DUE TO THIS SICK SOCIETY WHERE ONE MAN HAVE ENOUGH POWER TO...

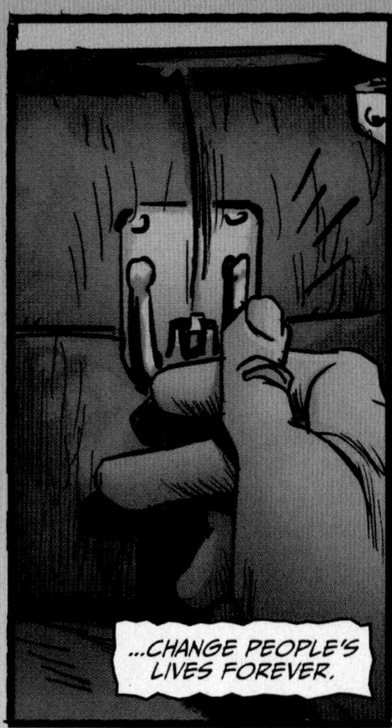
...CHANGE PEOPLE'S LIVES FOREVER.

I HAD PROMISED MYSELF I WOULDN'T SEEK ANSWERS...
...NOR FIGHT BACK.
BUT IT'S STRONGER THAN ME...

...IT'S IN MY SOUL.
IT'S PRIMAL--

THIS PLACE.
SUCH A LONG TIME--
IN MY PRAYERS I PLEDGED TO YOU I WOULD NEVER COME BACK HERE SINCE THAT DAY.

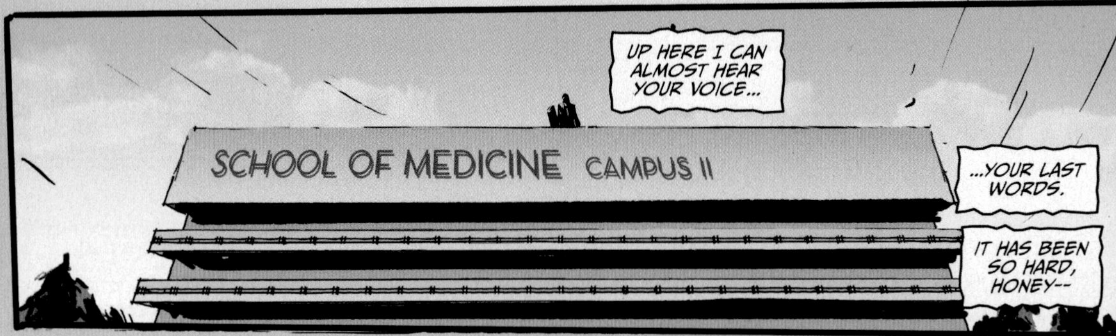
UP HERE I CAN ALMOST HEAR YOUR VOICE...
SCHOOL OF MEDICINE CAMPUS II
...YOUR LAST WORDS.
IT HAS BEEN SO HARD, HONEY--

I KNOW VERY WELL THAT WHAT I'M ABOUT TO DO IS A DESPERATE ACT.

IT'S GONNA TOUCH SO MANY PEOPLE AROUND HERE...

EVERYTHING AFTER

WORDS: JUSTIN JORDAN
ART/COLORS: TOM FOWLER
LETTERS: TAYLOR ESPOSITO

A FEW MONTHS BEFORE THE SHOOTING, SOME OF MY FRIENDS AND FAMILY WENT TO LAS VEGAS.

NOTHING UNUSUAL ABOUT THAT. VEGAS IS A TOURIST DESTINATION. SO EVEN PEOPLE FROM DEEPLY RURAL PENNSYLVANIA END UP THERE SOMETIMES.

BUT WHILE THEY WERE THERE, THEY MET A BARTENDER THEY REALLY LIKED. SO MUCH SO, THAT I GOT TO HEAR ALL ABOUT HER WHEN THEY GOT BACK.

THE TRIP ENDED AND STORIES WERE TOLD AND THAT WAS THE END OF THAT.

UNTIL A PSYCHOTIC MAN SHOT FIVE HUNDRED PEOPLE.

THE BARTENDER THEY MET WASN'T SHOT. BUT SHE WAS THERE. AND MONTHS AFTER MEETING HER, MY FAMILY SAW HER ON THE NEWS. SHE COMFORTED A MAN WHO HAD BEEN SHOT. A MAN WHO DIED.

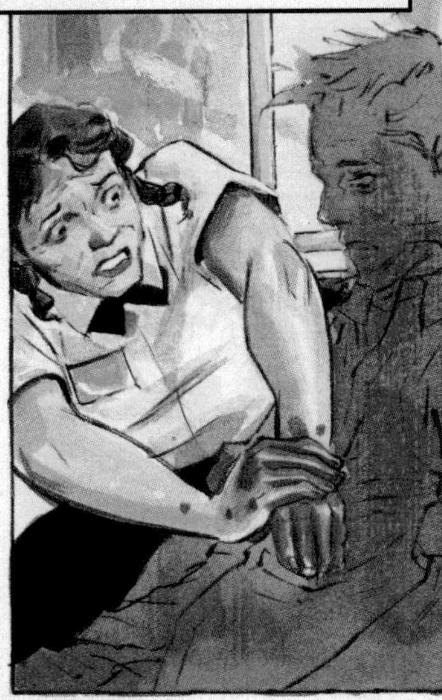
SHE STAYED WITH HIM FOR HOURS. SHE TALKED TO HIS FAMILY, HIS GIRLFRIEND ON THE PHONE.
HE WAS FROM BRITISH COLUMBIA. SHE'D NEVER MET HIM. HE WAS A STRANGER TO HER. HIS FAMILY, HIS LOVED ONES, WERE STRANGERS TO HER.

IT'S TEMPTING TO THINK THESE KINDS OF TRAGEDIES ARE DISTANT THINGS. BUT NOTHING IS REALLY DISTANT.
SHE MADE A DIFFERENCE, A SMALL ONE, IN MY FAMILY'S LIFE. A HUGE ONE IN ANOTHER FAMILY'S.

NOTHING IS DISTANT.
EVERYTHING MATTERS.

EVERYONE MATTERS.

EVEN IF WE ONLY SEE IT AFTER.

JESSE SLAYS THE DRAGON
Credits:
Script: Amy Chu
Art: Gabriel Walta
Lettering: Alexander Chang

Once upon a time*, in an ordinary town just past midnight,

a beautiful princess went to a party.

But she was in the wrong place at the wrong time.

Because it was in that flash... that burst of light...

...when her life changed.

The princess survived.

But now she could see everything was different.

Jesse knew she was still beautiful.
But the dragon was still there, lurking.
*based on a true story

So she put on her favorite lipstick...
--and she waited..
When the dragon raised its ugly head
Jesse charged into battle (rocking to her favorite band Behemoth...)
...and she smote that foul breathing bastard dead.
THE END

ENOUGH!

A Simple
Twist of Fate.

written by
Jeff Boison

with art by
Tyler Boss

I HATE YOU!

BREAKING NEWS

BREAKING NEWS
PRESIDENT CALLS SHOOTING "A HORRIBLE ACT OF EVIL"

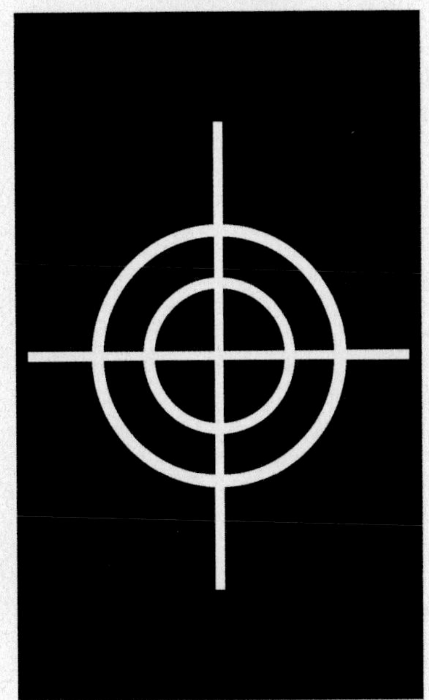

BREAKING NEWS
GUN STOCKS SOAR
AOBC 14.22 ⬆ 1.68 RGR 53.45 ⬆ 6.08 OLN 38.25 ⬆ 2.35

BREAKING NEWS
SENATE MAJORITY LEADER:
"ALL THOSE AFFECTED ARE IN OUR THOUGHTS AND PRAYERS."

AMBULANCE

I LOVE YOU.

Aubri

UNTIL THAT MOMENT, IT HAD BEEN A GOOD DAY. MY GRADES WERE UNDER CONTROL. I WAS GETTING OVER A BREAKUP. MY LIFE WAS TAKING A POSITIVE TURN.

Six Weeks

STORY BASED ON AN INTERVIEW WITH EYEWITNESS:
AUBRI
WORDS: JARRET KEENE
ART: CRAIG CERMAK
COLORS: MARISSA LOUISE
LETTERS: TAYLOR ESPOSITO

I WAS EXCITED TO BE WITH FRIENDS IN THE FRONT ROW OF A JASON ALDEAN CONCERT.
WE INSTANTLY KNEW IT WAS GUNFIRE. PEOPLE AROUND ME WERE SHOT IN THE HEAD. I HAD SHARED SMILES WITH THEM SECONDS BEFORE.
UNLV
NOW THEY WERE DYING.

SOMEHOW MY FRIENDS AND I WEREN'T HIT. WE RAN TOWARD THE GATE WE CAME IN, EVEN THOUGH WE'D BEEN STANDING NEXT TO AN EXIT.
MY FRIENDS CUT THEIR FEET ON BROKEN GLASS AND BEER CANS.

IT HAPPENED THAT ANOTHER FRIEND OF OURS ARRIVED LATE, DRIVING IN FROM A HIKE IN ZION. WE TEXTED HIM FOR HELP.
NEVADA
235DM1
HE PICKED US UP IN HIS CAR JUST AS WE MADE IT OUT, ZIPPING US AWAY.

WE SKIPPED THE HOSPITAL AND WENT TO A FRIEND'S HOUSE. WE DIDN'T TALK TO EACH OTHER, ONLY TO LOVED ONES.
WE COULDN'T PROCESS IT.

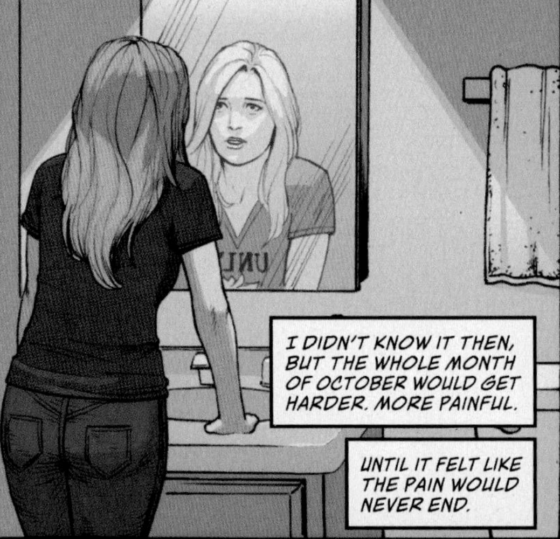

I DIDN'T KNOW IT THEN, BUT THE WHOLE MONTH OF OCTOBER WOULD GET HARDER. MORE PAINFUL.
UNTIL IT FELT LIKE THE PAIN WOULD NEVER END.

THE NEXT DAY WAS TOUGH. I WANTED THINGS TO RETURN TO NORMAL. BUT WHEN I SHOWED UP FOR MY CLASS, THE PROFESSOR SAID...
I ASSUME YOU'RE LATE BECAUSE OF THE SHOOTING, TOO.

I WAS SHOCKED. HIS WORDS HURT ME. THEN AGAIN, HOW WAS HE TO KNOW?
NOT MANY ENGLISH MAJORS ARE COUNTRY FANS, I GUESS.

I DIDN'T SAY ANYTHING IN RESPONSE.
GOT CHEER?
I JUST WALKED OUT.

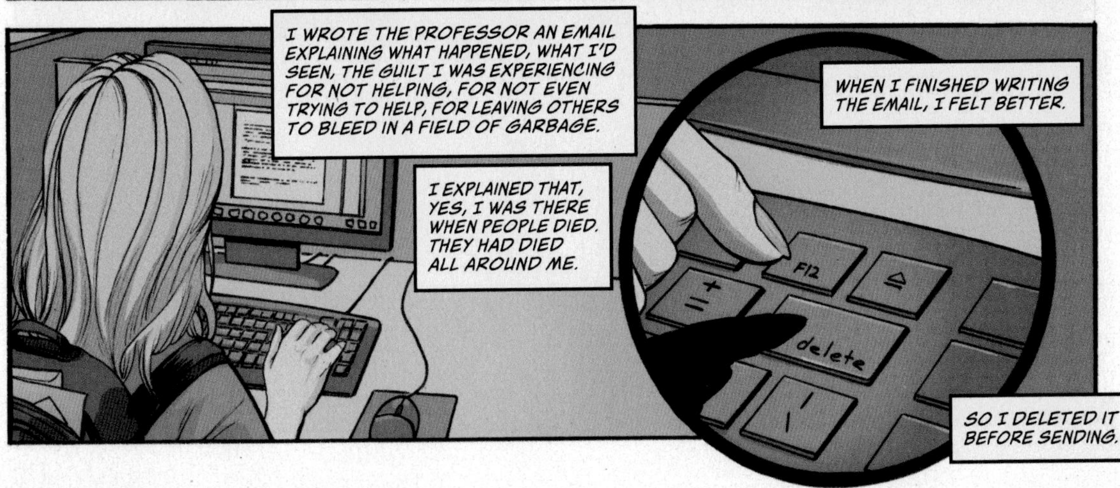
I WROTE THE PROFESSOR AN EMAIL EXPLAINING WHAT HAPPENED, WHAT I'D SEEN, THE GUILT I WAS EXPERIENCING FOR NOT HELPING, FOR NOT EVEN TRYING TO HELP, FOR LEAVING OTHERS TO BLEED IN A FIELD OF GARBAGE.
I EXPLAINED THAT, YES, I WAS THERE WHEN PEOPLE DIED. THEY HAD DIED ALL AROUND ME.
WHEN I FINISHED WRITING THE EMAIL, I FELT BETTER.
F12
delete
SO I DELETED IT BEFORE SENDING.

THE WEEK GREW DARKER. MY MENTOR FROM HIGH SCHOOL DIED.
SHE WAS THE ONE WHO HAD INSPIRED ME TO FIND A JOB AS A CHOREOGRAPHER, A JOB IN WHICH I WAS NOW STRUGGLING.

THEN MY FATHER HAD HEART SURGERY. IT DIDN'T GO WELL.
I NEARLY LOST HIM, TOO.
I FELT LIKE I WAS CRACKING APART, CRUSHED UNDER THE WEIGHT OF THINGS.

I WROTE SOME POEMS, BUT I COULDN'T GET ANY CRITICAL DISTANCE.
I COULDN'T WORK ON THEM THE WAY I USUALLY DID. THE PROCESS FOR ME HAD CHANGED.
I WAS WORRIED I'D NEVER WRITE AGAIN.

WORSE, I WAS LETTING DOWN MY CHEER STUDENTS. MY PASSION HAD ABANDONED ME.
I SAW PITY IN THEIR FACES. THEY WANTED TO HELP BUT DIDN'T KNOW HOW.
CMS
CMS
CMS
CMS
CMS

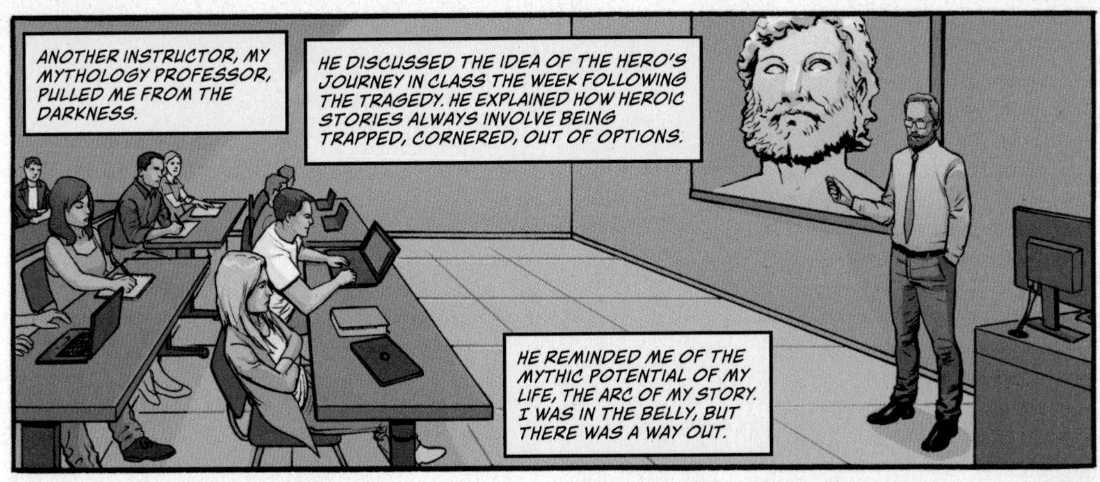
ANOTHER INSTRUCTOR, MY MYTHOLOGY PROFESSOR, PULLED ME FROM THE DARKNESS.
HE DISCUSSED THE IDEA OF THE HERO'S JOURNEY IN CLASS THE WEEK FOLLOWING THE TRAGEDY. HE EXPLAINED HOW HEROIC STORIES ALWAYS INVOLVE BEING TRAPPED, CORNERED, OUT OF OPTIONS.
HE REMINDED ME OF THE MYTHIC POTENTIAL OF MY LIFE, THE ARC OF MY STORY. I WAS IN THE BELLY, BUT THERE WAS A WAY OUT.

I TOOK EVERYTHING MY PROFESSOR TAUGHT ME AND FED IT BACK TO MY CHEER GROUP. A FEW OF THEM HAD FRIENDS AND FAMILY WHO'D BEEN HURT AT THE SHOOTING.
WE WORKED THROUGH OUR PAIN BY TRAINING FOR THE NEXT COMPETITION.

WE DUG DEEP INSIDE OURSELVES AND PERFORMED AT OUR VERY BEST.
CMS
CMS
CMS
CMS

BEFORE THE SHOOTING, MY CONFIDENCE WAS LACKING. CHEESY AS IT SOUNDS, I'M STRONGER FROM THE ORDEAL.
I EVEN PATCHED THINGS UP WITH MY BOYFRIEND. WE GOT BACK TOGETHER.

I LEARNED TO THINK OUTSIDE OF MYSELF AND BEYOND MY OWN PAIN. I LEARNED TO CONSIDER THE SUFFERING OF OTHERS.
I'VE GROWN AS A RESULT.

I ENDED UP HAVING A SUCCESSFUL SEMESTER. I EARNED "A" GRADES AND WROTE SOME OF MY BEST POEMS YET IN MY CREATIVE WRITING WORKSHOP.

OH, AND THAT FIRST PROFESSOR WHO'D BEEN THOUGHTLESS? WE GET ALONG GREAT NOW. HE'S A TERRIFIC TEACHER.
WE HAVE CONVERSATIONS ABOUT THINGS THAT MATTER, IN BOTH LITERARY STUDIES AND IN LAS VEGAS.

WHAT'S MORE, I STARTED MY OWN CHEER-CHOREOGRAPHY BUSINESS. I'M NO LONGER WORKING FOR SOMEONE ELSE.
I'M MY OWN BOSS.

MY FRIENDS ARE DEALING WITH SURVIVOR'S GUILT AND NIGHTMARES.
I'M THE YOUNGEST OF THE BUNCH, BUT I FEEL I CAN SUPPORT THEM THROUGH THIS.

I'LL ALWAYS MAKE TIME FOR THEM.
I LISTEN AND TELL THEM THEY'RE LOVED AND NEEDED.
BECAUSE THEY ARE.

WE CONTINUE TO HANG OUT AND SPEND TIME TOGETHER DOING FUN STUFF--
--LIKE SNOWBOARDING AT MAMMOTH MOUNTAIN IN CALIFORNIA.

THIS MIGHT SOUND SILLY. BUT I REDISCOVERED A SONG I'D WRITTEN AND RECORDED A COUPLE OF YEARS AGO.
IT'S CALLED "WINGS."

IT'S A SONG THAT COMFORTS ME NOW. THERE'S A VERSE IN IT THAT GOES...
"TWO OF THEM CAN'T
WORK A NINE-TO-FIVE
TOO YOUNG, TOO WILD
TOO MUCH GOING ON
IN THEIR MINDS."

PLAYING THE SONG AGAIN, I'M REMINDED OF THE POSITIVE PERSON I USED TO BE, BEFORE ALL THIS CRAZY STUFF HAPPENED. I HAD A REALLY GOOD, REALLY EASY LIFE.
AND YOU KNOW WHAT? I FEEL LIKE I CAN BE THAT PERSON AGAIN. WELL, NOT THE **SAME** PERSON, OF COURSE.
IT ISN'T EASY.

SOMETIMES IT FEELS LIKE THINGS ARE GOING REALLY WELL.
SOMETIMES I FIND MYSELF BACK IN A DARK PLACE.
CMS
CMS
CMS
CMS

I'M TAKING IT DAY BY DAY. MOMENT BY MOMENT. BECAUSE, WELL, THAT'S ALL I CAN DO.
I MIGHT NEVER BE WHO I WAS BEFORE.
BUT MAYBE I CAN BE SOMEONE BETTER.

A Primer to the Second Amendment

Once upon a time, the average American gave little thought to the Second Amendment, and the NRA focused on hunting and teaching Boy Scouts how to shoot safely. Of course this is no longer the case, but when did the Second Amendment so strongly come to the political forefront, and why?

Essay by **CHRISTINA RICE** Illustration by **RICHARD PACE**
Production Design by **BERNARDO BRICE**

Modern-day Americans tend to regard the Bill of Rights, including the Second Amendment, in an almost mythical light. However, those first ten amendments were in fact a compromise Federalist Founding Fathers made in order to get enough colonies-turned-states to ratify the Constitution. Then as now, there was a fierce debate over a strong federal government vs. states' rights. Those who favored the latter were fearful that the Constitution gave too much power to the former. The Bill of Rights was a promised concession to be tacked onto the founding document, though it took James Madison a full year after the Constitution was ratified to even draft the ten amendments.

Why was a right to bear arms even included? At that time, militias, or citizen armies, were a part of everyday life. Every (white) male was expected to be a member of the local militia and essentially be indefinitely on call. In many of the colonies, members of a militia were even required to purchase and maintain their own guns. Police forces did not exist, so communities were tasked with banding together to protect their own property and citizens. Militias were a major method for achieving this. This is where the Second Amendment comes in.

Having been under the thumb of a monarchy for over a century, many of the Founders were reluctant to give the Federal Government too much power, including military power. After all, without the militias, the colonies could have never staved off British troops and gained independence. It makes sense that many were vehemently opposed to a centralized standing army that could potentially overpower the people. The Second Amendment was included in the Bill of Rights to protect the militias and alleviate these fears. While the amendment clearly addresses the militias, does its vague wording and oddly placed commas also protect an individual's right to own guns? It would be up to the courts to decide that.

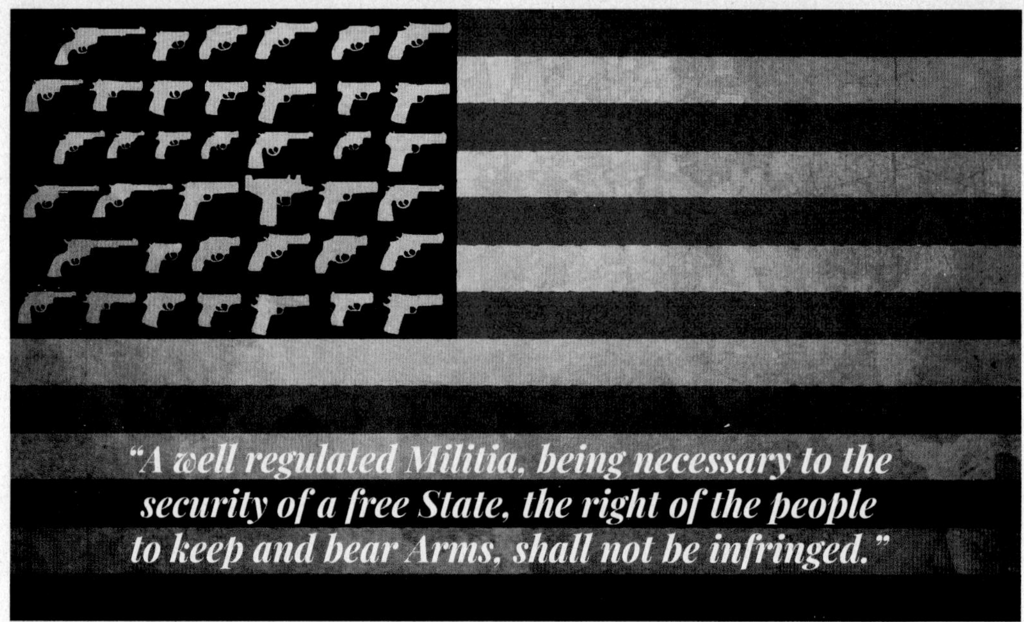

"A well regulated Militia, being necessary to the
security of a free State, the right of the people
to keep and bear Arms, shall not be infringed."

The United States has a longstanding history with guns. The earliest settlers needed them for hunting, and as relations with Native Americans deteriorated with westward expansion, the gun was the easiest way to assume victory in that realm. But as parts of the country became more industrialized, militias became less necessary, and as civil rights expanded beyond the white male, attitudes towards guns began to change.

In 1876, *The United States vs. Cruikshank* was the first case regarding the Second Amendment to come before the Supreme Court. Three years earlier, a militia made up of white men aggressed against a black militia in a standoff at a Louisiana courthouse. When the dust cleared, at least 100 African Americans lay dead, many having been killed after they had surrendered. Among the charges brought by the Federal Government against the white instigators was that an infringement of Second Amendment rights occurred when the freedmen's guns were confiscated. The Supreme Court disagreed, stating that the Second Amendment only applied to actions taken by the Federal Government, not individuals or even states (at the time, Louisiana law prevented African Americans from owning guns). The ruling did not make it any clearer who "the people" of the Second Amendment were, but it did serve to water down the Fourteenth Amendment, paving the way for state and local laws to usher in the Jim Crow era.

Supreme Court cases addressing the Second Amendment did not come on the docket often. When they did, the Court usually maintained that only Congressional law constituted infringement under the Bill of Rights. State gun control laws were allowed to stand. Even when the National Firearms Act was passed in 1934 as a response to guns that were wielded by Prohibition-era gangsters, the Supreme Court upheld it with *United States vs. Miller*, stating that weapons like sawed-off shotguns were not necessary for maintaining a well-regulated militia. This ruling was the first that dealt directly with Congressional infringement on the Second Amendment, though it still did not clarify if it included an individual right to bear arms.

This all changed in 2008 with *District of Columbia vs. Heller.* In this landmark 5-4 decision, the Supreme Court stated that the Second Amendment did indeed protect an individual's right to possess firearms unconnected to a militia. Two years later, another 5-4 decision in *McDonald vs. City of Chicago* stated that the Second Amendment applied to state as well as federal government. This overturned the Court's 1876 decision.

After 200-plus years of steering clear of defined Second Amendment decisions, why the change? There are many factors at play, including an increase in the appointments of conservative-leaning judges over the last few decades. But arguably, the most decisive contributor is the rise of the gun lobby, led by the NRA.

The National Rifle Association was formed in 1871 in response to the average Union soldier's lack of marksmanship during the Civil War. While the organization did keep an eye on gun legislation, for many years its focus was on education, marksmanship, and firearms in a recreational capacity. As late as 1967, the NRA claimed to have "no partisan political leaning," and "is a non-profit, educational organization, supported by the membership fees of public-spirited citizens and clubs." The old guard of the NRA leaned more and more away from politics, and in the 1970s even planned to move the national headquarters from Washington DC to Colorado.

In May of 1977, a radical gun rights faction of the NRA staged a coup at the organization's national meeting and took control. Often referred to as the "Revolt in Cincinnati," these events launched an extremely powerful gun lobby that has become closely aligned with the Republican Party. The NRA's stringent views on the Second Amendment matched with their money and political connections has certainly been a driving factor in opposing gun legislation and even preventing federal research on gun violence.

Given the United States' long and enduring history with firearms, the existence of guns in our country is an inescapable reality. Recent Supreme Court decisions regarding the Second Amendment are unlikely to be overturned. However, these rulings do not mean that a right to bear arms obliterates a responsibility to be sensible with that right.

Bibliography

Abumrad, Jad (Producer). October 11, 2017. More Perfect: The Gun Show [Audio podcast]. Retrieved from https://www.wnycstudios.org/story/gun-show

Hardy, David T. Origins and Development of the Second Amendment. Southport, Connecticut: Blacksmith Corporation, 1986,

National Rifle Association of America: Americans and Their Guns. Harrisburg, Pennsylvania: Stackpole Books, 1967.

Sommers, Michael A. Individual Rights and Civic Responsibility, the Right to Bear Arms. New York, New York: The Rosen Publishing Group, 2001.

Waldman, Michael. The Second Amendment, a Biography. New York, New York: Simon & Schuster, 2014.

WHY HERE?
WRITER MARK MILLAR
ARTIST ALEX SHEIKMAN
COLORIST MARISSA LOUISE
LETTERER BERNARDO BRICE
ASSISTANT EDITOR RACHAEL FULTON
ALL THESE MASS SHOOTINGS OUT THERE. IT BREAKS MY FRIGGIN' HEART.
WE'RE THE GREATEST COUNTRY IN THE WORLD. WHY DOES THIS KEEP HAPPENING?
POINT BLANK

BREAKING NEWS
SHOOTING
WELL, PSYCHOTROPIC DRUGS ARE CLEARLY A FACTOR. NINE TIMES OUT OF TEN THESE GUYS HAVE A HISTORY.
I SUSPECT IT'S A CELEBRITY THING. THE HIGHER THE BODY COUNT, THE WIDER THEIR PICTURES GO, RIGHT?

A LOT OF PEOPLE THINK IT'S MENTAL ILLNESS, BUT THAT'S A SMALLER FACTOR THAN ANYONE WOULD IMAGINE.
POINT BLANK
HALF THE SHOOTERS HAVE HAD PERSONALITY DISORDERS, BUT THEY'RE JUST AS LIKELY TO SHOW NO SIGNS AT ALL.

Reservoir
Hogs
THE FIXER
IT'S HOLLYWOOD I BLAME. ALL THESE MOVIES WITH PEOPLE GETTING SHOT?
WHAT ABOUT COUNTRIES LIKE ENGLAND AND GERMANY?
THEY GET ALL THE SAME MOVIES WE DO, BUT STUFF LIKE THIS IS VIRTUALLY UNHEARD OF.

ISLAMIC FUNDAMENTALISM?
PRETTY MUCH NONE OF THESE GUYS HAVE BEEN **MUSLIM** WHEN YOU SEE THE NUMBERS.
ABSENT FATHERS? THE ***COPYCAT*** PHENOMENON?
BULLETS FLY
DRIVE BY SHOOT BY

CRIMINALS ***SELLING GUNS*** ON THE ***BLACK MARKET?***
NOT WHEN MOST OF THEM HAVE BEEN BOUGHT ***QUITE LEGALLY.***

SO WHAT THE HELL IS ***GOING ON*** HERE?
WE'RE THE RICHEST COUNTRY IN THE WORLD WITH THE ***GREATEST OPPORTUNITIES.*** WHY ARE WE ***LEADING THE PACK*** WITH THIS PROBLEM?

I'VE NO IDEA, MY FRIEND...
ME NEITHER.
LIKEWISE.

GUN SHOP
CLEARANCE
BILLY'S GUN BAR
I GUESS SOME THINGS IN LIFE JUST HAPPEN FOR ***NO REASON.***
GUN SHOP
GUN SHOP
BLOWOUT SALE
SAVE 50%
END

FIRST PERSON SHOOTER
WRITTEN BY DARICK ROBERTSON
& R. ERIC LIEB
ART BY DARICK ROBERTSON
LETTERING BY CRANK!
THERE ARE MYTHS, ABOUT MONSTERS.
WELCOME BACK, MR. PADDOCK!
THAT YOU MUST INVITE THEM IN.
BUT WHAT IS A MONSTER?
WHAT DO THEY LOOK LIKE?
FESTIVAL TONIGHT IN VEGAS
OF COURSE!
WE HAVE A SUITE FACING NORTHEAST, LET'S SEE... ON THE 32ND FLOOR. WOULD THAT BE ALL RIGHT, SIR?
WOULD YOU KNOW IF ONE WAS STANDING IN FRONT OF YOU?
WITH ALL THESE BAGS IT'S EASIER TO TAKE THE SERVICE ELEVATOR, YA KNOW?
ONE OF THE PERKS FOR FREQUENT GUESTS LIKE YOURSELF.
HOW COULD YOU KNOW WHAT THEY WERE PLANNING?
WHAT DARK SECRETS THEY HIDE WITHIN.
THANK YOU, SIR! ALWAYS HAPPY TO DO WHATEVER IT TAKES FOR OUR VALUED M LIFE REWARDS MEMBERS.
AND WHAT IF THE MONSTER BLENDED IN?
WHAT IF THE MONSTER WAS FOLLOWING THE RULES?
ALL PERFECTLY LEGAL! HELL, I ONCE SOLD BAYONETS AS "TENT PEGS!" TENT PEGS!
YOU BEST BELIEVE THAT WAS LEGAL, TOO!
SUCH AS THEY ARE.
Google
WHAT IF THE MONSTER DOESN'T SEEM LIKE A MONSTER?
JACKS OR BETTER
BET 6
CREDIT

PLAYER ONE READY
WHAT IF THE MONSTER IS LARGER THAN JUST ONE PERSON?
OR TWO?
DOES THE CULTURE MAKE THE MONSTER, OR DOES THE MONSTER REFLECT THE CULTURE?
OR IS THAT TOO EASY AN EXPLANATION?
WHAT IF THERE IS NO EXPLANATION?
NO REASON FOR THE HORRORS THEY COMMITTED?
WHAT IF THE MONSTER WENT TO GREAT LENGTHS TO HIDE THEIR PREPARATION?
IT'S A "FIX-IT" TICKET, REALLY. JUST BRING PROOF OF CORRECTION AND YOU SHOULD BE ALL SET.
GAVE THE AUTHORITIES LITTLE REASON TO QUESTION THEIR ACTIVITIES?
PLANNED METICULOUSLY?
HOW COULD YOU STOP SUCH A MONSTER?
HOW DO YOU KEEP THE MONSTER OUT?
OCTOBER 1ST, 2017
10:05 PM
HOW?

Chad & James

THE RECORDING

Written by VAN JENSEN
Art by ERIC KIM
Colors by CHRIS O'HALLORAN
Lettering by BERNARDO BRICE

Adapted from the eyewitness accounts of Chad and James, as told to Van Jensen.

Chad and James were hired to set up a livestream of the concert.

Feeds going to the concert website, to the Facebook pages of some of the artists performing.

A pretty simple gig, once everything was set up. Point the cameras. Make sure everything keeps working.
This was the last night. The last act going on stage.

They had packed up all the gear that they could. The past two nights, they'd walked out into the crowd. Enjoyed some music, then headed back to their hotel.
But this night...

They had access to the hospitality tent. A perk of the job. The bartender remembered they were from Kentucky; their bourbon of choice was Wild Turkey 101, neat.
A toast to a job well done.

POP POP
POP

Then they heard it. Fireworks? The bartender said Jason Aldean always did have pyrotechnics in his act.

Then they started to hear the screams. And, as the music stopped, everything became surreal.

They decided to run for their production trailer. Everyone was scrambling, stampeding.
People sprinted for any safe haven. They didn't know where the bullets were coming from. What was happening.

They were all strangers inside. Scared. Stuck in place. There was nothing they could do except wait.

And watch.

James is a cinematographer. It was instinct, taking out his phone, recording. People would run. Then the shooting would start, and everyone would drop. When it stopped, most got up again. But not all.
Chad wanted so badly to look away. But he couldn't pull himself from what he saw.

One guy walked out onto the field even as bullets rained down. He lifted up both hands and extended his middle fingers. Chad remembers wondering, "Is he drunk? Does he have nothing to lose?"

The shooting stopped. Police finally arrived. Told them to leave. Just as they'd come together, the group disappeared into the crowd.

Walking away, Chad felt guilty. Why had they escaped unhurt when others hadn't?

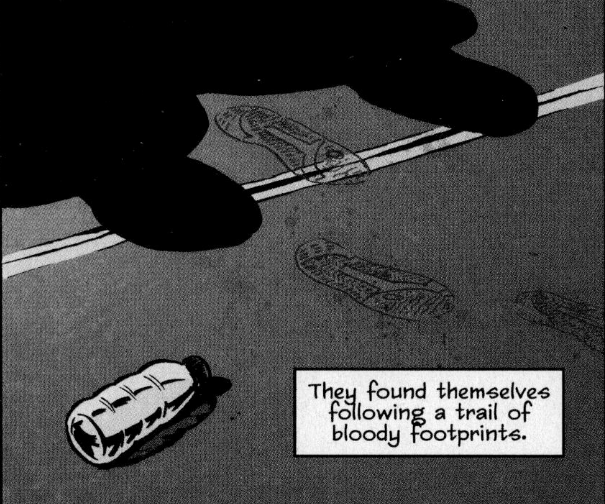
They found themselves following a trail of bloody footprints.

Until, suddenly, it ended. Who the blood belonged to, what happened, a story they would never know.

Back home, Chad tried to block it out, to avoid it. His girlfriend asked him to talk to someone.

One night, he finally opened up to her about what he'd seen. The weight of it all set in.

#VEGAS STRONG
A month later, Chad had to go back to Las Vegas to retrieve their video gear. When he went to the trailer, he half expected his unfinished bourbon to still be sitting there.

The bourbon was gone.
He stood there and let himself feel it. Let himself have the closure he needed. He stood there until it felt complete...

Then he opened his eyes, walked out, and never looked back again.
He headed home, but he was missing one piece of their equipment...

The recorder was gone, and the footage with it. Lost. Maybe taken by the F.B.I. They'll never know.

James still has the videos from his phone.

He hasn't been able to bring himself to watch them.

WORDS

by Neil Gaiman
Paint by
J.H. Williams III
Lettering by
Todd Klein

Let me go back
to the words
that made me.

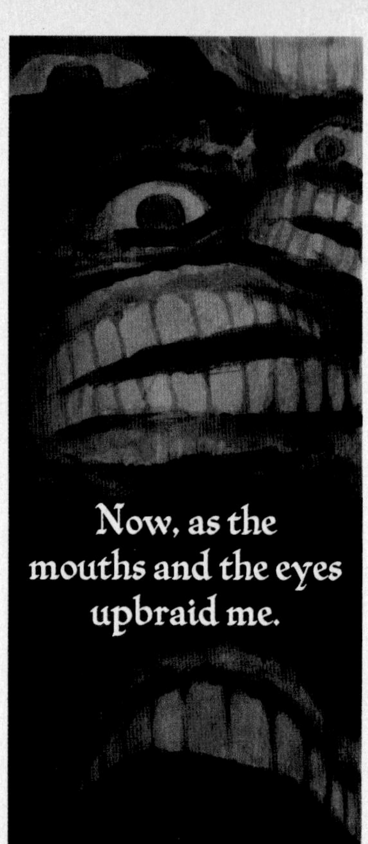

Now, as the
mouths and the eyes
upbraid me.

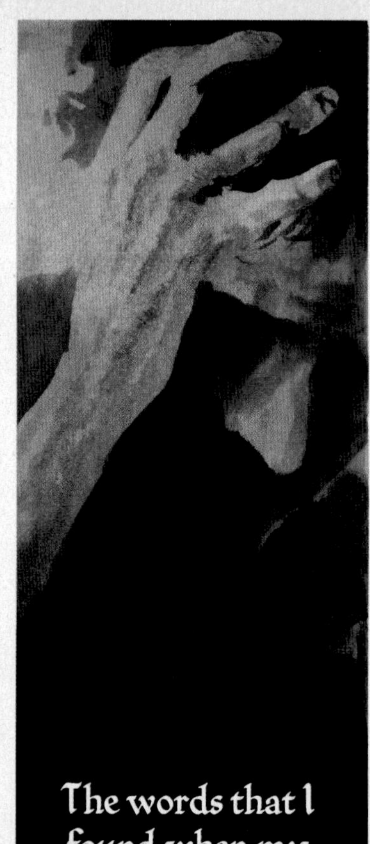

The words that I
found when my
mind betrayed me.

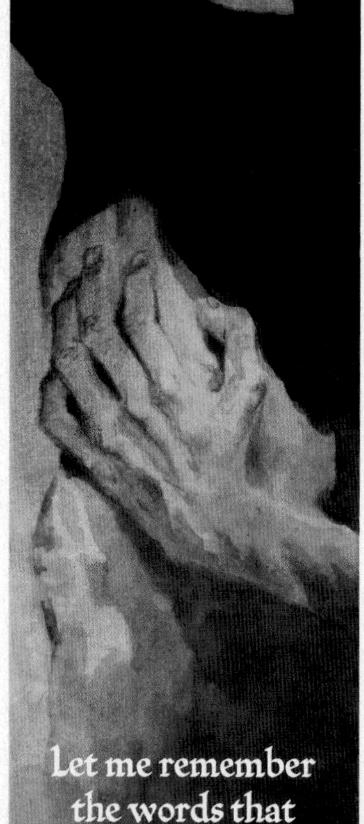

Let me remember
the words that
wound me.

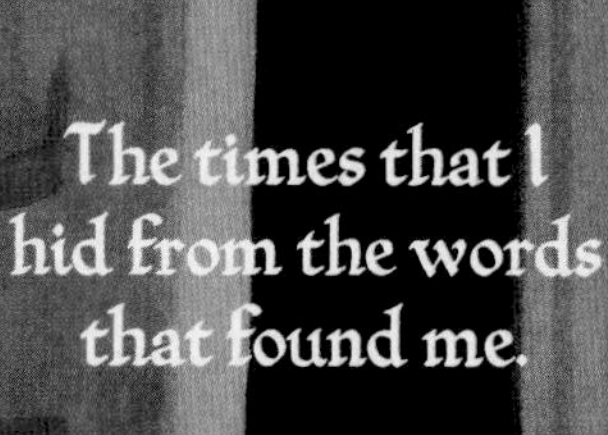

The times that I
hid from the words
that found me.

The words that
I hear when
the night comes
round me.

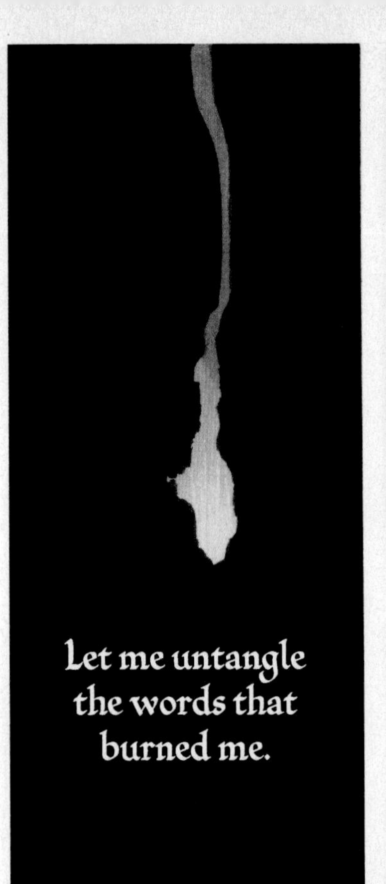
Let me untangle
the words that
burned me.

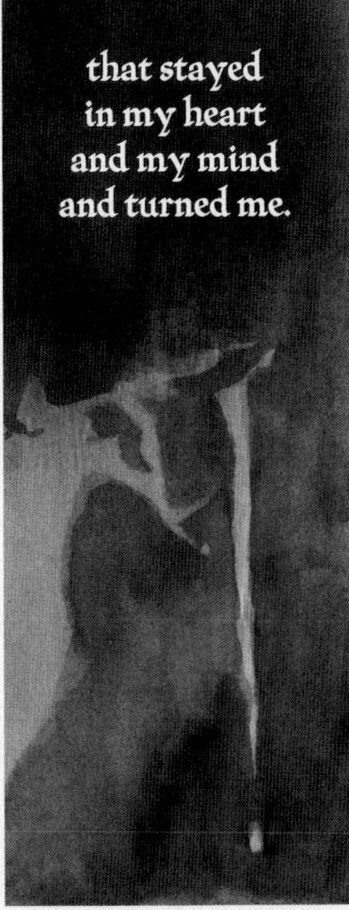
that stayed
in my heart
and my mind
and turned me.

Here in the twilight
the children
spurned me.

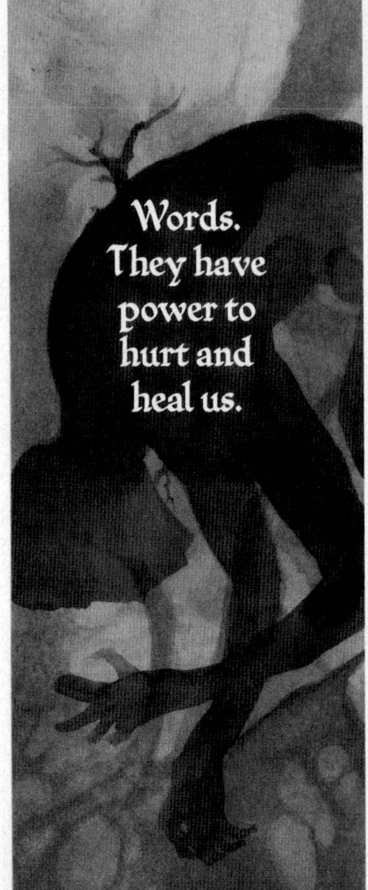
Words.
They have
power to
hurt and
heal us.

open our insides
and show us
the real us.

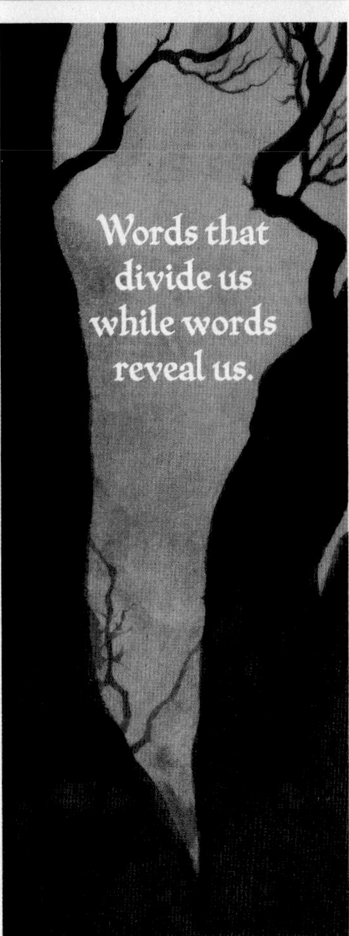
Words that
divide us
while words
reveal us.

You must imagine the words that built me.
insults that opened my chest and spilled me.
words that were worse than the shots that killed me.
This is the end of the words you give me.

This is for you,
you will all
outlive me.
This be
my epitaph:
Please,
forgive me.

BULLY
WRITTEN BY JOSHUA HALE FIALKOV
ART BY NOEL TUAZON
LETTERING BY BERNARDO BRICE
"WHAT'S WRONG, FAGGOT?"
"LITTLE DUDE'S CRYING! HE'S GONNA GET AIDS ON YOU!"
I DIDN'T DO ANYTHING--
YOU EXIST, BITCH, THAT'S ENOUGH--
WHAT'D YOU SAY, JARED?
NOTHING, DALE. EVERYTHING'S COOL, RIGHT, KARL?
THEY WERE KICKING ME AND CALLING ME "GAY".
GOT A PROBLEM WITH HOMO-SEXUALS?
N...NO...
CAUSE MAYBE I'M GAY. HELL, MAYBE YOU'RE GAY. YOU KNOW SO MUCH ABOUT IT, RIGHT?
W-- WHAT...?
LET HIM GO DALE.
HE WAS ATTACKING--
I DON'T CARE.
DALE USED HATE SPEECH, MR. WALLACE. HE MADE FUN OF US FOR BEING HOMOS--
ER...
GAY.
OH COME ON, MAN! THEY WERE KICKING THE CRAP OUT OF--
ALL FOUR OF YOU, SHUT UP, AND GO TO THE OFFICE. NOW.

GET BACK TO CLASS.

YOU'RE DEAD, FAGGOT.

MR. WALLACE, HE WAS TRYING TO PROTECT ME--
IT'S A ZERO TOLERANCE SCHOOL, KARL, DALE'S HAD MORE THAN ENOUGH CHANCES.
THEY'RE GOING TO KILL ME.

LISTEN, JUST, STAY AWAY FROM THEM. WAIT FOR THEM TO LEAVE THE CAFETERIA BEFORE YOU GO IN, IF THEY'RE ON YOUR BUS, WALK, IF THEY WALK--
BUT THEY ARE THE BAD GUYS.
I KNOW IT FEELS LIKE THAT NOW, KARL. BUT, IT'S JUST HIGH SCHOOL.

"JUST STAY OUT OF THEIR WAY AND YOU CAN PROTECT YOURSELF."

NO BOYFRIEND NOW, *HUH*, ***PUSSY?***
NO.

TOLD YOU WE WERE GOING TO KICK YOUR ASS--

END

HERE WE ARE AGAIN...

GHOST

WRITTEN BY
W. HADEN BLACKMAN
ART AND COLORS BY
RICHARD PACE
LETTERS BY
BERNARDO BRICE

END THE
GATHERED IN THE HOPES SOMEONE WILL NOTICE THE SEA OF SIGNS...

HEAR OUR CHANTS AND DEMANDS...

AND ACTUALLY DO SOMETHING.
OUR KIDS!
MAJORITY LEADER, YOU ARE COMPLICIT! SPEAKER, YOU ARE COMPLICIT!
WAIT...WE HAVE NEWS? THE VOTE'S IN?

BUT THE SIGNS, THE SHOUTING, JUST SHOWING UP--IT ALL DOES ABOUT AS MUCH GOOD AS SENDING AN OUTRAGED TWEET FROM THE COUCH.
THE BILL... IT DIDN'T... IT DIDN'T PASS.

AT LEAST THEN, I'D BE AT HOME.

NOT IN ANOTHER CHEAP MOTEL ROOM, COUNTING HOW MANY YEARS OF MY LIFE HAVE BEEN STOLEN BY THESE WASTED TRIPS, THESE USELESS RALLIES.

TRYING TO STAY AWAKE BECAUSE I CAN'T BEAR TO FACE HER...

I CAN'T DO THIS ANYMORE, SWEETHEART.

NO ONE WILL LISTEN TO ME. NO ONE CARES ABOUT YOU.

YOU DO.

I'M JUST ONE VOICE.

YOU'RE NOT THE ONLY ONE WHO HAS LOST SOMEONE YOU LOVE.

AND THEY ALL HAVE VOICES TOO.

EVENTUALLY, THERE WILL BE ENOUGH OF US.
AND ENOUGH OF YOU.

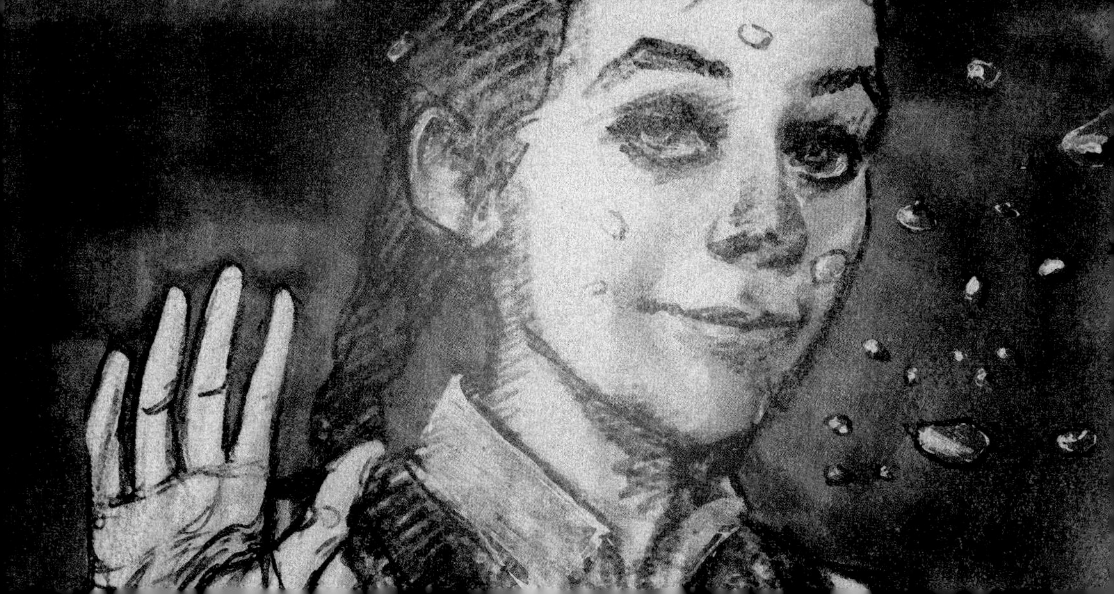

SHE IS RIGHT, MY DAUGHTER.
ALL WHO'VE LOST FRIENDS AND LOVERS, PARENTS AND CHILDREN, WE WILL BRING OUR HEARTACHE AND OUR ANGER...
I DON'T KNOW HOW MANY OF US IT WILL TAKE. A MILLION, TEN MILLION...
BUT, SOMEDAY SOON, THERE WILL BE TOO MANY VOICES TO IGNORE.
Seal Beach, CA
2011

Tether

by Wendy Wright-Williams
Painted by J.H. Williams III
Letters by Todd Klein

Your hand entwined in mine weaves our past
with the present
You will always be here

A blast of light and a path is lit
My chest lurches forward with knowing,
but my mind won't abide those sounds
The whistle, the pop
The scream
My head arches and contorts my body away
I didn't choose this course
I will not be made to choose this way

Your fingers slip
Our future loses its grip

Where do I go from here?
I walk backwards
My back towards the march forward
I can't turn my face from yours
You've become a hologram,
projected from somewhere I can't reach

Autumn

ARE YOU OK?
AS TOLD BY EYEWITNESS: AUTUMN K.
SCRIPT BY: MARIAH McCOURT
ART BY: ARIELA KRISTANTINA
COLORS BY: BRYAN VALENZA
LETTERING BY: BERNARDO BRICE
MANDALAY BAY
ROUTE 91 HARVEST
I WAS LOOKING FORWARD TO GOING TO THE SHOW FOR WEEKS.
EVERYONE KNEW I WOULD BE THERE, ALL WEEKEND.
JASON ALDEAN WAS FINISHING ONE OF THE LAST SONGS OF HIS SET.
IT WAS JUST SOME POPS AT FIRST.
POP
POP
LIKE FIREWORKS.
POP POP POP
I LOOKED UP BUT THERE WEREN'T ANY.
POP
POP
I LET EVERYONE TELL ME IT WAS OK.
I KNEW SOMETHING WAS WRONG WHEN MY MOM SAID--
EVERYTHING IS FINE BUT WE NEED TO START MOVING AWAY FROM HERE.
NOW.

IT WASN'T FIREWORKS.
POP POP POP
POP POP POP POP
BUT WE LOST MY AUNT AND BEST FRIEND AND THE OTHERS WE WERE WITH.
POP
POP POP POP POP
POP POP
POP POP POP
MY MOM SAID, "STAY TOGETHER. STAY TOGETHER."
YOU CAN'T GO THAT WAY!
HELP US!
THEY ARE HURT! SOMEONE HELP!
ARE YOU OK? ARE YOU OK? ARE YOU OK?
MY MOM WENT TO SEE WHAT SHE COULD DO.
HE WAS TRYING TO COMFORT ME...
ARE YOU OK? IT'S GOING TO BE OK.
...AND HE'D BEEN SHOT.
MY MOM FOUND MY BEST FRIEND AND WE HID IN OUR TRUCK.

I REMEMBER BEING CROUCHED DOWN BY THE VIP TAPE. THEN A TRASH CAN. THEN A POLICE TRUCK. WE COULDN'T STAY THERE BECAUSE IT MIGHT HAVE BEEN A TARGET.
I LOOKED DOWN AND SAW BLOOD ON THE SIDEWALK.
POP POP POP POP POP POP POP POP POP POP POP POP POP POP POP POP
THE SMELL... I REMEMBER THE SMELL. THICK. IRON-Y.
I THOUGHT I WOULD BE SICK.
I WOULDN'T LEAVE WITHOUT MY MOTHER.
"ARE YOU OK?"
"I'M OK. I'M NOT HURT."
WE KEPT MOVING, MY MOM TRYING TO HELP PEOPLE AS WE WENT.
WE KEPT GETTING NEWS ALERTS ON OUR PHONE OF CONFLICTING INFORMATION. CAR BOMBS, OTHER SHOOTERS, BUT MY MOM SAID IT WAS NOT ON THE SCANNER.
WEEEE-WOOOOOH
WE WERE IN OUR TRUCK FOR HOURS.
SOMEHOW MY STEPDAD GOT TO US.
MY BEST FRIEND KEPT ASKING ME IF I WAS OK.
HAVE YOU EVER SEEN A ZOMBIE MOVIE?
IT WAS LIKE THAT. DESOLATE. ALL YOU COULD HEAR WERE SIRENS.
MY SENSE OF TIME WAS LOST.

SOMEHOW WE GOT HOME. IT WAS MAYBE 2:00 AM.
THE BACK OF MY SHIRT WAS COVERED IN BLOOD.
SOMEONE WHO WAS HURT WAS THAT CLOSE TO ME...
THEY TOUCHED ME AND I DIDN'T KNOW...
AUTUMN, YOU'RE OK. WE'RE ALL OK.
AUTUMN, TIME TO GET UP!
I WENT TO SCHOOL BECAUSE I COULDN'T STAY HOME AND THINK ABOUT IT, ALONE.

MY FRIENDS WERE SO GLAD I WAS OK.

I WAS TRYING TO KEEP MY MIND OFF IT.

SOME OF MY TEACHERS WERE UP ALL NIGHT.

WORRYING ABOUT ME.

AT LUNCH, SOME OF THE OTHER KIDS THOUGHT IT WOULD BE FUNNY TO MAKE GUNSHOT SOUNDS.

I DIDN'T KNOW PEOPLE COULD BE SO IGNORANT AND **INSENSITIVE.**

POP

POP

I WAS SO TIRED.

POP

CHIP

Milk

I COULDN'T DEAL WITH THE HALLWAYS FOR A MONTH.

cafe
I'M NOT THE SAME PERSON I WAS.
EXIT

BUT NOW PEOPLE TREAT ME LIKE I'M JUST "THE GIRL FROM THE SHOOTING".
EXIT
SHO
SEASON

AND I REALLY WISH PEOPLE WOULDN'T ASSUME THAT BECAUSE I WASN'T HURT PHYSICALLY, THAT I'M OK.
THAT I SHOULD BE OVER IT.
THIS IS PART OF ME **FOREVER.**
JUST BECAUSE YOU DIDN'T SEE ME CRYING TODAY...
THAT DOESN'T MEAN ON THE INSIDE, I'M NOT SHAKING.
WHEN YOU'RE LOOKING IN FROM THE OUTSIDE, YOU DON'T UNDERSTAND.
I'M **NOT** OK.

DECEMBER 2012
IT'S ME. ARE YOU WATCHING THE NEWS?
OH, YEAH. I JUST...
NEIL
I'VE BEEN CRYING SINCE I HEARD...I CAN'T STOP.
LEFT WORK EARLY. I NEED TO...I WANT TO GET THE BOYS FROM SCHOOL.
YOU'RE TOO LATE. I HAVE THEM ALREADY.
...NEWTOWN, CONNECTICUT, WHERE SENSELESS TRAGEDY HAS OCCURRED...
BREAKING NEWS
COME HOME.
HOW I LIVE NOW
STORY & LETTERS BY NEIL KLEID PENCILS & INKS BY NICK PITARRA COLORS BY KEN SYD

—USED TO NOT WORRY, BUT AS WE HAVE MORE KIDS AND THE CULTURAL CLIMATE CHANGES, IT *REALLY* FREAKS ME OUT.
EVERY TIME I TURN ON THE NEWS, THE PARENT INSIDE *SCREAMS* IN HORROR.
JUNE 2017
WELCOME TO *TRUMP'S AMERICA*.
OH, I'D *LOVE* TO BLAME THE ADMINISTRATION, BUT THIS HAS BEEN GOING ON FOR YEARS.
AURORA AND ORLANDO... VIRGINIA TECH, SANDY HOOK...
HOW DO YOU DROP YOUR KIDS AT SCHOOL WHEN THERE'S A CHANCE THEY MAY *NEVER COME BACK?*
THIS COUNTRY HAS A *SERIOUS* GUN CONTROL PROBLEM...!
BULLSHIT. THE PROBLEM IS MENTAL ILLNESS.
WHICHEVER IT IS, HOW DO I PROTECT MY KIDS IF *I'M* AT WORK AND *THEY'RE* STILL AT SCHOOL?
IT'S JUST LIKE *ISRAEL*. WHAT IF YOU GET ON A BUS AND SOME BOMBER *BLOWS IT TO PIECES?*
OH, *VERY* COMFORTING. NOW PASS THE WINE.

THE COMMUNITY NEEDS TO TAKE *EXTRA* STEPS. OUR SCHOOL ADDED SECURITY—
SO DID OURS. BUT NOT EVERY SCHOOL *WILL*. AND WHAT HAPPENS AT A CONCERT...OR ON A SUBWAY?
—AND AS FOR THE MOVIES, GET A *LICENSE TO CARRY*.
NO *WAY*. I'D BE MORE AFRAID TO HAVE A GUN WHERE THE KIDS MIGHT GET IT THAN FEEL SAFER WITH IT AT HOME.
WE *COULD* JUST "HOME ALONE" OUR FRONT STEPS.
YOU JUST NEED TO TEACH THEM THAT IT ISN'T A TOY.
C'MON. IF YOUR FIVE-YEAR-OLD COMES ACROSS A GUN, HE'S *NOT* GOING TO—?
WE HAVE A GUN UPSTAIRS. IT'S *NEVER* BEEN A PROBLEM.
...YOU *DO?*

NEVER AGAIN.
WE'RE NEVER SENDING OUR KIDS THERE FOR A PLAY DATE AGAIN.
HE SAYS IT'S SECURE. GUN LOCKED UPSTAIRS, BULLETS IN HIS STUDY.
SO SOMEONE BREAKS IN, HE HAS TO SNEAK PAST THEM TO LOAD IT? HOW DOES THAT HELP?
HOW MANY TIMES HAVE OUR KIDS BEEN THERE AND WE DIDN'T KNOW, NEIL?
HE SAYS IT ISN'T A PROBLEM, LAURIE.
YEAH. IT ISN'T A PROBLEM... UNTIL IT IS.
NEVER AGAIN.

OCTOBER
2017
JACK
Owen
...LAS VEGAS, WHERE YET ANOTHER *TRAGIC SHOOTING* HAS OCCURRED...
JACK
OWEN
Pokémon
Harry Potter
FIELDER
45
COME *HOME*...
END

THE WOMAN AND THE MAN
WRITER GAIL SIMONE
ARTIST RYAN KELLY
COLORIST GIULIA BRUSCO
LETTERER BERNARDO BRICE
THE MAN AND THE WOMAN.
THE WOMAN AND THE MAN.
THE HAND ON THE GUN.
AND THE GUN IN THE HAND.

THE MAN AND THE WOMAN.
THE WOMAN AND THE MAN.
THE HAND ON THE GUN.
AND THE GUN IN THE HAND.

THE MAN AND THE WOMAN.
THE WOMAN AND THE MAN.
BEANS
THE HAND ON THE GUN.
WALKER ELEMENTARY
AND THE GUN IN THE HAND.
Law enforcement agencies say that there is increasing evidence of a connection between mass shootings and domestic violence.
Between the years of 2009 and 2016, 54% of mass shooters also killed a domestic partner or family member.
In nine of the ten deadliest incidents during that time, the shooter has been accused of or charged with domestic abuse.

VEGAS

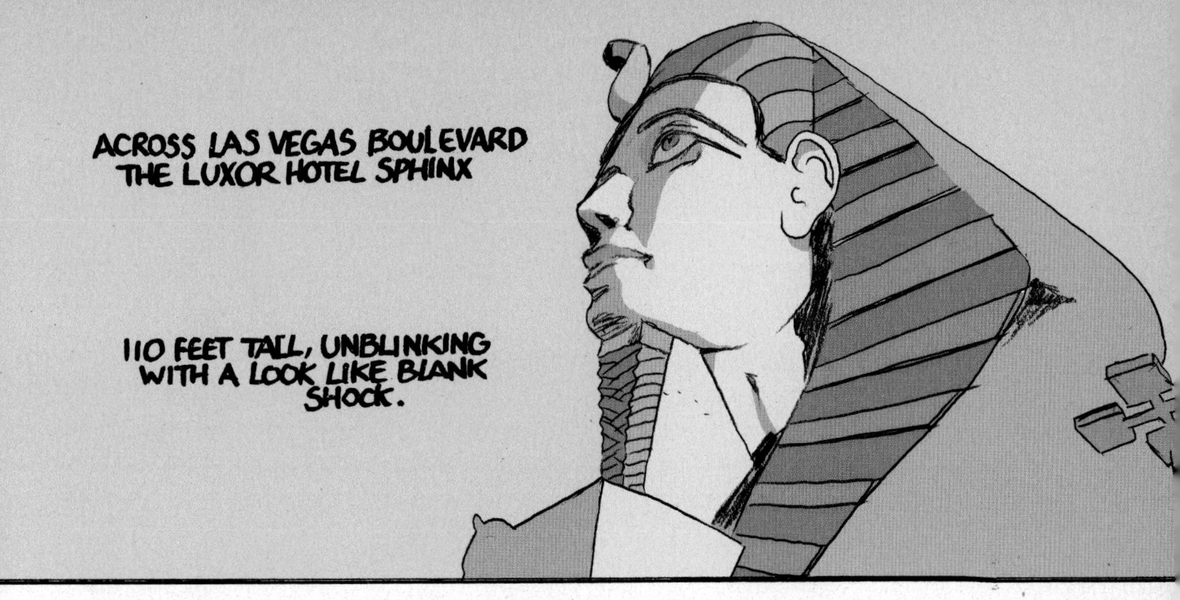

ACROSS LAS VEGAS BOULEVARD THE LUXOR HOTEL SPHINX
110 FEET TALL, UNBLINKING WITH A LOOK LIKE BLANK SHOCK.

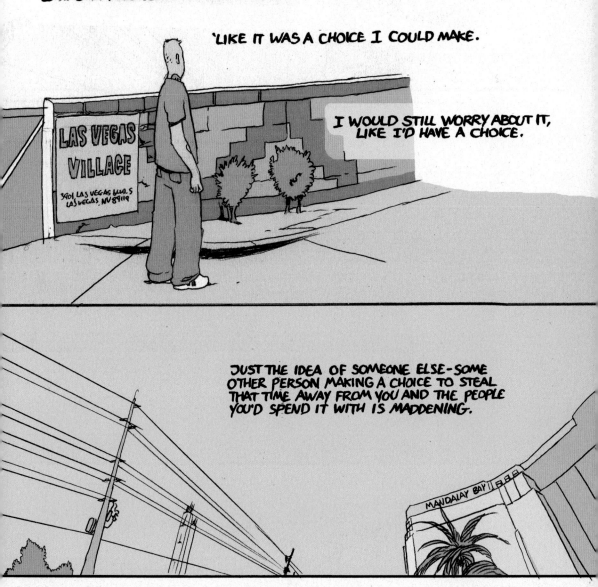

SHE WOULD JOKE ABOUT HOW I WASN'T ALLOWED TO DIE BEFORE HER.

'LIKE IT WAS A CHOICE I COULD MAKE.

LAS VEGAS VILLAGE

3901 LAS VEGAS blvd. S LAS VEGAS, NV 89119

I WOULD STILL WORRY ABOUT IT, LIKE I'D HAVE A CHOICE.

JUST THE IDEA OF SOMEONE ELSE-SOME OTHER PERSON MAKING A CHOICE TO STEAL THAT TIME AWAY FROM YOU AND THE PEOPLE YOU'D SPEND IT WITH IS MADDENING.

MANDALAY BAY

AT THE SAME TIME, HALF A WORLD AWAY.
THE GREAT SPHINX OF GIZA, FATHER OF DREAD~ SITS BEHIND A GUARDRAIL OF CHAINS RAN BETWEEN STONE BOLLARDS.

MILLENNIA HAVE PASSED IN FRONT OF ITS STONE FACED - STONE FACE.

OVER A HUNDRED GENERATIONS OF THE BEST AND WORST LIFE HAS TO OFFER.

BRANDON.

WHY?
THESE PEOPLE ARE SO CRUEL TO EACH OTHER. DESTROYING INDIVIDUALS THEY DON'T EVEN KNOW, OFTEN WITH NO DISCERNIBLE REASON.
THESE HORRIFIC EVENTS THIS SPECIES INFLICT ON EACH OTHER ARE OF GREAT CONCERN.
BUT, RELATIVELY SPEAKING, RARE.
PERHAPS A RECURRING ANOMALY?
DESPITE THE CONSTANT WARRING, THE GREAT MAJORITY APPEAR TO BE FULL OF KINDNESS, COMPASSION, AND EMPATHY.
NO NEED TO CLEANSE THIS PLANET JUST YET.

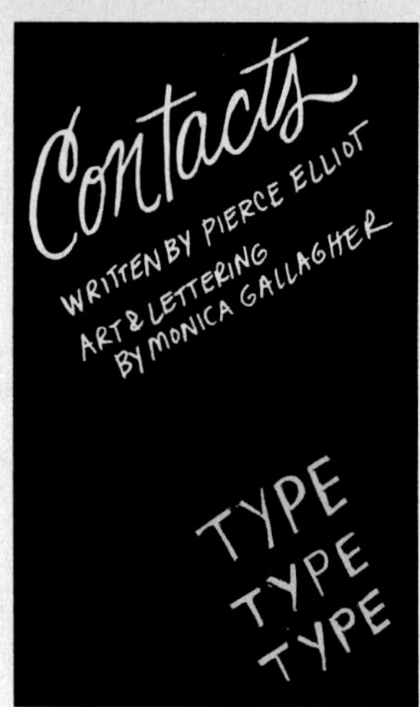
Contacts
WRITTEN BY PIERCE ELLIOT
ART & LETTERING BY MONICA GALLAGHER
TYPE TYPE TYPE

BING!
New iMessage
To: Jeff
Route 91 Incident
Karla has marked herself as safe
Eric has marked himself as safe
Jim has marked himself as safe
Space
return

Hey Jeff, text me when you get this. Hope you're ok.
Delivered
TYPE TYPE TYPE
BING

Allen
Tim! Are you alright? I saw the news I didn't think you were there, but I wanted to make sure you were fine.
Now
TYPE TYPE
I'm alright, has Jeff contacted you yet? I couldn't remember if he was working on the strip tonight.
Delivered

Allen
I sent him a text not too long ago and I haven't heard anything, but will let you know if I do.
Now
BING
Mom
Honey are you ok?
I'm alright Mom I wasn't at the concert.
Delivered
WHOOSH

BING
Karla
Tim, I saw that you didn't mark yourself safe and I just wanted to make sure you were ok.
Veronica
Tim are you ok? Have you heard from Jeff? I thought he was working on the strip tonight?
BING

TYPE TYPE
I'm alright Veronica, I just texted him and I'm still waiting for a reply.
Delivered
WHOOSH

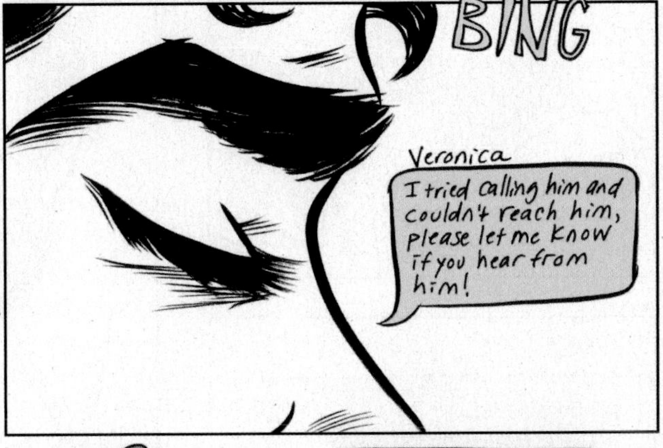
BING
Veronica
I tried calling him and couldn't reach him, please let me know if you hear from him!

BEEP BEEP
ALERT
Stay clear of Mandalay Bay and surrounding areas until further notice.

FWEET FWEET
@starving_artist_41
@Tim_Tam_87 Oh my god, please tell me you're alright!
@joebobfan
@Tim_Tam_87 Bro I just heard! You alright? Friends and family ok?

(012)345-6789

It's Jeff, I left my phone at home so I'm using a coworker friend's phone.

BING

Jason

WORKING THE LINE

Jason Harris
Story/Script

Ollie Masters
Script

Sina Grace
Pencils/Inks

Shaun Struble
Colors/Letters

MAYBE I CAN FIND A WAY TO HELP FROM HERE.

HEY CHEF, CAN YOU DONATE SOME FOOD?

I'M IN THE BLOOD BANK RIGHT NOW, STILL WAITING TO GIVE BLOOD. THE LINE IS LOOOOOOOOONG.

PAISAN, CAN YOU BRING SOME PIZZAS TO THE BLOOD BANK ON WEST CHARLESTON?

I'M ALREADY ON IT.

OKAY. I'LL GET YOU FOOD THERE. CAN YOU CALL SOME PEOPLE AND GET SOME STUFF DONATED TO THE RED CROSS STATION?

WHAT ARE YOU DOING TONIGHT?

MEET US AT THE EMERGENCY ROOM ENTRANCE AT SPRING VALLEY HOSPITAL AT 8.

THE BEGINNING.

THIS IS RAD.
LET'S DO THIS.

WHAT WOULD YOU LIKE?
DO YOU REALLY HAVE LOBSTER TAIL ON THAT TRUCK?
ONE ORDER OF LOBSTER TAIL, CHEFS!

WAITING
HEY, ARE YOU GUYS HUNGRY?

We need 3 pastas, 15 tacos and 8 orders of tots.

MY BROTHER GOT SHOT AT THE FESTIVAL. WE'VE BEEN HERE ALL DAY. THIS REALLY HELPS.

JOLENE IS MAKING FRIENDS.

EVERY DAY, WE KEEP GROWING AND WE'RE ABLE TO FEED MORE AND MORE PEOPLE.

HEY, BRO. I LOVE WHAT YOU'RE DOING. DO YOU WANT TO MAKE IT EVEN MORE PERSONAL?

WHAT DO YOU HAVE IN MIND?

HI, BRITNEY. WE HEARD YOU WERE ONE OF THE VICTIMS AT THE ROUTE 91 FESTIVAL.

YOUR FRIENDS TOLD US YOU WERE HOME RECOVERING. WE JUST WANTED TO MAKE THINGS A LITTLE BETTER.

SOMETIMES PEOPLE WOULD ASK ME HOW I'M FEELING BUT REALLY...
7AM: WAKE UP.

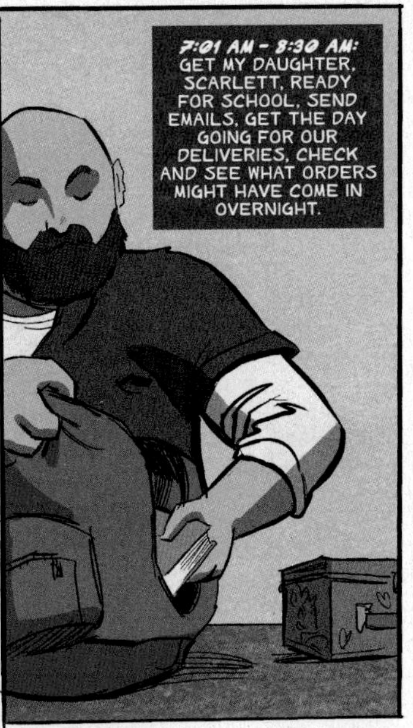
7:01 AM - 8:30 AM: GET MY DAUGHTER, SCARLETT, READY FOR SCHOOL, SEND EMAILS, GET THE DAY GOING FOR OUR DELIVERIES, CHECK AND SEE WHAT ORDERS MIGHT HAVE COME IN OVERNIGHT.

8:31 AM - 9:15 AM: DROP SCARLETT AT SCHOOL, GET TO WORK.

9:16 AM - 5 PM: PRETEND TO DO MY JOB / COORDINATING. SPEND LITERALLY ALL DAY MAKING CALLS, SENDING MESSAGES, FACILITATING DROP-OFFS.

5:01 PM - 6 PM: PICK UP MY KID. LET MY DOG OUT.

6:01 PM - 7 PM: MAKE DELIVERIES.

7:01 PM - 9 PM: BE AT FOOD TRUCKS. BEGIN PLANNING FOR TOMORROW.

9:30 PM: PUT MY KID TO BED.

10 PM - 12 AM: SEND EMAILS, LOCK IN SCHEDULE FOR TOMORROW, ETC.
...I DON'T HAVE TIME TO FEEL ANYTHING.

AND IT KEPT GOING--
I'VE BEEN OUT ALL MORNING. THE FBI NEEDS 100 LUNCHES. WE ALSO NEED 40 MEALS FOR GRIEF COUNSELORS.
I'M STARTING A LIST OF WHO NEEDS FOOD, WHICH RESTAURANTS WILL SUPPLY IT AND PEOPLE WHO WILL DELIVER IT.
I'LL LET YOU KNOW WHEN WE HAVE AN ORDER, YOU LET ME KNOW WHEN YOU FILL IT.
CAN YOU SEND BREAKFAST TO THE FBI?
DO YOU NEED ANY DELIVERIES DONE TODAY? I'M OFF.
HEY, I CAN SUPPLY 50 LUNCHES TODAY. LET ME KNOW WHERE YOU NEED THEM.
HEY, I'M A MASSAGE THERAPIST. I HAVE A TEAM OF FIVE. DO YOU KNOW ANYONE WHO COULD USE OUR HELP?
TWO WEEKS LATER.
WE DID WHAT WE COULD. WE FED A LOT OF PEOPLE.
BUT NOW THAT THINGS ARE BACK TO NORMAL, ALL I CAN THINK IS, HOW DO WE KEEP HELPING PEOPLE?

I'M A CRITIC. IT'S NOT MY KIND OF MUSIC.
I SHOULD HATE IT.
ROUTE 91 HARVEST
BUT... LET ME TELL YOU A STORY.

CRITICS

WRITER: KIERON GILLEN
ARTIST: JAMIE McKELVIE
COLORIST: DEE CUNNIFFE
LETTERER: HASSAN OTSMANE-ELHAOU

BACK AROUND 2K, I SPENT A WEEK IN A SMALL CITY IN NORTH AMERICA...

I HIT A DANCE CLUB. THE BEATS WERE FAMILIAR, BUT THE CROWD BEMUSED ME.
THEY FACED THE DJ AND DANCED IN ROWS, LIKE THEY WERE WATCHING AN INDIE BAND...

THE SAME WEEK, I HIT A COUNTRY CLUB.
THE BAND ROARED, THE PLACE SWEATED AND TWIRLED, AND I DID TOO...

THIS WAS MORE OF A DANCE CLUB THAN THE DANCE CLUB.
MY PEOPLE.

THIS ISN'T *THAT,* OF COURSE.

THIS IS A STADIUM CROWD.
IT'S ABOUT SIZE, COMMUNALITY, TOGETHERNESS.

EVEN IF I DON'T LIKE THE ROAD, IT DOESN'T MATTER. I LOVE THE DESTINATION.
PEOPLE, TOGETHER. WHATEVER IT IS, IT'S THE BEST OF US.

WHO COULD HATE THAT?

NOT ME. AND WHATEVER DID, IT WOULD BE THE WORST OF US.

HUH?

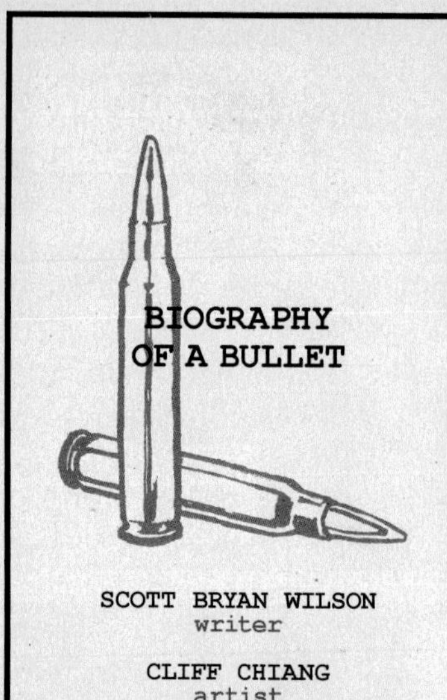

BIOGRAPHY
OF A BULLET
SCOTT BRYAN WILSON
writer
CLIFF CHIANG
artist

The simple bullet, given life.
The name written on it is invisible.

The bullet doctor makes sure it is healthy before releasing it into the wild.

It is joined with others, forming a temporary family.

To be given the best opportunities for adoption and to be put to best use, the bullet is driven all over the country, past mountain, heather, hill, cornfield, and dale.

The bullet uses its slick plumage to attract a buyer.

At last: a home.

Every bullet dreams of the day when it is finally mated.

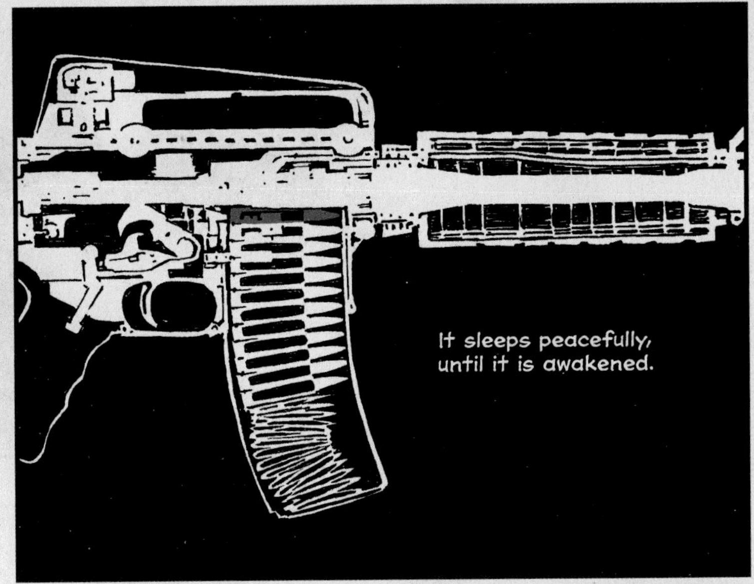

It sleeps peacefully, until it is awakened.

It's impossible to see in motion, so rapidly does it move to execute with perfection the one task it was born to achieve.

And as it performs that task—ending human life—its brief life also comes to an end.

Invisible names.
Sent all over the country, where they lay dormant, before being put to work—
—in places like—

LANDO. NEWTOWN. FORT HOOD. SAN YSIDRO. BLACKSBURG
USTIN. SUTHERLAND SPRINGS. LITTLETON. CARSON CITY.
NCHO TEHAMA. MENASHA. CHATTANOOGA. TUCSON. KILLEE
UMBUS. LOUISVILLE. MANCHESTER. BINGHAMTON. HIALEA
NTA BARBARA. COLORADO SPRINGS. KALAMAZOO. DALLAS
RORA. BROOKFIELD. FORT WORTH. SEATTLE. TUNKHANNOC
ALTURAS. SEAL BEACH. FRESNO. RED LAKE. PARKLAND.
RTHAGE. OAK CREEK. NORCROSS. SANTA MONICA. ROSEBER
ESSTON. BATON ROUGE. KIRKERSVILLE. MIAMI. THORNTON
FAYETTEVILLE. MERIDIAN. TAMPA. HONOLULU. OAKLAND.
ANTA. ORANGE. GARDEN CITY. WATKINS GLEN. OLIVEHUR
MELROSE PARK. CORPUS CHRISTI. EDGEWOOD. GOLETA.
CRANDON. DEKALB. ROYAL OAK. SUNNYVALE. LAS VEGAS.

For my cousin, Jeremiah Jones, murdered by an unknown gunman on June 18, 1995. —SBW

RECONSTRUCTION
BY MALACHI WARD
In the wake of the Civil War, the task at hand was the reintegration of the South into the Union, and to integrate the newly freed black community into the life of American citizenship.
But this time of reconstruction was tumultuous and often bloody.

It was frequently unsafe for freedmen to excercise their right to vote. It became common to carry firearms as protection against racist "Redeemer" militias and mobs.
The gun was the most effective tool against that violence, and the flood of available guns following the Civil War magnified the role of firearms in the Reconstruction era.

For many black people, firearms provided the only path to voting for government officials that truly represented them.
SEN. HIRAM REVELS
REP. ROBERT B. ELLIOTT
REP. BENJAMIN S. TURNER
REP. JOSEPH RAINEY
REP. ROBERT DeLARGE
REP. JOSIAH WALLS
REP. JEFFERSON LONG
For "Redeemers", firearms were a tool to take freedom from others.

To both parties, the gun was no longer a banal reality of frontier life, but an instrument of ideals.
L 11:57:20-63 AM
"When men sow the wind it is rational to expect that they will reap the whirlwind."
Frederick Douglass

EVERYONE KNOWS THE ANSWER TO SOLVE THE PROBLEM

story, lay-outs and lettering by CHRIS WISNIA

finishes by BILL SIENKIEWICZ

colors by JEROMY COX

I THINK IT'S EASY TO GET EMOTIONAL, DUE TO THE NATURE OF THESE CRIMES, BUT IF YOU TAKE A STEP BACK AND LOOK AT THE ACTUAL NUMBERS...

...MASS SHOOTINGS ARE ONLY ONE TWENTIETH OF ALL HOMICIDES...

WHAT, SO–?

—ON THE ***WORST*** YEAR. IT'S ACTUALLY MORE LIKE—

—SO IT'S OKAY WITH YOU IF—

THERE ARE THREE TIMES MORE SUICIDES THAN ***ALL HOMICIDES***—

WELL, ***ALL*** OF THESE ARE ***FIREARM*** PROBLEMS, AND—

—YES, AND FOUR TIMES MORE DRUG OVERDOSE DEATHS THAN ***ALL HOMICIDES,*** AND EIGHT TIMES MORE CAR ACCIDENT DEATHS—

GUN DEATHS ARE PREVENTABLE—

SOMEONE NEEDS to do something.
So much injustice.
AND THAT'S JUST A FRACTION, BECAUSE TWO THIRDS—
—TOTALLY PREVENTABLE, IF WE JUST—
—HEART DISEASE, STROKE, ALZHEIMER'S, CANCER, DIABETES, FLU—
—YOU CAN'T JUST IGNORE—
NO, BUT YOU HAVE TO KEEP THINGS IN PERSPECTIVE. THIS PARTICULAR TERRIBLE CIRCUMSTANCE GETS SENSATIONALIZED IN TERMS OF TAKING PRIORITY AMONG ALL THESE SOCIETAL ILLS WITH DWARFINGLY SUPERIOR NUMBERS.
TELL THAT TO... THEY LOST THEIR DAUGHTER. THEY LOST THEIR—
No one should have to suffer like this.
LOOK. THE CONSTITUTION DOESN'T ENFORCE RIGHTS. GUNS DO.
THE GOVERNMENT IS OUT TO TAKE AWAY OUR RIGHTS.
OH, WHAT RIGHTS DID YOU LOSE AGAIN? YOU STILL HAVE A GUN. WHAT DID YOU LOSE IF THERE ARE COMMON SENSE SAFETY PRECAUTIONS?
TAXI DRIVER (1976) Martin Scorsese director
MORE GUNS, LESS CRIME. STUDIES FIND CRIMINALS ARE AFRAID TO COMMIT CRIMES WHEN THEY DON'T KNOW WHO HAS GUNS—
I'm so Alone.
I don't fit in.
I'm A freak.
ONE 1997 STUDY. YOU'RE IGNORING THE DOZEN STUDIES SINCE THAT CONTRADICTED IT.
IF YOU REALLY FEEL YOUR RIGHTS ARE VIOLATED, A LAWYER WOULD BE WAY MORE EFFECTIVE THAN A GUN.
I cannot shake this feeling of helplessness. And fury.

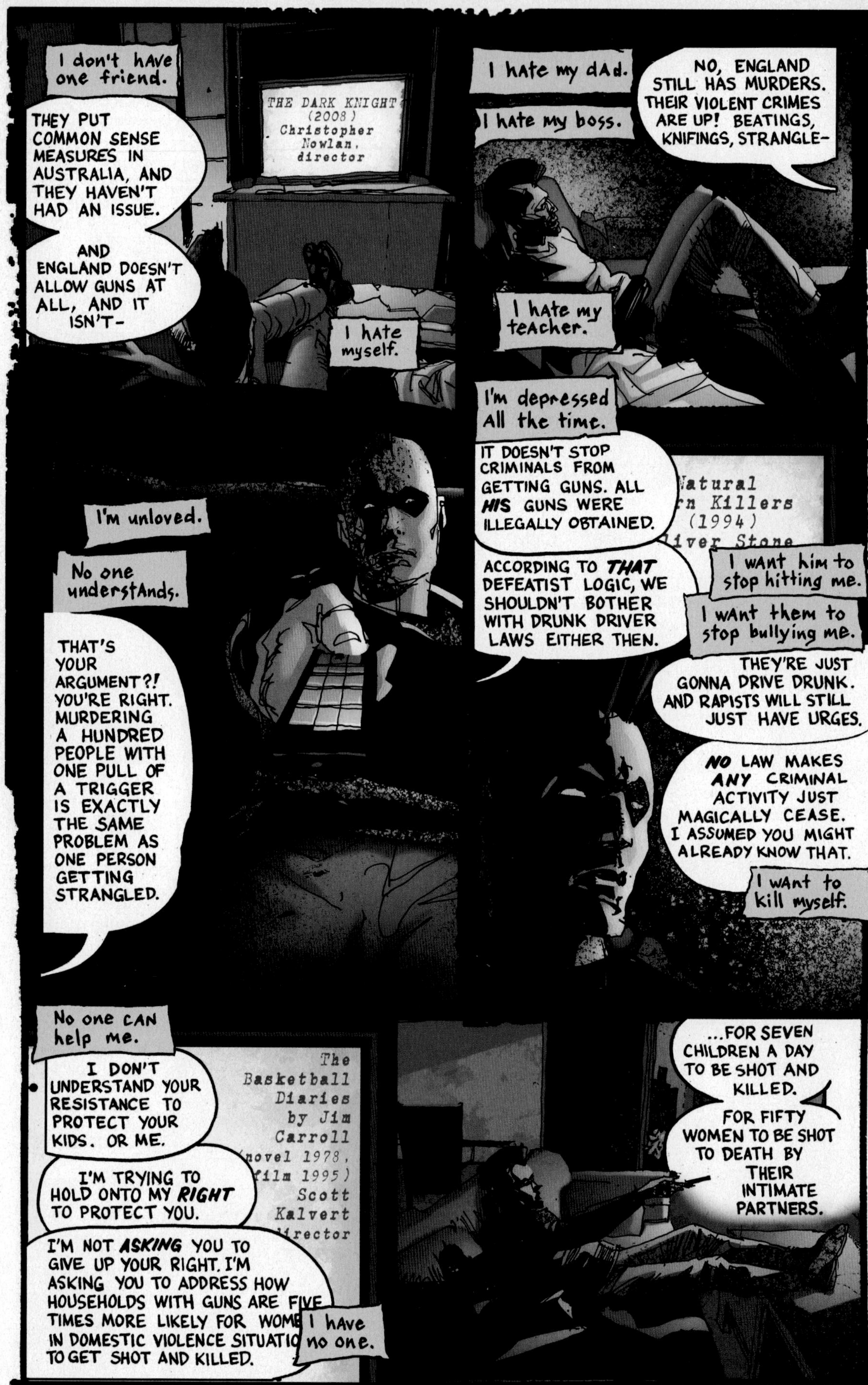
I don't have one friend.
THEY PUT COMMON SENSE MEASURES IN AUSTRALIA, AND THEY HAVEN'T HAD AN ISSUE.
AND ENGLAND DOESN'T ALLOW GUNS AT ALL, AND IT ISN'T-
THE DARK KNIGHT (2008) Christopher Nowlan, director
I hate myself.
I hate my dad.
I hate my boss.
NO, ENGLAND STILL HAS MURDERS. THEIR VIOLENT CRIMES ARE UP! BEATINGS, KNIFINGS, STRANGLE-
I hate my teacher.
I'm depressed All the time.
IT DOESN'T STOP CRIMINALS FROM GETTING GUNS. ALL HIS GUNS WERE ILLEGALLY OBTAINED.
I'm unloved.
No one understands.
ACCORDING TO THAT DEFEATIST LOGIC, WE SHOULDN'T BOTHER WITH DRUNK DRIVER LAWS EITHER THEN.
I want him to stop hitting me.
I want them to stop bullying me.
THAT'S YOUR ARGUMENT?! YOU'RE RIGHT. MURDERING A HUNDRED PEOPLE WITH ONE PULL OF A TRIGGER IS EXACTLY THE SAME PROBLEM AS ONE PERSON GETTING STRANGLED.
THEY'RE JUST GONNA DRIVE DRUNK. AND RAPISTS WILL STILL JUST HAVE URGES.
NO LAW MAKES ANY CRIMINAL ACTIVITY JUST MAGICALLY CEASE. I ASSUMED YOU MIGHT ALREADY KNOW THAT.
I want to kill myself.
No one can help me.
I DON'T UNDERSTAND YOUR RESISTANCE TO PROTECT YOUR KIDS. OR ME.
I'M TRYING TO HOLD ONTO MY RIGHT TO PROTECT YOU.
I'M NOT ASKING YOU TO GIVE UP YOUR RIGHT. I'M ASKING YOU TO ADDRESS HOW HOUSEHOLDS WITH GUNS ARE FIVE TIMES MORE LIKELY FOR WOME IN DOMESTIC VIOLENCE SITUATIO TO GET SHOT AND KILLED.
I have no one.
...FOR SEVEN CHILDREN A DAY TO BE SHOT AND KILLED.
FOR FIFTY WOMEN TO BE SHOT TO DEATH BY THEIR INTIMATE PARTNERS.

Doom video game (1993)
I don't care Any more.
...TWO INJURIES WITH GUNS FOR EVERYONE KILLED BY THEM...
...MORE THAN ONE MASS SHOOTING FOR EVERY DAY OF THE YEAR...
THE DOPE SHOW Marilyn Manson (2003)
BODIES Drowning Pool (2001)
RONNIE, Metallica (1996)
Here comes Satan, Im the antichrist, Im going to kill you." -Eminem
I FEEL SAFER WITH MY GUNS.
They'll All be sorry tomorrow.
They will All pAy.
Someone has to do something.
MOM, DAD...
I'VE BEEN HAVING THESE REALLY INTENSE, DISTURBING THOUGHTS THAT LEAD TO ULTRA VIOLENT FANTASIES, AND I'M FEELING JUST ABOUT READY TO START ACTING THEM ALL OUT RIGHT NOW.
COUNTRIES WITH MORE GUNS HAVE MORE GUN DEATHS AND THE MOST SUICIDES.
THERE'S ONE GUN FOR EVERY PERSON IN THE U.S., INCLUDING INFANTS.
GUNS ARE USED FOR SELF-DEFENSE LESS THAN 1% OF ALL VICTIM-PRESENT CRIMES, AND ITS EFFECTIVENESS IS NO GREATER THAN CALLING FOR HELP.
IF GUNS ARE SO UNSAFE, THEN WHY IS VIOLENT CRIME DOWN 41% OVER THE LAST TEN YEARS, DESPITE OWNERSHIP AT A RECORD HIGH?
BECAUSE THE INCREASE IS WITH OWNERS OF MULTIPLE GUNS. THE NUMBER OF HOUSEHOLDS WHO OWN THEM HAS DROPPED. 3% OF AMERICANS OWN 50% OF ALL GUNS.
I GOT DAD'S GUN DOWN FROM THE CLOSET, AND TOMORROW—
LATER! CAN'T YOU HEAR WE'RE BUSY?
WHEN DID HE GET HOME?
WELL I THINK—

"74% of gun owners feel that a firearm is essential to their freedom." (1)

"For every time a gun in the home was used in a self-defense or legally justifiable shooting, there were four unintentional shootings, seven criminal assaults or homicides, and 11 attempted or completed suicides." (2)

Everyone knows the answer to this problem. We don't feel safe without our guns, and we are less safe with them.

NOTES

Pages 1 and 2

(1) Centers for Disease Control and Prevention, National Vital Statistics Reports vol. 65, Number 5 (2016). www.cdc.gov/nchs/data/nvsr/nvsr65/nvsr65_05.pdf

(2) Centers for Disease Control and Prevention, Deaths: Leading Causes for 2014, www.cdc.gov/nchs/fastats/deaths.htm

Page 2

(3) NPR, Australians Urge U.S. To Look At Their Gun Laws (2012), www.npr.org/2012/12/21/167814684/australians-urge-u-s-to-look-at-their-gun-laws

Pages 2-4

Psychology Today, The Mind of the Mass Murderer (2014) www.psychologytoday.com/blog/saving-normal/201405/the-mind-the-mass-murderer

(4) Richard Rowe, Here's Why Gun Control Doesn't Make Sense Right Now (undated), https://www.ranker.com/list/arguments-against-gun-control/richard-rowe

(5) Huffington Post, Why the Arguments Against Gun Control are Wrong (2017), www.huffingtonpost.com/entry/why-the-arguments-against-gun-control-are-wrong_us_59d6405ce4b0666ad0c3cb34

Page 2, panel 3; page 3, panels 1, 4 and 6; page 4 panel 2

Following high profile violent acts, the media and politicians are quick to speculatively blame the films, video games, and music that we ALL watch.

(6) www.listverse.com/2014/06/24/10-attempts-to-blame-murder-on-music/

(7) www.ranker.com/list/movies-blamed-for-killings/jacob-shelton

(8) www.thegamer.com/15-despicable-crimes-that-got-blamed-on-video-games/

"Such claims are not based on research evidence and these claims may distract society from more substantive causes of violence, such as poverty, lack of treatment options for mental health... and educational and employment disparities." - Division 46 of the American Psychological Association, (9) "Societal Violence and Video Games: Public Statements of a Link are Problematic" (2017). www.thecut.com/2017/05/psychologists-stop-blaming-mass-shootings-on-video-games.html

(10) CNN, Mass Shootings in America are a Serious Problem (2017), www.cnn.com/2016/06/13/health/mass-shootings-in-america-in-charts-and-graphs-trnd/index.html

Pages 3 and 4

(11) Everytown, Gun Violence by the Numbers (2017), www.everytownresearch.org/gun-violence-by-the-numbers/

Page 5

(12) The Skeptic Society, Mass Public Shootings & Gun Violence: Part I (2017), www.youtube.com/watch?v=yrK0excqg00

The Guardian, America's passion for guns: ownership and violence by the numbers America's passion for guns: ownership and violence by the numbers (2017), www.theguardian.com/us-news/2017/oct/02/us-gun-control-ownership-violence-statistics

Rantt.com, Fact Checking Four Of The NRA's Favorite Anti-Gun Control Myths (2017) www.rantt.com/fact-checking-four-of-the-nras-favorite-anti-gun-control-myths-c45c615b338c

Washington Post, More Guns Less Crime? Not Exactly (2014), www.washingtonpost.com/news/wonk/wp/2014/07/29/more-guns-less-crime-not-exactly/?utm_term=.0b9232a2036c

Scientific American, More Guns Do No Stop More Crimes, Evidence Shows (2017), www.scientificamerican.com/article/more-guns-do-not-stop-more-crimes-evidence-shows/

Josh

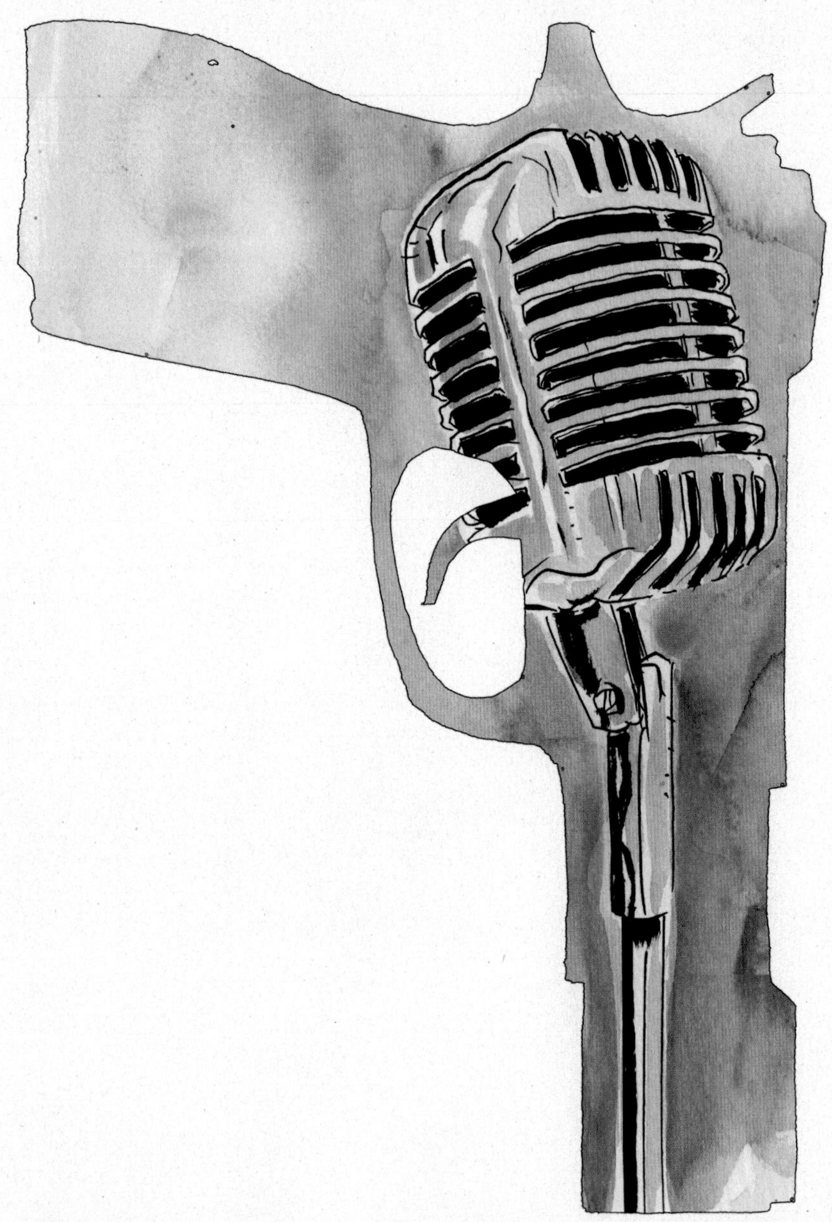

SING

Essay by **JOSHUA ELLIS**
Illustrations by **JEFF LEMIRE**
Production Design by **BERNARDO BRICE**

When Steven Paddock started shooting, I was singing.

The Huntridge Tavern is one of the oldest bars in Las Vegas. It sits off the Strip in a residential neighborhood that was the preferred hangout of small-time gangsters and casino moguls back in the Rat Pack days, and is now mostly hipsters with families and aging punks obsessed with the midcentury ModCon architecture, or working class Latino families - the kind of hood where one neighbor might have a house show with indie bands one night in their backyard and the other neighbor might have a quinceañera the next night with a bouncy castle for the kids and crates of Negro Modelo.

The bar itself is perfect. It's small, narrow, with a couple of red naugahyde booths with Formica tables that have seen better centuries. It's smoky — you can still smoke in bars in Vegas if they let you — and the walls are wood paneling like something out of a seventies porno, and if I walk in after nine PM on any given night in this 24-7 town, I'm likely to see my buddy Thom Chrastka drinking Jameson and reading through a script for a play he's in or doing sound tech for, or my friends Ken and Cindy from the great band The All-Togethers arguing about old movies, or the artist Jesse Smigel in a corner roundly condemning the perpetual sad state of the local art scene. And all of this is as likely to be accompanied by an old Tom Waits or Nick Cave or Merle Haggard song on the jukebox as Sublime or Kendrick Lamar or Gaga. It's a particular kind of heaven if you're a particular kind of person, in other words.

"Every couple of years now, it seems, I spend a night hitting refresh on Twitter and sending frantic texts to make sure that people I care about aren't lying somewhere with a bullet in them."

Sunday nights, I host an open mic at the Huntridge. This is a generational thing for me: my mother, a singer-songwriter, used to host the legendary open mic at the Bluebird Cafe in Nashville, and I grew up in bars like the Huntridge as a small boy, sitting off at the end of the bar with a Roy Rogers and a C.S. Lewis book, watching her play down on Greenville Avenue and in Deep Ellum in Dallas in the 1980s. I am not a particularly successful or well-regarded musician, but I've been doing it my whole life and I like doing it, at least well enough to haul my nearly forty-year-old ass down to a dive bar with my cheap sound system every Sunday and play to a room that varies between ecstatically enthusiastic and openly hostile, depending on whether I'm interrupting a football game or not. Sometimes nobody shows up and I play my repertoire of obscure covers solo all night — songs like "I'll Be Your Lover, Too" by Van Morrison or "Lungs" by Townes van Zandt or "Right Here, Right Now" by Jesus Jones. (I like to cover the waterfront.) Sometimes Ken and Cindy show up with their upright bass and mandolin and it turns magic, and sometimes a total stranger walks in and brings the house down. I show up every week no matter what, though.

October 1, 2017 was a Sunday.

That night, we'd had John Emmons, the local poet and sort of itinerant artist figure, who brought his Stratocaster with the Korg Kaossilator stuck on it so he could do bleepy Krautrocky jams over house beats; Eli and Garrett Curtsinger from the amazing band Indigo Kidd, who were stoned and giggling Pixies covers on bass and acoustic guitar; I can't remember who else.

I had just finished playing — I can't remember what song — and gone to the bar for a smoke and a shot of whiskey when the news came on the TV behind the bar. At first we thought it was just some dipshit shooting at another dipshit down on the Strip sidewalk, which happens occasionally... but it became clear after a few minutes that wasn't the case.

People's phones started lighting up with texts and alerts. Twitter. Facebook. There were shooters up and down the Strip in multiple casinos. Shots fired at the Mandalay Bay, the Luxor, Caesar's, the Venetian. One girl's friend who was a sommelier at the Paris texted her that they'd been evacuated into the wine storage as a panic room.

The Huntridge Tavern is less than a mile off Las Vegas Boulevard, but we were a long way north of where all of this was going down. We couldn't hear the gunfire or anything. But we could hear the sirens as every cop car and ambulance in Clark County went barrelling down Maryland Parkway or Charleston, towards the south end of the Strip.

There seems to be a general consensus in the rest of the world that Las Vegas consists of the Strip and a couple of trailer parks directly behind it; when my friend Melissa used to go on out-of-state speech and debate field trips in high school, people asked her if she lived in a casino.

But this is a city of two million people; we're larger than San Francisco or Seattle, for example. Most of my friends don't work on the Strip or in a casino. They're lawyers and coders and Lyft drivers and bartenders and writers.

But all of us know somebody who works on the Strip... and that night all of us waited to hear from those people. My friend Thom Chrastka I mentioned before? He works at the Mandalay Bay. He sets up light electrical stuff and audiovisual gear for trade shows...and festivals.

Really hoping you weren't working tonight man, I texted him, and waited for an answer.

It occurred to me, then, how sick I was of these late nights, these terrified vigils. My family lives in Aurora, Colorado, and were precisely the sort of nerds to be going to the midnight premiere of a Batman movie in 2012. I'm friends with a couple of the members of the band Eagles of Death Metal, who survived the shooting at their Paris concert in 2015 by hiding under the bodies of their dead fans.

Every couple of years now, it seems, I spend a night hitting refresh on Twitter and sending frantic texts to make sure that people I care about aren't lying somewhere with a bullet in them.

I have been very lucky so far.

Somehow, almost everyone I know was lucky in Vegas that Sunday night. No one I knew was shot or killed. Some friends and relatives of friends, but everybody I knew personally made it out.

I'm ok. Not at work. My guys are safe, Thom Chrastka messaged me, not long after I hit him up.

Eventually we realized we weren't going to find anything else out tonight, and I started breaking down my PA and loading up my guitar in my truck. Nobody much felt like playing anymore. And I had that deep body/deep mind exhaustion that only seems to show up in the 21st century when there's some sort of absurd and horrible event like this. I had it the night of Aurora, chugging coffee and waiting to hear back from my cousins. I had it the day of the Paris attacks, standing around in a parking lot hitting every feed and social network over and over while, in the dark on the other side of the world, my friends were literally dodging bullets.

I remember standing with my best friends on an apartment balcony here in Vegas on September 12th, 2001, looking up at something none of us had ever seen before: a sky with no contrails, a silent sky with no planes in it.

This is normal now.

I went home and I slept, and I waited to hear what was going to happen next.

***

A couple of nights later, I found myself in a parking lot outside University Medical Center, handing out food and drinks to exhausted trauma center medical personnel, cops, security guards and wounded people.

My buddy Jason Harris, a local comedian, had, along with some other restaurant owners and businesspeople, mobilized a bunch of locals to come out and make sure that the ER folks and trauma folks and first responders who had been working so hard were taken care of. I picked up my friend Jessi and we headed down to UMC, where a couple of food trucks were set up next to folding tables full of donated catered food from pizza joints and indian buffets and everything in between. I went to Wal-Mart and bought four or five cases of bottled water along with crackers, cookies, chips, dip and sugar-free snacks.

There were dozens of volunteers in that parking lot — tattooed hipsters, old folks, Summerlin housewives, queer folks, straight folks, white folks, black folks, Hispanic folks — the entire cross-section of Las Vegas's diverse population. I talked to a young country fan with a scruffy beard and a bullet in his arm. I gave glass bottles of ginger tea to nurses who looked like they were about to pass out. I got hugged by a surgeon with a German accent for bringing sandwiches into the trauma ward.

I saw the wreckage of Steven Paddock's madness there. I would be happy if I never saw that again.

People think this isn't a real city, but we stepped up in those nights after the shooting. We raised money and we took care of each other. We cried with each other and we held each other at candlelight vigils and in the parking lots of local hospitals and in our own homes at night. You see bumper stickers with the #VegasStrong hashtag on them everywhere here now, but it is a simple fact. We were strong. We remain strong.

As I stood by a cinderblock retaining wall in that parking lot, I thought about Tom Petty, who died the day after the shooting, and I sang one of his songs to myself, too quietly for anyone else to hear:

Well, I won't back down
No, I won't back down
You can stand me up at the gates of Hell
But I won't back down

Vegas didn't back down. And we kept singing. Sometimes that is all you can do. And sometimes it's enough.

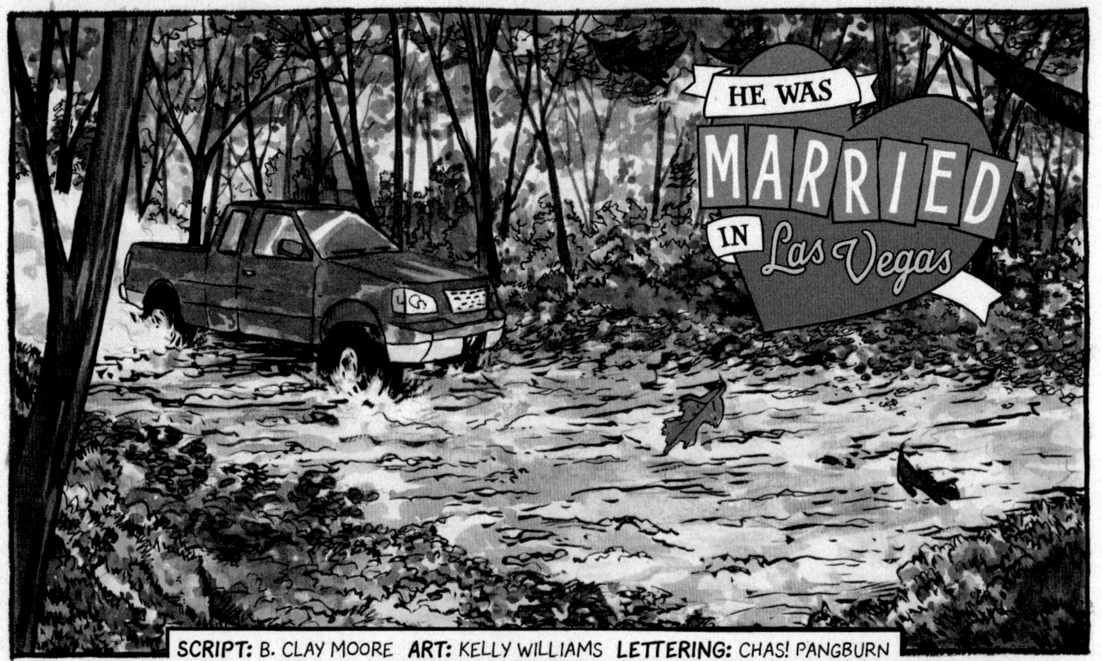
HE WAS
MARRIED
IN Las Vegas
SCRIPT: B. CLAY MOORE ART: KELLY WILLIAMS LETTERING: CHAS! PANGBURN

...PADDOCK FIRED MORE THAN 1,100 ROUNDS FROM HIS SUITE ON THE 32ND FLOOR OF THE NEARBY MANDALAY BAY HOTEL, KILLING AT LEAST FIFTY PEOPLE.

THE CONTROVERSY SURROUNDING PADDOCK'S USE OF LEGALLY MODIFIED BUMP FIRE STOCKS...
WELCOME
TO Fabulous
LAS VEGAS
NEVADA

...WHICH ALLOWED HIS SEMI-AUTOMATIC RIFLES TO FIRE AT A RATE SIMILAR TO THAT OF A FULLY AUTOMATED WEAPON...

WELCOME
To Fabulous
LAS VEGAS
NEVADA

PROUD MEMBER
NRA
I'D RATHER
BE HUNTING

WELCOME
to Fabulous
LAS VEGAS

END.

STICKING TO YOUR GUNS

STORY BY ROB ROSE
ART BY MATT STRACKBEIN

I FORGET HOW BREATHTAKING THIS PLACE CAN BE DURING THE HOLIDAYS, SAM.

YOU COULD ALWAYS MOVE BACK HOME, PETER.

AND DITCH MY FAILING ACTING CAREER? NOT A CHANCE. MARK MY WORDS, IN THREE DAYS I'LL BE BACK IN L.A., RUBBING SUNSCREEN ALL OVER MY INFLATABLE FRONT YARD SNOWMAN.

IN THAT CASE, THE CLOCK IS TICKING. TIME TO SUCK IT UP AND FACE THE MUSIC, BABY BRO.

DOESN'T MAKE THIS ANY EASIER THAT IT SOUNDS LIKE JEFFREY DAHMER'S MAN CAVE.
GNAAAAAASH!
IT'S NOT NEARLY AS FRIGHTENING INSIDE, YOU BIG BABY. HE'S ACTUALLY CONVERTED IT INTO A PROPER WOOD SHOP.

YOU ASKED ME WHAT I WANTED FOR CHRISTMAS. THIS IS WHAT I WANT. FOR MY BROTHER AND MY HUSBAND TO FINALLY PUT AN END TO THEIR HOLY WAR.
HE STARTED IT BY CALLING ME A SNOWFLAKE.
IS THAT RIGHT? I SEEM TO RECALL SOMEONE SCREAMING UNCONTROLLABLY THAT HE WAS "KNOWLEDGE INTOLERANT."

GNAAAASH!
ANY CHANCE THAT PARTICULAR DETAIL SLIPPED HIS MIND?

TRUTH IS, I DON'T CARE WHO STARTED IT. YOU'RE GOING TO BE AN UNCLE AGAIN AND YOU'VE MISSED THE LAST TWO YEARS WITH HOLLY. PLEASE, NO MORE LOST TIME. IF NOT FOR ME, DO IT FOR YOUR NIECES.
I CAN'T SPEAK FOR HIM, BUT I PROMISE YOU AND THE LITTLE ONES A HERCULEAN EFFORT ON MY END.

I KNEW I COULD COUNT ON YOU. AND PETER, JACK'S A GOOD MAN. I WOULDN'T HAVE MARRIED HIM OTHERWISE. SO GO EASY ON HIM, OK?

ME, GO EASY ON HIM?

HE'S A GOOD MAN, HUH...?

THEN WHY IS THIS STARTING TO FEEL LIKE EVERY OPENING SCENE ON FORENSIC FILES?!
GNAAAAAASH!

IF THAT'S SUPPOSED TO BE A TENNIS RACKET, I'VE GOT SOME TERRIBLE NEWS, JACK...
WELL, IF IT ISN'T MR. SAFE SPACE. COME ON IN. AND CLOSE THE DOOR. THE FRIGID AIR CONTRACTS THE WOOD.
IT'S THE HOLIDAYS SO I'M GOING TO LET THAT SLIDE.

SO...WHAT ARE WE BUILDING?
NOT BUILDING, REPAIRING. THE WIFE'S PRESENT. BEEN PROMISING TO FIX IT FOR YEARS.
HOW CAN I HELP?

CALL ME OLD FASHIONED, BUT I'D PREFER A HAMMER.
LET ME GUESS, YOU HAVE A PROBLEM WITH NAIL GUNS TOO?
ONLY IF THEY'RE USED IN A MASS SHOOTING.
THAT'S FUNNY. YOU GONNA BAN MINI-VANS THE NEXT TIME SOME PSYCHO PLOWS ONE INTO A CROWDED FARMER'S MARKET?
OH WAIT, I GOT IT, YOU'LL FORCE A BAN ON FARMER'S MARKETS

THAT'S THE PROBLEM WITH ALL YOU GUN NUTS. YOU THINK IT'S ALL JUST A BIG JOKE! THERE'S NOTHING FUNNY ABOUT MASS CASUALTIES IN THE WORK-PLACE, OR AT CONCERT VENUES. OR ELEMENTARY SCHOOLS FULL OF CHILDREN GETTING--
I'M GONNA HAVE TO STOP YOU RIGHT THERE. TO PAINT US ALL AS A BUNCH OF GUN-HUGGING MONSTERS WHO DON'T CARE ABOUT THOSE INNOCENT CHILDREN...
...OR THOSE GOOD FOLKS IN SAN BERNADINO OR LAS VEGAS IS WRONG! IT'S LIBERAL SPIN AND YOU KNOW IT!

YOU'RE RIGHT. THAT WAS UNFAIR. JESUS, I PROMISED MY SISTER I WOULDN'T DO THIS. I DIDN'T EVEN MAKE IT TWO DAMN MINUTES. I'D LIKE TO APOLOGIZE, JACK.
MY APOLOGIES TOO. SEEING AS I KINDA STARTED IT WITH THE SAFE SPACE CRACK. SEEMS THIS GUN CONTROL ISSUE'S TURNED US ALL INTO LUNATICS.
FROM CONGRESS ON DOWN, THIS ENTIRE COUNTRY IS IN DIRE NEED OF SOME BASIC COMMON GROUND.

THE ENTIRE COUNTRY'S A LOT TO TACKLE. MAYBE WE START WITH JUST THE TWO OF US. WHAT DO YOU SAY, JACK?
I SAY, YOUR SISTER'S ABOUT TO GRACE ME WITH ANOTHER BEAUTIFUL CHILD. I CAN'T THINK OF A MORE SOLID PIECE OF COMMON GROUND THAN FAMILY.

SO NOW THAT WE'RE FRIENDLY AGAIN...HAVE THESE HANDS EVER EVEN HELD A GUN?
WHATEVER IDEA'S ROLLING AROUND IN THAT HEAD OF YOURS, IT'S STILL WAAAAY TOO SOON, JACK!
CAN'T SAY I DIDN'T TRY.

AND FINALLY, TO BOTH MY HUSBAND AND MY BROTHER. FOR NOT ONLY REPAIRING MY POOR DINING ROOM TABLE, BUT FOR PLACING THAT SAME EFFORT AND CONVICTION INTO REPAIRING THEIR OWN RELATIONSHIP. I LOVE YOU BOTH SO DEARLY. CHEERS!

CLINK CLINK
CHEERS! CHEERS!
TO MY BROTHER-IN-LAW, JACK. FOR NOT ONLY REMINDING ME WHY WE SHOULD NEVER JUDGE A BOOK BY ITS COVER, BUT FOR HELPING ME TO RECOGNIZE THAT OUR HUMANITY LIES NOT IN OUR SHARED COMMON BELIEFS, BUT IN OUR SHARED COMMON GROUND. CHEERS EVERYONE!

CLINK CLINK
CHEERS! CHEERS!
PETER, IT TOOK A MAN OF GREAT CHARACTER, AND EVEN GREATER COURAGE TO WALK INTO MY WOOD SHOP ALONE THIS AFTERNOON. FOR THAT I'M TRULY GRATEFUL.
AND IF TWO STUBBORN MULES LIKE US CAN SOMEHOW MANAGE TO OPEN OUR MINDS AND HEARTS TO THE IDEA OF BETTER SOLUTIONS, WHILE STILL STICKING TO OUR GUNS, THEN PERHAPS THERE'S HOPE FOR THE REST OF THE COUNTRY. MERRY CHRISTMAS, EVERYONE!

NOW, IN HONOR OF TODAY'S MINI-MIRACLE, AND AS A SYMBOL OF MY WILLINGNESS TO COMPROMISE, I OFFER UP MY SWORN DUTY AS OFFICIAL TURKEY CARVER, TO MY BROTHER IN-LAW. MAY HIS CUT BE AS SHARP AS HIS TONGUE!
THANKS ANYWAY, JACK. I APPRECIATE THE GESTURE, BUT NO MEAT FOR ME. GUESS SAM NEVER TOLD YOU...I'M A VEGAN NOW.

HE'S A WHAAAAAT?!
GREAT! HERE WE GO AGAIN!
THE END

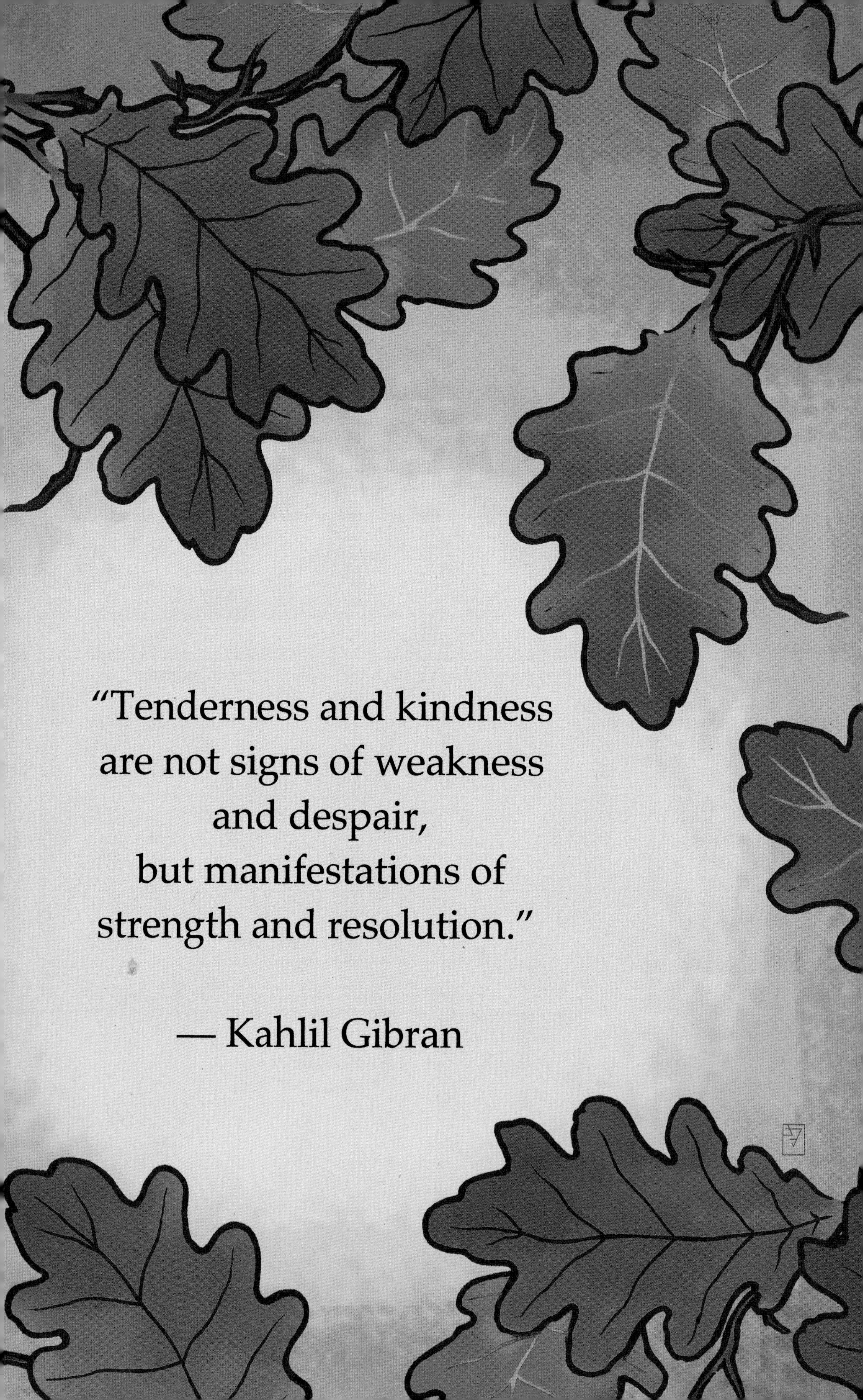
"Tenderness and kindness
are not signs of weakness
and despair,
but manifestations of
strength and resolution."
— Kahlil Gibran

Pieces of a Man

LIVING IN MANHATTAN IN THE LATE 1980S WAS AN ***INSANE*** ADVENTURE.

THAT'S ME BACK THEN...

...WHEN I STILL HAD HAIR, AND YOU COULD BUY NUNCHAKUS IN TIMES SQUARE.

I JUMPED INTO MY FIRST MOSH PIT AT THE ***24-7 SPYZ*** RECORD RELEASE PARTY FOR "HARDER THAN YOU," LONG BEFORE THE TERM ***AFROPUNK*** WAS COINED...

...AND HUNG OUT IN HARLEM ***BEFORE*** IT WAS GENTRIFIED.

I DRANK TOO MUCH, MOSTLY ATE ***HOT DOGS*** FROM GRAY'S PAPAYA PRINCE ON EIGHTH AVENUE, AND DIDN'T GIVE MUCH THOUGHT TO ***TOMORROW***.

TO BE ***SELF-ABSORBED*** AND ***OBLIVIOUS*** TO THE WORLD AROUND ME WAS SO MUCH ***EASIER*** IN MY YOUTH.

YET THERE WAS SOMETHING A LITTLE TOO ***RAW*** AND ***REAL*** FOR ME ABOUT NEW YORK.

I REMEMBER THIS ONE TIME, AT A SUBWAY STOP NEAR PENN STATION...

ME, GOING DOWN TO THE SUBWAY, CIRCA 1989.

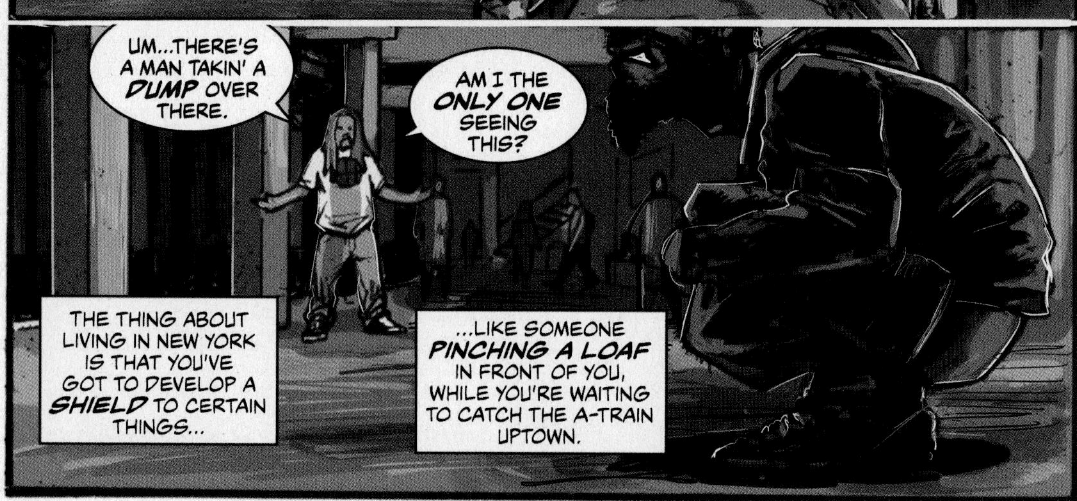

UM...THERE'S A MAN TAKIN' A DUMP OVER THERE.
AM I THE ONLY ONE SEEING THIS?
THE THING ABOUT LIVING IN NEW YORK IS THAT YOU'VE GOT TO DEVELOP A SHIELD TO CERTAIN THINGS...
...LIKE SOMEONE PINCHING A LOAF IN FRONT OF YOU, WHILE YOU'RE WAITING TO CATCH THE A-TRAIN UPTOWN.

I'VE THOUGHT ABOUT IT A LOT OVER THE YEARS -- IT'S ONE OF THOSE IMAGES BURNED INTO MY BRAIN.
SOMETHING THAT CAN NEVER BE UNSEEN.
AND HONESTLY, IF THERE WAS A SINGLE MOMENT IN NEW YORK THAT BROKE MY SPIRIT...
PUBLIC ENEMY
...IT WAS RIGHT THEN AND THERE.
WHAT'S WRONG WITH YOU PEOPLE?!
DON'T YOU SEE ANOTHER HUMAN BEING DEFECATING ON THE PLATFORM?!
THIS IS SO WRONG!
WHAT'RE WE ALLOWING OURSELVES TO BECOME?!
I COULDN'T LIVE IN A CITY WHERE YOU HAD TO SHUT OFF YOUR HUMANITY IN ORDER TO KEEP FROM BEING SUCKED INTO THE INSANITY.
SO I DECIDED TO LEAVE.
DON'T GET ME WRONG...I DIDN'T LEAVE FOREVER.
I STILL GO BACK TO VISIT. BUT EVERY SINGLE TIME, SOMETHING HAPPENS.
RIDING THE SUBWAY WAS ALWAYS THE MOST DIFFICULT -- TOO MUCH HUMANITY.
I JUST COULDN'T SHUT IT OUT.
NOT THEN. AND NOT NOW.

DURING A TRIP IN 2014, I HADN'T BEEN ON THE SUBWAY PLATFORM MORE THAN A MINUTE WHEN I SAW IT HAPPEN.
A STREET MUSICIAN WAS SINGING A SONG, BUT THAT'S NOT WHAT I NOTICED.
...WATCHIN' THE SHIPS ROLL IN...
IT WAS THIS GUY, RIGHT HERE. CLEARLY, SOMETHING WAS WRONG WITH HIM.
HE WAS HAVING A TOTAL EMOTIONAL BREAKDOWN. ANYONE COULD SEE IT...
...BUT EVERYONE WAS CHOOSING NOT TO SEE IT.
ANOTHER HUMAN BEING WAS FALLING TO PIECES IN FRONT OF ALL OF US, AND NOBODY WAS DOING A THING TO HELP HIM.
HEY, MAN... ARE YOU OKAY?
NO... I'M NOT.
IT WAS EVERYTHING I HATED ABOUT NEW YORK.
CAN I DO ANYTHING TO HELP?
I...I JUST... I GOT ALL THIS SHIT INSIDE ME. YOU KNOW?
AND...IT'S KILLING ME. I DON'T KNOW HOW TO GET IT OUT.
YOU CAN'T KEEP THESE THINGS INSIDE, MAN.
YOU GOTTA FIND SOMEONE TO TALK TO, SO

MAN, NO ONE GIVES A %#@$ ABOUT ME.
THAT'S NOT TRUE. I GIVE A %#@$ ABOUT YOU.
I'M STANDING RIGHT HERE, TALKING TO YOU RIGHT NOW -- GIVING A %#@$.
...LOOKS LIKE NOTHING'S GONNA CHANGE...
LOOK AT ME. I'M TELLING YOU, WHATEVER IT IS YOU'RE CARRYING, GIVE IT TO ME.
LET ME TAKE IT, SO YOU DON'T HAVE TO KEEP IT ANYMORE.
...AND THIS LONELINESS WON'T LEAVE ME ALONE...
I WAS JUST A TEENAGER WHEN THIS SONG CAME OUT -- A KID. YOU KNOW?
I DIDN'T KNOW ANY BETTER.
THIS MAN, HE TOLD ME A BUNCH OF BULLSHIT ABOUT ALL THE THINGS I COULD DO, AND THE DIFFERENCE I COULD MAKE.
AND I WAS SO YOUNG, AND I BELIEVED HIM, AND SO...YOU KNOW...

...AND SO I WENT TO VIETNAM.
HE TOLD ME HIS STORY.
AND I LISTENED.

WHY ARE YOU DOING THIS FOR ME?
YOU'RE A HUMAN BEING, AREN'T YOU? YOUR LIFE HAS SOME VALUE, DOESN'T IT?
YEAH, I'M A HUMAN BEING.
WELL, WE ALL NEED TO BE REMINDED FROM TIME TO TIME.
YOU MATTER. I MATTER. WE ALL MATTER.
NO ONE'S EVER DONE ANYTHING LIKE THIS FOR ME.
HEY, MAN, THAT'S MY TRAIN. BUT IF YOU NEED ME TO STAY WITH YOU...
NO. I'M GOOD. THANK YOU.
I... THINK...
...I THINK YOU JUST SAVED MY LIFE.
David F. Walker - writer
Damon Smith - artist
John Jennings & Jeremy Marshall of Motherboxx Studios - colorists

Information obtained from *GunViolenceArchive.org*

Gun Violence Archive (GVA) is a not-for-profit corporation formed in 2013 to provide free online public access to accurate information about gun-related violence in the United States. GVA will collect and check for accuracy, comprehensive information about gun-related violence in the U.S. and then post and disseminate it online.

GVA is not, by design an advocacy group. The mission of GVA is to document incidents of gun violence and gun crime nationally to provide independent, verified data to those who need to use it in their research, advocacy or writing.

GUN VIOLENCE Archive **INCIDENTS IN 2018**

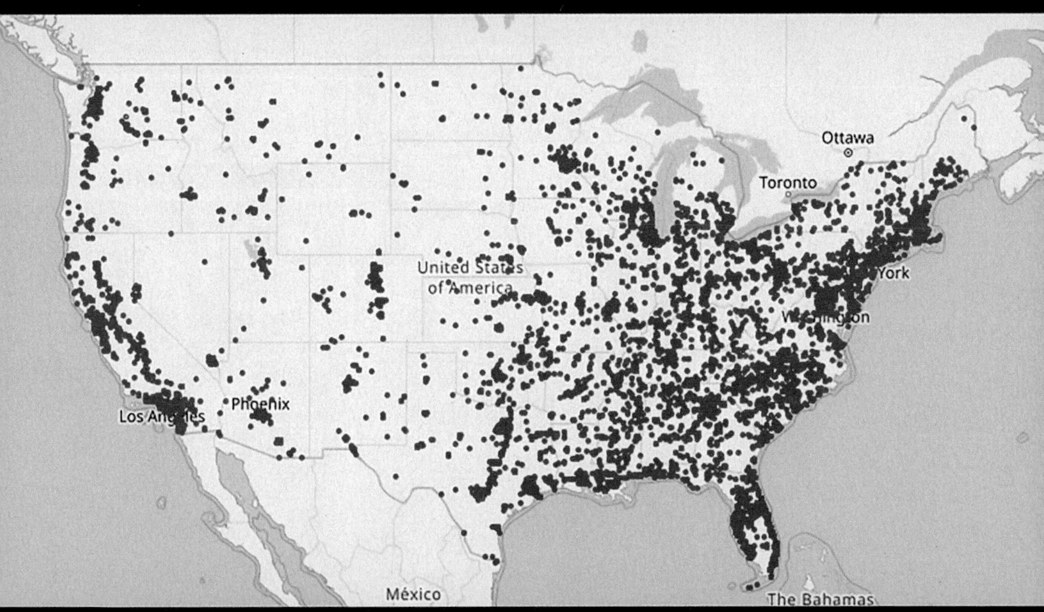

January 1 - April 30, 2018 gunviolencearchive.org

Total Number of Incidents: **18,720**

Number of Deaths[1]: **4,681**

Number of Injuries[1]: **8,279**

Number of Children (age 0-11) Killed or Injured[1]: **195**

Number of Teens (age 12-17) Killed or Injured[1]: **817**

Mass Shooting[2]: **79**

Officer Involved Incident (Shot or Killed)[2]: **87**

Officer Involved Incident (Subject-Suspect Shot or Killed)[2]: **755**

Home Invasion[2]: **680**

Defensive Use[2]: **538**

Unintentional Shooting[2]: **537**

Gun violence and crime incidents are collected/validated from 2,500 sources daily. Incidents and their source data are found at the *gunviolencearchive.org* website.

1: Actual number of deaths and injuries
2: Number of INCIDENTS reported and verified

22,000 Annual Suicides not included on the Daily Summary Ledger.

Numbers on this table reflect a subset of all information ccollected and will not add to 100% of incidents.

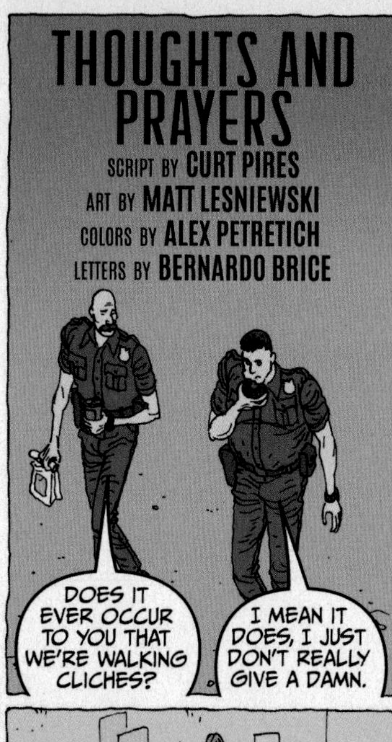
THOUGHTS AND PRAYERS
SCRIPT BY CURT PIRES
ART BY MATT LESNIEWSKI
COLORS BY ALEX PETRETICH
LETTERS BY BERNARDO BRICE
DOES IT EVER OCCUR TO YOU THAT WE'RE WALKING CLICHES?
I MEAN IT DOES, I JUST DON'T REALLY GIVE A DAMN.

YOUR WIFE ON LINE ONE.
OKAY, PUT HER THROUGH.
HEY, HONEY.
DON'T FORGET.
NO, YOU'RE RIGHT LINDA. THAT'S WHY REFORM IS SO KEY. WE'RE NOT TRYING TO TAKE AWAY ANYONE'S SECOND AMENDMENT HERE.

WHAT?
STACY'S BIRTHDAY. CONCERT TONIGHT. YOU'RE TAKING HER. DON'T FORGET.
COURSE I WON'T.
YOU TOTALLY WOULD. I LOVE YOU.
I LOVE YOU TOO, BABY.
GUN CONTROL
WE'RE TRYING TO PROTECT PEOPLE. WE'RE SAYING IT SHOULDN'T BE EASY TO WALK INTO A STORE AND BUY A MILITARY GRADE--

I'M GONNA SMASH HIM TONIGHT.
UH HUH?
I'M SO GONNA SMASH HIM TONIGHT. JUST YOU WAIT.
I BELIEVE YOU.

EXCITEMENT IN THE AIR TONIGHT FOR THE CONCERT-- WHICH IS JUST ABOUT TO GET UNDER--

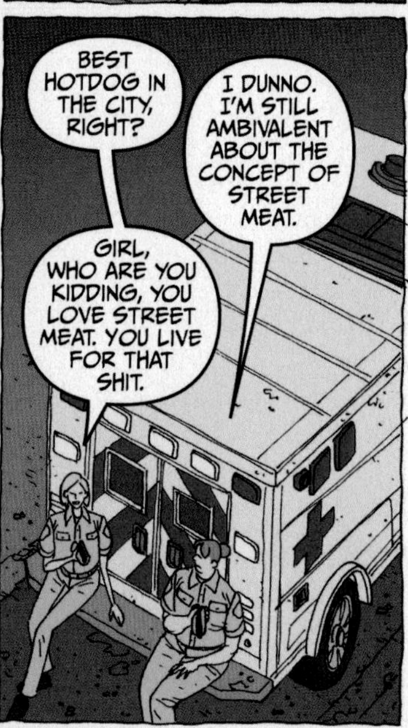
BEST HOTDOG IN THE CITY, RIGHT?
I DUNNO. I'M STILL AMBIVALENT ABOUT THE CONCEPT OF STREET MEAT.
GIRL, WHO ARE YOU KIDDING, YOU LOVE STREET MEAT. YOU LIVE FOR THAT SHIT.

WISH THEY'D JUST GO BACK TO THEIR OWN GODDAMN COUNTRY.
YEAH. YOU COME HERE AND YOU LIVE BY OUR FREAKIN' RULES, AIN'T NO GODDAMN--
...

HEY BABY, SORRY I MISSED YOU. I JUST WANTED--JUST WANTED TO CALL. KNOW THINGS AIN'T BEEN--AIN'T BEEN RIGHT LATELY AND THAT'S MY FAULT. I LOVE YOU. I MISS--
YOU SHOULD SEE IT HERE. WAY THE STRIP LIGHTS UP AT NIGHT--WAY THE LIGHTS CASCADE. NEVER GET TIRED OF IT. WE GOTTA BRING KIRA HERE SOM--
BILL! YOU'RE ON IN FIVE.

HEY, WAYNE. JUST WANTED TO DROP YOU A LINE. I WANT TO REASSURE YOU THAT YOU HAVE ABSOLUTELY NOTHING TO WORRY ABOUT REGARDING THE BILL.
THE PARTY IS GOING TO STAND ITS GROUND. YOU'VE DONE TOO MUCH FOR US OVER THE YEARS FOR US TO DO OTHERWISE...

WE'VE GOT A 246 AT THE STADIUM. I REPEAT, 246 AT THE STADIUM. ALL ACTIVE UNITS PROCEED.
ON OUR WAY.
DAMMIT.

I WANT NACHOS. CAN WE GET NACHOS?
WE CAN GET NACHOS, PRINCESS. WE CAN GET ALL THE NACHOS.

YEAH, I'LL BE HOME SOON. I MISS YOU TOO, BABY.
UH, SIR...
YEAH, LINDA?
...
WHAT IS IT?
THERE'S-- THERES BEEN A SHOOTING.

HOW LONG YOU THINK TILL HE'S ON?
I DUNNO. I FORGET. ANYTIME NOW, I BET.
I NEED ANOTHER BEER. YOU NEED ANOTHER BEER.
HELL YEAH, I NEED ANOTHER--

ALL AVAILABLE UNITS...

RIGHT THIS WAY, PLEASE...

HOW Y'ALL DOING TONIGHT-- I'M EXCITED TO...

I ASSURE YOU, WE ARE--
UH, SIR. THERE'S-- THERE'S A SITUATION.
WHAT?

LET'S GET THIS F#$%!
BANG
BANG
DADDY, WHAT'S THAT SOUND?
GET DOWN, BABY! GET DO--
GET DOWN! GET--
F#$%!
THERE'S BEEN A SHOOTING.

$@&#%*!
MY--MY GOD. IT'S--IT'S A GODDAMN--
KEEP YOUR HEAD ON STRAIGHT. WE DON'T' HAVE TIME TO FREAK OUT. RIGHT NOW WE'RE ALL THESE PEOPLE HAVE.
JESUS CHRIST. JESUS--
SIR, WE HAVE TO GET YOU OUT OF HERE.
BREAKING

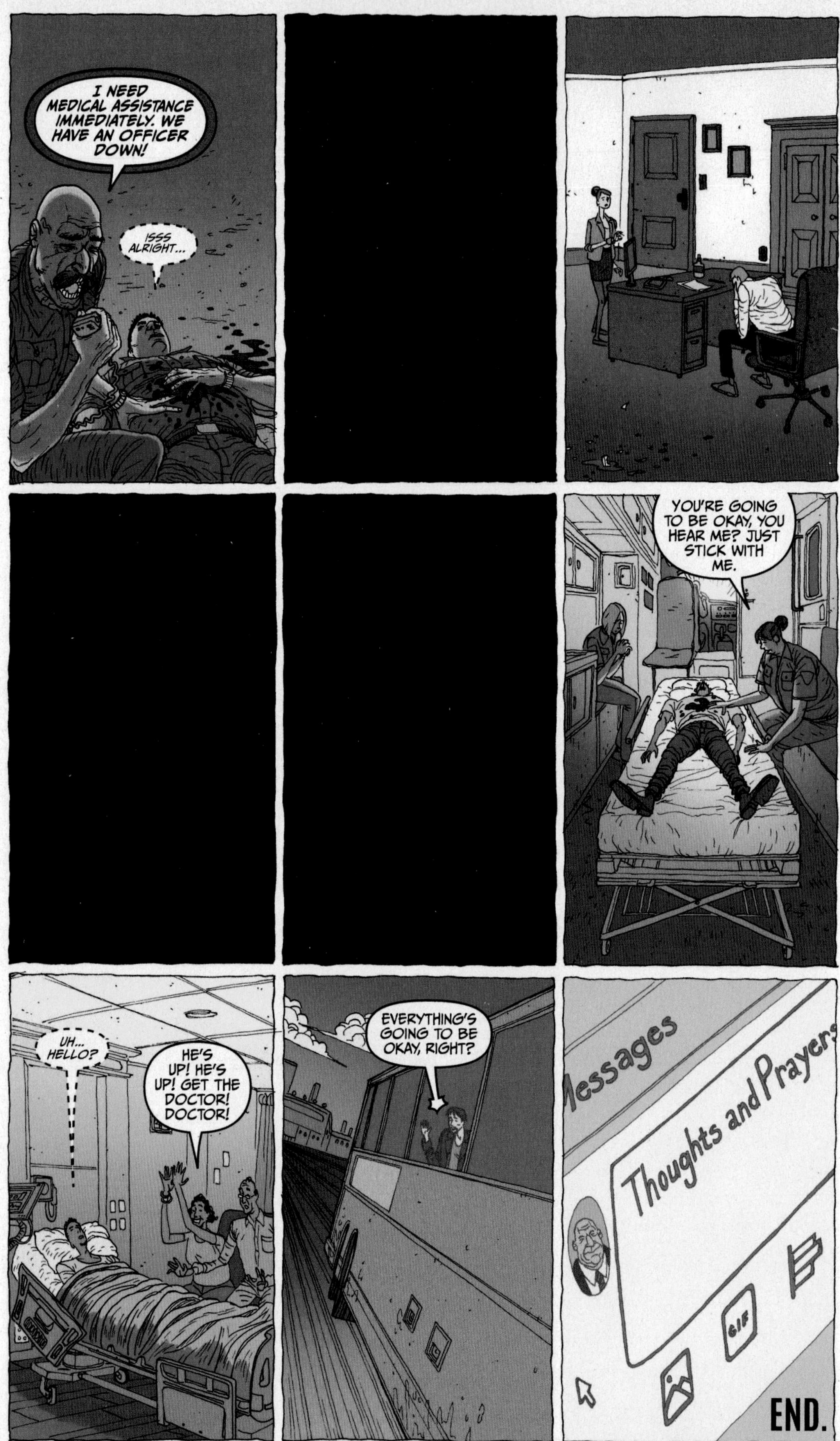
I NEED MEDICAL ASSISTANCE IMMEDIATELY. WE HAVE AN OFFICER DOWN!
ISSS ALRIGHT...
YOU'RE GOING TO BE OKAY, YOU HEAR ME? JUST STICK WITH ME.
UH... HELLO?
HE'S UP! HE'S UP! GET THE DOCTOR! DOCTOR!
EVERYTHING'S GOING TO BE OKAY, RIGHT?
Messages
Thoughts and Prayers
GIF
END.

Leala

WE WERE SO EXCITED.
A HELPING HAND
Script by Alex Segura, based on a witness account by Leala Tyree
Art by Kelsey Shannon
Letters by Janice Chiang

WE WERE HAVING A BLAST.

WE'D FOUND A PERFECT SPOT. I'D EVEN BOUGHT A NEW PAIR OF SHORTS FOR THE SHOW.
LATER, I'D CALL THEM MY "RUN FOR MY LIFE" SHORTS.
BUT I DIDN'T KNOW THAT YET.
66
VEGAS

THE FUN WAS CONTAGIOUS.
OUR NEW FRIEND JUDY HAD TO BE TAKEN AWAY AFTER PASSING OUT TWICE.
SHE WAS ONE OF THE LUCKY ONES.

ASK ANY OL' BARSTOOL IN THIS TOWN
ASK MY NEW FOUND PARTY CROWD
SURE I TAKE MORE JACK IN MY COKE NOW
A LITTLE MORE HIGH IN MY SMOKE NOW...
EVERYONE WENT NUTS WHEN JASON ALDEAN TOOK THE STAGE. CHRISTIAN IN PARTICULAR. IT WAS WHY HE CAME TO THE SHOW.

RATT-AT-ATAT-TATT...!!!
HOW'D THEY GET FIREWORKS IN HERE?
WE HAD TROUBLE JUST GETTING OUR PLASTIC FLASKS IN-

THAT'S WHEN WE KNEW IT WASN'T FIREWORKS.
WE'RE GUN OWNERS. WE KNOW THE SOUNDS AND SMELLS OF GUNFIRE.
THAT'S WHEN OUR LIVING HELL BEGAN.
BRAAAAPP-ATT AT-TAT-TAATTT!!

WE STAYED LOW.
MY BODY WAS SHAKING. I WAS PULSING WITH FEAR.

BRRAAATTAA TATATA-ATT AT-TAT!!
WE STAYED LOW AND INCHED FORWARD. AND WE DID THE ONLY THING WE KNEW TO DO.
WE REACHED OUT TO THE PEOPLE WE LOVE.
...ROB, HEY BRO, I DON'T KNOW IF I'M GONNA MAKE IT...
DAD...WE'RE IN TROUBLE...
FOR MAYBE THE LAST TIME.

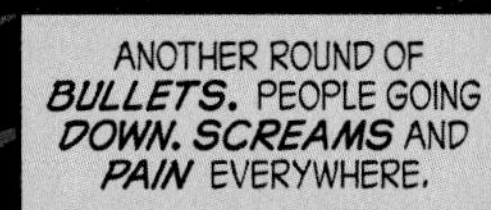
ANOTHER ROUND OF BULLETS. PEOPLE GOING DOWN. SCREAMS AND PAIN EVERYWHERE.

BRAAATA-TAAT!

THAT'S WHEN WE RAN.

DON'T LOOK BACK, MOM.

WE EXIT ON GILES STREET. SECURITY IS TRYING TO GET US TO GO SOMEWHERE, BUT I SEE OUR TRUCK.
I SEE ESCAPE FROM THIS HELL.

PLEASE, HELP ME. WE'RE NOT FROM HERE. MY DAUGHTER'S BEEN SHOT.
WE DON'T HAVE A CAR.

WE'LL COME BACK FOR YOU!
WE RAN.

LET'S GO. GO! GO!

WE STEPPED ON THE GAS.
BEEEP!
BEEEP!
BEEEEP!
BEEEEEEP!

A NEVADA HIGHWAY PATROL UNIT PICKED US UP AND LED THE WAY.
WE REACHED 100 MILES PER HOUR. AT LEAST.

ONCE WE GOT TO THE HOSPITAL, THEY TOOK THE GIRL.
EMERGENCY

THAT'S WHEN WE REALIZED THE DAD HAD BEEN SHOT, TOO.

EVEN IN THE WAKE OF UNIMAGINABLE TRAGEDY, SOME HOPE APPEARS.

THE FAMILY WE MET THAT NIGHT AND TOOK TO THE HOSPITAL—CHRIS, TAYLOR AND RACHAEL—ARE DOING WELL. BETTER.

WE'RE THANKFUL TO THE NHP TROOPER WHO GUIDED US TO THE HOSPITAL. TRAVIS SAVED LIVES.

AND I'M GRATEFUL TO MY OWN FAMILY—DEVIN, CHRISTIAN, HEATHER—AND THE LIFE LESSONS I TOOK AWAY FROM THAT HORRIBLE NIGHT.
LOVE YOUR FAMILY. LET GRUDGES GO. LIVE YOUR LIVES. LIFE IS SHORT.
EMBRACE YOUR TIME ON THIS EARTH.

THIS ONE ISN'T EASY FOR ME, BUT NOTHING ABOUT THIS COMIC IS EASY.
THE HERO FANTASY

THE HERO FANTASY

BY **PAUL TOBIN** WITH PICTURES BY **DUSTIN WEAVER** AND LETTERING BY **BERNARDO BRICE**

THIS IS A STORY ABOUT MY PERSONAL JOURNEY WITH THE "HERO FANTASY."

"YEARS AGO, I USED TO HAVE CONSTANT FANTASIES ABOUT WHAT I WOULD DO IF I WAS AT THE SCENE OF A MASS SHOOTING. WHAT WOULD I HAVE DONE? HOW WOULD I HAVE REACTED?

"AND IN ALL THESE FANTASIES, I WAS FOREVER STEPPING IN TO SAVE THE DAY WITH SOME AMAZING HEROICS...

"AND THEN PEOPLE WOULD CHEER WHAT A GREAT GUY I WAS, AND WOMEN WOULD WANT TO SLEEP WITH ME. ALL THAT CRAP."

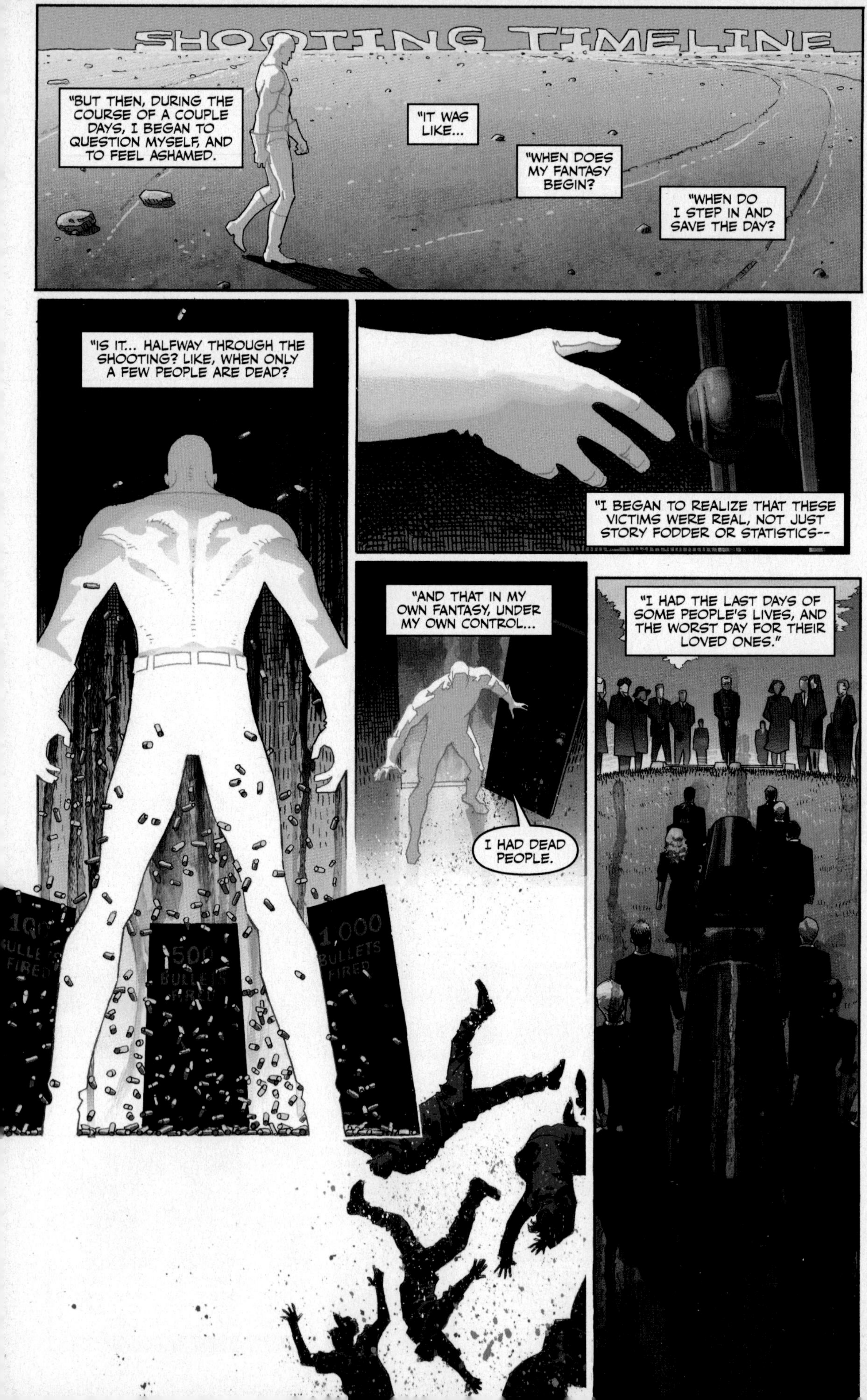

SHOOTING TIMELINE

"BUT THEN, DURING THE COURSE OF A COUPLE DAYS, I BEGAN TO QUESTION MYSELF, AND TO FEEL ASHAMED.

"IT WAS LIKE...

"WHEN DOES MY FANTASY BEGIN?

"WHEN DO I STEP IN AND SAVE THE DAY?

"IS IT... HALFWAY THROUGH THE SHOOTING? LIKE, WHEN ONLY A FEW PEOPLE ARE DEAD?

1,000 BULLETS FIRED

"I BEGAN TO REALIZE THAT THESE VICTIMS WERE REAL, NOT JUST STORY FODDER OR STATISTICS--

"AND THAT IN MY OWN FANTASY, UNDER MY OWN CONTROL...

I HAD DEAD PEOPLE.

"I HAD THE LAST DAYS OF SOME PEOPLE'S LIVES, AND THE WORST DAY FOR THEIR LOVED ONES."

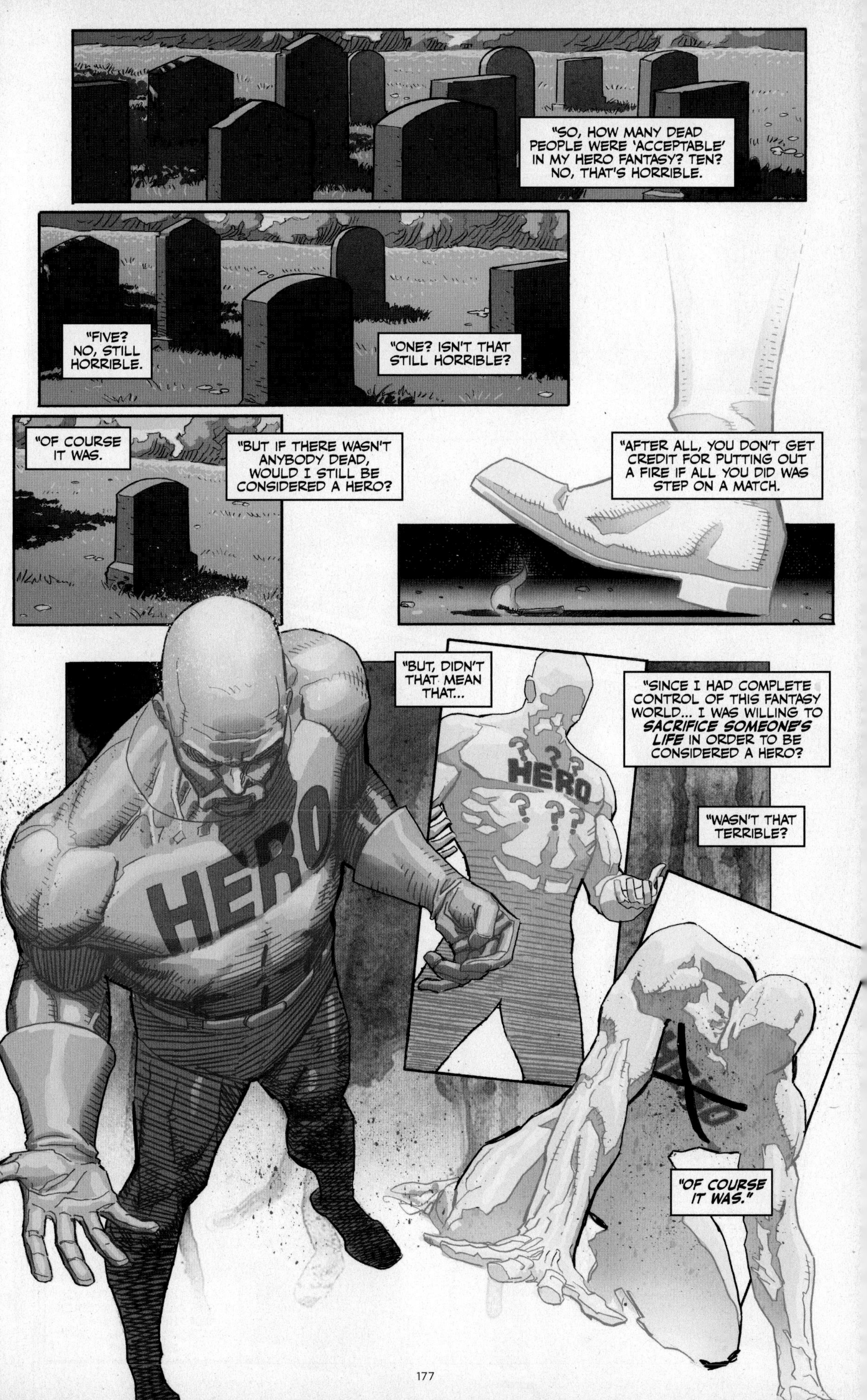
"SO, HOW MANY DEAD PEOPLE WERE 'ACCEPTABLE' IN MY HERO FANTASY? TEN? NO, THAT'S HORRIBLE.
"FIVE? NO, STILL HORRIBLE.
"ONE? ISN'T THAT STILL HORRIBLE?
"OF COURSE IT WAS.
"BUT IF THERE WASN'T ANYBODY DEAD, WOULD I STILL BE CONSIDERED A HERO?
"AFTER ALL, YOU DON'T GET CREDIT FOR PUTTING OUT A FIRE IF ALL YOU DID WAS STEP ON A MATCH.
HERO
"BUT, DIDN'T THAT MEAN THAT...
HERO
"SINCE I HAD COMPLETE CONTROL OF THIS FANTASY WORLD... I WAS WILLING TO ***SACRIFICE SOMEONE'S LIFE*** IN ORDER TO BE CONSIDERED A HERO?
"WASN'T THAT TERRIBLE?
"OF COURSE IT WAS."

"AND SO I KEPT WALKING THE TIMELINE BACK IN MY FANTASIES.
SHOOTING TIME LINE
"I WOULD ENVISION STOPPING THE SHOOTER AFTER THE FIRST SHOT--
"--WHICH WOULD MISS.
"BUT THAT WAS STILL TERRIFYING PEOPLE.
"SO THEN I TURNED THE DIAL BACK FURTHER, HEROICALLY APPREHENDING THE SHOOTERS WHEN THEY WERE ON THE WAY TO THE SCHOOL OR WHEREVER--
LAX GUN LAWS
ANOTHER MASS SHOOTIN
HISTORY OF TROUBLED RELATIONSHIPS
TROUBLED LONER
"I REALIZED IT WAS STILL APPALLINGLY WRONG TO *DREAM* OF TERRIFIED REAL-LIFE PEOPLE BEING NEARLY SHOT DEAD.
"AND THEN EVENTUALLY I WAS ALL THE WAY BACK TO THE BEGINNING, ERADICATING THE EVENT ENTIRELY."

BECAUSE THAT'S THE WAY IT SHOULD HAPPEN, EVEN IN YOUR FANTASIES, WHEN YOU'RE TALKING ABOUT REAL PEOPLE.

NOW, I'VE LEFT THOSE FANTASIES BEHIND AND MOVED INTO REAL LIFE--

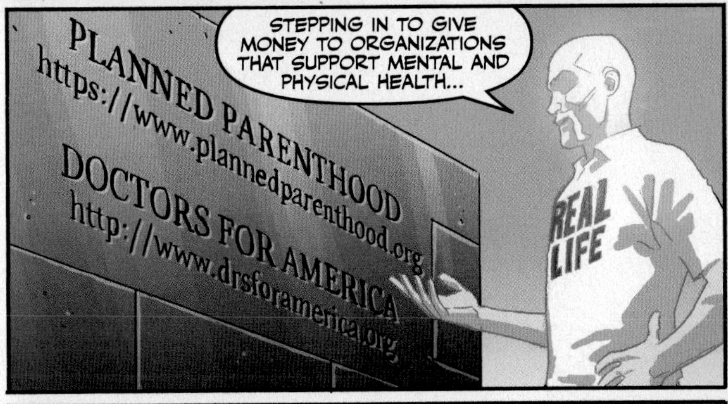

STEPPING IN TO GIVE MONEY TO ORGANIZATIONS THAT SUPPORT MENTAL AND PHYSICAL HEALTH...
PLANNED PARENTHOOD
https://www.plannedparenthood.org
DOCTORS FOR AMERICA
http://www.drsforamerica.org
REAL LIFE

"WHO PROVIDE AID AND COUNSELING FOR THOSE WHO ARE TOO OFTEN MARGINALIZED...
THE TREVOR PROJECT
https://www.thetrevorproject.org

"WHO SUPPORT REASONABLE GUN CONTROL...
BRADY CAMPAIGN
https://www.bradycampaign.org
VIOLENCE POLICY CENTER
http://www.vpc.org
GIFFORDS LAW CENTER TO PREVENT GUN VIOLENCE
http://lawcenter.giffords.org

"AND WHO ARE HONESTLY MAKING A DIFFERENCE IN THE REAL WORLD--
"RATHER THAN JUST STANDING AROUND BELIEVING THAT 'HERO' MEANS THERE'S STILL BLOOD ON THE FLOOR."
end

THIS IS PAU.

HE'S NOTHING SPECIAL. JUST A YOUNG GUY, A LONG WAY FROM HOME.

HIS GLIDER ARRIVED THIS MORNING ON THE TRANSPORT FROM HIS HOME WORLD AND HE'S TAKING IT ON ITS MAIDEN FLIGHT.

THE LONG FLIGHT

STORY BRIAN HABERLIN

ART BRIAN HABERLIN & GEIRROD VANDYKE

SCRIPT DAVID HINE

VIANNA ISN'T A PERFECT WORLD BUT IF THE COLONISTS WORK HARD ENOUGH, IT COULD BE AS CLOSE TO PARADISE AS IT GETS.

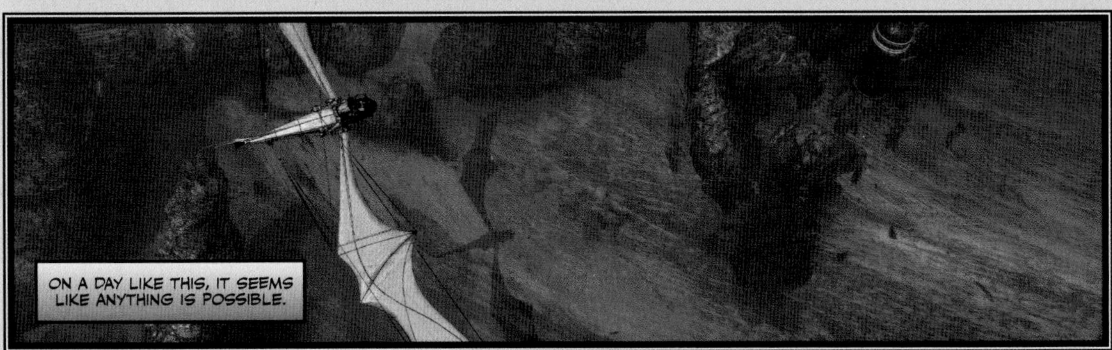
ON A DAY LIKE THIS, IT SEEMS LIKE ANYTHING IS POSSIBLE.

PAU ISN'T A HERO. HE HAS NEVER FACED ANY REAL DANGER...
...NEVER BEEN TESTED.

NOT YET...

WHAT THE HELL WAS *THAT?*

THOSE GUYS DON'T HAVE ANY WEAPONS. THEY'RE SITTING DUCKS!

IN TIMES OF DANGER, WHEN THE ADRENALINE KICKS IN, THERE ARE TWO NATURAL HUMAN REACTIONS...

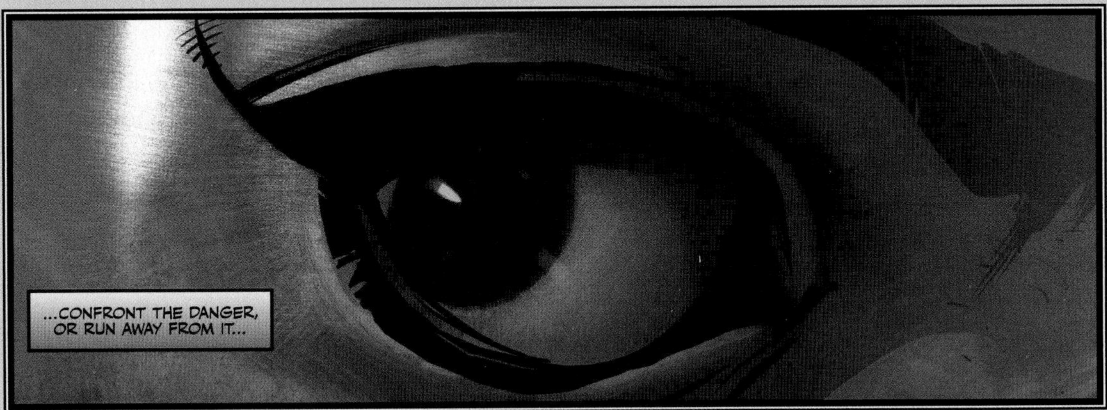
...CONFRONT THE DANGER, OR RUN AWAY FROM IT...

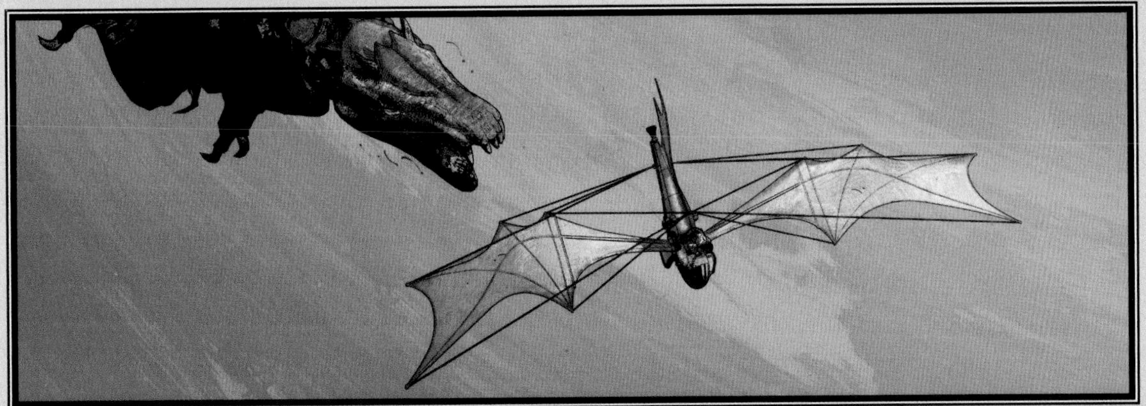

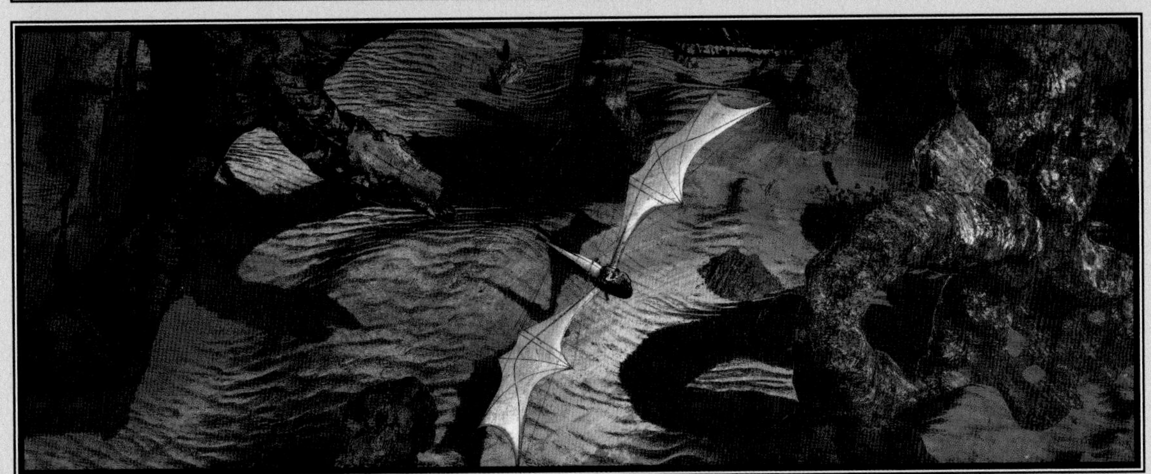

YOU COULD SAY PAU MADE A CHOICE.

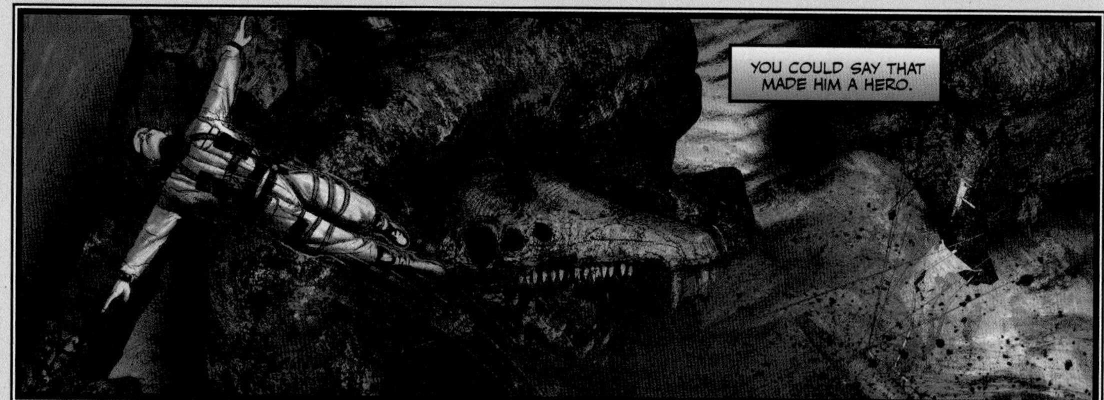
YOU COULD SAY THAT MADE HIM A HERO.

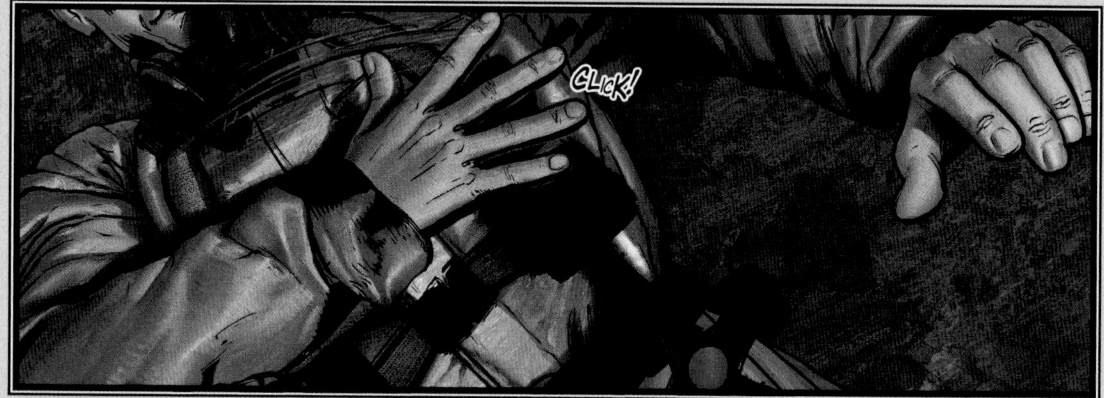
CLICK!

HE WILL SHRUG AND TELL YOU THAT THERE WAS NO CHOICE.
DEDICATED TO THOSE WHO RUN TOWARDS DANGER.

WHAT
CAN
BE
DONE

WRITTEN AND DRAWN BY GREG PAK
COLORS BY TRIONA FARRELL
LETTERED BY SIMON BOWLAND
KTHOOOM

IN OCTOBER 2017, A MAN FIRED ON A CROWD IN LAS VEGAS, KILLING 58 PEOPLE AND INJURING 851 MORE.
HE HAD BOUGHT HIS GUNS LEGALLY AND HAD NO CRIMINAL RECORD OR HISTORY OF MENTAL ILLNESS.
BUT HE'D USED DEVICES CALLED "BUMP STOCKS" TO CONVERT MANY OF HIS GUNS INTO MACHINE-GUN-LIKE, RAPID-FIRING WEAPONS.

BRIEFLY, DEMOCRATS AND REPUBLICANS IN THE UNITED STATES CONGRESS SEEMED OPEN TO BANNING BUMP STOCKS.

A FEW WEEKS LATER, A MAN MURDERED 26 PEOPLE IN A CHURCH IN SUTHERLAND SPRINGS, TEXAS.
KTHOOOM

HE HAD BEEN CONVICTED IN 2012 IN A MILITARY COURT OF ASSAULTING HIS WIFE AND TODDLER, CRIMES WHICH SHOULD HAVE LEGALLY PREVENTED HIM FROM EVER BEING ABLE TO BUY A GUN.
BRIEFLY, DEMOCRATS AND REPUBLICANS SEEMED WILLING TO PUSH FOR REFORMS TO THE NATIONAL INSTANT CRIMINAL BACKGROUND CHECK SYSTEM TO HELP ENSURE PEOPLE WITH SUCH CONVICTIONS WOULD BE PREVENTED FROM BUYING GUNS.

KTHOOOM

KTHOOOM

KTHOOOM

KTHOOOM

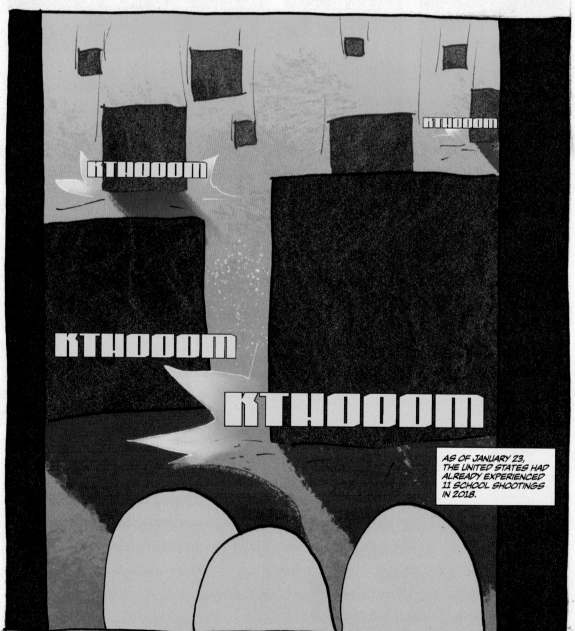

AS OF JANUARY 23, THE UNITED STATES HAD ALREADY EXPERIENCED 11 SCHOOL SHOOTINGS IN 2018.

BUT THE US CONGRESS HAD NOT PASSED ANY NEW, SENSIBLE, BIPARTISAN GUN CONTROL LEGISLATION.

"NOTHING CAN BE DONE" HAS BEEN THE MESSAGE...
...AGAIN AND AGAIN AND AGAIN.

BUT...

...BUT...

...MASSACHUSETTS, NEW JERSEY, AND DENVER, COLORADO, BANNED BUMP STOCKS.

COLUMBIA, SOUTH CAROLINA, BANNED BUMP STOCKS.

YES. **COLUMBIA, SOUTH CAROLINA.**

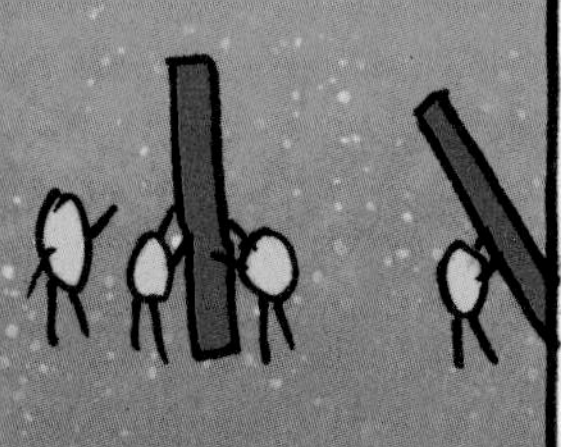

AND IN THE WAKE OF THE HORRIFIC FEBRUARY 14 MASS SHOOTING AT THE MARJORY STONEMAN DOUGLAS HIGH SCHOOL IN PARKLAND, FLORIDA...

...THOUSANDS OF PEOPLE HAVE FOLLOWED THE LEADERSHIP OF THE STUDENT SURVIVORS, RALLYING, PROTESTING, AND CALLING THEIR REPRESENTATIVES.

IN MARCH, FLORIDA PASSED A LIMITED GUN CONTROL BILL BANNING BUMP STOCKS, RAISING THE MINIMUM AGE FOR BUYING GUNS TO 21, AND CREATING A THREE-DAY WAITING PERIOD FOR BUYING GUNS.

THE FLORIDA BILL DIDN'T BAN ASSAULT RIFLES.

IT ALSO POTENTIALLY PUTS MORE GUNS IN SCHOOLS BY ALLOWING AUTHORITIES TO ARM SCHOOL EMPLOYEES.

AND FIVE MONTHS AFTER LAS VEGAS AND A MONTH AFTER PARKLAND, THE UNITED STATES CONGRESS STILL HAS PASSED NOTHING.

BUT NEVER, EVER LET ANYONE TELL YOU...

...THAT NOTHING CAN BE DONE.

REFERENCES:

https://www.nytimes.com/2017/10/04/us/politics/bump-stock-fire-legal-republicans-congress.html
https://www.denverpost.com/2018/01/22/denver-bans-bump-stocks/
https://www.reviewjournal.com/news/politics-and-government/nevada/state-law-prevents-las-vegas-others-from-banning-bump-stocks/
https://www.nytimes.com/2018/03/08/us/florida-gun-bill.html
https://www.nbcnews.com/storyline/texas-church-shooting/air-force-head-says-texas-gunman-s-court-martial-should-n819506
https://www.dallasnews.com/opinion/editorials/2018/03/02/cornyns-fix-nics-proposal-gun-checks-isnt-cure-start

Sarah & Savannah

I'D ALREADY WORKED ALL DAY AT THE HOSPITAL WHEN THE CALL CAME IN.

FINDING SAVANNAH

SCRIPT BY KELLY SUE DECONNICK ART BY JOËLLE JONES

COLORS BY DAVE STEWART LETTERS BY BERNARDO BRICE

FROM THE EYEWITNESS ACCOUNT OF SARAH ANGELO

THERE'S BEEN A SHOOTING ON THE STRIP.

MY NAME IS SARAH ANGELO, AND I RUN CT SCANS.
IN AN EVENT LIKE THIS ONE, THE PEOPLE WHO ARE HURT WORST COME TO ME.

THE WORLD'S MOST POWERFUL PAIR OF EYE GLASSES!
I CAN SEE WHAT'S GOING ON INSIDE YOU.

STEP ONE: RESCUE
I NEED YOU TO TRY AND LAY STILL SO WE CAN GET A PICTURE, OKAY?
IT HURTS!
SO MANY PEOPLE WERE HURT SO BADLY, IT WAS OVERWHELMING.
THERE WAS ONE, THOUGH... SHE WAS SO YOUNG. YOUNG ENOUGH TO BE MY KID.
OF COURSE IT HURT. THE BULLET HAD EXPLODED IN HER ABDOMEN, HITTING HER STOMACH, SPLEEN, LUNGS AND LIVER.
I KNOW, SWEETHEART. AND I AM SO SORRY, BUT WE NEED TO GET A PICTURE SO THAT WE'LL KNOW HOW TO HELP YOU.
WHAT'S YOUR NAME? CAN YOU TELL ME YOUR NAME?
SAVANNAH.

STEP TWO:
REHABILITATION
THE NEXT DAY, I WENT TO VISIT HER IN THE ICU. ON MY OWN TIME.
IN MY TWENTY YEARS, I'VE NEVER DONE THAT BEFORE.

I'M NOT SURE WHY I DID IT THIS TIME.
KNOCK KNOCK?

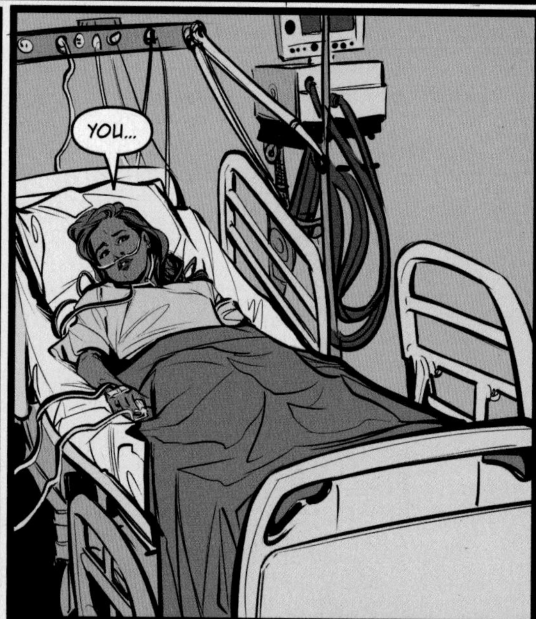
YOU...

I REMEMBER YOU.

WILL YOU COME BACK TOMORROW?
I WENT BACK ALMOST EVERY DAY FROM THEN ON.

SAVANNAH WILL HAVE BULLET FRAGMENTS IN HER LIVER FOR THE REST OF HER LIFE. HER BODY WILL NEVER BE THE SAME.
GET WELL SOON
NOTHING WILL EVER BE THE SAME.

I JUST WANT TO LIVE IN A GLASS BOX ALONE.
SHE COULDN'T WATCH THE NEWS.

SHE WATCHED THE SAME MOVIE OVER, AND OVER, AND OVER AGAIN.

TRAUMA MADE SAVANNAH'S WORLD VERY, VERY SMALL.

I DON'T THINK I'LL EVER FORGET YOU.

GO ON NOW. YOU'RE READY.

AEROMEXICO

GOODBYE, SARAH.

STEP THREE: RELEASE

THE WATERSHED
DAN EVIE IS
MATT CLAY: ONE STEP AT A TIME
PG13
PRODUCED & DIRECTED BY
GARY SPENCER MILLIDGE
OPENS WED MAY 30

It's payback time, suckers! I'm gonna get my revenge on *all* of you...
One step at a time!
Mr Clay...

Huh..?
Mr. Clay...why do you have to go around shooting people?
Hey, beat it, kid! You're gonna get hurt if you hang around here!
Why are guns your answer to everything?
I need my guns to stop the bad guys. Now, *beat it.*

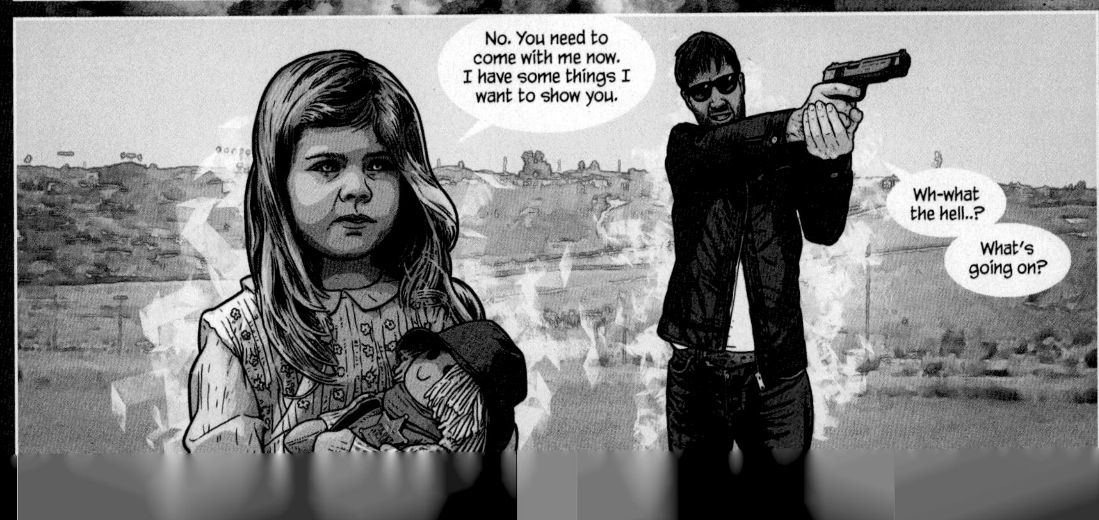
No. You need to come with me now. I have some things I want to show you.
Wh-what the hell..?
What's going on?

Where are we? What is this place?
This is **San Ysidro, California.** It's on the border between the US and Mexico in San Diego County.
It's known as the *Gateway to the Americas* because it's the busiest land border in the world. Almost 30,000 people call this place home.
In 1984, a forty-one year-old man armed with an Uzi, a pump-action shotgun, and a handgun, killed **twenty-one** adults and children and injured another **nineteen** at a *McDonald's* restaurant in the town.

Wait...we're somewhere else now?

This is **Killeen, Texas.** It's a military boom-town next to Fort Hood. **Elvis** lived here for a while when he was drafted into the US Army. Over 125,000 people live here.

In 1991 a thirty-five-year-old man crashed his pickup truck through the wall of a *Luby's Cafeteria,* then shot and killed **twenty-three** people. There were also **twenty-seven** wounded.

Kid, did you bring me here somehow?

Yes. And now we're in **Sandy Hook,** a neighborhood of Newtown, a small scenic town in southwestern Connecticut, with a population of about 12,000, about sixty miles from New York City.

In 2012 a twenty year-old man gunned down **twenty** children aged six and seven, and **six** adults at the local elementary school.

Jesus...that's terrible. But what's all this got to do with me?

You'll see.
This is the city of **Orlando,** in central Florida. They call it the *City Beautiful.* It's home to *Walt Disney World* and other theme parks. Over 275,000 people live here.
In 2016 a twenty-year-old man opened fire inside *Pulse,* a gay nightclub, in the city center. **Forty-nine** people were killed and **fifty-eight** wounded. It's America's most deadly terror attack since **9/11.**

OK, now where are we?

This is **Sutherland Springs**, about thirty miles east of San Antonio, Texas. It was founded in 1851 when a Dr. John Sutherland Jr. set up a post office and stagecoach stop. Fewer than five hundred people live here now.

In 2017 a man wearing black tactical gear and a skull mask walked into the **First Baptist Church** during Sunday worship and shot dead **twenty-six** people. **Twenty** others were injured.

Blacksburg, Virginia. An historic college town between the Blue Ridge and Allegheny Mountains, home to about 40,000 people.

In 2007 a student went on a shooting spree across the campus of *Virginia Tech*, killing **thirty-two** and wounding **seventeen** others.

Yeah, I remember seeing it on the news. Sure seems peaceful enough here now though.

It is. But a few minutes of madness change these communities - the places where these people live - forever. Things eventually get back to normal...but...a different sort of normal.
Who *are* you, kid?
I'm your conscience...*America's* conscience, if you like. Or maybe her future.
There are more places where I could take you. Columbine, Colorado...the University of Texas...Parkland, Florida...San Bernardino... Edmond, Oklahoma...

Or, here. In 2012, a man killed **twelve** and injured **seventy** in a movie theatre in **Aurora, Colorado.**
In the last fifty years, there have been over *one-and-a-half-million* gun-related deaths in the USA, about two-thirds from suicide.
On average, that's about 30,000 deaths by firearms every year. Another 70,000 people are injured by guns.
I get it. Guns are bad. But what can be done about it? Everyone's got a gun.

This doesn't look like America.
No. This is Dunblane, in Scotland, a quiet, rural commuter town at the entrance to the Scottish Highlands just north of Glasgow and Edinburgh. About 8,000 live here.
In 1996 the worst mass shooting in the United Kingdom's history took place at Dunblane Primary School.
Poor little kids. That's heartbreaking. What a tragedy.
The gunman used legally owned handguns to kill sixteen children, aged five and six, and their teacher. Tennis player Andy Murray was a pupil at the school and in the building at the time of the massacre.
After a huge public outcry, the British government eventually banned all handguns. There has been just one mass shooting in the country since the laws were tightened.
OK, where next?
This is the historic site of Port Arthur, on the Tasmanian Peninsula, in Australia. In the nineteenth century it was a penal settlement where the British sent their convicts. It's Tasmania's top tourist attraction.
Six weeks after the events at Dunblane, an assailant went on a shooting spree and killed thirty-five people and wounded twenty-five more. It was Australia's deadliest mass shooting.
Despite heavy opposition, Australia's Prime Minister John Howard pushed through a federal gun amnesty and changed gun laws, including rigorous background and identification checks and a ban on automatic and semi-automatic shotguns and rifles.
Gun deaths in Australia have since declined and there have been no mass shootings since the Port Arthur massacre in 1996.
But Britain and Australia are not the US. We can't just ban all guns. The NRA and the gun lobby wouldn't stand for it.

You're right. There would be considerable resistance if a total ban was suggested. There are already over ***three hundred million*** civilian-owned firearms in the US.

But an American is twenty-five times more likely to be killed by gunfire than people in other developed countries. And **fifty times** more likely than in the UK.

Most of the rest of the world are perplexed by America's apparent obsession with guns.

So, why is it so different here? Why are we all so obsessed with guns?

It can be traced back to the American Revolution, the American Frontier experience and romantic notions of the Wild West, perpetuated by television and film.

By necessity, early settlers always carried an American longrifle to hunt for food and to defend themselves against animals, bandits and Native Americans.

This is no longer the case of course, but the idea of a right to own a gun is entrenched in the American psyche.

This looks like Vegas.

Yes, **Las Vegas, Nevada.** World famous for its casinos and live entertainment. Over 600,000 live in the city while forty million tourists visit every year.

It's now also famous for suffering the deadliest mass shooting in modern American history.

On October 1st, 2017, a gunman opened fire from a hotel window into a crowd of 20,000 attending the Harvest Music Festival and killed **fifty-eight** people. There were also **five hundred** injured.

So...what's the answer? How can we stop this... madness?

The only real solution is to reduce access to firearms. As you say, a blanket ban is impractical, but there are some relatively uncontroversial first steps that can be taken.

Stricter gun licensing. Expanding gun buy-back programs. Compulsory training. A federal database to track gun sales. Banning assault-style weapons like the AR-15.

And even most gun aficionados are in favor of tighter background checks.

But people have to defend themselves and their families, right?
Most guns kept at home are never used for self-defense. It's more likely that an unstable person will use a gun to threaten other family members, and in particular, man-on-woman domestic violence.
States with more gun ownership have more gun deaths. Indeed, countries with more gun ownership have more gun deaths.
What about the *Second Amendment?*
It probably wasn't ever intended to give citizens the right to own any weapon they chose...it's even arguable that it's actually nothing to do with self-defense.
At the time the Amendment was added to the Constitution, firearms were muzzle-loaded, single-shot weapons which took time to reload. Semi-automatic guns or even six-shooters could not have been conceived of.
America has changed. There's no need to hunt for food. There's no longer any need to defend oneself from invading foreign armies or hostile forces. The Second Amendment is an irrelevant relic from a bygone era.
In a world without guns, people will still be killed and injured. But the answer to guns is not more guns. More guns lead to more deaths. And they are far too lethal to be so freely available to anyone who wants one.
People must demand change, else nothing will change. Surely, Americans cannot stand by and allow all this pain and suffering to continue?
It will not be easy. But nothing worthwhile ever is.
One step at a time, right?
Hey, you wanna get a milkshake or something? Do little future ghost girls drink milkshakes?

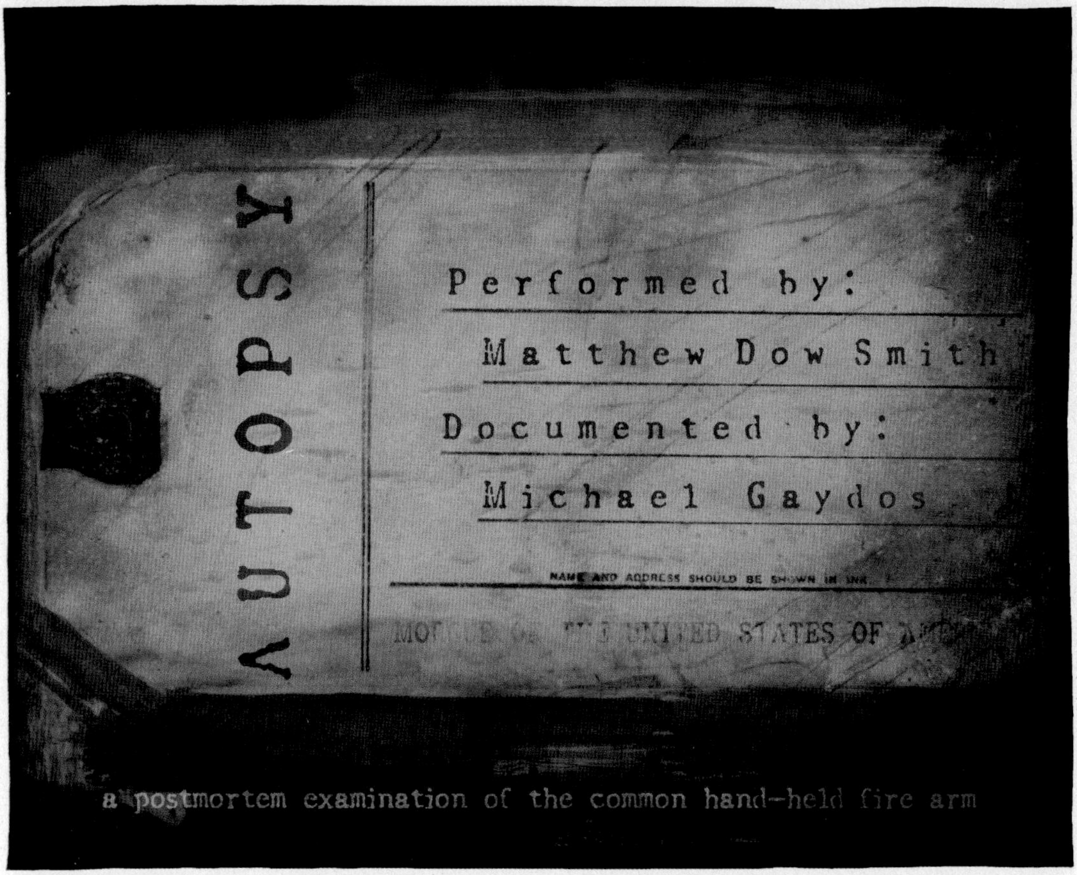

AUTOPSY

Performed by:

Matthew Dow Smith

Documented by:

Michael Gaydos

a postmortem examination of the common hand-held fire arm

No one knows for sure who made the first gun.

Best guess is someone in China around 100 AD.

Whoever made it, never gave it a name. At least, not one that we've heard.

It was just a bamboo tube, a spear and some gunpowder.

A simple device.

A machine.

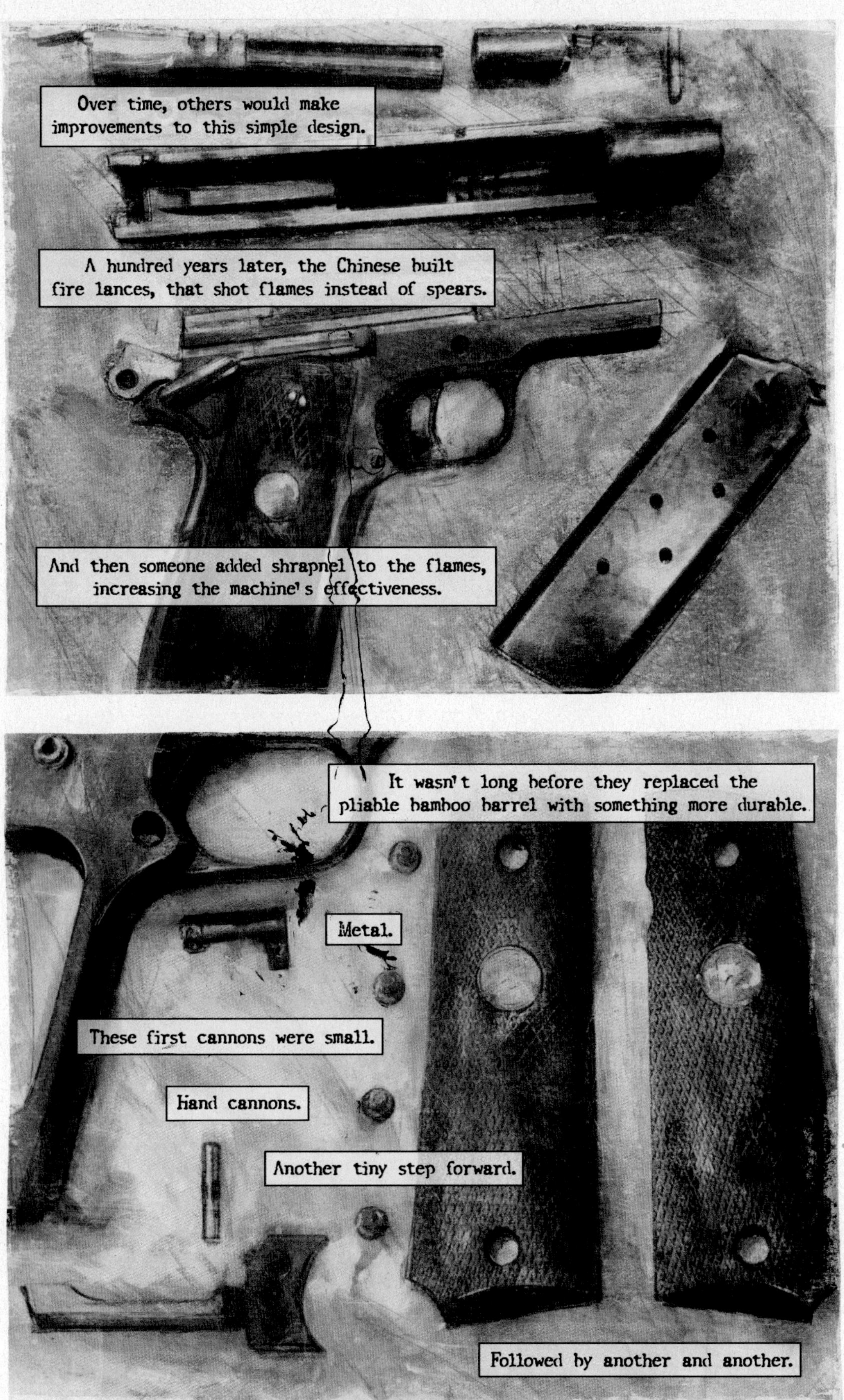
Over time, others would make improvements to this simple design.
A hundred years later, the Chinese built fire lances, that shot flames instead of spears.
And then someone added shrapnel to the flames, increasing the machine's effectiveness.
It wasn't long before they replaced the pliable bamboo barrel with something more durable.
Metal.
These first cannons were small.
Hand cannons.
Another tiny step forward.
Followed by another and another.

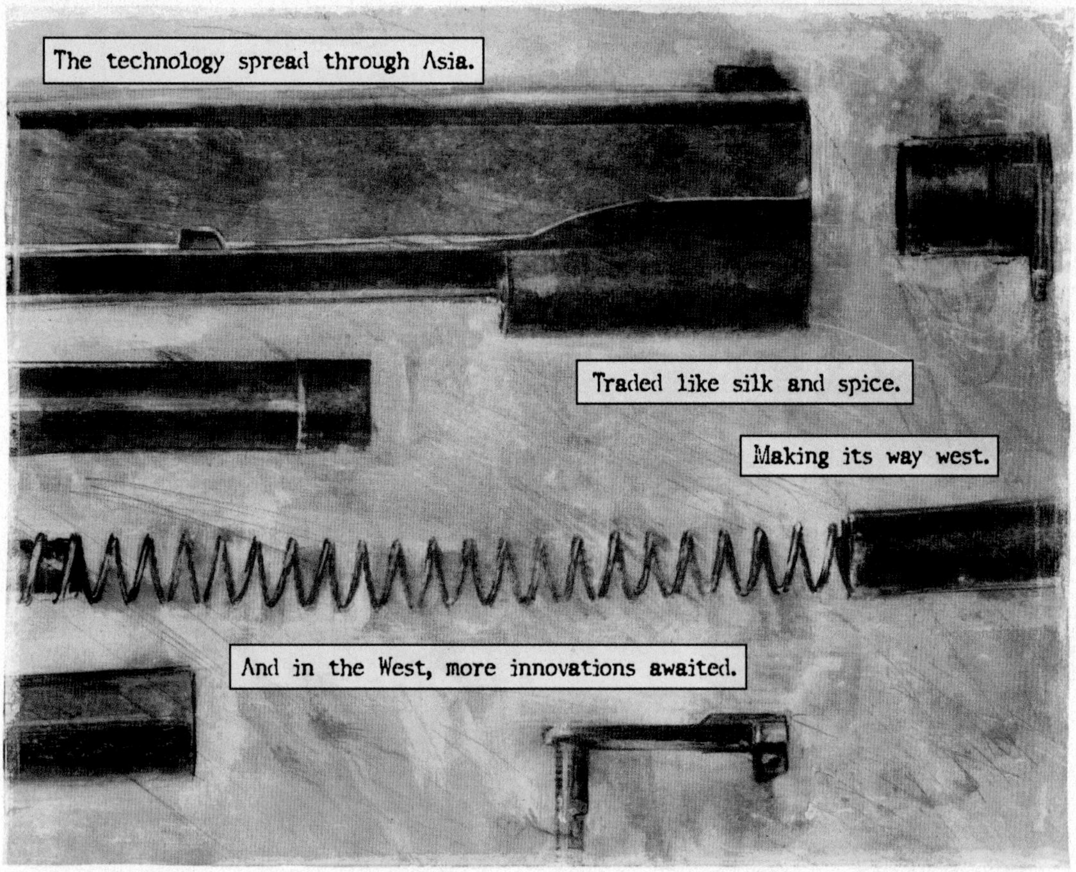

The technology spread through Asia.

Traded like silk and spice.

Making its way west.

And in the West, more innovations awaited.

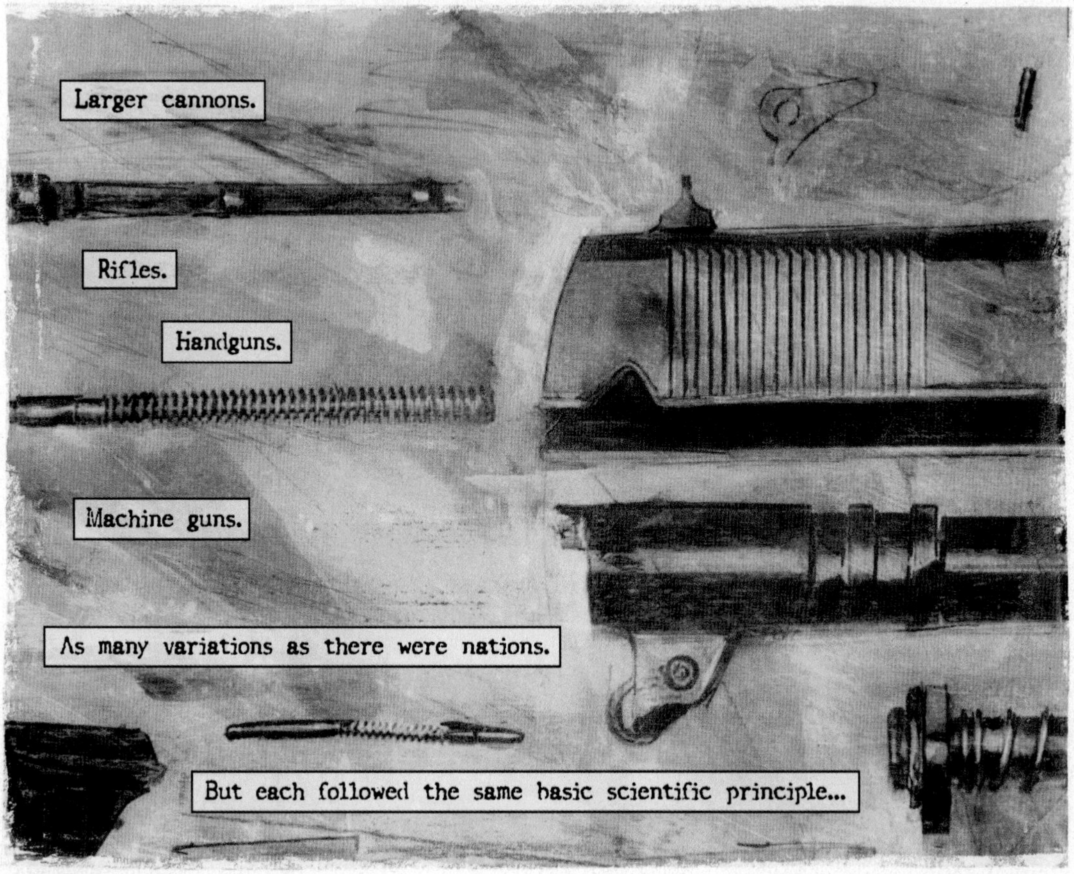

Larger cannons.

Rifles.

Handguns.

Machine guns.

As many variations as there were nations.

But each followed the same basic scientific principle...

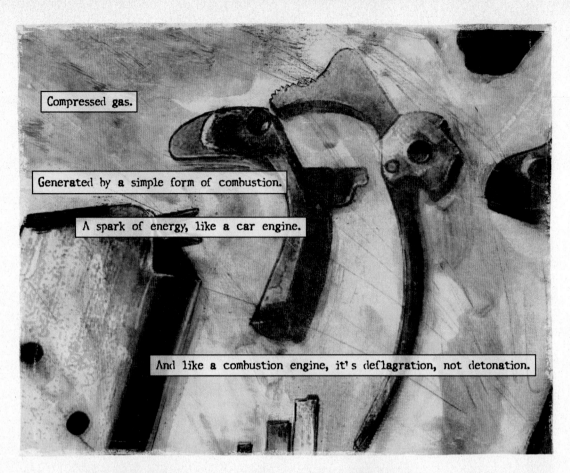

Compressed gas.

Generated by a simple form of combustion.

A spark of energy, like a car engine.

And like a combustion engine, it's deflagration, not detonation.

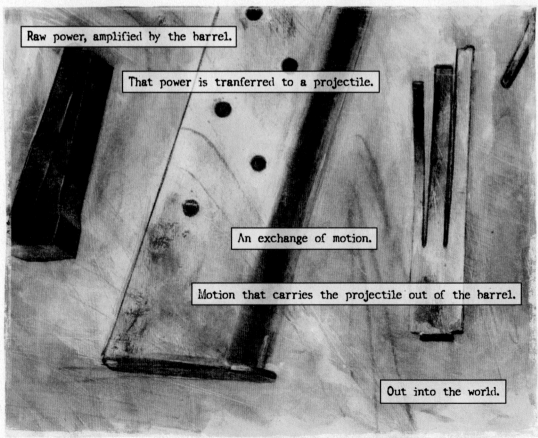

Raw power, amplified by the barrel.

That power is tranferred to a projectile.

An exchange of motion.

Motion that carries the projectile out of the barrel.

Out into the world.

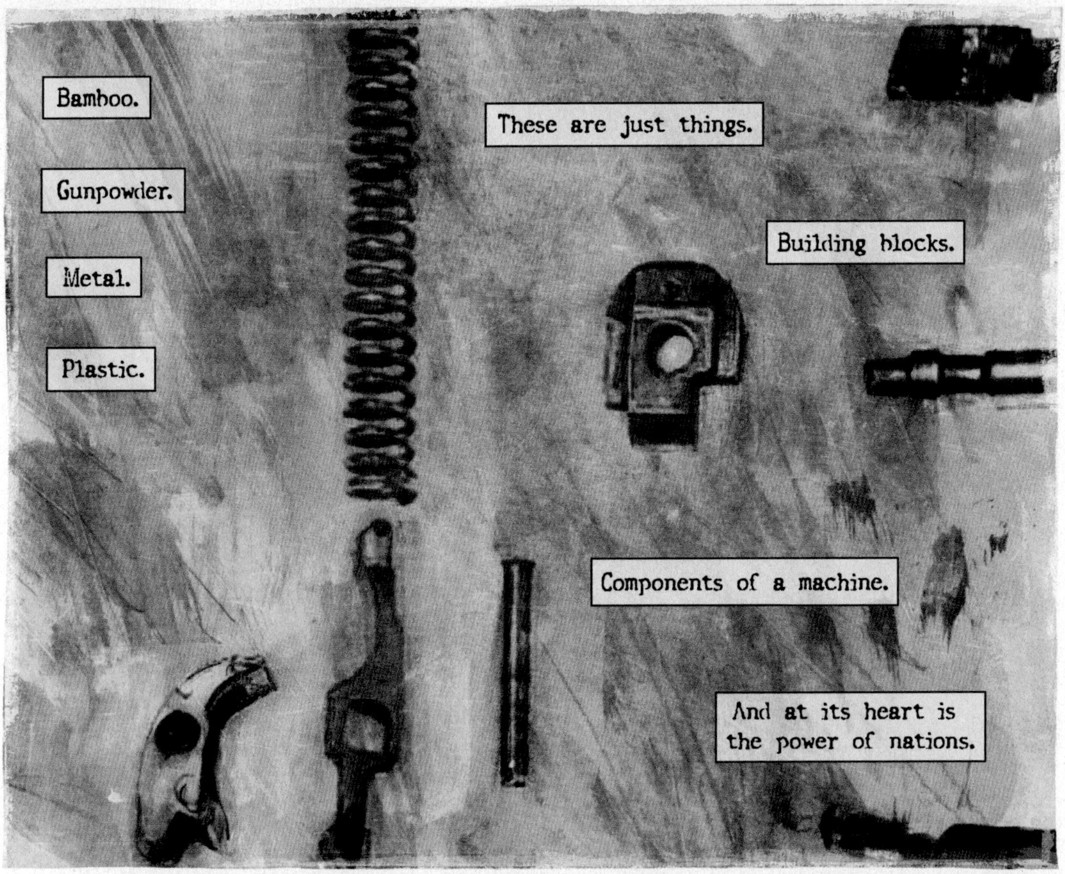

Bamboo.

Gunpowder.

Metal.

Plastic.

These are just things.

Building blocks.

Components of a machine.

And at its heart is the power of nations.

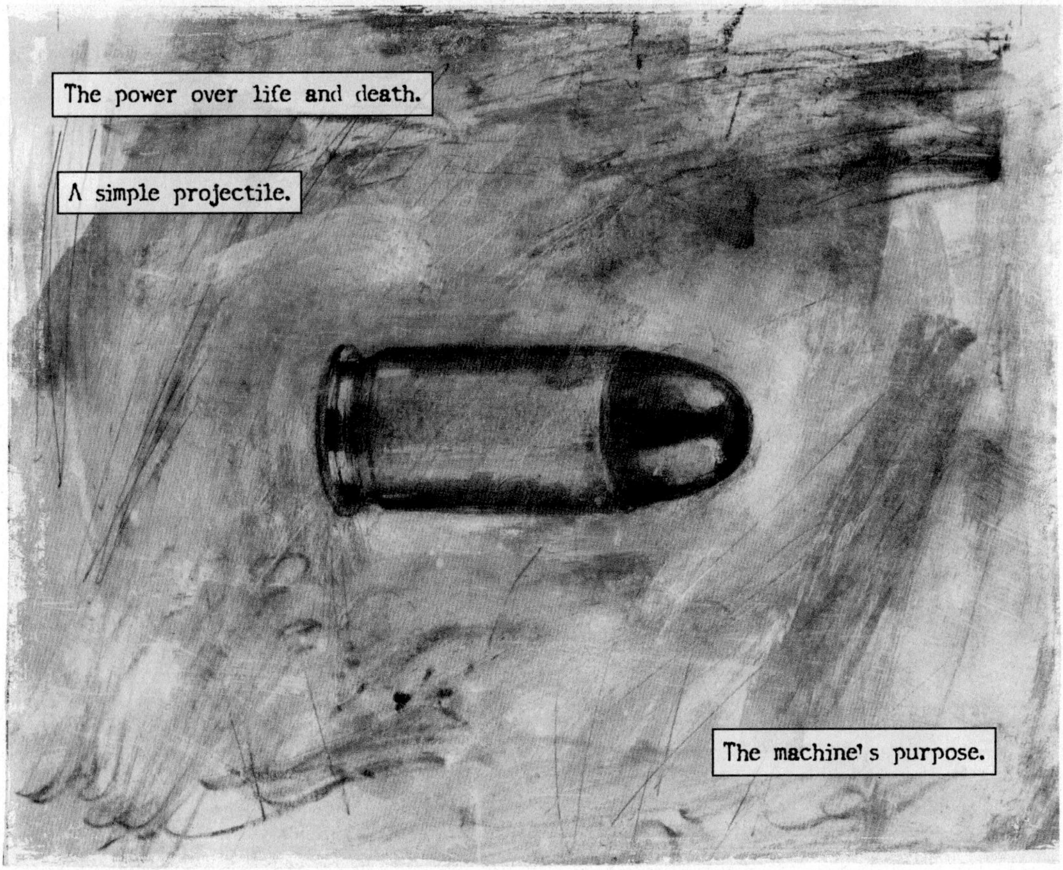

The power over life and death.

A simple projectile.

The machine's purpose.

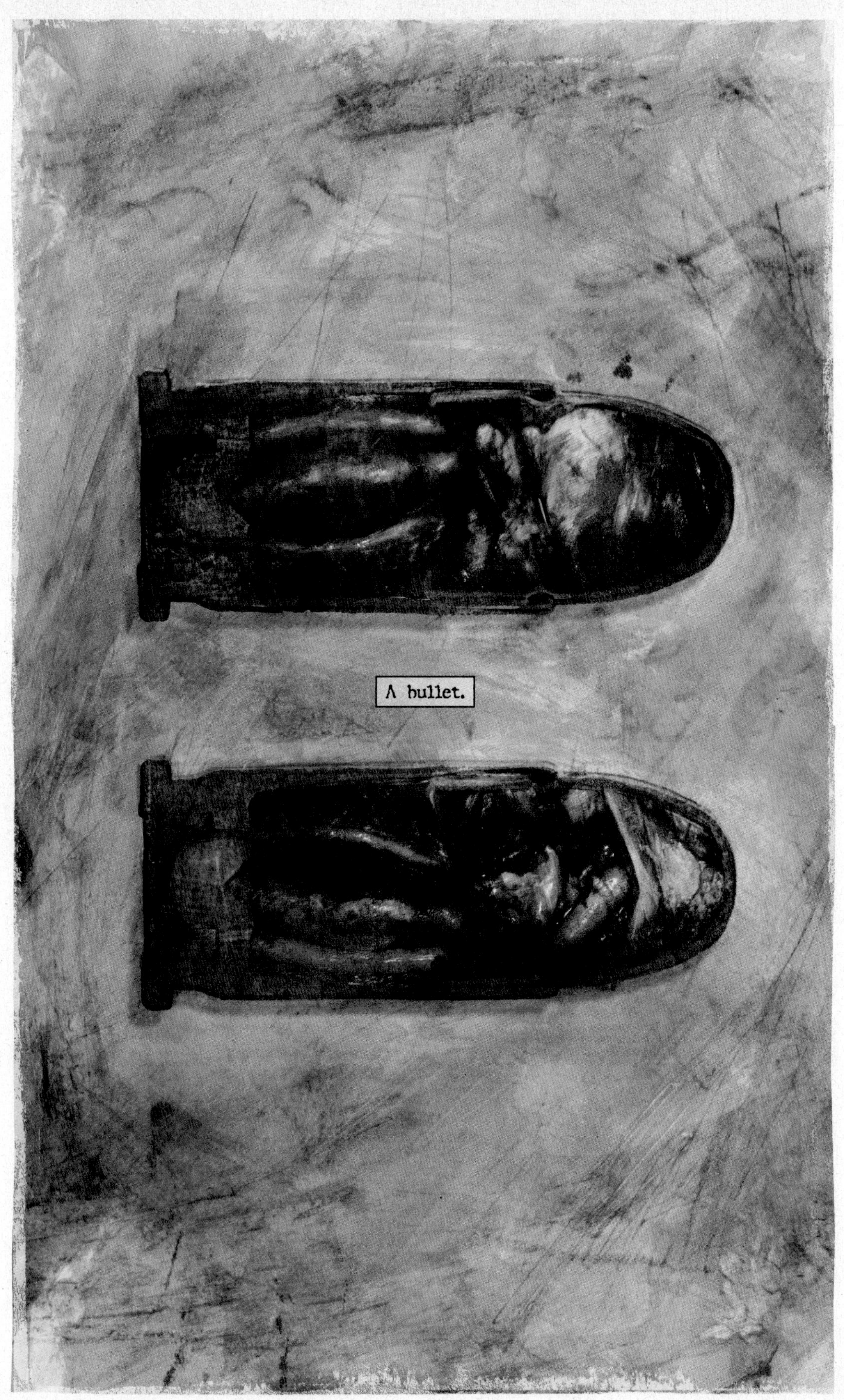
A bullet.

CLEMENT DUNWOODY IS THE DEADLIEST MAN IN THE TERRITORY.
EVERYONE SAYS SO -- AIN'T A SINGLE SOUL WHO DON'T.
IT'S 1781.
ON A DAY IN OCTOBER STILL GRAY AND COLD EVEN AFTER THE RAIN QUIT.
DARYL TRAINOR IS A DENTIST, N'HE AIN'T KNOWN FOR MUCH ELSE, SURE NOT FOR BEING DEADLY...
...THOUGH TIMES ARE, HE TAKES A DRILL TO SOMEONE'S TEETH, THEY MIGHT WISH THEY WAS DEAD.
IT'S 2018... ON A COLD DAY IN OCTOBER TOO.
'COURSE, DARYL'S WEARING THAT JACKET HIS WIFE GOT HIM, CHRISTMAS LAST, SO HE DON'T GIVE THE WEATHER NO MIND.
N'THESE ARE THE WOODS OF SOUTHERN VIRGINIA...
...WHERE TIME DON'T GIVE MUCH OF A NEVER MIND, NEITHER.
THE DEADLIEST MAN
STORY BY JAMES ROBINSON
ART BY DEAN KOTZ AND STEFANO GAUDIANO
COLORS & LETTERING BY CASEY SILVER
DUNWOODY'S BEEN UP HERE SINCE JUNE, WHEN HIM N'THE OTHER PATRIOTS LOST THE BATTLE OF GREEN SPRING AND HE DONE LIT OUT.
DARYL'S BEEN UP HERE A COUPLE OF HOURS, BUT HE'S KEEPING AN EYE ON HIS WATCH. HE PROMISED HIS WIFE.

DUNWOODY KEEPS HIS EYES ON EVERYTHING AROUND HIM.
EVERY SIGHT...
...EVERY NOISE.
"RED," DUNWOODY THINKS, "A REDCOAT!"
"GOTTA BE, WHO ELSE'D BE ADLE-HEADED ENOUGH TO WEAR SOMETHING SO BRIGHT?"

"CAREFUL NOW."
"TAKE A BREATH... HOLD IT AND--"
"DARN."
"DON'T KNOW IF JOHNNY ENGLISH SAW WHERE MY SHOT COME FROM."
"N'SOUND WALKS THE TRICKSTER'S PATH OUT HERE -- SEEMS TO COME FROM NOWHERE N'EVERYWHERE."
"MEANS I STILL GOT A CHANCE."
AND THEREIN LIES THE MANNER OF DUNWOODY'S LETHAL REPUTATION -- NOT FROM HIS AIM, NO...
...BUT RATHER THE SPEED OF HIS RELOAD.
HE GETS TO IT -- WITH A CARTRIDGE HE ROLLED TIGHT HIMSELF THE NIGHT BEFORE.
GET THAT CARTRIDGE OPEN.
PUSH THE FRIZZEN FORWARD, PUT SOME POWDER IN THE FLASH PAN.
GET THE FRIZZEN BACK IN PLACE.
HOLD THE RIFLE UPRIGHT AND POUR IN THE REST OF THE POWDER.
DROP THE BALL DOWN THE BARREL.
PUSH THE CARTRIDGE PAPER -- THE WADDING, THAT IS -- IN THE BARREL TOO.
GET THE RAMROD FREE...
...AND USE IT TO RAM THE BALL AND WADDING ALL THE WAY DOWN.

"DONE!"
"N'THIS SECOND SHOT -- LL'BE THE ONE THAT--"
"WHAT DID I SHOOT?" DARYL THINKS. "DID I -- DID --?"
"IT ALL HAPPENED SO FAST--"
"-- TOO FAST."
DARYL TRIES TO STEADY HIS SHAKING HANDS AS HE HOLDS THE AR-15...
...AND HE WISHES HE WAS HOME.
END

Stephanie

MY HUSBAND ANOOP AND I WANTED TO GO TO "ROUTE 91" MONTHS BEFORE IT HAPPENED, BUT WE NEVER GOT AROUND TO ACTUALLY BUYING THE TICKETS.

DATE NIGHT

STORY BASED ON AN INTERVIEW WITH EYEWITNESS: STEPHANIE BALLOU
ARTIST: ISAAC GOODHART
COLOR ARTIST: KELLY FITZPATRICK
WRITER & LETTERER: HENRY BARAJAS

THE ONLY TICKETS LEFT WERE $500 V.I.P. TICKETS AND WE COULDN'T JUSTIFY SPENDING A THOUSAND DOLLARS AFTER HAVING OUR SECOND CHILD.

I MET THESE TWO GUYS THAT WERE WORKING THE CONCERT AT MY BAR.

VIP
THEY FIGURED I WAS A LOCAL AND GAVE ME TWO V.I.P. BADGES.

I IMMEDIATELY CALLED ANOOP AND DEMANDED HE MISS WORK AND TAKE OUR TWO BOYS TO HIS PARENTS' HOUSE.
HERE'S HIS INHALER. BE CAREFUL, HE BITES.

DON'T WORRY ABOUT US! HAVE FUN!
THE LYFT IS WAITING!
I LOVE YOU, DONNY.

YOU TWO LOOK NICE! WHERE ARE WE GOING?
MANDALAY BAY, SIR.

I CAN'T BELIEVE YOU'RE SKIPPING THE GYM TONIGHT STEPHANIE.
WHEN SOMEONE GIVES YOU PASSES TO ROUTE 91...

YOU GO TO ROUTE 91!

BANG SPACK CRACK

ALL OF A SUDDEN WE HEAR THE GUNSHOTS.

EVERYONE GET DOWN!

BUT AT THE TIME IT SOUNDED LIKE A HELICOPTER.

SPACK
HARVEST
WHAT'S GOING ON?!
I THINK IT'S FIREWORKS?!

BANG
IT'S GUNSHOTS!
CRACK

I COULDN'T BELIEVE WHAT WAS HAPPENING.
BANG
THUD
WHERE'S IT COMING FROM?!
CRACK
OH MY GOD!

I REMEMBER THINKING "I'M GOING TO DIE."
I THINK I BLACKED OUT.

WE HAVE TO GO!
JUST STAY DOWN, STEPHANIE!

WE HAVE TO GET THE HELL OUT OF HERE!

WHEEEEEOooo
WHEEEEEOooo

"DAD! I'M TELLING YOU THAT SOMEONE STARTED SHOOTING."
GRAND
POLICE

I'M WATCHIN' THE NEWS AND THEY HAVEN'T MENTIONED IT.
IT'S HAPPENING RIGHT NOW! ANOOP IS OUTSIDE WAITING FOR THE LYFT DRIVER.

THE SHOOTER IS HERE!
RUN!

HELP!

EASY!
WE'VE GOT HIM!

THANK YOU!

SKRREEEECH

OVER HERE! GET IN!

EVERYTHING REMINDS ME OF THAT NIGHT.

EVERY SOUND AND SCENT BRINGS ME BACK.
CRACK
SPACK
SPACK

I'M LUCKY TO HAVE MY LOVING FAMILY AND FRIENDS HELP ME GET THROUGH THIS.

I BURST INTO TEARS EVERY TIME I SEE A "VEGAS STRONG" SHIRT.

PEOPLE ASK ME "HOW DO I LIVE MY LIFE AFTER THIS?"
I TELL THEM I HAVE NO CHOICE.

MY BOYS NEED ME.

LUCKY
STORY CHRIS RYALL ART GABRIEL RODRÍGUEZ
COLORS NELSON DÁNIEL LETTERS BERNARDO BRICE
I USED TO STARE AT THE GUN IN MY DAD'S DRAWER.

GROWING UP, I HAD PLENTY OF FREEDOM.
YOU'VE SEEN *STRANGER THINGS* AND MOVIES SET IN THE EIGHTIES--MY CHILDHOOD WAS A LOT LIKE THAT, MINUS THE FAKE MONSTERS.

BUT THE REAL ONES LURKED. MY DAD WAS A COP, ATTEMPTING TO KEEP THOSE MONSTERS AT BAY.
HE STASHED MULTIPLE GUNS AROUND THE HOUSE. THE ONE THAT INTERESTED ME WAS THE SHINY ONE JUST LIKE DIRTY HARRY'S.
HIDDEN IN PLAIN SIGHT IN HIS DRESSER DRAWER.

MY PARENTS TRUSTED ME, THEIR SMART AND CAUTIOUS SON, NOT TO DO ANYTHING STUPID WITH IT.
AT TEN, I "ACCIDENTALLY" SHATTERED A NEIGHBOR'S SLIDING GLASS DOOR WITH MY WRIST ROCKET.

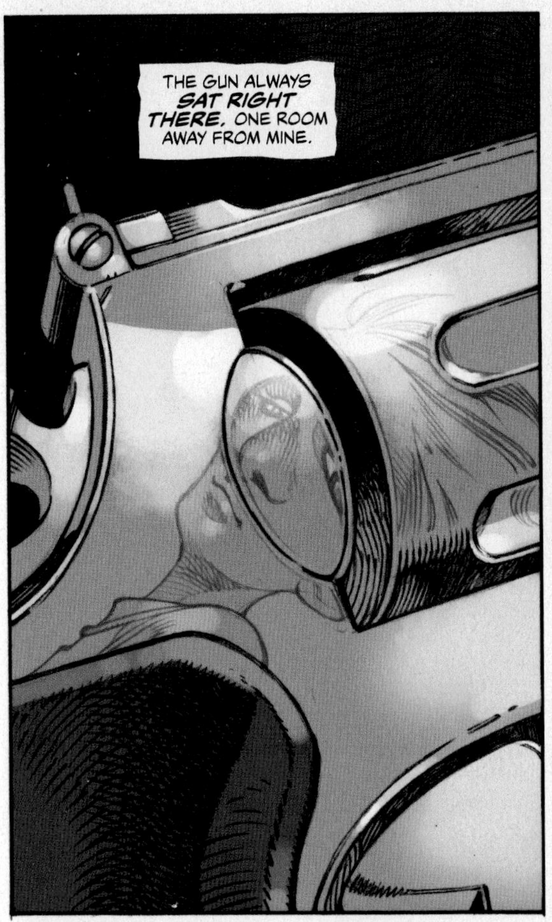
THE GUN ALWAYS SAT RIGHT THERE. ONE ROOM AWAY FROM MINE.

AT TWELVE, I CARRIED AROUND SHURIKEN--THROWING STARS. NEVER STUCK MYSELF OR ANYONE ELSE WITH THEM--NOT ME, I WAS THE SMART AND CAUTIOUS ONE, RIGHT?
INSTEAD, WE HURLED THEM AT TREES AND INTO WALLS OF NEARBY HOMES UNDER CONSTRUCTION.

THE GUN WAS HEAVY WHEN I HELD IT, LIKE ALL THINGS OF VALUE. MADE OF A SILVER SO SHINY I COULD SEE MY REFLECTION IN IT.
IT WAS BEAUTIFUL. IRRESISTIBLE.

AT FOURTEEN, WE HAD WEEKEND PAINTBALL FIGHTS. GOT A FEW WELTS BUT NOTHING SERIOUS, JUST IMPERMANENT BADGES OF HONOR. I LOVED IT. I WAS CAREFUL.

I ALSO PRACTICED WITH MY BROTHER'S WOODEN, FOAM-COVERED (TO BE SAFE) NUNCHUCKS.
PAINFUL WHEN I HIT MYSELF IN THE BACK OF THE HEAD, BUT NOTHING LASTING.

BUT SINCE I'D NEVER ACTUALLY BECOME A NINJA, I INSTEAD CLOSELY IDENTIFIED WITH GORDIE IN ***STAND BY ME.*** HE WAS SMART. CAUTIOUS.
AND HE MADE ME WONDER IF MY DAD'S GUN COULD SIMILARLY HELP ME WITH SOME OLDER BULLIES.

BLAM
BLAM
BLA
MY DAD TOOK ME TO THE SHOOTING RANGE ONCE. I WASN'T ALLOWED TO SHOOT, OR EVEN LEARN PROPER HANDLING. JUST SIT AND WATCH THE PROS.
HE AND HIS FRIENDS SURE DID MAKE IT LOOK ***FUN.***

I DISCOVERED THE GUN WASN'T ***THAT*** HEAVY. I BET I COULD HANDLE IT PROPERLY.

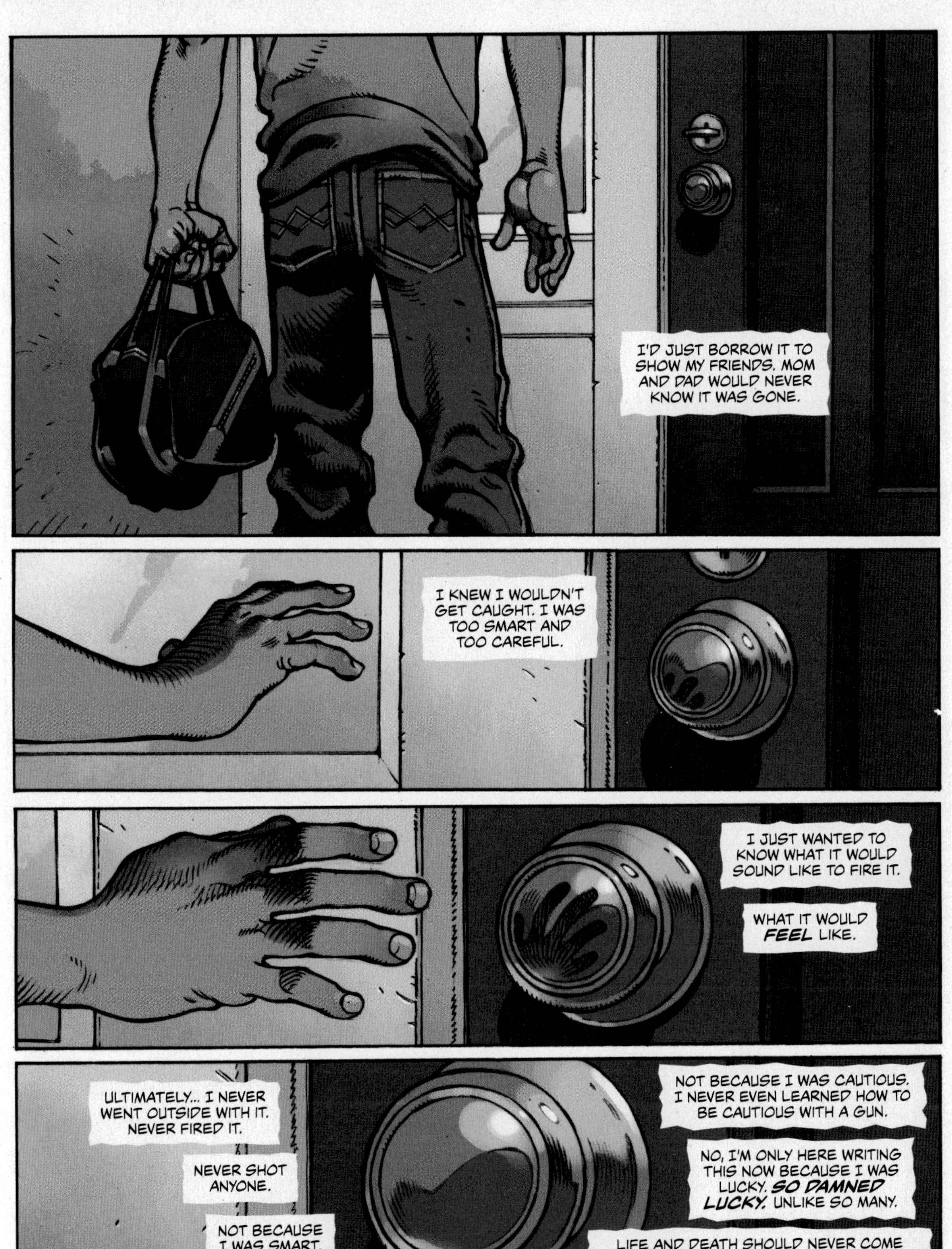

I'D JUST BORROW IT TO SHOW MY FRIENDS. MOM AND DAD WOULD NEVER KNOW IT WAS GONE.
I KNEW I WOULDN'T GET CAUGHT. I WAS TOO SMART AND TOO CAREFUL.
I JUST WANTED TO KNOW WHAT IT WOULD SOUND LIKE TO FIRE IT.
WHAT IT WOULD ***FEEL*** LIKE.
ULTIMATELY... I NEVER WENT OUTSIDE WITH IT. NEVER FIRED IT.
NEVER SHOT ANYONE.
NOT BECAUSE I WAS SMART. ***I WASN'T.***
NOT BECAUSE I WAS CAUTIOUS. I NEVER EVEN LEARNED HOW TO BE CAUTIOUS WITH A GUN.
NO, I'M ONLY HERE WRITING THIS NOW BECAUSE I WAS LUCKY. ***SO DAMNED LUCKY.*** UNLIKE SO MANY.
LIFE AND DEATH SHOULD NEVER COME DOWN TO ***LUCK***. WE ALL NEED TO BE MORE CAUTIOUS. WE ALL NEED TO BE SMARTER.

Nearly 6,000 children are treated for gun-related injuries every year. Guns kill approximately 1,300 children every year.

FOR YEARS THEY LAUGHED, TRYING TO *DISARM* THE PEOPLE OF THIS NATION. THE VIOLENCE FOLLOWING EVEN THEIR *CHILDREN* INTO THE LUNCHROOM.
WRITTEN BY **IVÁN BRANDON**
ART AND COLORS BY **PAUL AZACETA**
LETTERING BY **BERNARDO BRICE**

WHAT THIS SITUATION *NEEDS,* IS NOT LESS GUNS, BUT *MORE,* I SAID. ARMS GROWN ON FIELDS SO DENSE THE BAD GUYS CAN'T GET *THROUGH*.
I SAID TO THEM, WILL OUR CHILDREN RUN FROM DANGER? NOT *MINE,* I SAID.

AND NOW, NOT *YOURS.*

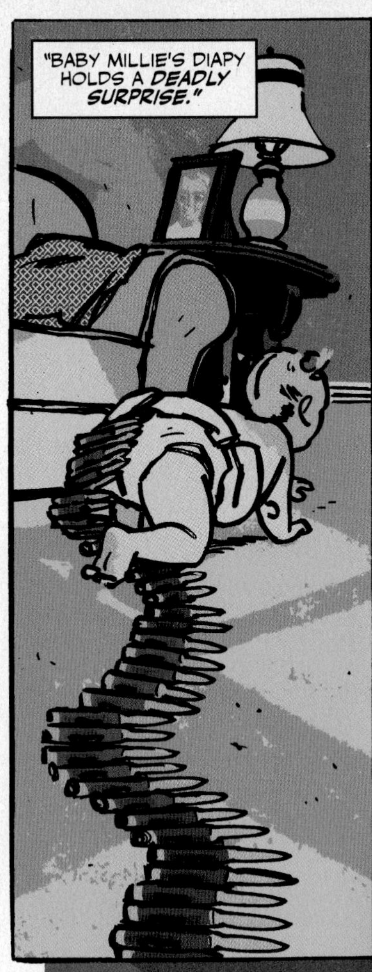

"BABY MILLIE'S DIAPY HOLDS A *DEADLY SURPRISE.*"

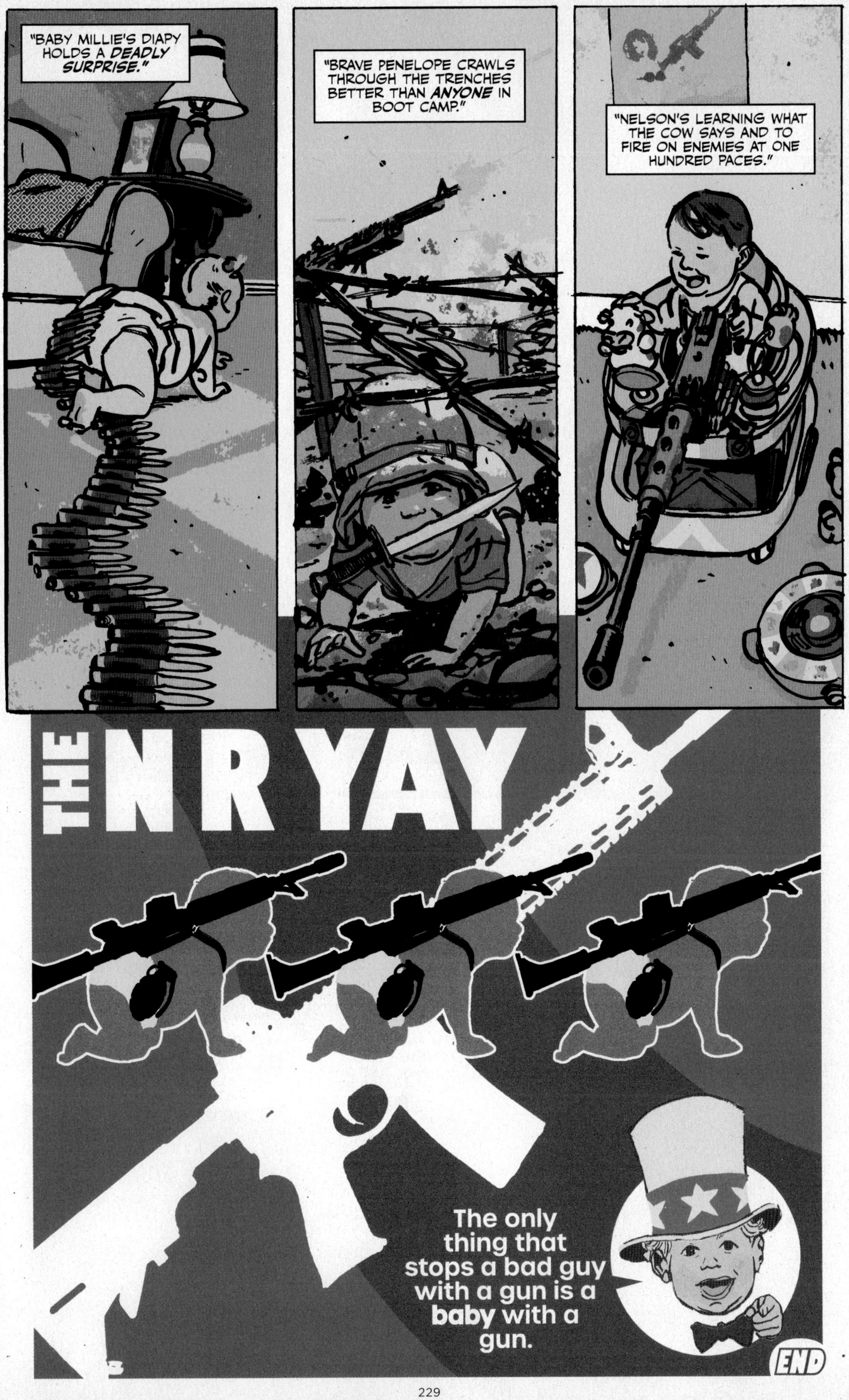

"BRAVE PENELOPE CRAWLS THROUGH THE TRENCHES BETTER THAN *ANYONE* IN BOOT CAMP."

"NELSON'S LEARNING WHAT THE COW SAYS AND TO FIRE ON ENEMIES AT ONE HUNDRED PACES."

THE N R YAY

The only thing that stops a bad guy with a gun is a **baby** with a gun.

END

"THE DECISION"
ILLIDGE
HEIGHT
BENNETT
DALHOUSE
IT'S HEAVIER THAN IT LOOKS.
AND COLD.
COLDER THAN I EVER IMAGINED.
I'M AFRAID TO HOLD IT.
AFRAID I'LL DROP IT.
AFRAID I WON'T.
I DON'T WANT THIS.
IT'S A GOD DAMNED EVIL THING.
NO GOOD COMES FROM IT.
BUT THAT'S NOT RIGHT, IS IT?
BECAUSE IF IT'S BETWEEN YOU AND THEM.
YOU AND YOURS.
AND MY BABIES.
AND THE ONLY THING THAT'LL SAVE THEM IS RAISING THIS TO YOUR FACE.
YOU TELL ME...

WHAT ELSE AM I SUPPOSED TO DO?
POLICE
YOU TELL ME!!
YOU ALRIGHT?

GO ON OUT OF HERE, NOW.
LEAVE MOMMY ALONE FOR A MINUTE.
NOT TODAY.
NOT GOING TO LET YOU MAKE ME THE ANIMAL YOU SAY I AM.
OR GIVE YOU AN EXCUSE TO END ME.
TOMORROW, HOWEVER...
KLUDD
JUST DON'T COME AFTER ME AND MINE TOMORROW.
LEAVE US BE.
END

MONDAY

HEY, DAD, IT'S LYNN.

JUST CALLING TO CHECK UP ON YOU.

DADDY'S *little girl*

WEDNESDAY

HI, DAD, IT'S LYNN... ***AGAIN.***

HAVEN'T HEARD FROM YOU IN A WHILE.

HOW'D YOUR ***DOCTOR APPOINTMENTS*** GO?

ARE YOU KEEPING UP WITH THE PROGRAM?

COULD YOU ***PLEASE*** JUST CALL ME TO LET ME KNOW YOU'RE OKAY?

WRITTEN BY Erica Schultz
ART BY Liana Kangas
COLOR ASSISTS BY Jamez Savage
LETTERS BY Cardinal Rae

THURSDAY

WE HAVEN'T SPOKEN IN DAYS.

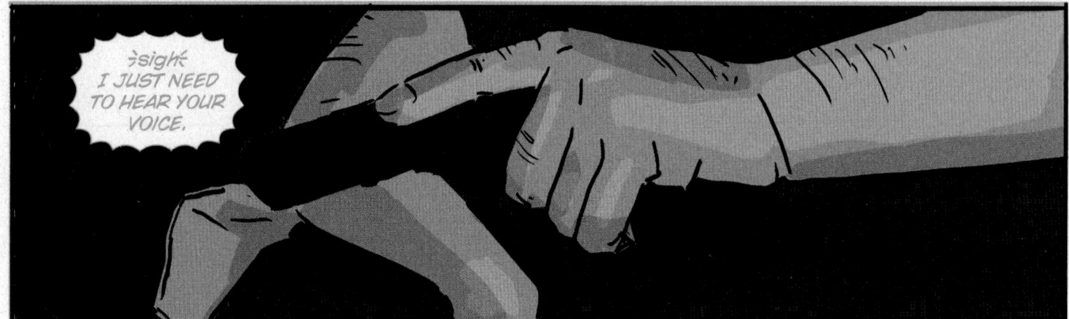
sigh
I JUST NEED TO HEAR YOUR VOICE.

I LOVE Y--
BEEEEEEEP

BEEEEEEEP
THE MAILBOX IS FULL.

DAMNIT.

DAMNIT.

FRIDAY

KNOCK KNOCK
SIR? IT'S THE POLICE. SIR, ARE YOU IN THERE?
THAT MAN IS DISGUSTING. HIS APARTMENT IS *FILTHY!*

SIR! WE'RE COMING IN!
OPEN IT UP.

I TRY TO EVICT HIM, BUT THEY SAY I *CAN'T* 'CAUSE HE'S "DISABLED" AND A VETERAN.
C'MON, HURRY UP.

WHAT'RE YOU DOING?
WHEN THE DAUGHTER CALLED FOR THE WELFARE CHECK, SHE SAID HE HAD A GUN.

43
CRAP...NOT AGAIN.

HE'S STILL GOT A PULSE.
CALL A BUS.

HOLY CRAP.

RANDY!
PDC AMMO

HE'S STILL BREATHING. CALL A BUS.

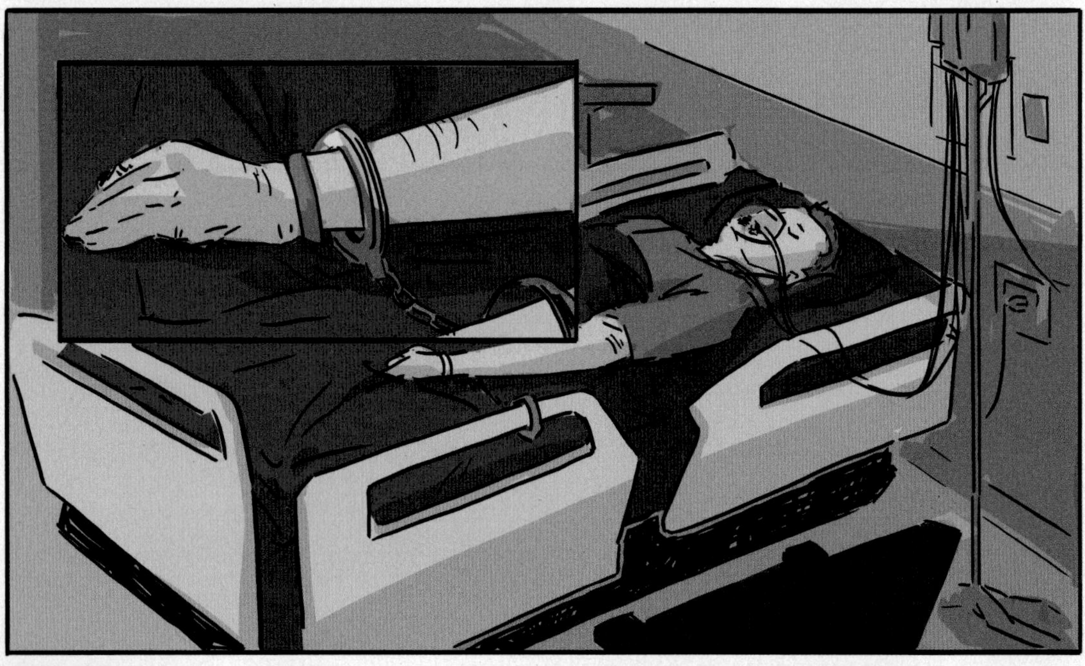

LATER
DAD!
OMIGOD, I'M SO GLAD HE'S OKAY.

HE WILL BE OKAY, RIGHT?

OFFICER? WHY IS HE-- WHAT'S WITH THE HANDCUFFS?

MA'AM...DID YOU KNOW YOUR FATHER WAS HOARDING WEAPONS?

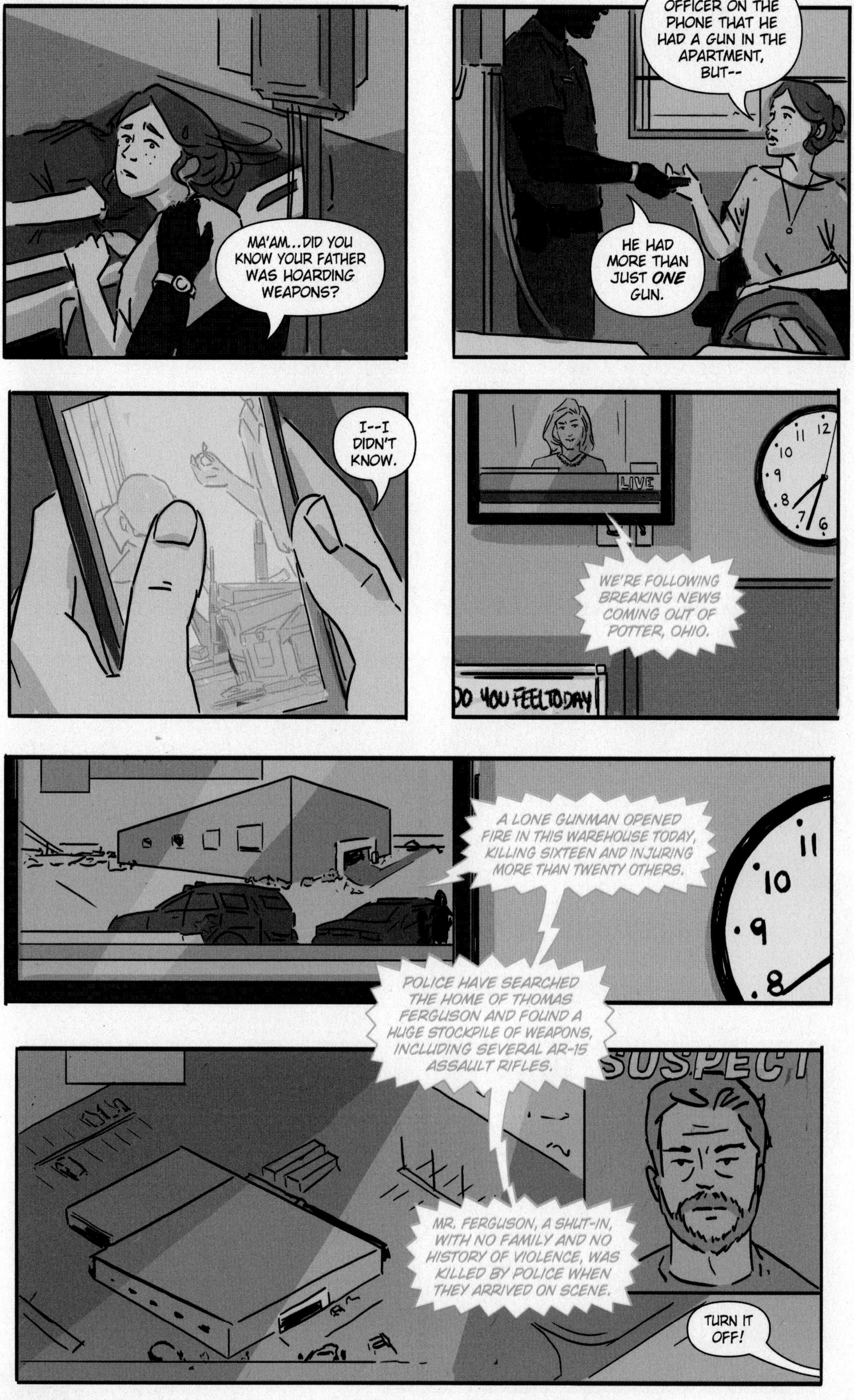

I TOLD THE OFFICER ON THE PHONE THAT HE HAD A GUN IN THE APARTMENT, BUT--
HE HAD MORE THAN JUST *ONE* GUN.

I--I DIDN'T KNOW.

LIVE
WE'RE FOLLOWING BREAKING NEWS COMING OUT OF POTTER, OHIO.
DO YOU FEEL TODAY
A LONE GUNMAN OPENED FIRE IN THIS WAREHOUSE TODAY, KILLING SIXTEEN AND INJURING MORE THAN TWENTY OTHERS.
POLICE HAVE SEARCHED THE HOME OF THOMAS FERGUSON AND FOUND A HUGE STOCKPILE OF WEAPONS, INCLUDING SEVERAL AR-15 ASSAULT RIFLES.
SUSPECT
MR. FERGUSON, A SHUT-IN, WITH NO FAMILY AND NO HISTORY OF VIOLENCE, WAS KILLED BY POLICE WHEN THEY ARRIVED ON SCENE.
TURN IT OFF!

THAT... COULD'VE BEEN HIM... OH, DAD...

NO...YOU KEPT REACHING OUT TO YOUR FATHER. YOU WERE THE REASON HE DIDN'T TAKE IT THAT FAR.
YOU DID THE RIGHT THING BY CALLING US.
BESIDES... THE DOCTOR SAID HE BARELY HAD THE STRENGTH TO LIFT ONE OF THOSE RIFLES.

COLD COMFORT, I KNOW, BUT--
I'M HERE.
I'M HERE, DADDY.

EEE
EEE
EEE
EEEEEEEEEEEEEEEEEEEEEEEEE

END.

Jennifer

ORDINARY DEVOTION

ESSAY BY JENNIFER BATTISTI
ILLUSTRATION BY GEOF DARROW
WITH COLORS BY DAVE STEWART
PRODUCTION DESIGN BY BERNARDO BRICE

> *"The cliched slogan, 'What happens in Vegas, stays in Vegas', has never been more untrue. What happens in Vegas radiates internationally. In my opinion, there isn't a more collectively experienced place on earth."*

Now, when I drive to the strip for work, carbonated grief presses against my chest at the light at Las Vegas Blvd. Is this fury? I look up at the tower where I work. It is a different shiny tower than the Mandalay Bay. There are so many windows in tower after tower lining the strip and I cannot stop seeing broken glass. The word "massacre" takes up all the space on the breakroom TV. I am under two miles north of the massacre. It is three days after a gunman opened fire into the crowd of a country music festival. I am learning about explosives stored inside the shooter's car in the parking garage. I am in a different shiny tower. There are so many towers.

Trauma is tricky. It begins to erode sleep. I cannot go to my kettle-bell class. Anything outside the hailstorm of news feels remote—a hologram of a former existence drained of all color and texture. How are people going to the GAP, making dentist appointments? I go to the welcome sign. The white crosses stretch on and on— a picket fence guarding our home after the kind of burglary for which there is no restoration. I go to the Remembrance Garden; there are mementoes, evidence of 58 lives. There is a Four Seasons record, a 45 rpm of "Too Many Memories", beside a studded black belt perched on a wooden milk crate. There is a scuffed up skateboard, a pair of cowboy boots; there are many— too many, colorings from children who have lost their mothers and fathers. There is a man who burns incense and plays the guitar. He is a veteran with PTSD. He is there everyday. The garden is heavy with a kind of healing I've never felt before, which is at once startling and familiar. Is this God?

***

Death becomes acutely inclusive when everyone has stake in the pot, when our lives become the "Big Blind" we take in the pursuit of pleasure. There is something so kindling about near misses, lucky breaks, survivor's guilt. In the wake of our nation's worst mass shooting in American history, a peculiar brand of kinship unfolded in the reflections of close calls. My co-worker turned down a free ticket for the Harvest 91 festival last minute. A friend's cousin was there, and survived a gunshot wound. A woman from my book study works in retail in the next hotel over. She was on lockdown until early morning. My high school classmate was a police officer who ran into the danger when everyone else was running away from it. Despite the tremendous growth in Las Vegas, we are still a small town, in which the majority are fused with the hospitality industry. In hearing these stories, the undercurrent beneath the details was, me too. If there is an anatomy to a tragedy, this is the connective tissue.

By definition, the word hospitality means: *"The quality or disposition of receiving or treating guests and strangers in a warm, friendly, and generous way."* In Las Vegas, hospitality is the spine of the strip— the brightest thread in every spirited swirl of psychedelic carpet blooming in every casino. We are a city fueled by hyper-vigilance to service. Our native tongue is, *how may I assist you? It would be my pleasure, how's the pressure, the temperature, the wine, the show, would you like large bills or small, we are: good morning, good afternoon, good evening, certainly, and we hope you've enjoyed your stay*. It isn't surprising that in the darkest of hours, our city showed up in the sort of five-star-service way we've been trained. The first responders and the blood donors cared for the trauma survivors while the community cared for the blood donors. The domino effect of kindness was a tender proof of our humanity, which only makes the many uncomfortable, inconvenient conversations we need to have much more necessary, in order to protect the fierceness of our resilience.

Vegas is my home— my native home. In under thirty minutes, I can reach the sagging, malnourished neighborhood known as "The Eastside", where I spent the first eighteen years of my life. My initials are still etched into the street-lamps. As a child, I used to go to the Circus Circus Midway show and marvel at the acrobats floating above the baccarat tables, while trapeze artists swung inverted to the careful call of bingo numbers in the background. When I turned sixteen, my older sister rented a cherry-red convertible Mustang and chaffered my friends and I up and down Las Vegas Blvd, back when "cruising the strip" was the way to spend a Saturday night. I have worked in casinos for over twenty years. I've scooped ice cream, worked for the Siegfried and Roy show, and for the last fourteen years, made a living out of making people feel comfortable as an esthetician in resort spas.

The cliched slogan, "What happens in Vegas, stays in Vegas", has never been more untrue. What happens in Vegas radiates internationally. In my opinion, there isn't a more collectively experienced place on earth. Geography and memory have a way of blending and becoming part of our personal histories. In that way, we all have a little neon running through our veins. Over the years, it's almost as if Vegas has developed its own ecosystem, able to evolve and thrive under the changing desires of tourism—so seamlessly it appears to adapt without any human influence (thanks to our magnificent marketing departments). Adaptation keeps the four-mile feast stocked with the most sought-after flavors. Vegas has been hand-sewn and customized for every tourist to discover the salve for their every itch. Every visitor who comes to Vegas gambles, shops, has the best Kobe beef they've ever tasted, sees a Cirque show, gets married in a drive-thru, rents a hummerzine for their bachelor party, gets a massage on their company retreat — every time they make a memory with Vegas as the setting, they

> *"In the wake of our nation's worst mass shooting in American history, a peculiar brand of kinship unfolded in the reflections of close calls."*

too own a piece of our city, they too, etch their initials into our street-lamps. Vegas belongs to everyone.

***

I live in a cul-de-sac in a suburban neighborhood where on most days families with young children stand in the street and talk to each other. There are always piles of bikes in driveways and sidewalk chalk baking in the sun. It is rare and precious. Two days after the shooting my neighbor and I talked about it. Horrifying, unimaginable, and then we sat in silence for awhile. She asked me if I wanted to see a praying mantis giving birth? I did. The mama mantis was cradled in the groove of the rear tire tread of her husband's pickup truck. Incredible, I said hovering over the green leaf of her body. Her lower half contracted. Her limbs unfurled—an accordion balancing her elongated thorax. Soon, we all leaned in, desperate for metaphor—we rejoiced through glances at the spectacular symbol the universe had placed in the safe cocoon of our gated community. A balm for the feelings which we had no words for. She was steadfast, laboring, procreating, praying. We hushed curious children as they leaned into the wheel-well, her majesty's chamber; the smell of rubber like the sweetness of the most sacred of offerings. It took hours of focused prayer and continuous pulses until a silky sac was released with close to 200 baby mantis eggs inside. We feverishly googled mantis facts: The eggs would hatch in eight weeks if the weather stayed mild. The mama mantis would die soon after giving birth— the ultimate sacrifice; the last particular praying mantis thing she would ever do, this ordinary devotion.

The sun was setting. The street-lamps blinked on. We ushered our babies inside and washed the day off of their soft faces. My neighbor said he'd move the sac in the morning to a nearby bush, where they would be safe. The mama mantis would likely leave in the night, purpose letting her go easily. She'd have the privacy to die. But something went wrong. By morning, the sac hardened into a husk. The ootheca was cemented to the tire—already plumping on the bliss of biology. Inside, each nymph was tucked into its own tiny pod like a pomegranate seed. A razor would have surely sliced into the eggs. There was no way to move them, and people need to get to work. The halo of the evening's promise was gone by the time the sprinklers chirped on. Even divinity doesn't come through. My loneliness let up a bit, seeing how the earth is neutral; that no species is exempt from pointless devastation. My neighbor said a prayer while he backed up his truck. That same morning, I dressed my five-year-old for kindergarten, where she is working on the letter S, and then I drove to work and recommended the places I love in our city to tourists: The Italian restaurant with photographs of the Rat Pack lining the walls, Hoover Dam, and the Neon Boneyard museum—a place where we honor our spectacular glittered and improvable history, not imploded but restored through story and light by the people of Las Vegas, who know hospitality as intimately as desert heat—in a place where caring for strangers is an ordinary devotion.

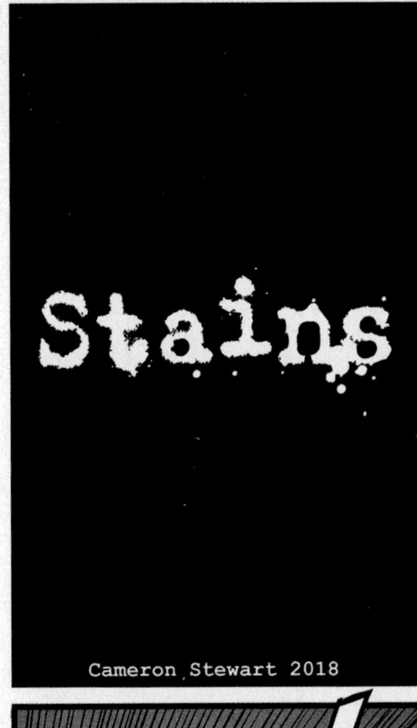
Stains
Cameron Stewart 2018

BANG

BANG
BANG
BANG
BA

BANG
BANG
BANG
BANG
BANG
BANG
GUNWAR
ASSASSINETTE

BANG
BANG
SPY SPOUSE
99 Targets
EXPLORER
BANG
BANG
BANG
KID DEMON
GRAVEYARD DETECTIVE
The UMBRA

BANG
STAFF
BANG
BANG
BANG
BANG
AMERICOP

BANG BANG
BANG
BANG
BANG
BANG
BANG
BANG

BANG BANG
FAN-CON
BANG BANG

BANG
NEESON
BANG
BANG
BANG BANG

BANG BANG
BOOM
BANG BANG
BANG
BANG BANG BANG

BANG
BANG
BANG

BANG
Play
Recently Added
THE PENALIZER
My List
BANG
ASSASSINETTE
THE BUSINESS OF GUNS
GRAVEYARD DETECTIVE
Because You Watched Bullet Hoarders

BANG BANG BANG
HAHAHA
BANG BANG BANG

HEADSHOT!!
+1000
BANG BANG

BANG
BANG
BANG
BANG
BANG
"NEWS"

BANG BANG BANG
BANG
BANG BANG
NRA
BANG BANG

BANG
BANG
BANG
BAN

BANG
COUNTY GUN FAIR
NO I.D. REQUIRED
BANG
BANG
SALE!

BANG
BANG
BANG
BANG

BANG
BANG
BANG
BANG

BANG
BANG
BANG

BANG
BANG
BANG
Room Service

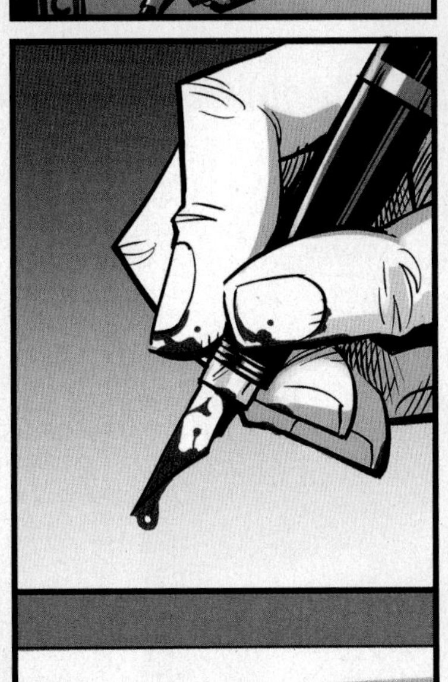

THE RANGE
WRITER JASON STARR
ARTIST ANDREA MUTTI
COLORIST VLADIMIR POPOV
LETTERER BERNARDO BRICE
OCTOBER 1, 2017.
INSTINCTS.
SOMETIMES I LISTENED TO THEM, SOMETIMES I IGNORED THEM.
I HATE GUNS.
CASINO ROYALE

I USUALLY LISTENED.
THIS ISN'T GUNS, KYLE. THIS IS FUN.
AT THE RANGE YOU GET TO USE THE SAME MACHINE GUNS FROM LETHAL WEAPON AND THE M-SIXTY RAMBO USED.
RAMBO. LIKE HE WAS A REAL PERSON.
POKER

I THINK YOU'RE THE ONLY DUDE FROM TEXAS WHO DOESN'T OWN A GUN.
I GOT THREE GUNS AT HOME.
GOOD FOR YOU.

WE'RE NOT EVEN TALKING ABOUT OWNING GUNS. YEAH, I'M A SECOND AMENDMENT GUY, BUT THIS IS DIFFERENT. THIS IS JUST A DAY OF FUN, LETTIN' LOOSE. LIKE... LIKE GOING TO A WATER PARK.
YEAH, A WATER PARK WITH AUTOMATIC WEAPONS.

WHAT ABOUT YOU GUYS? YOU COMIN', RIGHT?
HELL YEAH.
WHY NOT? IT'LL KEEP ME AWAY FROM THE BLACKJACK TABLE AND SAVE ME A TON OF SCRATCH.
IT'S DOWN TO YOU, KYLE. COME ON, THIS IS VEGAS. YOU'RE SUPPOSED TO LEAVE YOUR COMFORT ZONE HERE.
SERIOUSLY, HOW MANY TIMES ARE WE GONNA TURN 40 ANYWAY?

WHAT'RE YOU GONNA DO, HANG OUT HERE AND PLAY KENO ALL DAY WITH THE OLD LADIES?
I DIDN'T WANT TO RUIN EVERYONE ELSE'S GOOD TIME, SO I DECIDED TO NOT GO WITH MY INSTINCTS.
BUT IN THIS CASE...

MY INSTINCTS WERE DEAD WRONG.

I HAD A TOTAL BLAST.

IT WAS SO AWESOME, AND SO MUCH COOLER THAN I'D EXPECTED.
LIKE I WAS IN BLACK OPS, PLAYING A LIVE-ACTION VIDEO GAME.

I'D NEVER BEEN A BIG DRUGGIE.
DID COKE IN COLLEGE A FEW TIMES, BUT THIS WAS SO MUCH BETTER THAN COKE.

THE ULTIMATE SHOOTING EXPERIENCE
WE GOTTA HIT THIS PLACE AGAIN FOR OUR FIFTIETH!
SEE? WHAT'D I TELL YOU?

YEAH, YOU WERE RIGHT.

LATER ON WE HEADED OUT TO THE MUSIC FESTIVAL.
THIS BETTER NOT SUCK.
IT WON'T.
I WAS WAITING FOR THEM TO PLAY "MY KINDA PARTY", ONE OF THE ONLY ALDEAN SONGS I KNEW.
BUT THEN...
I DIDN'T THINK IT WAS REAL.
I STILL FELT SO JUICED UP FROM THE DAY AT THE RANGE, I THOUGHT THAT'S ALL IT WAS...
...MORE FANTASY.
BUT MY INSTINCTS TOLD ME OTHERWISE.

SOMEHOW I FOUND COVER...
BUT IT WAS TOO LATE FOR MY BUDDIES.
I PROBABLY SCREAMED LOUDER THAN I'VE EVER SCREAMED BEFORE, BUT I COULDN'T HEAR ANYTHING.
IT WAS LIKE I WAS IN A SILENT MOVIE.
I COULD'VE JUST STAYED THERE, I GUESS.

BUT I LISTENED TO MY INSTINCTS AGAIN.
I **HAD** TO SAVE HIM. IT WASN'T EVEN A CHOICE.
I COULD SEE IT IN HIS EYES.
I KNEW IF WE'D HAD A CHANCE TO SPEAK, HE WOULD'VE TOLD ME HOW SORRY HE WAS FOR **EVERYTHING.**
HOW **WRONG** HE'D BEEN.
I WANTED TO TELL HIM THAT IT WASN'T JUST HIM. I WAS WRONG TOO.
BUT WE DIDN'T HAVE A CHANCE TO SPEAK.
WELL...
...I DIDN'T.
END

SHAKEN, NOT DETERRED
MATTHEW SORVILLO - WRITER
SEAN PHILLIPS - ARTIST
THE REAL QUESTION IS, WHY DOES IT *KEEP* HAPPENING?

RIGHT? THIS DOESN'T HAPPEN ANYWHERE ELSE. WHY CAN'T WE JUST GET SOME COMMON SENSE LEGISLATION--
LIKE IN AUSTRALIA OR THE U.K.

I SIGNED THIS ONLINE PETITION I SAW. WE NEED TO GET WEAPONS LIKE THESE AWAY FROM THESE GUN NUTS.
FORWARD ME THAT LINK.
YEAH, ME TOO.

WE NEED TO MAKE OUR LAWMAKERS LISTEN. WHY ARE THESE DAMN THINGS LEGAL TO BEGIN WITH?
THE 2ND AMENDMENT IS GONNA COME UNDER ATTACK, YOU WAIT AND SEE.

HELL, THIS IS PROBABLY A FALSE FLAG ANYWAY. JUST AN EXCUSE TO COME AFTER OUR FREEDOMS.
THEY SAY HE ACTED ALONE. I SAY BULL AND SHIT.

HE SUPPOSEDLY HAD UPWARDS OF TWENTY RIFLES IN HIS ROOM. YOU SEE ALL THE CAMERAS THEY HAVE EVERYWHERE? HOW'D HE MANAGE GETTING ALL 'EM GUNS UP THERE WITHOUT NOBODY NOTICING?

THAT'S WHAT I BEEN SAYIN'. THIS IS THE MOST HEAVILY SURVEILLED CITY ON EARTH. EYE IN THE SKY SEES ALL, BUT DIDN'T CATCH HIM? COME ON, NOW...
DEFINITELY STAGED. BUNCHA CRISIS ACTORS JUST LIKE ALL THE OTHER TIMES.

SO... WHAT DO WE DO?
SHOULD WE FLY HOME? IS IT EVEN SAFE HERE?
LIKE IT'S SAFE TO BE ANYWHERE THESE DAYS? THESE THINGS HAPPEN ALL THE TIME NOW.

SHOULDN'T THEY SHUT DOWN THE STRIP OR SOMETHING? LIMIT CROWDS SO IT DOESN'T HAPPEN AGAIN?
I'M SUPPOSED TO GET MARRIED TOMORROW. IS IT OKAY FOR US TO ENJOY OURSELVES? IS THAT DISRESPECTFUL?

I WAS JUST SAYING THAT TO MY HUSBAND.
WE'VE WAITED ALL YEAR FOR THIS VACATION. IS IT OKAY FOR US TO HAVE FUN IN LIGHT OF ALL THIS?
I KNOW IT'S A TRAGEDY, AND I DON'T WANT TO SEEM UNCARING, BUT IS IT OKAY FOR US TO CELEBRATE?

IN THE SERVICE INDUSTRY, YOU'RE FORCED TO BITE YOUR TONGUE A LOT.
EVEN WHEN YOU ASK US OUR OPINION, WE CAN'T REALLY SPEAK FREELY. WE'RE AT WORK.
BUT HERE'S WHAT YOU SHOULD KNOW...
LAS VEGAS IS A REAL CITY. A MILE FROM THE STRIP IN ANY DIRECTION, PAST THE FAKE VOLCANOS, THE PHONY EIFFEL TOWER, AND THE DANCING FOUNTAINS...
...YOU'LL FIND HOUSES AND HOSPITALS, GROCERY STORES AND ELEMENTARY SCHOOLS, POST OFFICES AND PARKS.
SO, PLEASE, DON'T ADD INSULT TO THE HEARTBREAKING INJURY OUR COMMUNITY HAS SUFFERED BY DENYING THIS UNSPEAKABLE ACT OF VIOLENCE EVEN TOOK PLACE.
YOU HAVE QUESTIONS ABOUT HOW THIS COULD HAVE HAPPENED. HOW NO ONE HAD SEEN SOME WARNING. BUT IN A CASINO THE CAMERAS AREN'T WATCHING YOU, THEY'RE ONLY WATCHING THE MONEY.
SAD, BUT TRUE.
AND TO THOSE WHO WONDER WHY OUR LAWMAKERS WON'T ACT WHEN 96% OF THE COUNTRY SUPPORTS BACKGROUND CHECKS FOR ALL GUN PURCHASES*...
YOU ALREADY KNOW WHY? THEY'RE ONLY LOOKING AT THE MONEY TOO.

BUT THE MOST IMPORTANT THING FOR YOU TO KNOW IS HOW TRULY WE NEED YOU. ALL OF YOU.
SO, YES, ENJOY YOURSELVES BECAUSE THAT'S WHY WE'RE HERE.
AS STUNNED AS OUR COMMUNITY WAS, WE STILL SHOWED UP TO WORK THE NEXT MORNING, PUT ON OUR SMILES, AND MADE SURE OUR GUESTS ENJOYED THEIR STAY.
BECAUSE *THAT* IS THE HEART OF THIS CITY. WE ARE AMERICA'S BARTENDER. WE PLAY HOST TO THE ENTIRE WORLD AND WE DO IT BETTER THAN ANYONE.
WE WORK, WE SMILE, WE HAPPILY LISTEN TO YOUR TROUBLES, EVEN WHILE MOURNING OUR OWN.
BECAUSE IF YOU STOP COMING, AND YOU STOP HAVING FUN, AND YOU DECIDE TO STAY HOME FOR FEAR OR FOR SADNESS, THAT WOULD HURT THIS COMMUNITY MORE THAN 100 GUNMEN.
PFFFT!
AND IT'S TRUE. SOMETIMES TOURISTS CAN BE RUDE, UNTHINKING, AGGRAVATING, AND SELF-ENTITLED...
AND WE STILL LOVE EVERY SINGLE ONE THAT STEPS UP TO OUR BAR.
BECAUSE WE DON'T GET TO BE WHO WE ARE WITHOUT YOU.
(*ACCORDING TO GALLUP, OCT. 5-11, 2017 - HTTP://NEWS.GALLUP.COM/POLL/1645/GUNS.ASPX)

"You could see it on the people who were there.

"Not a single person was untouched by this experience.

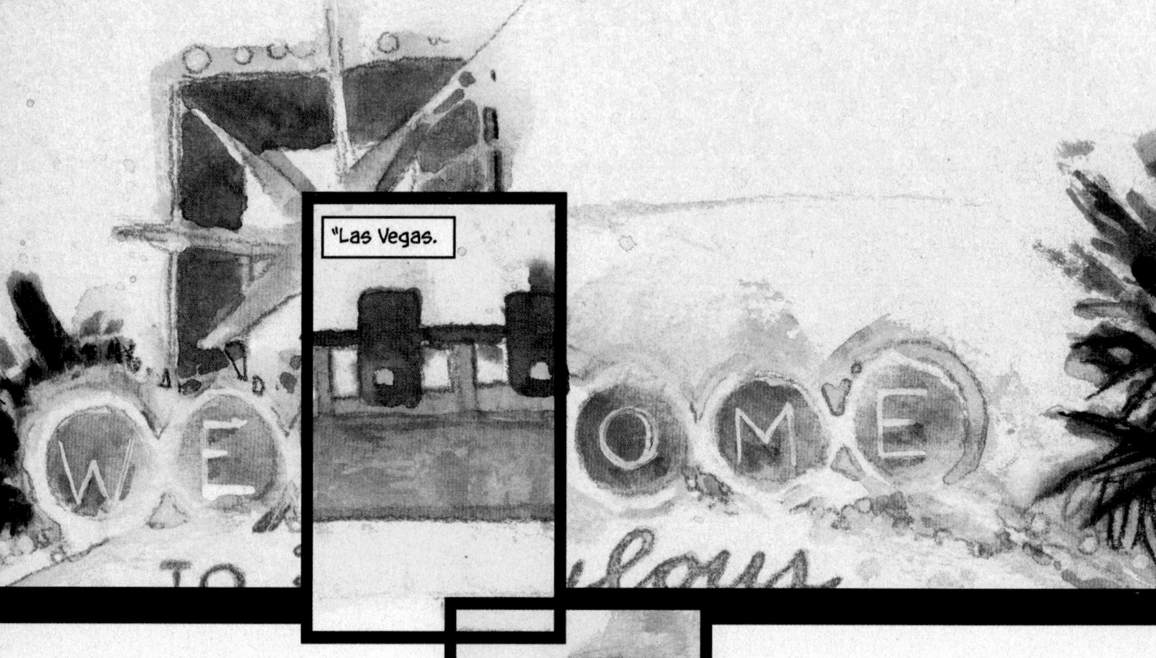

"I work on the strip - serve at a restaurant.

"It was a normal night at work, but it was weird.

"Every cell in my body was telling me not to go to work that night.

"Not to leave my house.

"Something was just...off.

The Red Light

By Ray Fawkes, from an interview with Bonnie Hilts

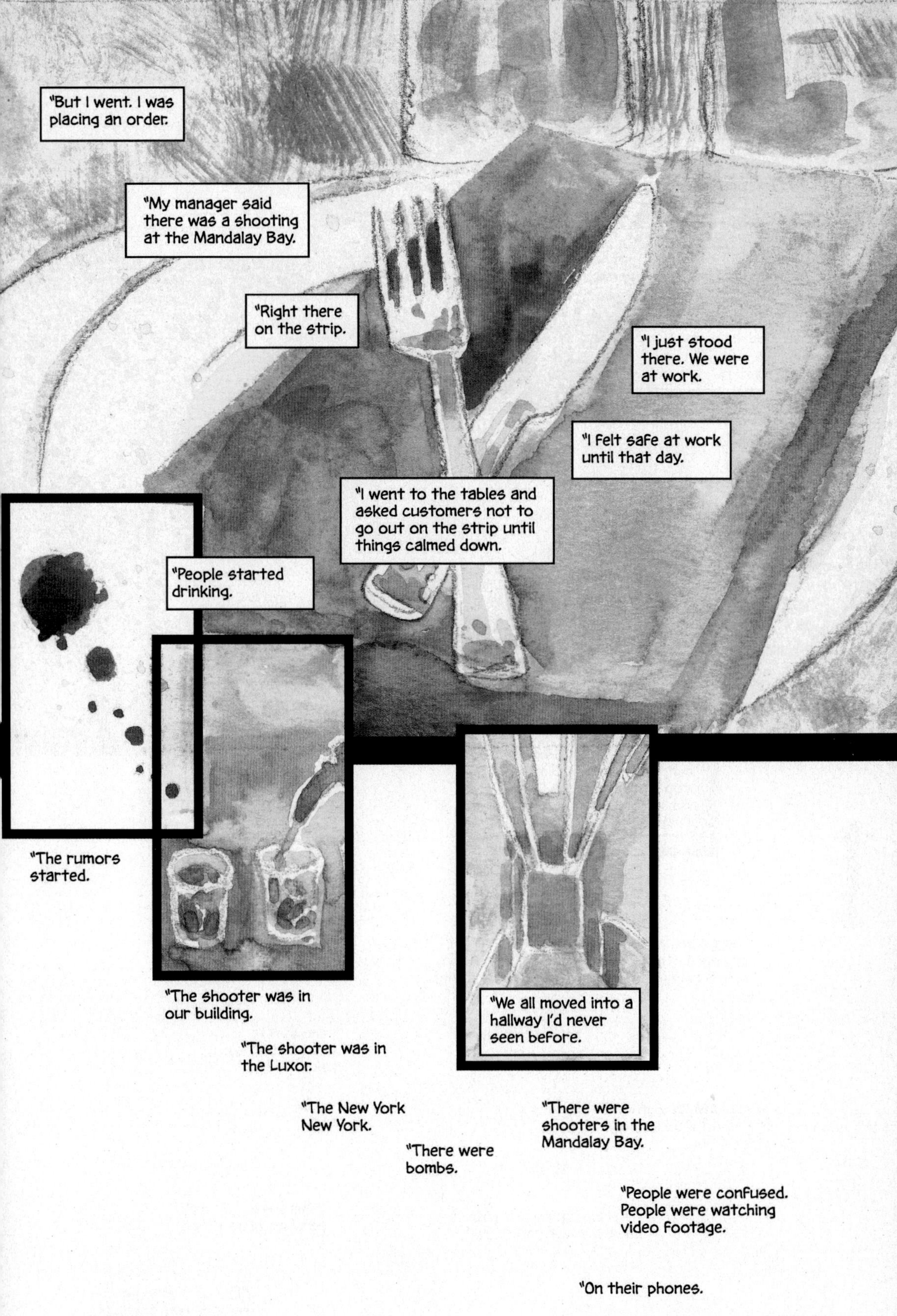

"People were confused. People were watching video footage.

"On their phones.

"This is the definition of terror.

"The gunshot sounds in the videos made me jump.

"They were packing the freight elevator with people, sending them to the basement.
"Then they said we couldn't go that way.
"I couldn't get to the exits I knew.
"People were making gun jokes, not understanding.
"But everybody would stop at the corners and be afraid to look, afraid to go on.
"I broke and shouted at people watching videos on their phones.
"SWAT was outside, keeping us inside.
"We were trapped for our own good.
"They sent us back into the restaurant.

"I was on the phone with my husband.

"People were texting me. My mother, my brother, my sister.

"The hardest thing to do was hang up.

"I thought I wasn't going to make it home.

"Wendy called, crying. She said 'I wish I could be with you.'

"I said 'I don't want you here. It's not safe here.'

"There was so much panicky information.

"The only window to outside was through peoples' phones.

"It was close to 3 A.M. A security guard said 'we're going to let you go soon.'
"I just wanted to get out of there.
"I just left.
"I got down to my car and drove out. Nobody was there. No SWAT, no security guards.
"I turned the corner and there was the flood of police lights.
POLIC
"I knew there were bodies and I knew there were people...
"...I sat staring at the red light.

"And when it was green I got on the freeway and drove home.

"The adrenaline wore off and I had the full shakes.

"I just wanted to get home.

"And then when I did I thought:

"How are we ever going to recover?

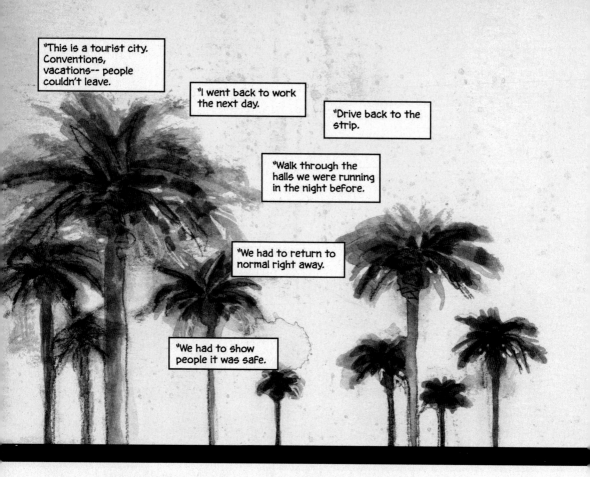

"This is a tourist city. Conventions, vacations-- people couldn't leave.

"I went back to work the next day.

"Drive back to the strip.

"Walk through the halls we were running in the night before.

"We had to return to normal right away.

"We had to show people it was safe.

"There were customers asking if I was okay.

"There were people acting like they weren't affected.

"There was a couple who were at the concert. They were separated during the shooting.

"But you could see it on the people who were there.

"Not a single person was untouched by this experience.

"There was a table of people -- media. They talked about it like-- they didn't think about the words they used.

"One reporter stopped to ask me something:

"How bad was your business affected?'

"I said:

"People have really been there for each other today."

MARY DOESN'T DANCE
North of England. 1987
Who wants to go first?
Siobhan?

I think I did a bad thing. He didn't want me to play with anyone, and it felt funny, bad funny, when he made me stay inside and do the touching game.
He said it was my fault. I'm a bad girl. My tummy feels funny when I think about it. I want to hurt myself.

I'D HAVE PUNCHED HIM IN THE THROAT! THEN CUT HIM. DON'T BE SUCH A WIMP!

Am I allowed to do that? It doesn't seem very nice.

I like your dog Siobhan, I had a dog, but he went away, 'cos he told me I had to cut my hair off. I liked my hair, but he said it made me look too nice, that boys would start liking me, and that's bad.

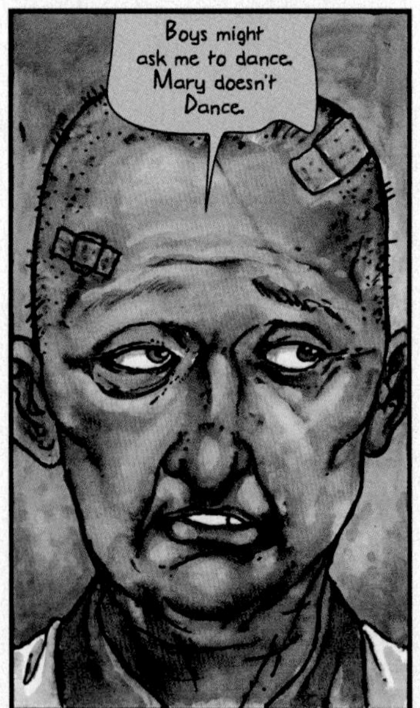
Boys might ask me to dance. Mary doesn't Dance.

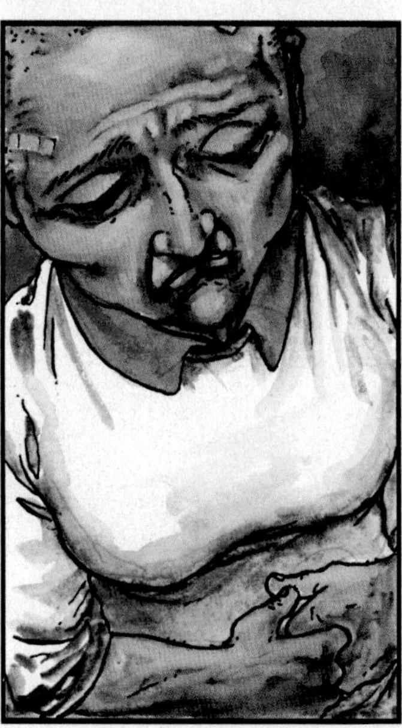

Tracy?

Hello everyone! I just had a bit of a wobble, but I'm fine, really. I'm good. I'm a nice person.

I just start the fires sometimes, it's the bad place, it needs to go away. They hurt me there, tricked me.
I dream about the place sometimes and then I start a fire. I'm ok now.

...only when the place is empty though, I wouldn't hurt anyone, I'm a nice person.
THAT'S DUMB!

Vince?
JEEEEZ! WHAT!... OH, I KICKED THE BLOKE IN THE SHOP, BUT HE STARTED IT, PUSHED ME AND SLAPPED ME HEAD! HE SAID HE DIDN'T WANT PEOPLE LIKE ME IN HIS SHOP.

BUT THEY DID ME, JUST BECAUSE I'M MENTAL, HE DIDN'T GET PUT AWAY, EVEN THOUGH HE STARTED IT!

Julie?
I saw it, but no one believed me because I get mixed up, but I did see it. it was bad.

No Julie, don't! lets get that seen to, come on.

Bad people took me to a house and made me play the touching game, they took my money as well, and kicked my dog.
no one believed me, until a man who wasn't mental told the police.

MARY DOESN'T DANCE.
That's right. It's a sin!

Hello.

THE BITER'S BACK!

Mr Saunders, said I was trespassing, but I wasn't, it was a public footpath, he hit me with a shovel, the police believed me, but the court said I was too unreliable, because I had a fit at the meeting with the judge-man.
Mary doesn't dance.

I left the flat when the fireman asked me to, I'm good really.

Tom?
I'm Jesus
NO YOU'RE NOT! STUPID!

You probably just don't recognise me because I'm not wearing my clown makeup today.
THAT'S STUPID!!

Vince?
She said we were related and that she'd help me with my money, help pay the bills. But she didn't she bought stuff, spent it all. she was really bad.
But she told the social worker that I said she could spend it all, I didn't, really. I do get mixed up and spend too much but I thought she was helping me stop that. Not nice that.
I got in trouble 'cos I shouted at her in the cafe.
Mary shouldn't dance, it's a sin
You're him, aren't you? you are you are!
Who!? I'm Vince...
No! You're him, you are. I told you I didn't dance! I've been a good girl, I have, honest!
I'M NOT PLAYING THE TOUCHING GAME ANYMORE, I DON'T LIKE IT!
MARY DOESN'T DANCE!!
Lots of boys wanted to dance with me they did, because I was pretty.
Mary doesn't dance Are you him? Are you? no... he's dead. Is he dead? I saw him yesterday.
GO AWAY!

This was a conversation that I witnessed between a family member and a number of her personalities that she manifested during a crisis with her schizophrenia. She didn't recognise me until the last panel. all the incidents the various personalities refer to actually happened. Only the names have been changed.

BLAM

BREAKING NEWS THIS EVENING AS A SHOOTER ...

SHOOTER

MONSTERS

Story
Lela Gwenn

Pictures
Matthew Dow Smith

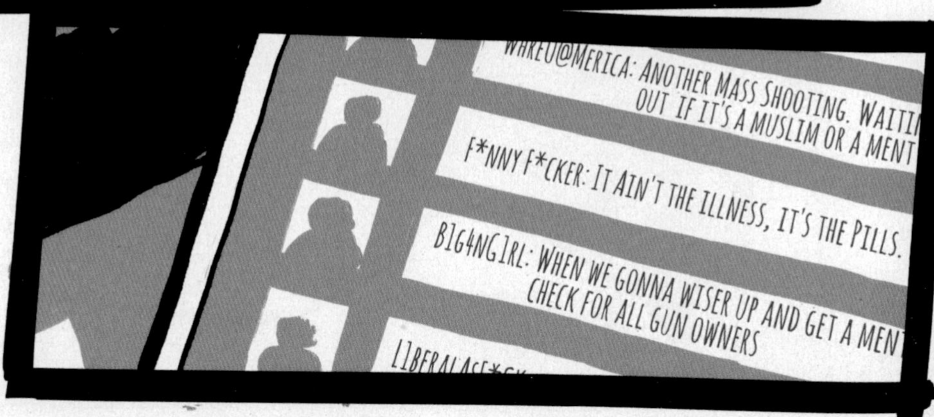
WHREU@MERICA: ANOTHER MASS SHOOTING. WAITI
OUT IF IT'S A MUSLIM OR A MENT
F*NNY F*CKER: IT AIN'T THE ILLNESS, IT'S THE PILLS.
B1G4NG1RL: WHEN WE GONNA WISER UP AND GET A MEN
CHECK FOR ALL GUN OWNERS

THESE ARE MY FRIENDS.
THIS IS WHAT THEY THINK OF ME.
BZZZZT
MORNING MEDS
PAUSE
EVERYONE HATES ME.
I'M A MONSTER.
THAT COULD BE ME.
BZZZT

MISSY
NOW
I'M CALLING.
PICK UP.
RING
DON'T GO ON THE INTERNET.
IT'S A SHIT-SHOW.
TOO LATE.
I'M A MONSTER.
RIDICULOUS. YOU THOUGHT THE LETHAL WEAPON MOVIES WERE NEEDLESSLY VIOLENT.
THERE ARE A LOT OF PEOPLE WITH BAD OPINIONS THAT MAKE THEM FEEL SMART.
THAT DOESN'T MAKE THEM RIGHT.
YOU ARE NEVER GOING TO HURT ANYONE.
WHAT YOU **ARE** GOING TO DO IS TAKE YOUR MEDS, EAT SOMETHING, AND IGNORE THE INTERNET TODAY.
I'LL CHECK ON YOU LATER.
THANKS, MISSY.
I LOVE YOU.
END.

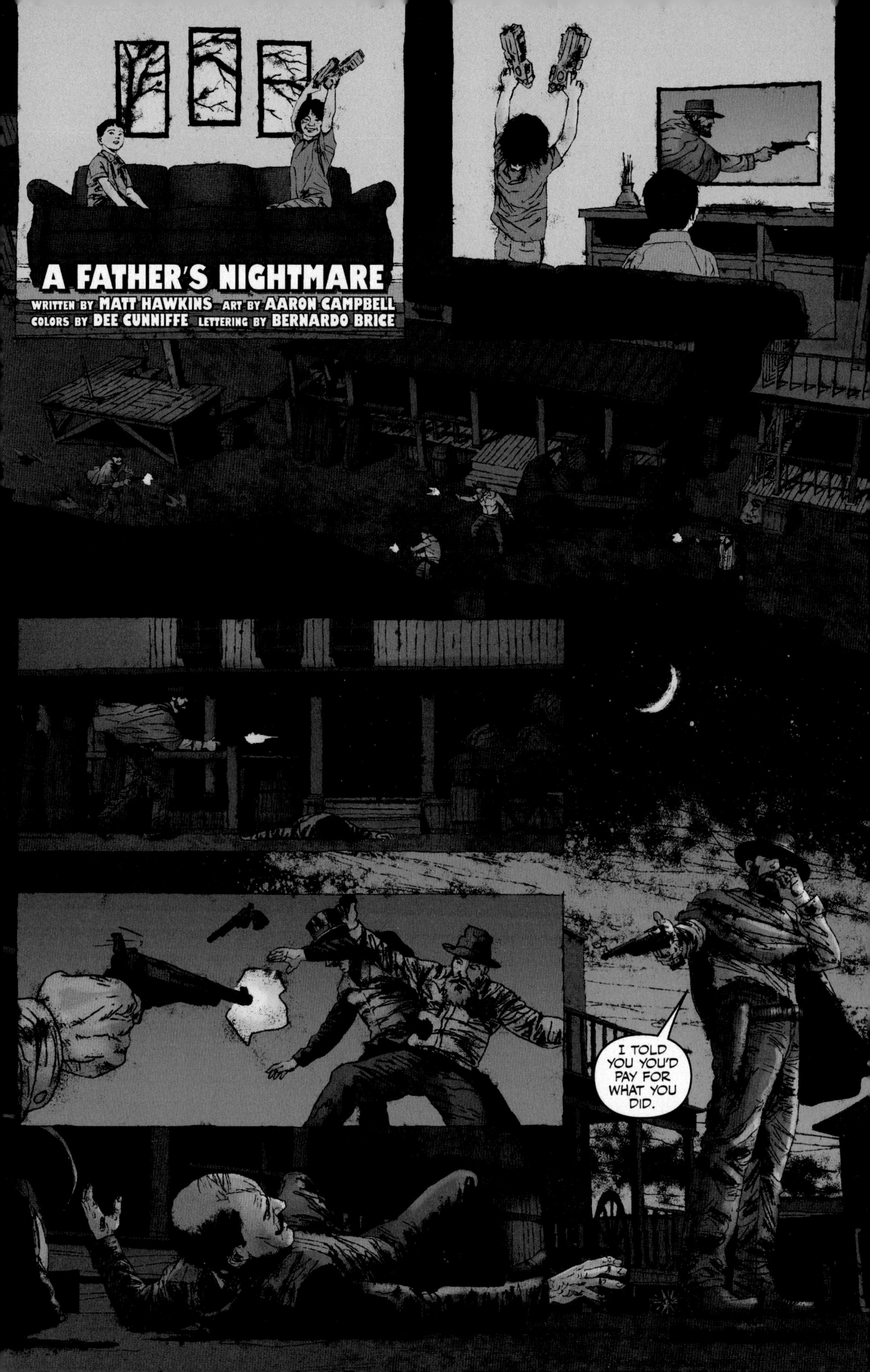
A FATHER'S NIGHTMARE
WRITTEN BY MATT HAWKINS ART BY AARON CAMPBELL
COLORS BY DEE CUNNIFFE LETTERING BY BERNARDO BRICE
I TOLD YOU YOU'D PAY FOR WHAT YOU DID.

BLAM

YOU'RE SUPPOSED TO DIE.
LUKE, WILL YOU PLAY?
OKAY.
BANG, BANG!
BANG, BANG!
BANG, BANG!
BANG, BANG!
BANG, BANG!
BANG, BANG!

YOU'RE GOING TO PAY FOR WHAT YOU DID.
BLAM

NO!

WHAT'S WRONG?

I HAD A NIGHTMARE... MARK SHOT LUKE WITH MY GUN.

WHAT ARE YOU GOING TO DO WITH IT?

I'LL DROP IT OFF AT THE POLICE STATION TOMORROW.

THEY HAVE SOME LAKERS TICKETS TRADE-IN PROMOTION GOING NOW.

END

"YOU ALL SET FOR THE TEST?"

"I...I THINK SO."

"GOOD. **GOOD.** BUT LOOK, WHATEVER HAPPENS JUST STAY FOCUSED AND YOU'LL DO GREAT. REMEMBER-- WINNERS **ACT,** LOSERS **DISTRACT.** GOT IT?"

"GOT IT."

"ATTABOY."

"DAD?"

"YEAH?"

"CAN I TAKE IT OFF FOR A WHILE? JUST... IT ***ITCHES."***

"NO, BUDDY. NO. I'M SORRY."

"BUT WHY?"

"BECAUSE IT'S NOT ***SAFE,*** THAT'S WHY."

I'M SORRY, MASON.

I'M SO, SO SORRY.

"MY ONE JOB IN THIS WORLD IS TO KEEP YOU SAFE."

...MALL SHOOTING...

...HEARD HE GOT HIT LIKE **SEVEN** TIMES...

GUYS, BEFORE WE GET STARTED I JUST WANNA SAY A WARM "WELCOME BACK" TO MASON HERE.

HE'S BEEN THROUGH A LOT THIS PAST COUPLE MONTHS, SO LET'S ALL LOOK OUT FOR HIM THIS SEMESTER, OKAY?

...UNCLE SAYS HIS DAD'S GONE **LOONEY TUNES...**

ARE YOU **SURE** YOU'RE UP TO THIS, MASON? THERE'S **NO SHAME** IN TAKING IT SLOW FOR A LITTLE BIT.

...HE THINK HE IS, IRON MAN?

I'M GOOD. **REALLY.** THANK YOU, MISTER O'SULLIVAN.

HEY, WHATEVER YOU NEED.

"OKAY GUYS, I DON'T WANNA HEAR SO MUCH AS A **HICCUP** FOR THE NEXT FORTY MINUTES, IS THAT CLEAR?

"USUAL RULE APPLIES: PENCILS AND PAPER **ONLY.** IF I SEE **ANYTHING** THAT SHOULDN'T BE HERE--PHONES, SMART WATCHES, **MAGIC EIGHT BALLS**--THEN IT'S **STRAIGHT** TO THE PRINCIPAL'S OFFICE.

"GOOD LUCK, GUYS. TURN OVER YOUR PAPERS, AND WHEN YOU'RE READY YOU CAN BEGIN."

TEST 7 - QUESTION 1
Page 1 of 4
Are you a member of a well regulated militia?
Yes
No
It's Complicated
QUESTION 2
QUESTION 2
The absence of political constraints upon the individual, such as the right to bear arms, roughly conforms to which definition of liberty proposed by social theorist Isaiah Berlin?
Negative liberty
Positive liberty
Paternalism
QUESTION 3
1.5 million people have lost their lives to gun violence on US soil since 1968.
In your view, is the right to bear arms compatible with Americans' unalienable right to Life, Liberty and the pursuit of Happiness?
Yes
No
Fake News
Are we in Hell?
Signs point to yes
Reply hazy. Try again later
My sources say no

"AND THEN WHAT HAPPENED?"

"I FINISHED THE TEST RIGHT BEFORE THE MAN SHOT HIMSELF.

"I HAD TO LEAVE THE LAST QUESTION THOUGH. IT WAS **HARD.**"

"NAH, YOU DID GREAT JUST KEEPING YOUR FOCUS WITH ALL THAT... EXCITEMENT GOING ON.

"HECK, I'M ***PROUD*** OF YOU."

THERE. NO REAL HARM DONE.

HOW DO YOU FEEL?

...

DAD, CAN I ASK YOU SOME-THING?

HIT ME.

MASON... THE REAL MASON, I MEAN...
WHAT ABOUT HIM?
AM I ANYTHING LIKE HIM?

MASON WAS...
NO. NO, YOU'RE NOT.
HOW AM I DIFFERENT?

End.

Scott & Heather

BUT STILL IT GETS IN. FLOATING ON AIR WAVES, MAKING OUR PHONES SHIVER AND SQUAWK.

WHAT'S WRONG? SOMETHING HAPPEN?

THE CALL

WRITTEN BY
SCOTT DAVID JOHNSON
PENCILS BY
PHIL HESTER
INKS BY
ERIC GAPSTUR
COLORS BY
MARK ENGLERT
LETTERING BY
BERNARDO BRICE

WHAT? LIKE ON THE CASINO FLOOR?

NO. THIS IS *BAD.*

I'VE WORKED ON THE STRIP FOR OVER TWO DECADES, AND SEEING IT BATHED IN CHAOS AND DEATH WAS HEARTBREAKING.
Breaking:
SHOOTING ON THE STRIP.
SAYS TWO ARE CONFIRMED DEAD. AT LEAST TWENTY INJURED.
AND NOW THERE'S REPORTS OF A SHOOTER AT NEW YORK-NEW YORK TOO.
WHAT THE HELL IS GOING ON OUT THERE?
OH, MY GOD, MY BOSS IS CALLING.
HELLO. YEAH, WERE WATCHING IT ON THE NEWS, RIGHT NOW.
YES. YES, I CAN. I'M--
OK. I'M ON MY WAY.
I GOT... I'VE GOT TO GO IN.
I DON'T WANT YOU TO.
OKAY.

SHE SAID THEY'RE CALLING IN EVERYONE THEY CAN.
OH MY GOD, IT'S THAT BAD?
I GUESS.

YOU WANT COFFEE?
I PROBABLY SHOULD, BUT I GOT TO HURRY.
I'LL FIGURE IT OUT.

IT'S OLD AND COLD, SORRY.
IT'LL BE FINE.
BUT WILL YOU? WILL YOU BE FINE? WE DON'T KNOW WHAT'S OUT THERE.

I KINDA DON'T WANNA GO.
I DON'T WANT YOU TO GO EITHER.
BUT I **HAVE** TO.
YEP, CAUSE YOU A BAD ASS NURSE.
HA. YES, I AM.
I JOKE. THAT'S WHAT I ALWAYS DO. DEFLECT THE REAL FEELINGS AND GO FOR THE LAUGH.

SERIOUSLY HEATHER, YOU WILL BE FINE. YOU DON'T HAVE TO GO ANYWHERE NEAR THERE TO GET TO THE HOSPITAL.
I KNOW.

I WANT TO TELL HER NOT TO LEAVE. THAT I NEED HER. LOVE HER, AND I CAN'T IMAGINE LIFE WITHOUT HER. BUT SHE KNOWS THAT, AND I KNOW THAT SHE HAS TO DO THIS. IT'S WHO SHE **IS**.

I'M TERRIFIED OF WHAT SHE WILL SEE.
I WISH I COULD PROTECT HER FROM THAT, BUT I KNOW I CAN'T.

I LOVE YOU.
I LOVE YOU TOO.
YOU'RE GOING TO BE GREAT--YOU BIG BAD ASS.

I DON'T CLOSE THE DOOR RIGHT AWAY.
I LIKE TO WAIT TO HEAR THE ENGINE OF THE CAR, MAKE SURE SHE IS SAFE. THAT NIGHT, I FEEL SHE IS ANYTHING BUT.

DADDY?
HEY, WHAT ARE YOU DOING UP?

WHERE'S MOMMY?
WELL, A LOT OF PEOPLE WERE HURT, AND SHE NEEDED TO GO TO THE HOSPITAL TO HELP THEM.
OH. OKAY. CAN I SLEEP IN YOUR BED?
OF COURSE.
I LOCK THE DOOR AND SET THE ALARM. TRY AND MAINTAIN THAT ILLUSION OF SAFE.

FROM MY STREET THE STRIP LOOKS PEACEFUL. YOU CAN'T TELL WHAT IS NORMAL RAZZLE DAZZLE AND WHAT IS EMERGENCY FLASHERS; IT'S ALL JUST AN AMBER HAZE.
I TRY TO IMAGINE HER DRIVING TOWARD THE CITY, HER TAILLIGHTS ADDING TO THE HAZE. ONE MORE LIGHT, ON THIS NIGHT OF DARKNESS.

In the ancient country of Orn, there lived an old man called the Bee-Man, whose whole time was spent in the company of bees.
He lived alone, traded in honey and had mostly been content.
But he learned, one day, from a Junior Sorcerer, that he'd been transformed by magic, and was not what he had originally been.
The Junior Sorcerer could not say what he'd been transformed *from...*
BZZT BZZT
...so the Bee-Man set out to wander the world and discover for himself his true form.*
This is a tale from his travels.
The BEE-MAN of ORN and the LIGHTNING LANDS
KURT BUSIEK writer
ANDREW MACLEAN artist
LEE LOUGHRIDGE color art
JOHN ROSHELL of COMICRAFT lettering
One day, after learning he had not been a bear, a dragon, or a cockatrice, he made his way up the western slopes of the Borious Hills...
...where he came upon a strange land.
BZZT BZZT
OH! OH!
WHAT *IS* THIS PLACE? ALL THIS LIGHTNING -- AND YET NO RAIN! WHAT COULD POSSIBLY --
*it's true! See "The Bee-Man of Orn" by Frank R. Stockton, originally published in 1887.

!

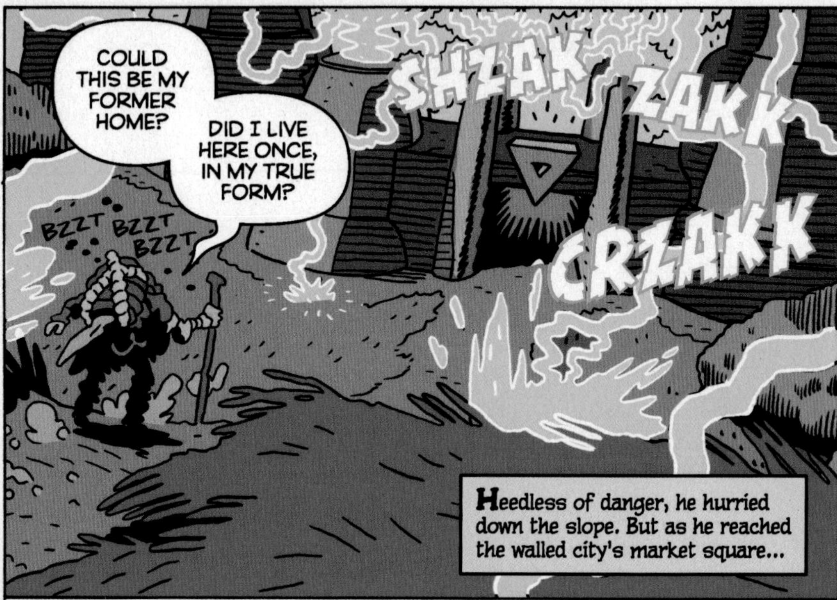
COULD THIS BE MY FORMER HOME?
DID I LIVE HERE ONCE, IN MY TRUE FORM?
BZZT BZZT BZZT
SHZAK ZAKK
CRZAKK
Heedless of danger, he hurried down the slope. But as he reached the walled city's market square...

SHRZAK
CZZ
ZAK
OH!
THEY'RE *KILLING* EACH OTHER! OH!

AH! I HOPE I WAS NOT ONE OF THESE...!

And when the battle was over...
BAM!

MA'AM! MADAM, HERE!
YOU STILL *BREATHE!* A MIRACLE!

BZZT
BZZT
BZZ
PLEASE --
GLORP!

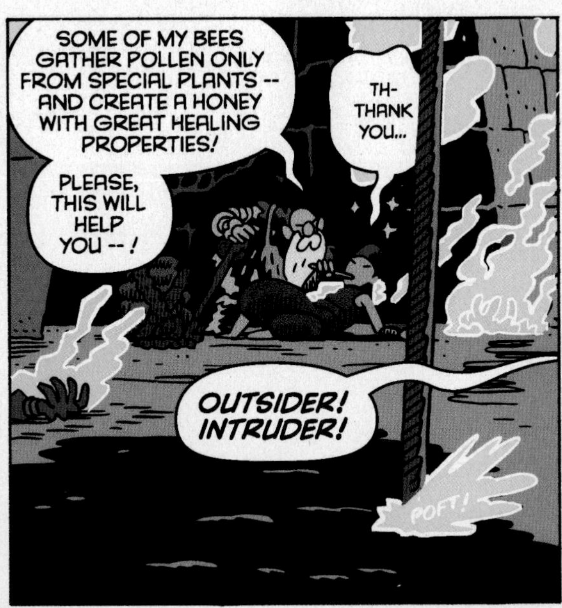
SOME OF MY BEES GATHER POLLEN ONLY FROM SPECIAL PLANTS -- AND CREATE A HONEY WITH GREAT HEALING PROPERTIES!
PLEASE, THIS WILL HELP YOU -- !
TH- THANK YOU...

TRY SOME OF THIS.

OUTSIDER! INTRUDER!
POFT!

WHAT ARE YOU DOING?
BY WHAT RIGHT DO YOU INTERFERE WITH THE GREAT LAND OF SHAKKARN?

Eh -- Ah -- I ONLY --

I WAS ONLY TRYING TO HELP HER.
THIS IS NOT HOW THINGS ARE DONE IN ORN.
I DO NOT UNDERSTAND.
HNEH! THAT'S 'CAUSE YOU'RE A FOOL OUTSIDER -- AN' YOU DON'T KNOW!

YOU DON'T KNOW ABOUT *SHAKKARN,* DO YA? DON'T KNOW A *THING!* BUT I'LL *TELL* YA...

"BACK WHEN SHAKKARN WERE NEW, THERE WAS MONSTERS -- GREAT, HUNGRIN' *WORMS!* THEY'D HA' DEVOURED ALL WHO SETTLED HERE!

"THEN THEM WIZARDS UP AND DECIDED THEY COULD DO AS THEY *PLEASED.* AND WHO'D *STOP* 'EM, THEM WITH THEIR MIGHTY SPELLS!

"THE LORDS DIN'T WANT TO *OUTLAW* THE WIZARDS -- NOT WHEN THEM MONSTERS MIGHT STILL BE *OUT THERE* --"

"AN' ALL SHAKKARNIANS *LEARNT,* FROM THE ELDEST TO THE SMALL. TO PROTECT THEIR LAND. AN' PROTECT *THEYSELVES!*

"-- WELL, THAT'S THE *PRICE,* INNIT? OF HAVIN' THE POWER T'*PROTECT!*"

BUT -- THE DEAD -- THE INJURED! HOW DO YOU ENDURE IT?

EHH...Y'GET USED T'IT!
Y'R TRIAL'S T'MORRER, RIGHT? YOU'LL SEE!
POP
SPAK

YOU STAND ACCUSED, FOREIGNER! OF VIOLATING OUR WAYS, BY COMING AMONG US WITHOUT SPELLS OF DEFENSE AND POWER!
I -- I --

ALL MUST MASTER THE LIGHTNING MAGICS, IF THEY SEEK TO REMAIN! WHAT SAY YOU, OUTLANDER?
I WOULDN'T WANT TO KNOW SUCH MAGICS!
THEY'RE MADNESS! THEY'RE --

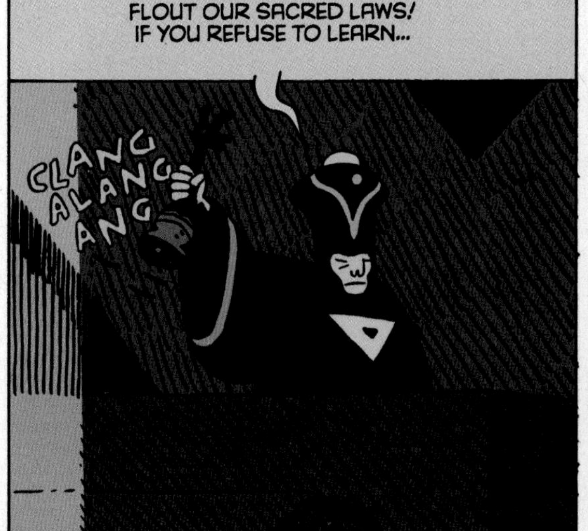
SILENCE! NONE MAY DEFY OUR TRADITIONS! NONE SHALL FLOUT OUR SACRED LAWS! IF YOU REFUSE TO LEARN...
CLANG ALANG ANG

...YOU ARE BANISHED FROM THESE LANDS! NOW, AND FOR ALL TIME!
WELL! THAT WAS VERY...
GO!
GO!
BZZT
BZZT

And so the Bee-Man left Shakkarn...
...and continued his journeys, seeking his true shape.
BZZT BZZT
He traveled far, and he saw many wonders.
And years later, he trudged along a half-familiar path...

WILL I FIND IT TODAY? MY FORMER HOME? THE ANSWER TO MY QUESTIONS?

Eh? WHAT IS THIS *RUIN*? THERE'S NAUGHT HERE BUT...
BUT...
BZZT BZZT BZZT

BZZT BZZT

NO...
NO, I COULD NOT HAVE BEEN FROM HERE...
BZZT

The animals and the thieves came to the village...
And they came hungry.
He had seen a blade on his journeys. He had watched one being made.
He was strong and of a keen mind and the fear of being weak and defenceless in the wilds made anger coil and writhe in his gut.
He would not be prey.
He would protect those he loved.
The blade was only for his family...
HUNGRY
ROB WILLIAMS JAVIER PULIDO
RRRRDNNAAAARR

The blade shook in his hand as it pierced the monster's chest.
It shook as he stabbed and gouged at the creature with a blind desperation. A wild unstructured panic that myths did not speak of.
He had pissed himself during the beast's assault.
But the bear tasted warm and good and the admiration of his people felt moreso.
He ate well. They all did. They had been hungry prior...
And the winter was coming...
The nearest village was well-stocked with food stores, he knew from his journeys.
He would provide for his village. For those who depended upon him and the blade.
For those who now looked to him for protection.
This was only done for his family.

AAAAAAHHH
They had come... They had heard of the blade. They had come to take it.
He would not allow that.
If they took it he would not be able to safeguard his people.
He would go back to being weak again...
He would be afraid again...

mals and
hieves came
he village...
And they came
hungry.
END
J.

Daniel

I HEARD A MEMORIAL HAPPENING OUTSIDE MY APARTMENT. SOMEONE READ EACH VICTIM'S NAME AND CHIMED A BELL.
ANDREA CASTILLA...
SANDY CASEY...

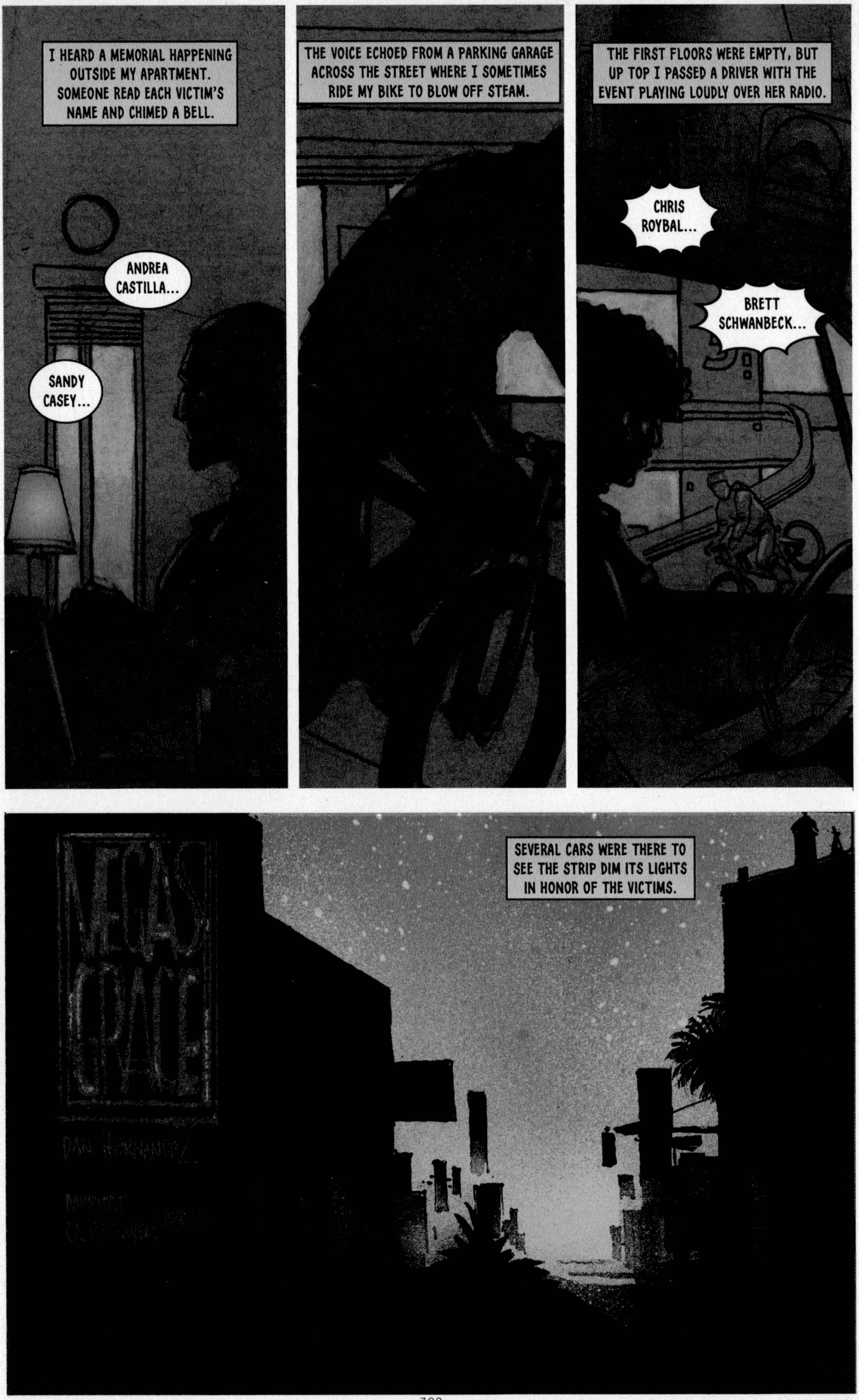

THE VOICE ECHOED FROM A PARKING GARAGE ACROSS THE STREET WHERE I SOMETIMES RIDE MY BIKE TO BLOW OFF STEAM.

THE FIRST FLOORS WERE EMPTY, BUT UP TOP I PASSED A DRIVER WITH THE EVENT PLAYING LOUDLY OVER HER RADIO.
CHRIS ROYBAL...
BRETT SCHWANBECK...

SEVERAL CARS WERE THERE TO SEE THE STRIP DIM ITS LIGHTS IN HONOR OF THE VICTIMS.

TRAGEDIES LIKE THIS ARE NOW A FACT OF AMERICAN LIFE.
WELCOME
TO FABULOUS
LAS VEGAS
NEVADA
I GREW UP IN COLORADO AND REMEMBER BEING IN CLASS WATCHING COVERAGE OF A SHOOTING IN NEARBY LITTLETON. WE HAD FRIENDS THERE, AT COLUMBINE HIGH SCHOOL.
DARK KNIGH
ON JULY 19, 2012, I WENT TO THE MOVIES IN AURORA WITH MY MOM. TEENS WERE LINED UP FOR THE PREMIERE OF THE DARK KNIGHT. I THOUGHT OF THEIR FACES THE NEXT DAY WHEN I HEARD 12 WERE KILLED AT A DIFFERENT THEATER IN TOWN.
A WRETCHED ACT OF VIOLENCE. A SUDDEN, SENSELESS LOSS. THESE ARE TERROR ATTACKS.
MESSAGES
ACTIVE SHOOTER ON THE STRIP!!
AND HAVING MET THE VICTIMS' FAMILIES MANY TIMES AS A JOURNALIST, I KNOW THEY NEVER GET OVER IT.

THEY DON'T WANT ANYONE ELSE TO EXPERIENCE THEIR LOSS. BUT HERE WE ARE AGAIN.

THAT NIGHT, POLICE LIGHTS OUTSHINED CASINOS ON THE STRIP, WHERE I HIT A ROADBLOCK.

I FOUND SURVIVORS AT A GAS STATION NEAR THE ROUTE 91 CONCERT GROUNDS. SOME HAD OTHER PEOPLE'S BLOOD ON THEM. THEY STOOD AROUND CALLING LOVED ONES.

I'M STILL SHAKING.
I WANT TO GO HOME.
IT WAS CHAOS.
THEIR TRAUMA WAS CONTAGIOUS. AS WE SPOKE, I FELT IT IN MY EYES AND THROAT.

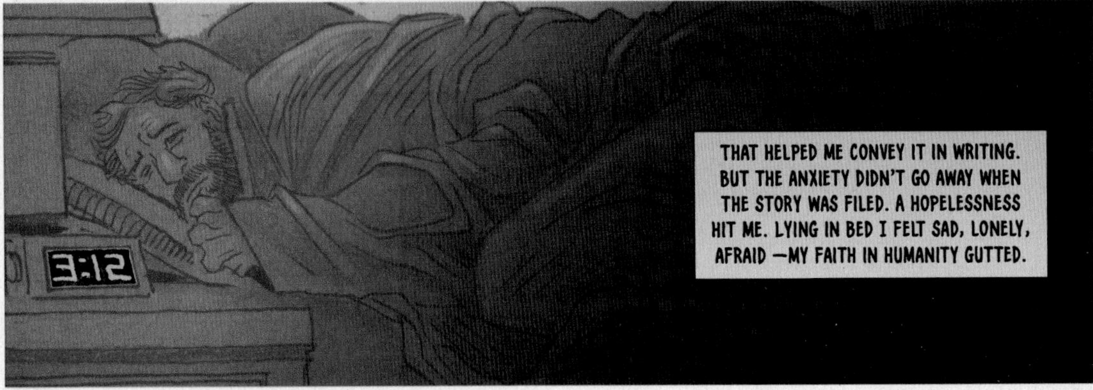
3:12
THAT HELPED ME CONVEY IT IN WRITING. BUT THE ANXIETY DIDN'T GO AWAY WHEN THE STORY WAS FILED. A HOPELESSNESS HIT ME. LYING IN BED I FELT SAD, LONELY, AFRAID —MY FAITH IN HUMANITY GUTTED.

BUT ON THE FOLLOWING MORNING, THE COMMUNITY COUNTERED THE SHOOTER'S EVIL. PEOPLE LINED UP TO GIVE BLOOD, DONATE PROVISIONS, AND OFFER RIDES FROM THE HOSPITAL. FLORISTS LAID FLOWERS, COUNSELORS WERE DEPLOYED THROUGHOUT THE CITY, AND MEMORIALS SPROUTED UP UNDER THE SLOGAN #VEGASSTRONG.

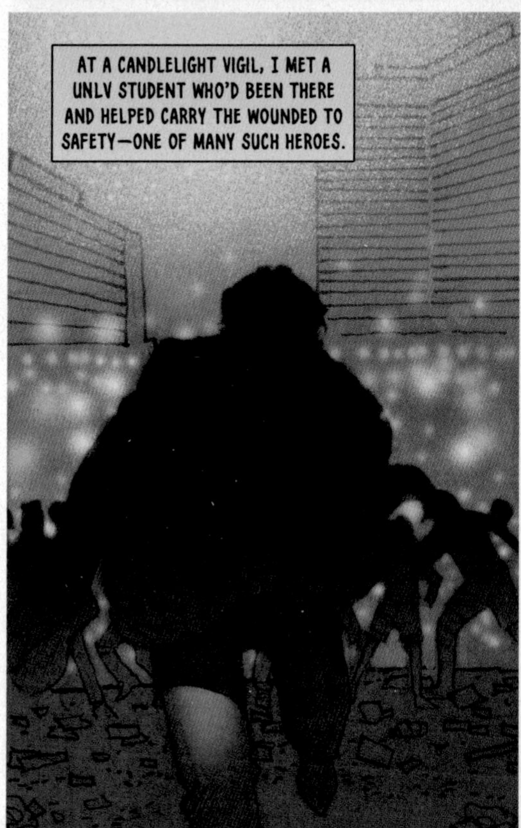

AT A CANDLELIGHT VIGIL, I MET A UNLV STUDENT WHO'D BEEN THERE AND HELPED CARRY THE WOUNDED TO SAFETY—ONE OF MANY SUCH HEROES.

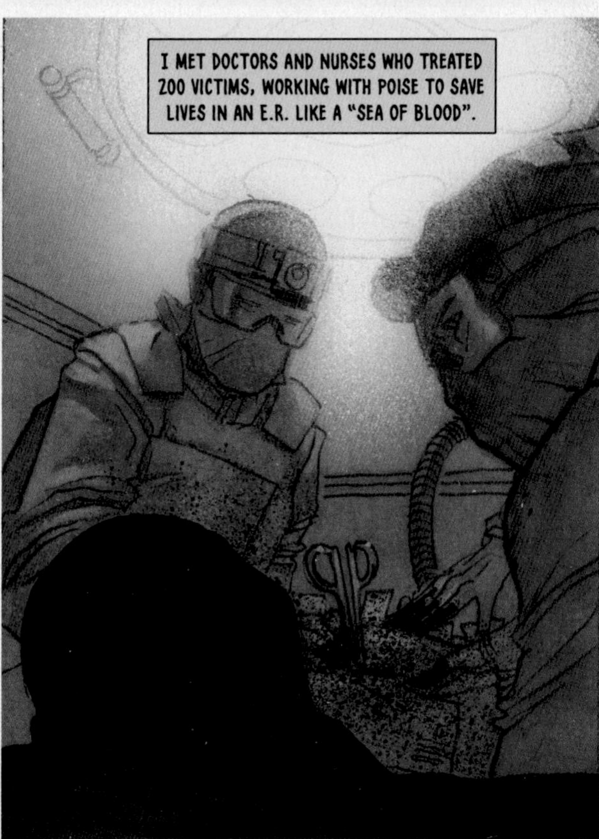

I MET DOCTORS AND NURSES WHO TREATED 200 VICTIMS, WORKING WITH POISE TO SAVE LIVES IN AN E.R. LIKE A "SEA OF BLOOD".

THE OPPOSITE OF VIOLENCE ISN'T PEACE, IT'S GRACE, AND THAT'S WHAT VEGAS SHOWED AS SOON AS THE TRAGEDY OCCURRED.

WE'RE GRATEFUL FOR THOSE WHO SURVIVED, AND THOSE WHO AVOIDED IT ALTOGETHER. BUT SIMPLY HOPING FOR CONTINUED SAFETY IS FOOLISH. IN THIS CLIMATE OF HATE, ISOLATION, AND FETISHIZED VIOLENCE, AT THE VERY LEAST OUR GOVERNMENT SHOULD LIMIT ACCESS TO WEAPONS LIKE THOSE USED BY THE MANDALAY BAY SHOOTER.

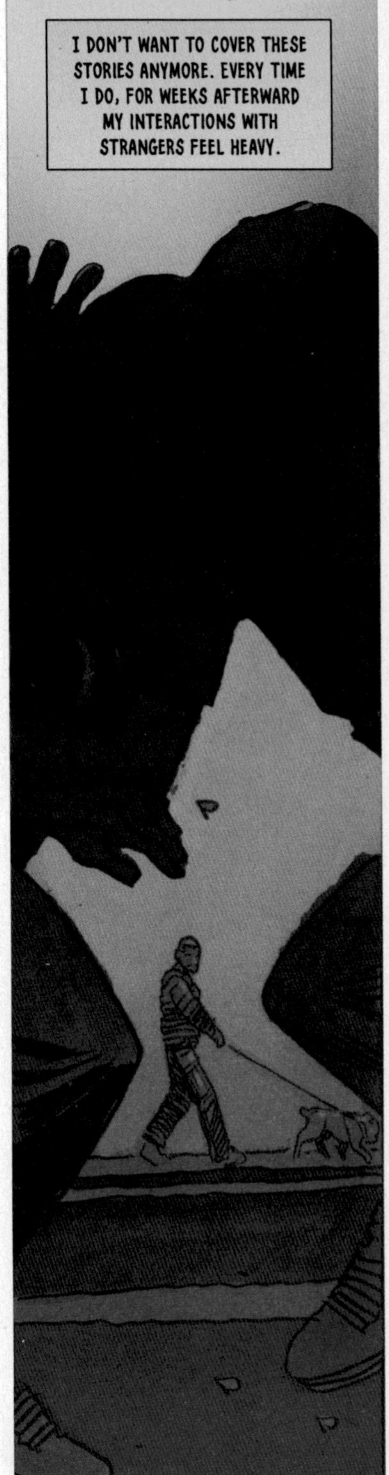

I DON'T WANT TO COVER THESE STORIES ANYMORE. EVERY TIME I DO, FOR WEEKS AFTERWARD MY INTERACTIONS WITH STRANGERS FEEL HEAVY.

HOW ARE YOU DOING?
YOU NEVER KNOW WHAT SOMEONE'S BEEN THROUGH...

YOU NEVER KNOW HOW MUCH TIME IS LEFT.

HALF A WORLD AWAY

I can't remember my dad's email address.

Just for a minute. Maybe two. A blip.

It's weird how we remember the big things--

WRITTEN BY LUCIA FASANO
ART BY TESS FOWLER
LETTERED BY BERNARDO BRICE

--the things we build our narratives around.

Big, basic facts that don't really say much.

I was raised Republican. I'm very Italian.

I'm from L.A.

My parents made cult horror films. Then my dad made Tombstone.

I moved to Portland.
My dad died when I was twenty-one.
What else? I was raised a witch.

I'm a feminist.
HEY, I WANTED YOUR FEMINIST OPINION ON ISIS.
YOU'VE SHOT GUNS? I THOUGHT YOU WERE A LIBERAL.
I AM!
DON'T YOU KNOW ME?

That isn't all there is to me, though.
I've told my story over and over.

I had a dad, now he's gone.
He was an artist, a filmmaker, and a gun enthusiast.
Fear of judgment makes me demure.

And the futility. How can I really explain?
The sound of him singing with me like Robert Goulet--
--Or nasaling like Michael Stipe?

Or that we shot guns. That he was a conservative, but progressive.
That he made me charitable.
Made me liberal.

Or how do I tell people how I got the call?
Me in Oregon, him in L.A., dying.
A word I couldn't say until now.

My best friend, a state away.
IT'S OKAY, DADDY, YOU JUST REST. WE'LL HAVE THE SCREENING WITHOUT YOU.
I LOVE YOU MORE THAN ANYTHING.
He felt half a world away.

HOLLYWOOD
ZOMBIE NIGHTMARE: A JOHN FASANO TRIBUTE
So I give the info I need.
And I move on with my life.

CDs F-H
What is his email?
And over time, things slip due to lack of use.
It comes back. Relief. Wince. Blip.

I go through my last emails with him. A few sweet ones, a few pointless. A few political.
WTF, REALLY?
Our last fight was over Hobby Lobby.
Y'know, the Supreme Court case about if a craft supply store should provide birth control to its employees.
YOU KNOW THE PILL ISN'T AN ABORTIVE. YOU KNOW THIS.
THERE'S A WAR ON WOMEN!
He called it what it wasn't, because Fox News did. This made no sense since my dad was pro-science, pro-birth control, pro-women.
He was defensive, felt out of control. The world was changing.
His daughter was changing.
Lucia Fasano
Romney's a freaking robot!
Binders full of women?? Seriously?
Yesterday at 10:00 pm.
Like · Comment · Share
72 people like this.
He supported the right to healthcare, but didn't think Obamacare was the right way.
Afraid of things becoming more dystopian.
It was the worried father in him.
It was the nerd in him. The secretly disabled person.
Not a woman hater or a bigot.
So why were we breaking our hearts over this?
THE THING IS THEY'RE JUST SAYING THIS STUFF TO GET ELECTED! IT'S NOT GOING TO HAPPEN!
IT'S ALREADY HAPPENING!
It felt so important, to change each other's minds. Like life or death.

When best friends grow apart, usually it's cause one moves away.

Or changes schools.
Or gets really into soccer.

But what about when it's your dad?
My dad's values were mine, which meant his politics, too.
WOOHOO!

Terrorists = violent = oppress women = bad, so war = stop terrorists = good?
Men = hurt women, women + guns = self defense.
Democrats = mainstream = racist = bad.
Bill Clinton = was in power = hurt women = bad.

My dad's interests were mine, whether it was old TV shows, monsters, musicals, comic books--

Or shooting.
I'LL NAME HER TWOEY!

And my interests were his. He was our number one advocate.
DO YOU HAVE ANY DRAGON BALL Z OR SAILOR MOON TOYS?
GUYS, GRAB THE POKÉMON CARDS.

HERE, GIVE MY CHRISTOPHER LEE DRACULA TO GERARD WAY AT THE SIGNING.
THANKS, DADDY.

YOU SING BETTER THAN REGINA SPEKTOR.

We always had each other's back.
He showed me the limitless beauty of the world--

--While preparing me for its dangers and darkness.

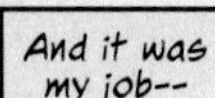
And it was my job--

--to carry and quell his fears.
IF YOU'RE EVER ABDUCTED, I WANT YOU TO SCRATCH THE BASTARD SO DEEPLY THAT WE CAN FIND THEIR DNA UNDER YOUR FINGERNAILS.

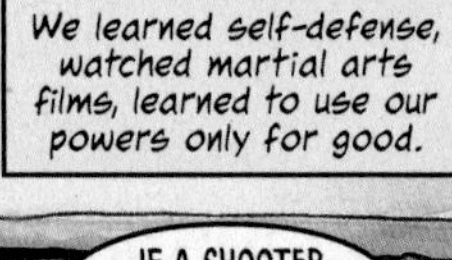
We learned self-defense, watched martial arts films, learned to use our powers only for good.

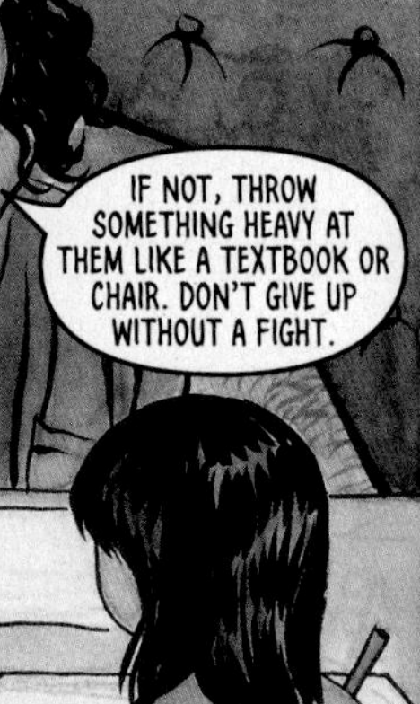
IF A SHOOTER COMES IN YOUR CLASSROOM, PLAY DEAD LIKE YOU'VE ALREADY BEEN SHOT.
IF NOT, THROW SOMETHING HEAVY AT THEM LIKE A TEXTBOOK OR CHAIR. DON'T GIVE UP WITHOUT A FIGHT.

JOHNNY! NEVER, EVER POINT A GUN AT ANOTHER PERSON. EVEN A TOY GUN. EVER!

A FOUR-YEAR-OLD TEXAS BOY WAS KILLED WHEN HIS BROTHER SHOT HIM IN THE HEAD WITH HIS DAD'S RIFLE, MISTAKING IT FOR A TOY.

He kept his guns locked up in his office. He worked from home, so he could spend as much time with us between writing, drawing, meetings, filming.

He hoped to break the cycle of his dad, a star football coach who showed his love by busting your chops.

I WORRY ABOUT YOUR BROTHER. HE GETS TOO WORKED UP ABOUT GIRLS.
So I went with him on most errands.

I TRIED TO SWERVE BUT HE RAN BACK AND I HIT HIM. ONE OF OUR LITTLE GUYS.

He taught me how to be a photographer.
He'd pull me out of class to take photos on our outings at gun ranges, celebrity shoots. A role he usually played.

He'd use them in his articles he'd write for gun magazines, in advertisements for different gun companies that his friends ran. I was a professional.
YOU HAVE SUCH AN EYE FOR COMPOSITION. LOOK HOW YOU GOT THAT SHELL IN MIDAIR.

I didn't shoot much, but when I did I felt like Annie Oakley, like Joan of Arc, like Artemis. I felt empowered. I felt badass. And I felt loved.

Diagram of a Liberal Boyfriend (circa 2010)
(Or as my dad called him, "My Little Commie")

Three years older than me.

Irreligious.

Can sing Leonard Cohen on the spot.

Always open to debate.

Soft.

Never has shot a gun.

Plays guitar.

Knows where a Planned Parenthood is.

I graduated high school, fell in love, started a band and moved in with my new boyfriend, Kyle. I went to L.A. City College, where issues of immigration, reproductive rights, tuition costs, and more were in my face. I joined Occupy LACC. My dad even bought me a Bitch Magazine subscription.

The world got scarier.
BREAKING NEWS
3 UC Santa Barbara Students shot
I HOPE TREVOR AND GIOVANNA ARE OKAY!
BREAKING NEWS
Shooting at Santa Monica City College
CAMI GOES THERE! ...I ALMOST DID.
BREAKING NEWS
Sandy Hook
WHO COULD HURT LITTLE KIDS AT SCHOOL?
WHAT IF THERE'S A SHOOTING RIGHT NOW?

My dad and I were horrified. And guns became something different to me.
THIS IS SO SICKENING. SOMEONE SHOULD'VE STOPPED IT.
To him they meant protection from violence. To me, the perpetuation.

I moved to Portland to attend Portland State. I organized a feminist music festival that my dad called my Lilith Fair.
WHAT BETTER WAY TO CELEBRATE FINALS THAN SHOOT SOME FRIENDS?
PSU PAINTBALL
Pictures I'd taken, people I'd met, movies I watched, video games, now made my stomach turn.
And each walk to campus felt like it could be my last.
THANKS FOR THE PEN.
Each dude I politely turned down, a risk.
IT'S TWOEY. SINCE I'M MOVING, I THOUGHT YOU'D WANT IT.
THANKS, DADDY.
I do feel safer with it.
I don't have any bullets.
HOW DID THEY FIND MY ADDRESS?
AMERICAN GUNMAN
REMINGTON R51
HILLARY WILL TAKE OUR GUNS
FIGHT ISIS AT HOME
I go it alone.
End.

IT IS WINTER 2002 IN YONKERS, NEW YORK.
WEEKS EARLIER, A CLOSE FRIEND OFFERED ME A JOB WORKING FOR VICTIMS ASSISTANCE OF WESTCHESTER, A NOT-FOR-PROFIT STATE-RUN AGENCY WITH AN OFFICE IN GETTY SQUARE, MORE COLORFULLY KNOWN AS "GHETTO SQUARE".
THAT PAST SEPTEMBER, I FINALLY GOT MY BIG BREAK IN AND WAS WORKING AS A FREELANCE WRITER FOR WILDSTORM COMICS. I VAINLY THOUGHT THE JOB WOULD PROVIDE VALUABLE EXPERIENCES TO INFORM MY FUTURE WRITING.
I GREW UP READING SUPERHERO COMICS, AND I PARTICULARLY LIKED STREET-LEVEL HEROES HELPING ORDINARY PEOPLE IN PRECISELY THE KIND OF PLACE THAT GETTY SQUARE IS. I HAD NO IDEA OF THE REALITY I WOULD FACE IN THE MONTHS AHEAD.
THE OFFICE WAS MADE UP OF A HANDFUL OF SMALL ROOMS IN DESPERATE NEED OF FRESH PAINT, WARMED BY MASSIVE RADIATORS OVER A COFFEE-STAINED CARPET.
AMY
WORDS & LETTERS: J.V. GRAY
ILLUSTRATIONS: JOHN BROGLIA

PARENTS, MOSTLY SINGLE MOTHERS, BROUGHT THEIR CHILDREN TO THE OFFICE, SO THERE WAS A PILE OF DIRTY PLASTIC TOYS AND FURNITURE PILED UP IN ONE CORNER OF THE WAITING AREA.
MY CO-WORKER WAS A BEARDED, LEFT-LEANING SOCIALIST IN HIS FIFTIES.
THE OTHER WAS A VERY OUTSPOKEN, AND DRIVEN WOMAN OF PUERTO RICAN DESCENT IN HER MID-THIRTIES. SHE WOULD FIGHT TOOTH AND NAIL AGAINST ANYONE AND EVERYONE FOR HER CLIENTS.
THE MAJORITY OF OUR CLIENTS WERE HISPANIC OR AFRICAN AMERICAN. MANY OF THEM DID NOT SPEAK ENGLISH.
AMONG THEM, WAS A YOUNG, MENTALLY CHALLENGED WOMAN, THE VICTIM OF MULTIPLE RAPES AND UNWANTED PREGNANCIES INFLICTED ON HER BY MULTIPLE PEOPLE IN HER ASSISTED LIVING COMMUNITY.
THERE WAS NO VIGILANTE TO COME SWOOPING DOWN FROM THE SHADOWS TO SAVE HER, NO DEVIL OF HELL'S KITCHEN TO SET THINGS RIGHT FOR THESE PEOPLE.
I WAS JUST FILING PAPERWORK ON THEIR BEHALF IN THE HOPE THEY'D GET SOME FINANCIAL COMPENSATION.

4 P.M. ON A MONDAY IN JANUARY 2002.
DAYS BEFORE HER SECOND BIRTHDAY, AMY SAT BETWEEN HER PARENTS CLUTCHING WINNIE THE POOH IN THE BEDROOM OF THEIR SECOND-FLOOR APARTMENT ON ELM STREET. THEY WERE A FAMILY OF IMMIGRANTS WHO ESCAPED EL SALVADOR LOOKING FOR A BETTER LIFE IN AMERICA.
MEANWHILE, A MAN IN A NEARBY BUILDING STUCK A HUNTING RIFLE OUT OF HIS WINDOW.
"TARGET PRACTICE" IS WHAT THE JURY WILL HEAR.
THE BULLET, WAS A POINTED, JACKETED TYPE DESIGNED TO PENETRATE BONE. IT WENT THROUGH A METAL HARDWARE SIGN AND RICOCHETED OFF THE INTENDED TARGET LEAVING A HOLE IN THEIR LIVES.
DURING MY FIRST WEEK ON THE JOB, THE GIRL'S PARENTS STOOD IN THAT UGLY YONKERS OFFICE LOBBY RADIATING A MIXTURE OF ANGUISH AND RAGE.
I'VE NEVER FELT THE EMOTIONAL RESONANCE THAT COMES FROM A FAMILY LOSING AN INFANT SO TRAGICALLY. IT BENDS YOUR SPINE AND INJURES YOUR SOUL AS A HUMAN BEING TO SEE SENSELESS, PREVENTABLE DISASTER.

AMY DIDN'T DIE IN A WAR-TORN FOREIGN COUNTRY. SHE DIED WATCHING A CARTOON SURROUNDED BY LOVE.
THEY BURIED THEIR CHILD, AND THE SHOOTER WENT TO JAIL. IT WAS JUST ANOTHER SENSELESS CRIME IN THE "GHETTO."
THERE WAS TALK IN THE OFFICE OF ORGANIZING AN EFFORT TO PUT FORTH NEW GUN LEGISLATION IN THE ANY'S NAME. TO MY KNOWLEDGE, IT DIDN'T HAPPEN, AND NOTHING CHANGED IN THE LARGER NARRATIVE OF GUN VIOLENCE.
I EVENTUALLY HAD TO WALK AWAY FROM THE JOB BECAUSE IT WAS IMPACTING MY MENTAL HEALTH. WALKING AWAY WAS A LUXURY. SO MANY PEOPLE THAT I HELPED AND THE PEOPLE IN THE COMMUNITY WERE TRAPPED THERE BY THEIR SOCIAL AND ECONOMIC PREDICAMENTS.
SIXTEEN YEARS LATER GETTY SQUARE IS STILL A PLACE OF VIOLENCE AND CRIME.

Bristlecone In Blue

by Jennifer Battisti
Art by J H Williams III

Ascending takes effort.
My hamstrings protest; dizzy spells,
a cold sharp ache coiling in my ears,
my mind like an open door—
all the flies let in, the bodies below, still
waiting on warm asphalt.

There seems no good reason to climb
mountains anymore.
We left our grieving city, the sound of
trauma still audible
beneath our heavy sips of air
switchback after switchback, then higher still
the silence first like a murder then solvent.

My heart blooms suddenly— the delinquency
of being alive.
We rest at Ponderosa, inhale
sun-baked butterscotch
from its bark, the sweetness, an infidelity.

The dead still stand here centuries later.
The canyon bursts open a boneyard of bristlecone
in blue, the sky so certain—
gnarled trunks support branches, poised
petrified lightening, limbs
held up in terror
and surrender.

Wind-carved fissures filled with
termite families burrow and devour
history, because the earth won't
waste one single thread.
Quiet is a tender animal at our feet,
a helix of sorrow and prayer held
in the den of its mouth.

There is nothing here to discover;
when we reach Raintree,
the oldest living thing in Nevada,
we are finally far enough away to
be seduced by hope.
The 3,000 year old tree is neither
boastful nor glum.

Beneath a heap of roots, thick as thighs, it forges
soil, tangled by time into braided bark.
It forks turbulent winds through waxy needles,
It asks us to unbutton our souls—

Carnage is compost here,
a harvest for those breathless and bruised.
at 10,000 feet, the air is too thin
to remember how we swore we couldn't go on.

Rachel & Bob

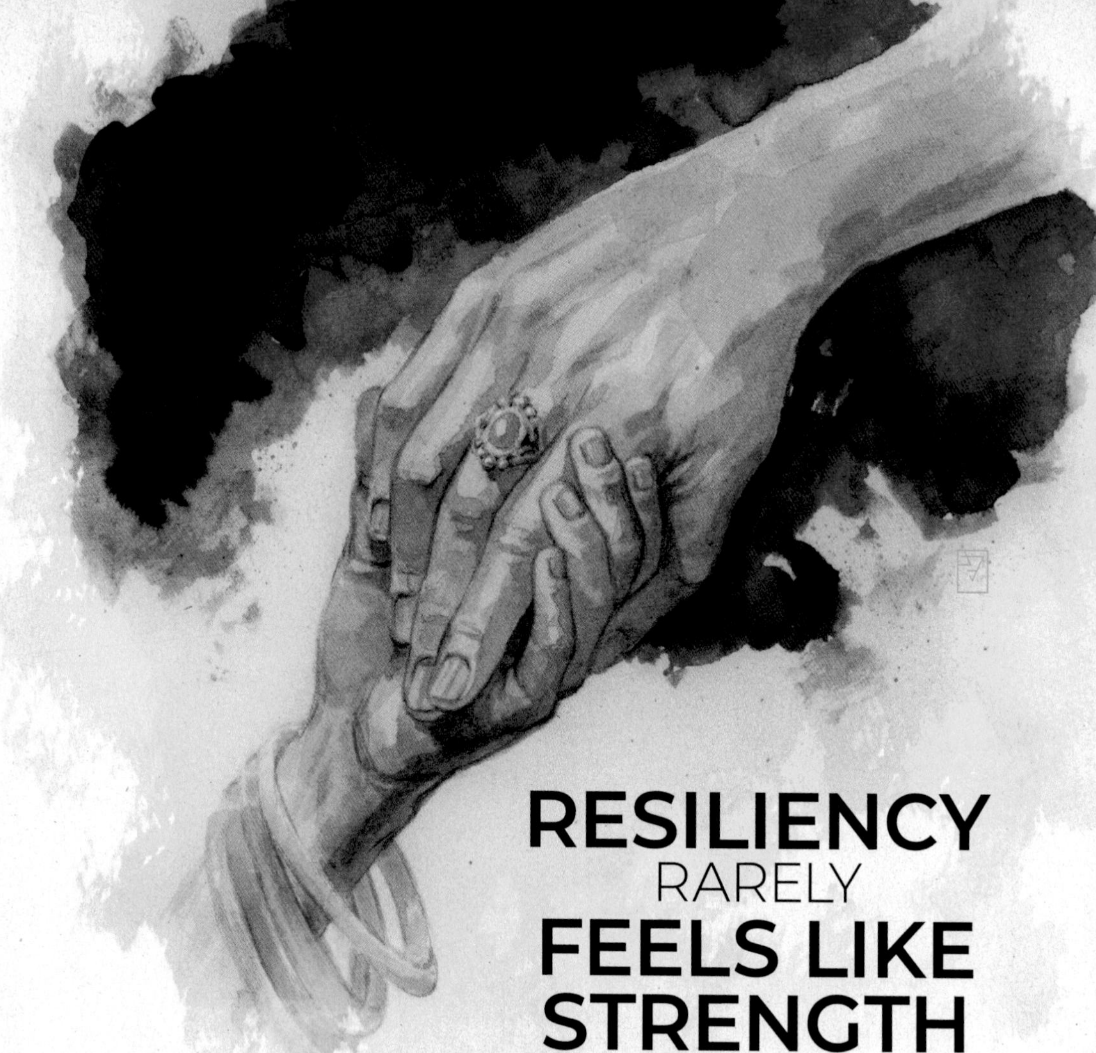

RESILIENCY RARELY FEELS LIKE STRENGTH

Essay by Las Vegas journalist **Rachel Crosby**
Illustration by **J.H. Williams, III** Lettering by **Bernardo Brice**

I WAS GETTING READY FOR BED when I got the text from my editor. Possible active shooter. Mandalay Bay.

No one wants to believe something like that, so I didn't. But I quickly changed my clothes, just in case.

My boyfriend got on Twitter.

"Rachel, this looks real," he said.

Videos were already circulating on social media, but I didn't watch. I heard them though. Gunfire. Screaming.

I took some deep breaths, got in my car and headed to the closest trauma center, a few miles from my apartment.

There, I waited for answers.

***

BOB WAS AT HOME in California. He had been texting his wife, Lisa, earlier that night. She was at the Route 91 Harvest Festival with friends, across the street from Mandalay Bay.

When Bob heard about the possible shooting, he tried to call and text her.

He waited for a response. But he never got one.

IT WOULD TAKE HOURS for officials to confirm the tragedy, so at the hospital, I used my eyes and ears instead.

People paced in the parking lot, screaming into cellphones.

Men and women in scrubs filed into staff entrances. Then more. And more.

A few nurses stepped out back for a smoke, the color drained from their faces.

Before the somber press conferences started, I got another text. This time, from a police source. More than 20 people were dead, he said.

I read the words. Then I read them again. I knew they were true but hoped they were wrong. My body begged me to throw up.

Trembling, I called my editor. Over the next few hours, "more than 20" climbed to "more than 50."

I reported through the night. Just before the sun rose, Las Vegas police allowed me to use the restroom. Inside a small, tan stall, I finally got the chance to cry.

***

AFTER HOURS OF WAITING in the dark, Bob woke his teenage son and drove to Las Vegas.

He imagined Lisa in a hospital somewhere, unable to use her phone but very much alive.

He didn't have to tell his son or his oldest daughter, who had driven to Las Vegas from college in Arizona to meet him. When he emerged from the room where he heard the news, they looked at his face and knew.

Together, they collapsed and cried. They were surrounded by so many other families, waiting for the same word.

***

IN THE FIRST FEW DAYS after the shooting, I didn't sleep much. I didn't eat at all. I had no desire to do anything but work. It was the only thing that felt normal.

That's when I got an email from Bob. He had spent the first few days after the shooting drowning in overwhelming grief. Still, he cared for his three children and managed to organize Lisa's arrangements. Her service was wonderful, he would later say. Thousands came.

We met in person at one of the Las Vegas memorials. He brought Brooke, his youngest child.

I mostly watched as they lingered near a white cross marked with the name "Lisa Patterson." I didn't want to interrupt.

I also didn't want to confront the reality in front of me — the one Bob and Brooke were now living in. I turned away a few times to collect myself. I wanted to say so many things, but I couldn't find the right words. So I took notes in near-silence.

The next day, we met at a park, where Brooke played as Bob talked. He opened up about his last conversation with Lisa, the race for information, the moment he found out. But he also opened up about *Lisa* — when they met, when they got married, when they decided to have children. All the years they spent together, suddenly cut short. When we parted ways, I felt like I knew her. I never did. But now I was grieving her, too.

***

A FEW WEEKS LATER, I visited Bob's home in California. There, I met with his two older children. We talked about Lisa, too. She had a presence that filled up a room. She loved to laugh. She always knew what to say.

What would she say now?

That night, Bob invited me to Brooke's school play.

In the audience, I sat alone until Bob waved me over. Then I sat with his family as the lights darkened and a woman announced over a microphone that the show had been dedicated to Lisa, who over the years had devoted many of her parenting hours to planning and producing similar shows.

When Brooke took the stage, she delivered her lines with such personality. It was a sight to see.

After the show, she realized I had come and gave me a huge hug, her family standing close by.

What do you do in that moment? What do you say?

How did I get here?

I told her she did a wonderful job as I hugged her back. Then I sat in my rental car in the theater parking lot and cried.

***

WEEKS PASSED, as did the holidays, when Bob reached out to me again. He said his family would be visiting Las Vegas soon. This time to spread some of Lisa's ashes at a small memorial garden the city had created the week of the shooting.

I had to work, but I rushed over to the garden as soon as I could.

When I arrived, the small ceremony had already started. I stood a few feet back, watching as the children collected a scoop of gray ash and sprinkled it at the foot of the tree marked with Lisa's name. Robert, the couple's son, kissed the tree's trunk.

Then little Brooke guided more and more people up to the tree, and without words, held out the small container with Lisa's ashes, suggesting they grab a scoop and sprinkle some, too.

As I watched, I thought about how thankful I was to ever meet Bob and his family, but how cruel that it happened in the wake of tragedy.

I turned around and commanded myself to keep it together. That's when Brooke walked up to me. Everyone was watching.

Embarrassed, I knelt down, wiped away my tears and gave her a hug. She simply smiled. I looked up at her in awe.

What a strong child, I thought.

Then she grabbed my hand and guided me to the tree, too.

REMEMBER

J.M. DeMatteis, writer **Mike Cavallaro**, artist/letterer

HOW COULD A BOY THAT AGE RESIST THE TALE OF JIM BOWIE AND DAVY CROCKETT LEADING A DESPERATE, DOOMED BID FOR FREEDOM--
REMEMBER THE ALAMO!
--BATTLING TO THE DEATH AGAINST AN ARMY OF FEARSOME BAD GUYS?
WELL, THEY TOLD US THEY WERE BAD GUYS--SO WE HAD TO BELIEVE THEM, RIGHT? OUR VIEW OF HISTORY...OF THE WORLD...WAS A LITTLE SIMPLER THEN.
AND A HELLUVA LOT MORE NAIVE.

BUT WE ATE IT UP--AND OUR PARENTS BOUGHT THE TOYS WE NEEDED TO LIVE OUT OUR WESTERN FANTASIES.
THAT PISTOL IN MY HANDS WAS MADE BY MATTEL. IT WAS CALLED A FANNER 50.
CAME COMPLETE WITH PLASTIC BULLETS AND FAUX PEARL HANDLE--AND IT MADE ME FEEL LIKE ROY ROGERS, THE LONE RANGER AND WILD BILL HICKOK ALL ROLLED INTO ONE.

BUT IT WASN'T JUST WESTERNS WE WERE OBSESSED WITH.
HERE I AM READY FOR WAR, WITH MY LIEUTENANT'S HELMET AND MY DAISY AIR RIFLE. YOU'D GIVE IT A CRANK AND THEN IT WOULD MAKE THIS EAR-POPPING RICOCHET SOUND.
I ADORED THOSE GUNS.
T-KOWW
NOW THERE'S A STATEMENT THAT I FIND TRULY DISTURBING. "I ADORED THOSE GUNS."

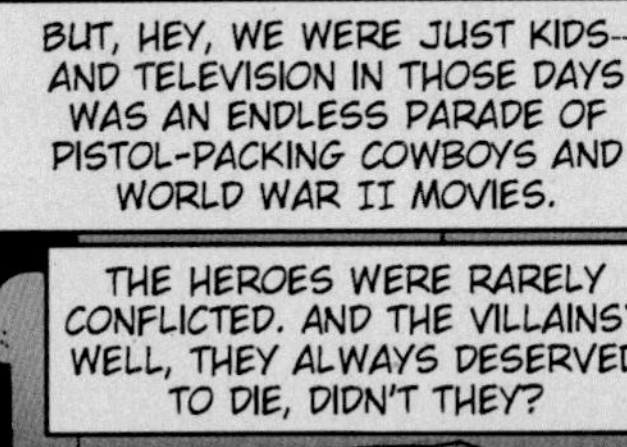
BUT, HEY, WE WERE JUST KIDS--AND TELEVISION IN THOSE DAYS WAS AN ENDLESS PARADE OF PISTOL-PACKING COWBOYS AND WORLD WAR II MOVIES.

THE HEROES WERE RARELY CONFLICTED. AND THE VILLAINS? WELL, THEY ALWAYS DESERVED TO DIE, DIDN'T THEY?
OF COURSE THERE WAS NEVER ANY BLOOD, EXCEPT PERHAPS A LITTLE SMEAR OF RED FOOD COLORING.

CHEYENNE BRODIE OR BRONCO LANE WOULD GET OFF A PERFECT SHOT, AN OUTLAW CLUTCHED HIS SIDE, FELL OVER--
--AND THAT WAS PRETTY MUCH IT. DEATH WAS NEAT AND CLEAN.
AND CHANCES ARE YOU'D SEE THE SAME ACTOR ALIVE AND WELL ON ANOTHER SHOW THE FOLLOWING WEEK. SO NO WORRIES, RIGHT?

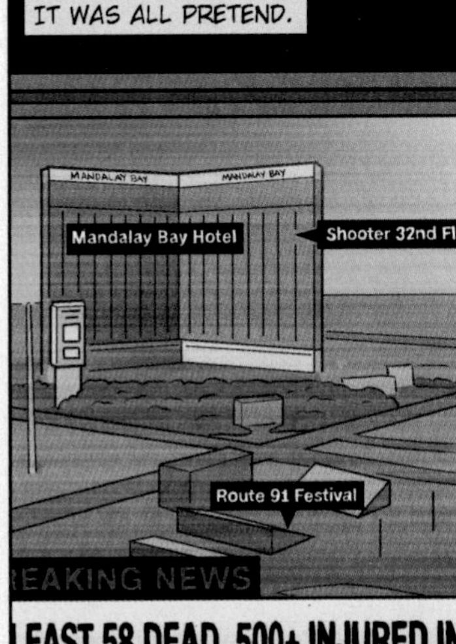
IT WAS ALL PRETEND.
MANDALAY BAY
Mandalay Bay Hotel
Shooter 32nd Fl
Route 91 Festival
REAKING NEWS
LEAST 58 DEAD, 500+ INJURED IN
LAS VEGAS LAW ENFORCEMENT OFFICIALS SA

THEN, IN THE FIFTH GRADE, PRESIDENT KENNEDY WAS ASSASSINATED. A CRAZY PERSON CROUCHING BY A WINDOW, CRADLING A RIFLE IN HIS ARMS, FIRED OFF THREE SHOTS--
CBS NEWS CBS NEWS CBS NEWS CBS NEWS CBS NEWS CBS NEWS CBS NEWS CBS NEWS
BULLETIN
--AND THE WHOLE DAMN WORLD EXPLODED.

A COUPLE OF DAYS LATER, JACK RUBY MURDERED LEE HARVEY OSWALD. ON LIVE TELEVISION. I MISSED IT, BUT MY BEST FRIEND BOBBY WAS WATCHING TV AS IT HAPPENED--
--AND I REMEMBER A GROUP OF US STANDING AROUND HIM, ABSOLUTELY MESMERIZED, AS HE TOLD US WHAT HE SAW.

AND THEN WE ALL WENT RIGHT BACK TO SHOOTING ***EACH OTHER.***

BUT SOMETHING FUNDAMENTAL HAD CHANGED. WE UNDERSTOOD (ALTHOUGH WE COULDN'T ARTICULATE IT OR EVEN ADMIT IT TO OURSELVES) WHAT A WEAPON COULD REALLY DO. I MEAN, LET'S FACE IT--
Tonight's Guest Star: John F. Kennedy as "Jack"
--NOBODY GLUED JFK'S HEAD BACK TOGETHER. HE WASN'T ON TELEVISION AGAIN THE FOLLOWING WEEK GUEST-STARRING ON AN EPISODE OF "LYNDON JOHNSON PRESENTS."

PRETTY SOON WE WERE WATCHING THE BIGGEST SHOW OF THE 60s--THE VIETNAM WAR--PLAY OUT ON OUR TVs EVERY NIGHT. AND IT WAS NOTHING LIKE THE BIG SCREEN FAIRY TALES JOHN WAYNE AND COMPANY FED US.
IT WAS UGLY AND BRUTAL. AND SAD.

NOT SURPRISING THAT A LOT OF THOSE MINIATURE COWBOYS AND SOLDIERS GREW UP TO BE VEHEMENTLY ANTI-WAR. ANTI-VIOLENCE.
"ALL WE ARE SAYING IS GIVE PEACE A CHANCE," RIGHT? "ALL YOU NEED IS LOVE."
NAIVE? SIMPLISTIC? ABSOLUTELY. BUT I STILL BELIEVE IT. I THINK JOHN LENNON DID, TOO--
END THE WAR NOW!
BRING THE TROOPS HOME
STOP THE WAR
Bring OUR BOYS HOME ALIVE!

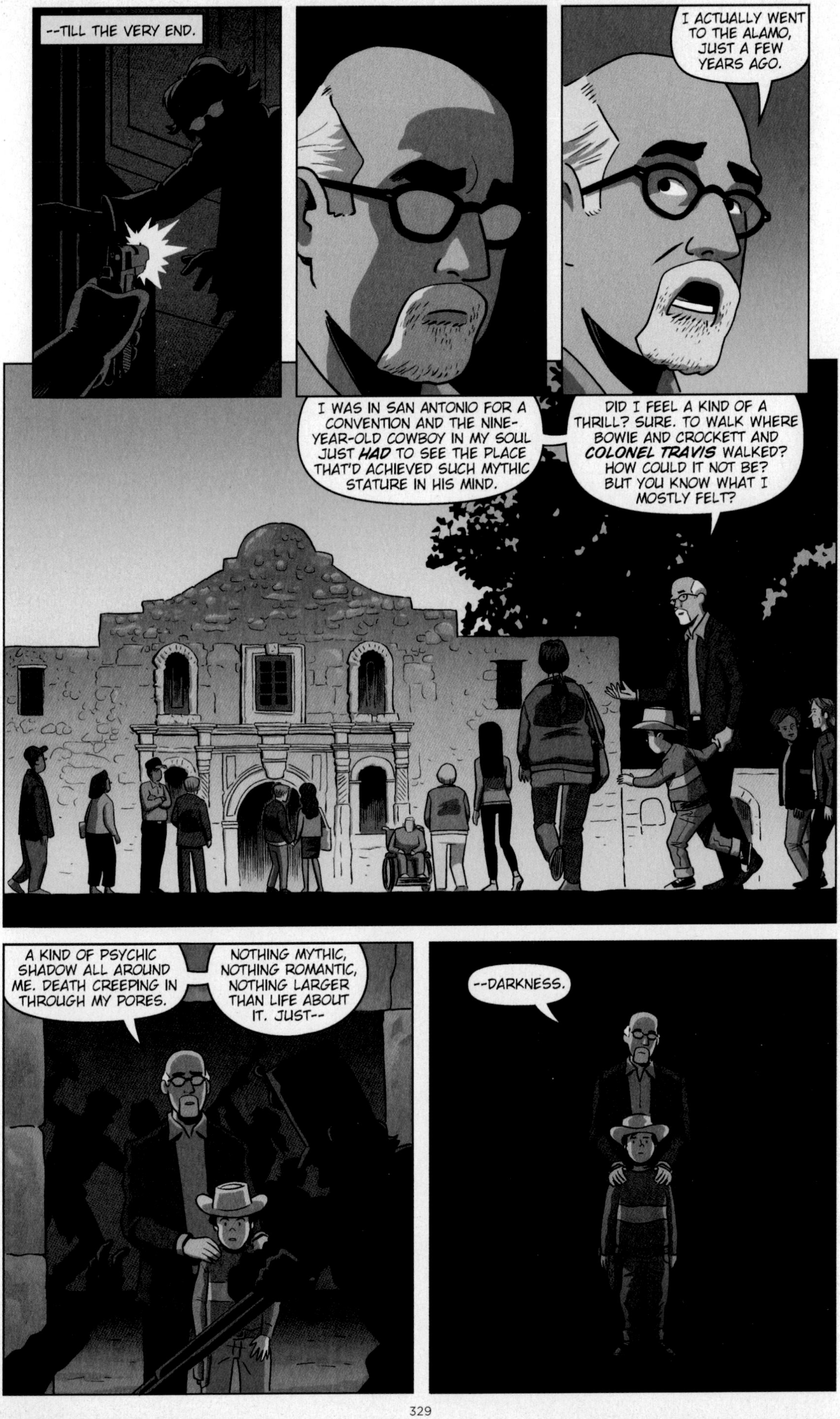

--TILL THE VERY END.

I ACTUALLY WENT TO THE ALAMO, JUST A FEW YEARS AGO.

I WAS IN SAN ANTONIO FOR A CONVENTION AND THE NINE-YEAR-OLD COWBOY IN MY SOUL JUST **HAD** TO SEE THE PLACE THAT'D ACHIEVED SUCH MYTHIC STATURE IN HIS MIND.

DID I FEEL A KIND OF A THRILL? SURE. TO WALK WHERE BOWIE AND CROCKETT AND **COLONEL TRAVIS** WALKED? HOW COULD IT NOT BE? BUT YOU KNOW WHAT I MOSTLY FELT?

A KIND OF PSYCHIC SHADOW ALL AROUND ME. DEATH CREEPING IN THROUGH MY PORES.
NOTHING MYTHIC, NOTHING ROMANTIC, NOTHING LARGER THAN LIFE ABOUT IT. JUST--

LOOK, I STILL LOVE A GOOD WESTERN AS MUCH AS ANYBODY. PROBABLY MORE.

BUT WHEN IT COMES TO GUNS--WE'RE NOT KIDS ANYMORE. WE KNOW BETTER.
AT LEAST WE SHOULD.
SO WHY, AFTER TWENTY CHILDREN AND SIX TEACHERS DIED IN NEWTOWN...AFTER FIFTY WERE CUT DOWN IN ORLANDO...AFTER FIFTY-EIGHT WERE SLAUGHTERED IN LAS VEGAS...AND THEN, A FEW MONTHS LATER, SEVENTEEN MORE DIED IN PARKLAND--

WHY, AFTER THIS STOMACH-TURNING PARADE OF HORRORS, DO SO MANY OF OUR ELECTED REPRESENTATIVES CONTINUE TO DO NOTHING?
MOST AMERICANS, INCLUDING THE MAJORITY OF GUN OWNERS, WANT STRICTER GUN-CONTROL LAWS--SO WHY DO THEY KEEP IGNORING THE WILL OF THE PEOPLE WHO ELECTED THEM?

THESE BASTARDS TAKE BOATLOADS OF MONEY FROM THE NRA--
--AND THEN OFFER UP "THOUGHTS AND PRAYERS" EVERY TIME THERE'S ANOTHER ONE OF THESE TRAGEDIES! THEY--

...I...
I'M SORRY. I'M NOT HERE TO DEMONIZE ANYONE. THAT'S NOT GOING TO HELP CHANGE THINGS.
AND I'M ALL *FOR* PRAYER. I BELIEVE, TO THE CORE OF MY BEING, THAT IT HAS POWER TO TRANSFORM THE HUMAN HEART AND SHAKE THE WORLD.

BUT THAT'S ONLY HALF THE EQUATION.
PRAYER ALONE ISN'T ENOUGH. GOD ACTS ***THROUGH*** US.

THOSE PEOPLE WHO DIED IN VEGAS WEREN'T ACTORS. THE MADMAN WHO MURDERED THEM WASN'T SHOOTING PLASTIC BULLETS.
THAT WAS NO FANNER 50...NO DAISY AIR RIFLE...IN HIS HANDS.

"REMEMBER THE ALAMO"? NO.
REMEMBER ***NEWTOWN***. REMEMBER ***VIRGINIA TECH***. REMEMBER ***ORLANDO***. REMEMBER ***PARKLAND***.
ANDALAY BAY

REMEMBER LAS VEGAS.

AFTERWORD
by Will Dennis

It's strange to work on a project that you wish was irrelevant.

Great storytelling isn't always topical (often quite the opposite) but as a creator, there should always be a goal of relevance; expressing some underlying truth that your audience can relate to — a connection that's made with them, for them or by them. You have to believe that you have something to say that's worth hearing.

And after the terrible events in Las Vegas on October 1st, 2017, a pair of creators living in that very city felt compelled to say something that they wish they didn't have to say. JH Williams III and his wife Wendy decided that something needed to be done — not only to help the survivors of this horrible massacre financially, but also to spark a conversation about guns in America. So they set out to curate a collection of stories that might help make sense of this epidemic of shootings that seems to be infecting our nation.

In order to make that idea a reality, they put out the call that they wanted stories that would not only convey the immediacy of the actual event from eye-witness survivors and Las Vegas locals, but include stories about gun control, domestic violence, gun legislation, political polarization, mental illness and the myriad other factors that revolve around these incidents.

And the call was answered by an incredible range of writers, artists, journalists, witnesses, locals, colorists, letterers, editors and so many more. Comics are an intensely collaborative medium and this book would have been impossible if not for the dozens of amazing people whose first response when they were contacted was "What can I do to help?" And for that I want to say a huge 'thank you' to each and everyone of them.

While all of the contributors are worthy of effusive thanks, there's a few that need special shoutouts:

Of course, to J. H. Williams III and Wendy Wright-Williams for having the vision to create this project and the willingness to put your own career to the side for these many months in pursuit of this lofty goal.

To Eric Stephenson and his fantastic crew at Image Comics — you really stepped up by agreeing to publish this book. As a company, you've made a huge difference in the lives of so many creators and fans and we can't thank you enough.

To letterer extraordinaire Bernardo Brice (one of the first contributors who volunteered to help) your unprompted offer to letter over ONE HUNDRED pages for free brought tears to my eyes. You ended up doing way more than that and if I can ever repay you with actual paying work someday, I promise I will.

Finally, to Michael Perlman... you offered to "help run the database" and ended up giving countless hours of your life over to seeing this book to completion. You were always there — early mornings, late nights, weekends, holidays and more — with a speedy reply, a handy spreadsheet, technical assistance and unwavering moral support. You got a crash course in comic book editing and came through every time. Thank you.

And while I'm very proud of the hard work that we all did on this book, I profoundly wish we didn't have to make it, and you didn't have to read it. But I'm glad you did, and for that, dear reader, I am forever grateful.

Peace,

WILL DENNIS
Editor

WHERE YOU LIVE

Contributors

Albuquerque, Rafael – Porto Alegre, Rio Grande do Sul, Brazil

Allred, Laura – Earth

Allred, Michael – Earth

Azaceta, Paul – West New York, NJ

Barajas, Henry – Los Angeles, CA

Battisti, Jennifer – Las Vegas, NV

Bendis, Brian – Portland, OR

Bennett, Deron – Keyport, NJ

Bidikar, Aditya – Pune, Maharashtra, India

Blackman, W. Haden – Seal Beach, CA

Boison, Jeff – Rockville Centre, NY

Boss, Tyler – Brooklyn, NY

Bowland, Simon – Macclesfield, Cheshire, England

Brandon, Ivan – Brooklyn, NY

Brice, Bernardo – Santiago, Chile

Broglia, John – Long Island, NY

Brusco, Giulia – London, England

Burton, Ryan – Houston, TX

Busiek, Kurt – Portland, OR

Campbell, Aaron – Albuquerque, NM

Cavallaro, Mike – Raritan, NJ

Cermak, Craig – Chicago, IL

Chiang, Cliff – Brooklyn, NY

Chiang, Janice – Woodstock, NY

Chu, Amy – Princeton, NJ

Cipriano, Sal – Brooklyn, NY

Cox, Jeromy – Portland, OR

Crank, Christopher – Cincinnati, OH

Crosby, Rachel – Las Vegas, NV

Cunniffe, Dee – Athboy, County Meath, Ireland

Dalhouse, Andrew – Houston, TX

Daniel, Nelson – Chile

Darrow, Geof – somewhere on Earth

Davison, Al – Coventry, West Midlands, England

DeConnick, Kelly Sue – Portland, OR

DeMatteis, J. M. – Hudson Valley, NY

Dennis, Will – Brooklyn, NY

DiMotta, Michael J. – Portland, OR

Duarte, Gustavo – Sao Paulo, Brazil

Duran, Aaron – Portland, OR

Dysart, Joshua – Los Angeles, CA

Elliott, Pierce – Las Vegas, NV

Ellis, Joshua – Las Vegas, NV

Englert, Mark – Palmdale, CA

Esposito, Taylor – Kearny, NJ

Farrell, Triona – Dublin, Ireland

Fasano, Lucia – Los Angeles, CA

Fawkes, Ray – Toronto, Ontario, Canada

Fialkov, Joshua Hale – North Hollywood, CA

Finnegan, Marco – Temecula, CA

Fish, Tim – Boston, MA

Fitzpatrick, Kelly – Portland, OR

Fowler, Tess – Los Angeles, CA

Fowler, Tom – Ottawa, Ontario, Canada

Fulton, Rachael – London, England

Gaiman, Neil – Woodstock, NY

Gallagher, Monica – Baltimore, MD

Gapstur, Eric – Coralville, IA

Gaydos, Michael – NY

Gillen, Kieron – London, England

Goodhart, Isaac – Jackson Heights, NY

Grace, Sina – Los Angeles, CA

Graham, Brandon – Portland, OR

Gray, Justin – Ossining, NY

Gaudiano, Stefano – Issaquah, WA

Gwenn, Lela – DE

Haberlin, Brian – Laguna Niguel, CA

Harris, Jason – Las Vegas, NV

Hawkins, Matt – Los Angeles, CA

Height, Ray-Anthony – Compton, CA

Hernandez, Daniel – Las Vegas, NV

Hershewe, Talia – Reno, NV

Hester, Phil – North English, IA

Hine, David – London, England

Illidge, Joe – Brooklyn, NY

Jensen, Van – Atlanta, GA

Jock – Totnes, Devon, UK

Johnson, Scott David – Las Vegas, NV

Jones, Joëlle – Los Angeles, CA

Jordan, Justin – Six Mile Run, PA

Kangas, Liana – Highland Park, NJ

Keene, Jarret – Las Vegas, NV

Kelly, Ryan – St. Paul, MN
Kim, Eric – Toronto, Ontario, Canada
Kleid, Neil – Teaneck, NJ
Klein, Todd – Cape May Court House, NJ
Kotz, Dean – Brooklyn, NY
Kristantina, Ariela – Jakarta, Indonesia
Lieb, R. Eric – CA
Lemire, Jeff – Toronto, Ontario, Canada
Lesniewski, Matt – Ballston Spa, NY
Lockard, Greg – Granada, Andalucia, Spain
Loughridge, Lee – Newport Beach, CA
Louise, Marissa – Vernonia, OR
MacLean, Andrew – Beverly, MA
Masters, Ollie – Hove, East Sussex, England
McCourt, Mariah – Los Angeles, CA
McKelvie, Jamie – Edinburgh, Scotland
Mignola, Mike – Los Angeles, CA
Millar, Mark – from Scotland
Millidge, Gary Spencer – Leigh-on-Sea, Essex, UK
Moon, Fábio – Sao Paulo, Brazil
Moore, B. Clay – Kansas City
Moritat – Seattle, WA
Mulvey, Joe – Queens, NY
Mulvihill, Patricia – New York City, NY
Mutti, Andrea – somewhere on Earth
O'Halloran, Chris – Cork, Ireland
Oeming, Michael Avon – Earth
Otsmane-Elhaou, Hassan – Cheltenham, England
Pace, Richard – Toronto, Ontario, Canada
Pak, Greg – New York City, NY
Paknadel, Alex – Manchester, UK
Pangburn, Chas! – Cincinnati, OH
Parker, Tony – Vancouver, WA
Perlman, Michael – Cumming, GA
Perez, Pere – Barcelona, Spain
Petretich, Alex – Cleveland, OH
Phillips, Sean – Milnthorpe, Cumbria, UK
Pires, Curt – Calgary, Alberta. Canada
Pitarra, Nick – Texas
Popov, Vladimir – Belgrade, Serbia
Pulido, Javier – Las Palmas of Gran Canaria, Canary Islands, Spain
Rae, Cardinal – Hackensack, NJ
Rice, Christina – Los Angeles, CA
Rivera, Jules – Bronx, NY
Robertson, Darick – Northern CA
Robinson, James – Las Vegas, NV
Rodriguez, Gabriel – Santiago, Chile
Rose, Robert – West Hills, CA
Roshell, John – (at Comicraft) Santa Barbara, CA
Ryall, Chris – San Diego, CA
Scavone, Rafael – Porto Alegre, Rio Grande do Sul, Brazil
Schultz, Erica – Edison, NJ
Segura, Alex – Kew Gardens, NY
Shannon, Kelsey – Baton Rouge, LA
Sheikman, Alex – San Jose, CA
Sienkiewicz, Bill – CA
Silver, Casey – Seattle, WA
Simone, Gail – The Boonies, OR
Smith, Damon – Portland, OR
Smith, Matthew Dow – Washington, DC
Soma, Taki – Earth
Sorvillo, Matt – Las Vegas, NV
Starr, Jason – New York City, NY
Stewart, Cameron – Toronto, Ontario, Canada
Stewart, Dave – Portland, OR
Strackbein, Matt – Longmont, CO
Struble, Shaun Steven – Dallas, TX
Syd, Ken – Hutto, TX
Taylor, Larime – Las Vegas, NV
Taylor, Sylv – Las Vegas, NV
Tobin, Paul – Portland, OR
Tuazon, Noel – Scarborough, Ontario, Canada
Valenza, Bryan – Jakarta, Indonesia
Van Dyke, Geirrod – USA
Walker, David – Portland, OR
Walta, Gabriel Hernández – Granada, Andalucia, Spain
Ward, Malachi – South Pasadena, CA
Weaver, Dustin – Portland, OR
Wildgoose, Chris – Walkern, Hertfordshire, UK
Williams III, J. H. – Las Vegas, NV
Williams, Kelly – Blytheville, AR
Williams, Rob – Portishead, North Somerset, UK
Wilson, Scott Bryan – Bloomfield, NJ
Wisnia, Chris – Davis, CA
Wright-Williams, Wendy – Las Vegas, NV
Wucinich, Warren – Durham, NC (via Las Vegas, NV)

WHERE
WE LIVE
A Benefit for the Survivors
in Las Vegas